One Saturday

A NOVEL

by

TAMARA TILLEY

One Saturday

By Tamara Tilley

Library of Congress Cataloging-in-Publication Data is on file at the Library of Congress, Washington, DC.

ISBN 10: 0692662669
ISBN 13: 978-0692662663

Cover design by Scott Saunders
Cover images: Shutterstock

ARCHER
PRESS

OTHER BOOKS BY TAMARA TILLEY

FULL DISCLOSURE

ABANDONED IDENTITY

CRIMINAL OBSESSION

BADGE OF RESPECT

TO MY LOVE

❤

Acknowledgements

Thank you to the readers who have taken the time to contact me or written reviews for my previous books. Your words of encouragement are a great source of affirmation.

Thank you to my friends who urge me on with their constant reassurance and support.

Thank you to my family-Walter, my Moms, Christopher, John, Jennifer, Alex, Lorelei, Addison, Trey, Jackson, and Grant. I love you more than words can express.

Thank you to Bob Phillips and MaryLu Tyndall for helping me on my journey.

Thank you to Scott Saunders for creating the perfect cover for *One Saturday*.

Thank you to Nancy Archer and Charlene Ponzio for your editing skills and your wiliness to always review my stories.

Thank you to Michele Nordquist for your tireless efforts in editing and giving so generously of your time. You know my characters as well as I do. Words cannot express my gratitude.

Thank you to my Lord and Savior, Jesus Christ for the greatest story of all.

ONE

Amber Porter quickly looked both ways as she rushed across the street. Juggling two bags of groceries and her purse, she stepped up on the curb just as a clap of thunder reverberated from the charcoal-colored clouds overhead. "Oh come on, not yet!" she huffed as she hiked her purse up onto her shoulder.

Cutting through Riverbend Park, Amber hurried down the well-groomed jogging path, glancing every few seconds at the threatening clouds above. "Just a few more minutes and I'll be home. You can hold off that long," she mumbled to the sky determined to unleash the first storm of the fall season.

She shouldn't have gotten her hopes up. She should've known the mechanic was feeding her a line when he said it would only take him twenty minutes, thirty tops, to locate and diagnose the pinging sound that had bothered her for over a week. *Bring it right in. I'll have it fixed in no time.* Here she was two hours later—with an armload of groceries—walking home with the promise that her car would be ready on Monday. Monday!

She had thought it was a real coup to find a mechanic that worked on Saturdays. Well, that had backfired. Now she would be without her car for the entire weekend. Though the mechanic offered to give her a ride home—for a fee of course—she opted to walk. She lived just on the other side of Riverbend Park, and as long as she made it home before the first cloudburst, she would be fine.

Amber's hurried steps slowed under the weight of her groceries, but instead of getting more irritated, she decided to enjoy the beauty of her surroundings.

Nestled in a ravine between three neighboring cul-de-sacs, Riverbend Park was lined with aged pine trees and neatly trimmed shrubs. It was a haven in the middle of a bustling city. It was not a typical park as parks go. There was no jungle gym for kids to play on or baseball diamonds for little league teams. There wasn't even a sandbox for toddlers. Instead, there was a stately white gazebo positioned in the center of a sprawling lawn—manicured to perfection. A series of bridges crossed a gurgling creek, and large shade trees played the perfect hosts to picnic lunches and afternoon naps. It was a Victorian setting by design and spoke of the simplicity of a time gone by. Amber loved the park and used it quite extensively for photo shoots. Many of her clients chose the picturesque surroundings for wedding pictures, engagement sittings, and family portraits. Most Saturdays the park was teeming with people, but it was obvious the threatening storm had kept the normal weekend crowd away.

A low rumble stole Amber's attention, once again reminding her she needed to hurry.

Just a little ways to go.

Amber stayed on the jogging path that outlined the quaint park, her grocery bags growing heavier with every step. *Okay, so I guess having chili for dinner wasn't the smartest choice.* She chastised herself as she readjusted the plastic bags loaded down with cans of tomato sauce and kidney beans. "Just don't break on me," she said to the rustling bags.

Taking a deep breath, she puffed at the strand of hair that kept playing with her eyelashes, her thoughts drifting to the to-do list waiting for her when she got home. "Well, one good thing about the coming storm," she muttered, "it will force me to stay inside and get caught up on my work."

Though Amber was a disciplined person by nature, she loved the outdoors. Knowing fall would soon slip into winter, she had been spending all her free time outside enjoying the weather, the beauty of the changing leaves, and the crispness in the air that was so unique to this time of year. In doing so, she had neglected everyday chores like dusting and vacuuming, not to mention the numerous rolls of film that still needed to be developed for her appointments next week.

Her shoulders sagged slightly when she thought about her daily routine. She was a wedding/special occasions photographer by trade, and though she enjoyed her work, it was only a stepping stone to her true ambition. She aspired to be a serious photographer. She daydreamed of her work hanging in galleries and garnering the attention of those who appreciated true art. But for now, her clients consisted of those who wanted to pose with their dogs or have entire walls covered with eleven by fourteen glossies of their toddler sitting in a miniature chair, squeezing the stuffing out of a tattered old bear.

She chuckled. It wasn't that bad. She reveled in the fact that she could coax the perfect smile out of an ornery child or capture a memorable moment families would cherish forever.

Still, she wanted more.

She wanted to be known as a serious artist.

One day . . .

Amber continued down the twisting path—picking up her pace—determined to beat the threatening rain. With her internal task list distracting her, she wasn't really paying attention to her surroundings. When she looked up, she was startled to see a man just a few paces ahead of her, heading her way.

Amber slowed, uneasiness chilling her bones. Instinctively, she looked toward the heart of the park.

It was empty.

"Can I help you with your groceries?" the man asked as he approached her.

"No, thank you. I don't have far to go." Amber moved to step around him, but his steps mimicked hers.

"Are you sure?" he persisted, his smile more disturbing than friendly.

Amber could not continue to walk with his burly physique blocking her way. She glanced to her left, realizing how close the jogging path had veered to the shrub-lined perimeter.

Her pulse quickened.

"Nice day for a walk, isn't it?" A voice startled her from behind.

Amber spun around to see a second man behind her. Frantically, she looked again for anyone who could help her, just one person, but the park was hauntingly vacant. Her heart sank. She turned back to the man in front of her, his intentions obvious in his repulsive glare.

"Please, don't do this," Amber whispered as her heart raced.

"Listen, Jack, she's begging us."

The man in front of Amber stepped closer still, closing off any possibility of escape. Tears ran down her cheeks as the feeling of helplessness consumed her.

"Oh, don't cry, sweetheart," the man said as he brought his hand up and brushed the tears from her cheek.

The feel of his touch sent an electric shock through Amber's entire body. In an instant, she shoved her groceries at his chest and tried to bolt from between the two men.

It was a futile attempt.

Her groceries dropped to her feet as a hand that smelled of tobacco pressed roughly against her mouth—smothering her screams. She fought with every ounce of strength she had as the man dragged her deep within the nearby foliage. She twisted and kicked, connecting with his knee. He let her go for an instant, spewing a string of vulgarities. She sprinted forward but the other man tackled her to the ground, trapping her with the weight of his body. While he straddled her hips and tore at her clothes, the other man used his knees to pin her arms above her head and nearly suffocated her with his large calloused hands. Amber thrashed and writhed, trying to fight off her attackers—a reflex of the human soul—but it was useless against the two men who were fueled by the depravity of their sexual appetites. She squeezed her eyes shut, not wanting to look at the men—the animals—that were attacking her.

She prayed God would allow her to die.

She could not comprehend living with the knowledge of what was happening to her. The sounds her attacker made. The things he said as he violated her body. She had never heard such repulsiveness or felt such intense pain.

Just let me die, God. Please let me die. She repeated the plea as time stood still.

She felt the man shift his weight. *It's over.* Amber opened her eyes. Then she realized what was really happening. The men were merely switching positions. It was going to happen all over again.

As the men jockeyed for position, Amber's arms were momentarily free. She lashed out with a frenzy of strength she didn't know she had. She swung at her captors connecting with a nose, a jaw. She screamed at the top of her lungs before a hand clamped down to silence her. She sunk her teeth into the dirt-stained flesh and bit as hard as she could. The man yelled obscenities as he yanked his hand back from her clenched jaw and rose up on his haunches. She pulled her legs up, hoping to unseat the man when a single blow to her temple shot pain through her every limb. Her world turned to black.

Finally, God had answered her prayer.

TWO

Steven Levitt decided he would try to get in his daily jog before it started to rain. He and Bo—his ever-present canine companion—jogged the path that encircled Riverbend Park as part of their daily routine. Bo, his prized Labrador retriever, had been his father's hunting dog for years. When Steven's dad was tragically killed in an auto accident, Bo came to live with him. It was quite an adjustment for the frisky retriever who was used to bounding over brush and through water, extracting fallen fowl. The most Bo could hope to trap now were a few squirrels or raccoons that lived in the wooded areas backed up against Steven's residential sub-division.

Steven knew Bo missed his days of hunting, but the oversized pup seemed to love being at his side just as much. Bo even had his own hard hat that he wore when accompanying Steven on construction sites. Steven's crew loved Bo and treated him like a team mascot. Overall, it wasn't a bad life for the energetic canine.

"Ah, man . . ." Steven looked up and felt a few drops of rain pelt his face. "Come on, Bo, we need to pick up the pace if we're going to make it home before that cloud erupts." Steven pulled at the hoodie tied around his waist, slipped it on, and flipped the hood over his head.

Steven and Bo were circling the far side of the park when all of a sudden Bo let out a howl, raced ahead of Steven, and darted towards the bushes that outlined the path's perimeter.

Great, now he'll be on one of his wild goose chases.

"Leave the squirrels alone, Bo," Steven yelled as he continued down the path. When Bo failed to emerge from the bushes, Steven turned around, jogged in place, and with a firmer voice hollered for Bo to come. His usually obedient companion completely ignored his command.

Jogging back to where Bo veered off the path, Steven clapped twice and whistled for Bo, but the retriever still didn't respond. Steven was surprised by Bo's disobedience. Never before had the dog so blatantly disregarded a command.

Steven whistled once again for Bo, but was acknowledged by a howl instead of submission. "Come on, Bo, we don't have time for this," Steven said, his agitation growing. Stepping over a bag of trash, he split the bushes and walked to where Bo was standing stiff as a board. Bo's eyes were focused on an area deep inside the lush flora.

Steven was ready to scold Bo, when a chill rushed through him. There . . . by the ferns and the underlying brush was a woman's sandal.

Is that a body?

It took Steven a moment to comprehend what he was seeing. He approached slowly as if hurried footsteps would somehow disturb the victim. Then urgency kicked in and he rushed to the twisted form protruding from the vegetation. When he pushed back the shrubbery and saw the woman's bloodied face and obviously violated body, he froze. There was so much blood, and her clothes were . . .

A hot sensation stung Steven's entire body; heat and numbness seeped up his neck and face. He couldn't control it. His stomach was ready to heave. Stepping aside, Steven relieved himself from the acid that had gathered in his throat. He coughed and sputtered, his stomach voiding itself of its remaining contents. Panting as he dragged his sleeve across his lips, he pulled his cell phone from his pocket and dialed.

"911 operator, what is your emergency?"

"I'm at Riverbend Park." Steven turned towards the woman's body but quickly turned away. "There's a woman in the bushes."

"You said there's a woman in the bushes? Is that correct, sir?"

"Yes. She's been beaten and . . ." he couldn't say it.

"Is she alive?"

Steven swung around and looked at the woman again. *Could she be alive?* He hadn't even considered the possibility. She looked so . . .

"I . . . I don't know. I didn't check."

"Sir, I'm sending the police and an ambulance to your location, but I need you to check if she's alive. Can you do that, sir?"

His own discomfort was no longer important. Steven knelt alongside the body and gently pressed two fingers to the woman's neck. A faint pulse caused Steven to jump to his feet.

"She's alive! I felt a pulse, but please, you've got to hurry!"

"Sir, help is on the way, but I need you to stay on the line with me until help arrives. I need to know exactly where you are in the park."

"Uhh . . ." He squeezed his eyes shut and pinched at his brow, trying to gather his thoughts. "I was jogging. By the gazebo. Just look for a yellow lab sitting on the jogging path. I'm in the bushes off to the side."

Steven ran to the jogging path and called for Bo to follow. The dog responded hesitantly, his eyes drifting between the woman and his owner. With a little coaxing, Bo walked to the path and stood in front of Steven.

"Stay!"

Obediently, Bo lowered his hindquarters, hung his head, and whimpered.

"It's going to be okay," Steven assured him.

It has to be.

Steven ran back to the victim as the sky unleashed the torrent it had been threatening all day. Within seconds, large raindrops pelted him and the ground around him. Struggling to remove his jacket, he dropped his phone. He could still hear the voice of the emergency operator talking to him, but he didn't bother to pick it up. He needed to do something to protect the woman from the rain. She was the priority.

Using his jacket, Steven knelt beside the woman and tried to shield her face. But the rain had already mingled with the blood from her nose and mouth and trickled down her swollen cheek. Leaning close, Steven whispered, "Help is coming. Hang on. Can you hear me? You're going to be okay. I promise."

If only he could convince himself it was true.

His thoughts immediately went back to the summer he graduated college. He had told Jeff the same thing—that he would be okay. Steven had promised he wouldn't leave him alone. And then everything had gone horribly wrong.

Please don't let her die, God. Please don't let her die.

Steven's eyes stung from the tears that blurred his vision while he begged God to send help before it was too late. Reaching for the hem of the woman's gauzy skirt, he slipped it past her hips and down her scratched and bloodied legs, trying to give her a measure of privacy, as well as coverage from the rain.

He felt helpless to do anything more. He wanted to pull her close and protect her from the weather, but he was afraid he would only hurt her further or contaminate evidence if she didn't survive.

I can't think that way. She's got to make it.

Steven heard the muffled voice of the 911 operator as she continued to talk on his phone, but he didn't pick it up. She couldn't do or say anything to help the woman. It was up to him. He would stay with her until help arrived.

He'd made her a promise.

Nothing was going to make him leave. Not this time.

Hunching alongside the woman, Steven tried to block the rain as it intensified. He prayed out loud for God to save her, to get her the medical attention she so desperately needed.

Please, God, don't let it be too late this time.

❧❧❧❧

Amber's senses were assaulted by noises and smells she couldn't comprehend. The scent of earth and pine mingled with the iron smell of blood and the rancid tang of vomit. She was cold. She was wet.

Then she remembered where she was and what had happened.

But what was she hearing? What was that mumbling? It sounded like words from a prayer. But she knew they weren't her words or her thoughts. She had not prayed for God to save her. She had prayed to die.

She tried to open her eyes, but couldn't. It was as if a weight lay over her eyelids, preventing her from opening them. The voice was close. Someone was definitely hovering over her, but it wasn't the voice of one of her attackers. She would never forget those voices. No. Someone else was with her. Beside her. And somehow—oddly enough—she felt comforted knowing she wasn't alone.

❧❧❧❧

Steven heard sirens approaching and reached for her hand. "Help is coming; hang on." He saw the woman's eyelids flutter and realized she could hear him. "I'm right here. You're not alone. I promise I'll stay with you. I won't leave you alone." Steven felt her shaking hand give his a feeble squeeze. He held her hand a little tighter, stroking it for comfort. However, as he continued to coax her to be strong, her body began to convulse. Steven watched as tremors shook her body. It could be the dropping temperature or she could be going into shock. All he knew was she was running out of time.

"No. No. Come on. Don't give up. Help's almost here."

Bo began to bark, announcing the arrival of help. Steven turned to see a uniformed officer approaching him, his gun drawn.

"Step away from the body!" the officer shouted while pointing his weapon directly at Steven.

Immediately, Steven threw up his hands. "I'm the one who called 911," he tried to explain.

Two more men stepped through the bushes, guns drawn as they approached Steven. Their shouts joined with the first officer, directing him to move away from the body. They were in street clothes and ball caps, but the badges on their belts, the guns in their hands, and the command in their voices let Steven know they too were cops.

He needed to comply with the officer's instructions. With his hands in the air, he leaned down close to her ear. "I'm right here. I'm going to be right here."

"On your feet!" the uniformed cop yelled.

Steven stood and took a few steps to the side. The uniformed officer approached Steven, roughly spun him around, and searched him from head to toe before telling the other two officers he was clean.

Steven lowered his hands, but before he could begin to explain what had happened, the paramedics arrived. In an instant, the scene became one of chaos. One of the men wearing a ball cap walked over to Steven and pulled out a notepad. "I'm Detective Hastings. I need you to tell me exactly what you saw."

"I didn't see anything. It was Bo, my dog. He ran into the bushes, barking and howling. When I followed him I saw . . . I saw her just lying there."

"Did you touch anything or move anything?" the detective asked.

Steven looked at the men working on her, and then back at the officer. "I checked for her pulse . . . and pulled her skirt down."

"Why did you move her skirt?" the officer asked matter-of-factly.

"Why?" Steven repeated, doing nothing to hide his belligerence. "She was exposed. I was trying to give her some privacy and protection from the rain."

"Did you move or touch anything else?"

"No."

"And you're sure you didn't see anything?"

"I'm sure. If it wasn't for Bo, I wouldn't have seen her at all."

Steven tried to maintain his composure as Det. Hastings rephrased and asked him the same questions over and over again. When he was asked for the umpteenth time why he had touched the victim, Steven had had enough. "Look, I told you everything I know. Bo found her. I called it in and stayed with her until you guys arrived. That's it."

Steven watched as the other cop in the ball cap approached where he and the detective were standing. He was holding a plastic bag with a cell phone in it.

"Mr. Levitt, this is my partner, Det. Jones."

Steven acknowledged the introduction with a nod of his head, then pointed to the bag. "That's my phone."

Det. Hastings looked at him with an icy stare. "Then what was it doing with the victim?"

"I dropped it when I was trying to cover her up."

"Why were you trying to cover up the victim?" Det. Jones asked.

Steven let out a slow breath to keep from losing control. "Like I told your partner, I was trying to keep the rain off of her, so I took off my jacket and held it over her face. That's when my phone dropped out of the pocket."

The detectives exchanged skeptical glances.

"Check the call history," Steven said. "I dialed 911 from that phone."

Det. Jones handed the plastic bag to Steven. "Unlock it."

Steven pushed his passcode in through the plastic and handed it back.

The detective pushed a few buttons and scrolled through some pictures. When he was satisfied Steven was telling the truth, he turned to his partner. "They're ready to transport. Are you done here?"

"Is she going to be okay?" Steven asked.

His question was ignored while Det. Hastings continued to write in his little notebook. "Okay, Mr. Levitt, that's all for now, but I'll need to get ahold of you if we have any further questions. Here's my business card in case you remember anything more that might be of value."

Steven took the offered card, running his thumb across the embossed badge.

"Don't plan any out of town trips, Mr. Levitt," Det. Jones said, sarcastically.

"No problem. I'll be available."

"Then we'll be in touch." The detectives turned to leave.

"Wait. What about my phone?" Steven asked.

"It's evidence," Hastings said over his shoulder as he kept walking. "It will be returned to you when we're done with it."

"Hey!" Steven shouted to get their attention. "Is she going to be okay?"

The detectives stopped and shared a look. Then Det. Jones took a few steps towards Steven. "Are you *sure* you don't know the victim, Mr. Levitt?"

"No. Why? Is it illegal to care about someone you don't know?"

"Illegal, no, out of the ordinary, yes," Jones said, scrutinizing Steven before rejoining his partner.

Steven watched as the ambulance attendants carefully navigated the gurney through the foliage to the jogging path. He walked over to where Bo was still diligently standing guard in the rain and squatted down beside him. Bo whimpered at Steven but quickly turned his attention back to the emergency personnel moving slowly down the path.

"It's okay, boy. Come on, let's go home."

THREE

Voices swirled around her. Amber knew she was being asked questions and somehow those talking to her knew her name, but she was powerless to say anything. She listened as two men spoke back and forth. She heard words like bruises, swelling, bones, concussion.

She finally put it together.

She was in a hospital.

But why?

She tried to open her eyes but felt resistance. Her body was writhing in pain, and her throat burned when she tried to swallow. It took all the energy she had but was finally able to communicate what she needed.

"Water."

The men hushed for an instant before one of them spoke to her.

"Ms. Porter, I'm Dr. Troup. We'll get you something to drink in a moment, but first we need to know if you have any allergies we should be aware of?" Amber shook her head slightly, wishing she hadn't.

"Try not to move, Ms. Porter," the doctor said. "Is there anyone we can contact on your behalf? A relative?"

She thought about it, completely confused. *Why am I in the hospital?* She tried to think, to make sense of what was happening. *Was I in a car accident?* No. She remembered dropping off her car at the mechanic's.

"Ms. Porter, is there someone we should call?" the doctor

asked again.

She whispered, "No," wishing they would stop interrupting her train of thought.

"Ms. Porter, you're going to feel some slight pressure. Let me know when it hurts."

Amber gasped, the pain in her side taking her breath away.

"I'm sorry," the doctor said, his tone compassionate. "We'll get you something for the pain."

She was tired. Very tired. The voices seemed to quiet, and though she still heard beeping, it grew fainter and fainter. She was having a nightmare, that's all it was.

A nightmare.

❧❧❧❧

Steven tossed his keys and the detective's business card on the entry table, crossed the living room, and collapsed into his favorite leather chair. From this vantage point, he had a panoramic view of the city. It was usually therapeutic at the end of a hectic day, but not this afternoon. No amount of gazing out into the cityscape could erase the horrible images that would forever stain his consciousness.

He rested his head back on the chair and closed his eyes, welcoming the void of darkness, but flashes of the scene from the park played like snapshots in his mind.

Her face bloodied and swollen.

Her clothes torn and skewed.

Her body cut and bruised.

Then the scene warped to Jeff, his fractured femur protruding through his skin, the gash in his skull looking like something out of a horror film.

It was a day Steven would never forget.

On a whim, he and his best friend, Jeff, had gone on a day hike. Nothing too strenuous, just a relaxing hike. They planned on being back by dusk. But Jeff, ever the adventurer, decided to do some free climbing. Steven watched, admiring his friend's natural abilities. And then, in a split second, Jeff was free-falling and landed awkwardly on a buttress twenty feet above Steven.

It took Steven valuable time to climb to Jeff. He could hear him moaning, so he kept calling to him, letting him know he was coming. When he reached Jeff, Steven saw his fractured leg and immediately did what he could to stop the bleeding, but it was the gash on the back of Jeff's head that worried him most.

Jeff was conscious but in an incredible amount of pain. He held onto Steven's hand, begging him not to leave. Steven tried reasoning with Jeff, insisting he needed to go for help. But Jeff argued that it was a well-hiked path. Someone would come along who could go for help. Jeff made Steven promise—promise he wouldn't leave. After an hour went by with not a single hiker on the trail, Steven had no choice. He had to go for help.

He had broken his promise.

And when he had returned with a ranger and a medic, Jeff was dead.

It still haunted Steven after all these years, wondering what Jeff's final moments were like. Alone and afraid. His best friend abandoning him.

Steven had sworn he would never break another promise again.

Opening his eyes, Steven shot to his feet. Running his fingers through his wavy hair, he paced like a caged animal.

He couldn't get the woman out of his head. The condition she was in. He knew this kind of thing happened all the time. It was on the news and in the paper on a daily basis. But when faced with it, he still couldn't comprehend how someone could be that brutal to another human being.

Frustrated, Steven trudged to the bathroom and turned on the shower. Extra hot. He stripped off his clothes, wadded up each garment and angrily threw them across the room. He stood in the shower—his hands against the tile—and allowed the scalding water to wash over him. But no matter how hard he tried, he couldn't wash away the morose feeling weighing him down or the sick sensation twisting him into knots.

He was angry. Angry he hadn't gotten to the woman sooner. Angry he couldn't have done something more. If he'd been at the park even ten minutes earlier, maybe he would've been able to stop the assault, or at least identify the person responsible for the vicious attack.

He stepped from the shower, his mood no better than when he started. Scrubbing his scalp with his towel, he felt rage rising inside him.

Steven wandered from one room to another, unable to clear his thoughts. When he went to the pantry and filled Bo's dish with kibble, Bo raised his head and looked from the bowl to Steven, showing no interest at all. Instead of racing across the kitchen like he usually did, Bo lowered his head, rested his chin between his front paws, and let out a doggy sigh.

"I know how you feel, boy," Steven said, with a sigh of his own.

Crossing the living room, Steven stepped out onto the deck. Leaning his elbows on the rail, he stared out into the distance. Bo joined him, pressing his body against Steven's leg. They exchanged glances, then turned back to the view just beyond the rail.

I know this didn't take You by surprise, God. I just don't understand why You would allow something like this to happen?

Steven spent the next few hours in a funk, pacing his house, agitated that there hadn't been something more he could've done. Frustrated, he picked up Det. Hastings' business card from the entry table and reached for his phone . . . the phone he no longer had.

Grabbing his keys, wallet, and a jacket from the coat rack, he opened the front door.

Bo gave Steven a whimper and looked up at him with soulful eyes. Steven stopped and bent down to rub Bo's ears. "Sorry, boy, you can't go this time. But I'll be back soon, okay?"

Bo whimpered again, and hung his head begrudgingly, before slowly moving to his favorite spot alongside the sliding glass door. There he turned three complete circles before laying down in the patch of sun coming through the glass. Steven watched Bo settle in before he headed out the door.

The trip to the mall to replace his phone had been insane. After waiting in a forty minute line, the flirtatious clerk did everything she could to talk him into the latest upgrade. He explained that he didn't need a phone that was two millimeters thinner or a screen that was ten percent larger. He just wanted the same phone he already had. Finally, he settled on the next generation because the model of his current phone was no longer available.

After retrieving his information from his cloud account, and doing a quick charge at the store, Steven hurried to his car and dialed the number listed on the detective's business card.

"Hastings."

The gruff voice definitely belonged to the cop who had questioned him.

"Det. Hastings, this is Steven Levitt . . . from the park."

"Yes, Mr. Levitt, I know who you are."

Steven didn't miss the irritation in the detective's tone, but he continued anyway. "I was calling to find out what hospital the woman was taken to. I would like to make sure she's okay and maybe take her—"

"I thought you didn't know the victim?" Hastings interrupted.

"I don't, but I would still like to know how she's doing."

"The hospital will only give that information to immediate family."

"Then can *you* give me that information?"

There was a significant pause before the detective spoke. "She made it through surgery, but she's in and out of consciousness. The hospital will call us when she's awake and able to give her statement."

"Would it be against policy for you to let me know how she's doing once you see her?"

There was an audible sigh. "I could let you know her general condition, Mr. Levitt, but I won't be able to go into specifics."

"I understand."

"If there's nothing else Mr. Lev—"

"I would like to send her some flowers, to let her know

someone's thinking about her. Can you tell me what hospital she's at?"

"Persistent aren't we, Mr. Levitt?"

"I just want to make sure she's okay." Steven waited, sure the detective wasn't going to give him any more information.

"I can tell you she's *not* at General or Memorial, how's that?" the detective said dryly.

"Thank you, Det. Hastings. I appreciate it."

Steven headed for the only other hospital she could've been taken to—Valley Medical. Traffic was light, the passing storm keeping extra travelers off the streets. He stopped at the florist around the corner from the hospital and inspected each and every display. The choice of flowers was plentiful. There was everything from large, colorful bouquets in fancy woven baskets to long-stem roses in tall glass vases, and every bloom and vessel in-between. As he scanned the varied selection, a bouquet of miniature yellow roses stood out. They were small, delicate, and somehow seemed fitting.

Steven hurried through the sliding double doors of the hospital lobby, shook the rain off his jacket, then stopped. Now that he was at the hospital, he wasn't quite sure what to do or where to go. There was a volunteer seated at the information desk in the corner of the lobby, but she wouldn't be much help. How could he ask for a room number, when he didn't even know the woman's name? Not wanting to take the chance that he would be turned away, he quickly scanned the directory on the wall and headed for the ICU ward on the fourth floor.

When he stepped off the elevator, Steven was once again at a loss. He floundered a few steps from the nurses' station, not knowing what he was going to say. Finally, one of the women sitting behind the long white desk asked, "Can I help you?"

He walked up to the desk, setting the vase on the counter. "I'm not sure if you can help me because I don't even know who I'm here to visit."

The nurse eyed him curiously.

"You see," Steven continued, "there was a young woman

brought in today in serious condition. I don't know her name or who she is. It's just that I was the one who found her and called the police. I stayed with her until the paramedics arrived. I know you can't give out information regarding her condition, but if you could somehow get these flowers to her, I'd appreciate it."

The nurse looked at Steven and the bouquet of roses he had set on the counter. "Patients in the ICU are not allowed to have flowers, but I can put them on the window ledge outside her room. She'll be able to see them when she wakes up."

It was obvious to Steven that the nurse knew exactly who he was talking about. "Could you at least tell me her name?"

"I'm sorry, sir, that's confidential. How about you give me *your* name. When the patient wakes up I can tell her you're here."

"That's okay. I'll just wait."

Steven watched as the nurse took the flowers and set them on a ledge that protruded into the corridor. She glanced at him, then quickly looked through the large window that separated the patient's room from the hallway. She hurried in, but was only gone for a moment before she rushed back to the nurses' station.

"Call Dr. Troup and let him know the patient is conscious," the nurse said to one of her co-workers. "I'm going to call Det. Hastings and let him know she's awake."

When Steven realized Det. Hastings was on his way, he decided to hang around, hoping the detective would be willing to volunteer a little more information about the woman's condition, or at least let him know her name. He took a seat in the pale blue sitting area to wait.

❧❧❧❧

Amber was confused as she struggled to open her eyes. Her right eye fluttered open, but her left eye would not cooperate. Her breathing was hindered by a large weight on her chest, and when she tried to move, every inch of her body throbbed with pain. Feeling the pillow beneath her head and the stiff sheet that covered her, she realized she was in bed.

But it wasn't her bed.

"Ms. Porter?"

She heard an unfamiliar man's voice, and was startled by a shadowy figure at the foot of her bed.

"Ms. Porter, do you know where you are?" the ominous figure asked while moving closer to her side.

Amber could barely see him. She tried to focus, tried to understand where she was, and who the man talking to her was, but her mind would not cooperate.

"Ms. Porter, can you hear me?" the man asked.

She nodded, wincing at the pain in her head.

"Do you know where you are?"

She shut her eyes, trying hard to think. She remembered dropping her car off at the mechanics . . . she was walking home with her groceries . . . through the park . . .

Suddenly, the flash of a man's face appeared.

She cried out.

She clenched her eyes shut, trying to make the man's image disappear. When she felt a hand close around her arm, she pulled away and began to lash about violently. She had been attacked. Two men. They were here. They were back to finish what they had started. The man hovered over her, talking to her, but she refused to listen.

I have to get away. I have to fight.

Firm hands pressed against her shoulders while words were exchanged around her. Amber exerted what little energy she had, and as the voices grew more distant, her thoughts became more clouded. Her eyelids refused to open. She wanted to see who was talking to her, but she just didn't have the strength.

❧❧❧❧

Steven waited anxiously for the doctor to come out of the room. A security guard was on his fourth lap when the doctor, in a crisp white coat, and a nurse, in her bright floral smock, emerged from the first room on the right. Both looked grim as they walked toward the nurses' station. Steven picked up a magazine from the table next to him and quickly crossed in front of the nurses' station.

He leaned against the opposite wall—pretending to be engrossed in the magazine—while positioning himself to better overhear what the doctor had to say. The security guard passed by, glancing momentarily at him.

"She'll need supervision until we can determine she's not a danger to herself," the doctor said. "The restraints will hold her, but I'd like someone there when she wakes up. She's been through enough already. I don't want her to be afraid or feel further victimized by the restraints. Call me as soon as she's coherent."

Steven could hear the concern in the doctor's voice.

"It's tragic that a young woman like that should suffer so," the nurse said. "I sometimes wonder—in situations like these—if death would've been a more merciful end than the horror she will have to live with the rest of her life. I don't know if I could live with that kind of emotional baggage."

Steven was shaken by the nurse's statement. It was a miracle the woman was alive, not a curse. How could she feel that way and still call herself a nurse?

"I understand what you're saying," the doctor said, "but it's incredible sometimes what the human spirit can overcome. Let's just hope she's one of the success stories and not one of the statistics." Both doctor and nurse were quiet for a moment, no doubt wondering about the woman's future.

"Were we able to contact a relative?" the doctor asked as he handed the nurse the digital tablet he was holding.

"No. We know where she lives because of her driver's license, but she had no emergency contact information on her phone. The police are making some calls. They said they would let us know as soon as they had any information."

"Keep me posted," the doctor replied.

"It's heartbreaking, isn't it, Dr. Troup?" the nurse sitting behind the counter commented.

The doctor glanced back toward the room down the hall. "She's the same age as my Amy. I would be devastated if I got a call telling me my daughter had been viciously attacked and left for dead."

The doctor walked past Steven, where he stood with his nose stuck in the magazine. Steven waited to see if the nurses had any more to say.

"She has to live close to the park," the nurse in the floral smock said. "The detectives said it looked like she had been walking with her groceries when it happened."

Steven thought back to the pile of trash he had stepped over at the scene. *It must have been her groceries.*

"Did they say anything more?" the other nurse asked.

"Not much. Her license says she lives on Crescent Drive. I think that's where they were going next. Maybe once they talk with some of her neighbors, they'll know a little bit more about her," the first nurse replied.

The nurses began to discuss another patient so Steven turned toward the elevators, an idea rolling around in his head. Never one to sit around and wait for others, Steven decided he would head for Crescent Drive too, and see if he might be able to find someone who knew the woman. It wasn't right that she was lying alone in a hospital room on what had to be the worse day of her life. Surely one of her neighbors would know how to contact her family.

FOUR

Crescent Drive was a small cul-de-sac much like the one Steven lived on. The houses were smaller and older than the homes on his street, but every house was well maintained and the yards carefully manicured.

Surely the people who live in a neighborhood this small are close with their neighbors.

Steven drove down the street once and circled back around. The only parking available was at the arc of the street, so he drove back to that spot and sat, not sure what to do next.

As he observed people going in and out of their homes, dusk began to settle over the neighborhood. House lights popped on up and down the block, as soccer moms in minivans pulled into their driveways. That gave him an idea. He would just wait and see which house remained dark. Then he would ask a neighbor who lived there. It was a long shot, but he thought it might work.

❧❧❧❧

Det. Hastings emerged from the elevator, immediately making eye contact with Nurse Larsen. She got up from behind the desk at the nurse's station and approached him.

"I'm sorry, detective, but Dr. Troup had to sedate Ms. Porter. She was hysterical, and he was afraid she was going to injure herself further."

"Then I'll talk to her later." He glanced around the waiting room. "Where is the man you told me about?"

"I don't know. Henry was watching him for a while, but he just sort of disappeared. But he matched your description perfectly."

"Did he give his name?"

"No."

"Did he seem overly nervous or did he try to gain access to Ms. Porter's room?"

"No. He was quite calm and very polite. He even brought her flowers. He seemed willing to wait around even though I told him I wouldn't be able to give him any information. I saw him when I was with Dr. Troup, and then he was gone."

Hastings' cursed under his breath. "What about Ms. Porter? Did she say anything when she came to?" he asked.

"No. Like I said, she was hysterical and combative. When it was obvious she was a danger to herself, Dr. Troup had no choice but to sedate her. You're welcome to wait but it's going to be awhile before the sedative wears off."

Hastings had nothing better to do, so he decided to stick around and see if Levitt came back. In the meantime, he called Jones.

"Hey, Levitt made an appearance at the hospital. The nurse said he was calm, polite, and even waited around for a while. But never made an attempt to access her room."

"So, what do you think?" Jones asked. "You told him where she was to see what he would do."

"I don't know. I'm going to wait around and see if he shows up again. In the meantime, why don't you do a little digging? Call if you find anything."

Hastings had gone to the cafeteria for some coffee. He was just stepping off the elevator on the fourth floor when his phone vibrated in his pocket. "Hastings."

"Hey, Rick, we just got a call about a suspicious looking person hanging around on Crescent Drive."

"I'll be there in five."

Hastings hurriedly approached the nurse at the white counter. "I have to go, but please call me when Amber Porter is conscious." Hastings left before the nurse even had a chance to acknowledge him.

As he headed for Crescent Drive, Hastings ran through possible scenarios in his mind. Could the girl's attacker have stalked her? Maybe her attack hadn't been random after all. Maybe they were looking for a crazy ex-boyfriend or some guy she'd dumped that didn't take rejection well.

Hastings slowly approached Crescent Drive, pulled next to the curb, and killed his lights. He saw his partner's sedan just a few cars ahead of him. He keyed in his phone number and waited for a response.

"Okay, I'm behind you. What do we have?"

"See the white truck at the end of the street?"

Hastings craned his neck to see around an SUV. "Yeah."

"A neighbor called it in a few minutes ago. She said the truck had been parked there for a while. The driver is a male but she said he wasn't anyone she had ever seen before. I haven't been able to get a good look at him from this distance."

"Did you run the plates?"

"I can't see them from this angle, and I didn't want to spook him by moving in before you got here."

"Okay. I'm going to pull up closer and have a little talk with the guy. Watch my six, and if he makes a run for it, make sure he doesn't get past you."

Hastings cruised down the dead-end street. He pulled into a driveway close to the white truck, making sure he was out of the driver's peripheral vision. When he got a glimpse of Steven Levitt, he swore under his breath. *You've got to be kidding! I must be slipping,* Hastings chastised himself. *I'm usually a better judge of character than this.*

Obviously, Levitt was more than just an innocent passerby.

❧❧❧❧

Steven had narrowed it down to three houses. Even though he hadn't taken into account lights being on automatic timers, every other house had been alive with activity of some kind or another. He still wasn't sure what he would say when he approached the neighbors. He didn't have that part of his plan ironed out yet. He figured he'd come up with something by the time he knew which house was hers.

"Mr. Levitt, I see we meet again."

Immediately, Steven looked in his side mirror and watched Det. Hastings approach his vehicle. He cringed. When he saw the way the detective's hand rested on his weapon, he realized he might have had a lapse in judgment when he decided to play private eye. Taking a cleansing breath, he made sure his voice was calm and steady before he spoke. "I know this probably looks bad but I can explain."

"I'm sure you can, but right now, I need you to slowly extend your hands outside the vehicle."

"But I said I could explain."

"And I'm going to give you that chance. Please . . . extend your hands where I can see them." Hastings' voice was firm.

Steven slowly stuck his hands through the open window, knowing he was better off doing what he was told. When he saw an unmarked sedan pull up in front of him, he realized he was in a lot of trouble.

Hastings opened Steven's truck door while his partner stood to the side, his hand resting on his weapon, too. Having no choice, Steven slowly lifted his hands above his shoulders and stepped from his cab.

"Turn around and place your hands on the hood of the vehicle."

When Steven turned around to comply, he noticed the neighbors coming out of their homes. *I'm an idiot.*

"Mr. Levitt, am I going to find any weapons on you?"

"No, sir."

Hastings patted him down and then stepped back, allowing Steven to turn around.

"Mr. Levitt, I'm going to need you to accompany Det. Jones and me back to the station so we can get a formal statement from you."

"But I didn't do anything wrong. You can't charge me for just sitting in my truck."

"This will go a lot easier for you, Mr. Levitt, if you do what we ask. If we find out you had no involvement in the earlier attack, this will merely be a minor inconvenience. If you do not wish to go with us voluntarily, I'll charge you with interfering with an ongoing investigation. The choice is yours, Mr. Levitt, but you look like a smart man. I think you understand that going with us now would be your best option."

Steven knew he had no choice, and he also knew he had nothing to hide.

"What about my truck?"

"We'll leave it here for now. If things go well at the station, we'll bring you back to your truck and you can be on your way."

The detective led Steven to the backseat of the waiting sedan and closed the door behind him. "Mike, go ahead and let the neighbor know these two vehicles are going to remain parked here for a while."

Waiting for the other detective to return, Steven sat in the back seat, his heart racing. He was amazed how guilty he felt just being in the presence of a cop. Though he knew he had nothing to hide, he was afraid he would somehow not be able to prove his innocence. He leaned forward, elbows resting on his knees, and began to pray. Even though he knew he was in a lot of trouble, his first thought was of the woman lying in the hospital. Eventually, he would be able to explain his extremely poor sense of judgment, but her life was forever changed.

When they reached the station, Hastings asked Steven if he wanted a lawyer present during his questioning. Of course Steven declined, knowing he had nothing to do with the crime.

Steven sat in the interrogation room for three hours waiting for Hastings or Jones, or someone to come in and talk to him. He had watched enough crime dramas on television to know they were trying to make him feel uncomfortable. Agitated. Paranoid even. But since he had nothing to hide, it just made him mad.

When Hastings finally showed up to question him, Steven did

everything he could to answer the detective's questions precisely and without belligerence. Hastings asked him every question imaginable. He asked about his job, family, friends, his hobbies, social life, his sexual preference, and if any of his past partners would be available to talk with them. Then he stepped away for another hour before coming back and finally asking him questions pertaining to the day's events.

He had Steven outline his whole day, interrupting occasionally to ask about time frames and anyone who could verify his statement.

"Are you going to question these people?" Steven asked.

"Why? Is there something you need to clarify?"

Steven knew the minute he said it, he sounded like he was hiding something. "No. Everything I told you is true. It's just that my mother is not in the best of health. I'm afraid if the police were to show up at her door she would overreact and get upset. I don't want this to weaken her already fragile condition."

"We'll be very clear that we are questioning everyone that was at the scene. We will make it all seem very routine," Hastings assured him.

Steven's pulse race. *I was the only person at the scene. I'm their only suspect. Visiting the hospital and being found on Crescent Drive only makes me look guiltier.*

He tried to remain calm as he continued to answer all of the detective's questions. He realized he would have to explain himself to his mother, sister, brother-in-law, and Scott—his foreman and one of his best friends. He knew they would understand, that is, after they got over the initial shock that he was being questioned in a sexual assault and attempted murder case.

"You know, Mr. Levitt, I just don't get it. I don't understand why you keep inserting yourself in this case if you had no prior relationship with the victim."

Steven sighed. It took him over an hour to explain to the detective what happened that day with Jeff, and why it was so important for him to keep his word. "I don't expect you to understand how I feel. But I need to know that she's going to be okay."

"I don't think she's going to hold a perfect stranger to a promise he muttered in a moment of panic, that is if she was even coherent enough to know what you were saying."

"It doesn't matter. It's what I have to do."

Hastings stepped out into the hall.

❧❧❧❧

"So, what do you think?" Mike asked, as his partner stepped into the hallway.

"As guilty as it looked for him to have been on her street, and earlier at the hospital, I think he's telling the truth."

"Really?" Det. Jones was clearly disappointed. "I was hoping we got lucky."

"Well, we'll still question the people he was with today, but I have a feeling everything is going to check out just like he said."

"You really think he was on her street looking for someone who knew her?"

"As stupid as it sounds, yes. I think he somehow thought he was helping. You heard him. He said he made her a promise, and now he has this crazy idea it's up to him to take care of her."

"But that's ridiculous. If he's telling the truth, she doesn't even know who he is. What would make him feel like he's responsible for taking care of her?"

"I know, I know, it sounds irrational. But she was alone and scared; anything could've happened."

"She was also unconscious. I doubt she heard a thing he said."

"Regardless . . . Levitt feels a responsibility to her, and since we have nothing linking him to her attack, we've got to let him go."

❧❧❧❧

Steven looked up when both Hastings and Jones entered the interrogation room.

"Thank you for your cooperation, Mr. Levitt, you're free to go. But . . . let me remind you to stay close to home. You are still a person of interest in this investigation, and we reserve the right to call you in for further questioning."

"I understand." Steven stood. "I know you guys will probably think I'm crazy, but would it be okay if I visited with . . . with . . ." Steven sighed. "Man, I still don't even know her name."

"Her name is Amber Porter," Det. Jones snapped.

Hastings rubbed the back of his neck, clearly annoyed. "We can't prevent you from visiting her; that's up to Ms. Porter and hospital policies. But if she refuses to see you, and you pursue her further, then we'll have a problem."

"I understand."

Det. Jones and Hastings drove him back to his vehicle in silence. Steven caught Jones watching him in his rearview mirror, his stare cold and unnerving. Steven could tell the detective still wasn't convinced of his innocence. *Oh well, that's his problem.*

When the detective pulled up next to Steven's truck, the three of them got out. "Thank you again for your cooperation." Hastings extended his hand to Steven. "I must say, if your dog had not found Ms. Porter when he did, I don't think she would've made it."

Steven shook his hand, nodded to the other detective leaning against the unmarked sedan, and quickly got in his vehicle.

Steven drove away, knowing his first priority was to talk with his mom, and he knew he had to do it in person. She would not handle it well at all.

FIVE

"Steven, what are you doing here? It is plenty late," Rosa asked as she stood in the doorway of Steven's lavish childhood home. Rosa had been his parent's housekeeper since he was in high school and was very much a part of his family.

Steven bent down and gave her a light kiss on the cheek. "It's nice to see you too, Rosa. Is Mom still up?"

"Yes. She is in the den. We were just watching a movie."

Rosa closed the door behind them and walked with Steven to the far side of the house, his steps echoing in the long tiled hallway. His father had been a strong believer in the motto 'bigger is better.' The house was outfitted with several rooms for entertaining, most of them overlooking the pool area or the panoramic view of the city. But the room used most often by the family was the cozy den nestled downstairs. It was expansive, but decorated in such a way that it felt homey and warm.

Steven descended the steps, trying to formulate what he was going to say to his mother. She would believe him—that wasn't even in question—but he feared how she would react to her son being suspected of such a heinous crime. Her protectiveness for her children could only be compared to that of a lioness and her cubs. If she felt in the least that Steven had been mistreated, she would fall apart. That was exactly what he was hoping to prevent.

"Steven? What's wrong?" she said as he entered the room.

She was already onto him. It wasn't often he stopped by unannounced, especially at this late hour. He just smiled. "Who says anything's wrong?" He leaned down to give her a kiss.

"It's almost eleven o'clock at night. I dare say, you didn't stop by for a casual chat. Oh dear!" She sat up abruptly. "It's your sister, isn't it? Has something happened to Stacy? Or the kids?"

"No, no. Everyone's fine."

"Oh good," she sighed as she relaxed back against the cushions of the couch. "I just thought with it being so late that it had to be something very important or an emergency."

"Well, I do need to talk to you, but everything is going to be fine. I just need to tell you something that you might not want to hear."

His mother sat up a little straighter as if to brace herself. "I knew it. Nothing good happens at this hour of the night."

"I will leave you two alone," Rosa said as she turned to leave.

"No, Rosa, you need to stay. I want you to hear this as well, and I want you to hear it from me."

Steven sat forward on the couch opposite his mom. Rosa sat next to his mother, waiting for him to speak.

He paused, not knowing where to begin.

"Steven, you're scaring me. Please just tell me what's wrong."

He took a deep breath before he started. "This afternoon, when Bo and I went jogging . . . we found a woman. She'd been brutally attacked."

His mother gasped, one hand flying to her mouth, the other reaching over to clutch Rosa's hand. "Oh Steven, was she . . ."

"No. She's alive."

"Oh, thank God," she said, letting out the breath she was holding. "How horrible for her . . . and for you. What did you do?"

"I called 911 and stayed with her until the police arrived."

"Do they know what happened, or who did it?"

"No. Right now they only have one suspect . . . me."

Again, his mothered gasped. "Steven, how could they suspect you?" Her voice raised an octave. "You would never do such a horrible thing!"

"Now, Mom, you need to calm down. I'm not going to tell you

anymore unless you promise me you'll stay calm."

"Calm? My son is being accused of attacking a woman, and you want me to stay calm? I've never heard of such an injustice." Her tone was getting sharper as her words rushed together. "To think you stayed with this woman, possibly endangering yourself, and this is how they treat you? What if her attacker was waiting close by? What if he saw you? We need to call—"

"Mom, stop!" Steven's raised voice hushed her immediately. He softened his tone before he continued. "I'm not going to be able to talk to you about this if you're going to get all worked up."

She took a couple of breaths, Rosa patting her hand. "Is okay, Mrs. Levitt. They see that Steven is very good boy. They will not problem him."

"Thank you, Rosa." Steven smiled at the older woman's endearing broken English.

"Now, Mom, I'll tell you what happened, but you have to stay calm. I'm not worried in the least, and there is no reason to believe that my questioning will be made public, but I've got to let you know what happened because the police will be contacting you to verify my alibi."

"Alibi? But you don't need an alibi. You did nothing wrong."

Steven could tell his mother was trying to control her tone, but she couldn't control the trembling of her lips. "Come on, Mom . . ." Steven moved to sit beside her. As soon as he pulled her close she began to cry.

"This must be horrible for you, Steven. I'm sorry I'm making it worse."

"It's okay, Mom, really. I know you're upset, but you have to trust that the Lord will see us through this."

"But Steven, what if it gets out? What if people find out about this? Doesn't that bother you?"

Steven thought for a moment. "Actually, I'm more concerned about Amber—she's the girl that was attacked. I know I have nothing to be afraid of, but she . . ." He couldn't finish. When he thought about the condition he'd found her in and the nightmare she would have to live with, it made his run-in with the police seem petty.

"Oh, sweetheart, I'm so sorry. You must have been terrified."

"I was. When I realized she was still alive, I was afraid I wouldn't be able to help her in time. It seemed like an eternity before the paramedics showed up. I prayed with her and assured her I wouldn't leave her alone. I felt her squeeze my hand. I knew then she'd heard me. That's what got me into trouble."

"What do you mean?"

"When I went to the hospital and found out the police had nobody to notify regarding her attack, I felt like I needed to be there, or that I should be doing something to help her. They made it sound like she had no one. No family. No friends."

"So, what did you do?" his mom asked.

"I figured out where she lives. I thought maybe if I talked to one of her neighbors, I'd be able to find someone to stay with her. Well, I was waiting on her street when the police were called about a suspicious vehicle."

"Oh, Steven, no." His mother cringed, obviously understanding the implications.

"I know. It was dumb of me." Steven got up and paced the width of the room. "I didn't even think of the ramifications of getting involved."

"Well, of course you didn't. You were only trying to help."

"But that's not the way the police saw it. They picked me up for questioning. I had to give them a statement of everything I did today. That's why I had to talk to you. Since I had lunch with you and Stacy, they'll be calling you to confirm my statement."

"Have you talked to Stacy yet?"

"No. I wanted to talk with you first."

"But honey, Stacy and Connor could help you. You should've called them first."

Steven knew the point his mother was making. His sister had been a very prominent attorney before she decided to take on the full-time job of motherhood. She also happened to be married to the recently re-elected County District Attorney.

"But, Mom, I don't need their help. I told the police what they wanted."

"But—"

"Mom, if something more comes of this, you can bet I will have Connor right at my side, but nothing is going to happen."

"Okay, okay." She looked at Steven and sighed. "I'm just thankful you're all right. When I think of what could've happened. I mean, you could've gotten yourself killed."

"But I didn't, Mom." He patted her hand and smiled. "Look, I need to call Stacy before it gets any later. I would wait until tomorrow, but I would hate for Connor to get blindsided at work before I had a chance to talk to them."

"No, you need to tell them tonight. Right now. They'll understand the late hour."

Steven pulled out his cell phone and speed-dialed his sister's house.

"Hey, Connor, sorry to bother you this late at night but it's kind of important."

"No problem, Steven. What's wrong?"

Before he could say anything further, he could hear his sister telling Connor to put his phone on speaker.

"What is it, Steven, what's wrong? Is it Mom?" Stacy asked.

"No. Mom's fine. In fact, she's sitting right here," he said in his calmest voice.

"Then it's you. I knew it. I told Connor something was wrong, I could feel it. Spill it, Steven. What happened?"

As he began to explain, his sister's *lawyerese* kicked in full force. She peppered him with clear, concise questions. Connor chimed in with his own queries and assured Steven there was nothing to be concerned about. He hadn't done anything wrong.

"Unfortunately," Connor explained, "in this day and age, the good citizens sometimes get lumped in with the hardened criminals. The police were only doing their job by detaining you," Connor said, ever the diplomat.

"I know. That's why I cooperated and didn't see the need to pull you guys into this. I just hope none of it gets to the press. I would hate for a backlash to damage your reputation, Connor. You know . . . guilty by association."

"Don't worry about it. None of this is going to prove to be damaging. I would just make sure you don't interfere further."

"But I can still visit her, right?"

"You mean the woman who was attacked?" Connor clarified. "I wouldn't recommend it. You did your good deed by reporting it. I would keep your distance from now on."

"I can't do that, Connor."

❧❧☙☙

Stacy and Connor lay in bed, awake and restless.

"You understand, don't you?" Stacy asked her husband. "Steven's never forgiven himself for what happened to Jeff."

"But you told me, even if he'd stayed with Jeff, it wouldn't have changed anything. Jeff's injuries were fatal."

"But Steven wasn't there with Jeff when he passed. In his mind, he broke his promise."

"Yeah, I understand. I just hope he doesn't give the police reason to suspect him further."

"But he's done nothing wrong."

"Stacy, he interfered with a police investigation."

"He didn't know that. Now that he does, he won't do it again."

"I hope you're right."

SIX

Steven waited until morning to talk to Scott. He drove to the work site—business as usual—knowing he would find Scott in Levitt and Son's mobile office. Scott looked up from the plans in front of him and stretched back in his chair. "Unless you were abducted by aliens and hovered over the earth last night, I don't even want to hear your excuse for standing up Meagan."

"How about I was being questioned by the police because I found a woman beaten and raped in the park?" Steven said matter-of-factly as he crossed his arms against his chest.

The smile on Scott's face was quickly replaced with shock. "What are you talking about?"

"Just what I said." He plopped down in the chair opposite Scott's desk.

"Okay. Then run that by me again."

Steven went on to explain the events of the previous day. Scott sat mesmerized, too shocked to interrupt.

"So, now you know. I assume the police will be by sometime today to confirm my alibi."

They both sat in silence; Scott staring off into space, Steven thinking only of Amber, wondering how she was doing this morning.

"What are you thinking?" Scott asked.

"I'm just thinking about Amber. I don't think I'll ever be able to get those images out of my mind. It was horrible. How could someone do that to her? I mean . . . I know it happens all the time.

You hear about it every day on the news or read about it in the paper, but to see it . . . to see someone so bloodied and bruised. I think it was the worst thing I've ever witnessed."

Steven rode the elevator to the ICU. When he exited, he saw Det. Hastings talking with a nurse in the hall. When the detective saw Steven, he excused himself and walked towards him.

"How is she doing?" Steven asked immediately.

"Physically . . . better than last night. Emotionally . . . not so good. She was able to give us a statement this morning, but it was pretty difficult for her."

"But she's conscious?" Steven asked, knowing that would be an improvement from the night before.

"Yes. Despondent at times, but conscious."

"Have you found a relative?"

"Her sister. She's with her now."

"That's great." Steven sighed with relief to find out Amber would not have to go through this alone. "Do you think I could talk to her sister? Maybe if I explained why I'm here she'd understand."

Just then, a tall blonde exited Amber's room with Det. Jones at her side. Steven watched as the woman continued her conversation with the detective.

Hastings answered. "I know you just want to help, Steven. But I don't think Amber's going to feel strong enough or comfortable enough to want to see you. At least for now. As for talking to her sister, that's your call. But I wouldn't expect her to be too hospitable."

Steven realized the detective was probably right. Amber was going to be okay, and that was all that really mattered. As long as she had someone to help her . . . as long as she wasn't alone.

Steven turned around and headed for the elevator.

"Mr. Levitt?" Det. Hastings stopped him. "I thought you'd like to know you're no longer a suspect." Steven turned to the detective for clarification. "Ms. Porter was able to give us a vague description of her two assailants. When we showed her your picture, she was sure you weren't one of the men who attacked her."

"Thanks. I'll let my family know they won't be contacted." Steven was thrilled to be in the clear, but it took him a minute to absorb the rest of what Hastings had said. Amber had been assaulted not once, but twice.

Steven sat in his truck staring at the hospital doors. He was having a hard time leaving. If he could just see Amber once, let her know that he was praying for her, he would feel so much better. But he couldn't ignore what Det. Hastings had said. This wasn't about him, the promise he made, or the closure he thought he needed. This was about Amber and her recovery.

He turned the key in the ignition just as Amber's sister stepped through the hospital's automatic doors. Without even thinking, he killed the engine and bolted from his truck. "Excuse me . . . excuse me." He tried to get her attention as he crossed the parking lot. Finally, she stopped and turned.

"Are you talking to me?" Her words were clipped and abrupt.

"Yes." Steven stammered for a moment, unsure what he should say. "How's your sister?"

"Excuse me, who are you?" She took off her designer sunglasses to look Steven in the eyes; her own bloodshot and empty.

"My name's Steven. I'm the one who found her."

Her stare turned from him to nowhere in particular. "The doctor told me she's going to be fine . . . eventually."

Steven was surprised at how cold and uncaring her words sounded. She glanced at her watch and then back to Steven. "Did you want to talk to me about something?" Impatience was obvious in the way she planted her hand on her hip.

"I just wanted the chance to see Amber . . . to see that she was okay. I thought maybe if I explained to you why, you wouldn't mind if I went to see her."

"How is that my decision?" she huffed. "I have no say in that. You'll have to talk to her doctor."

She turned to leave, but Steven continued. "Maybe you could talk to him for me."

"Look, I'd like to help," she turned towards him, "but I have a plane to catch."

"You mean you're not staying?" Steven was shocked, and his tone did nothing to conceal his feelings.

"Look, I'm a very busy person. I came as soon as I was called and did what I was asked. But I don't have time to stick around and play nursemaid. Amber and I haven't been close for years. She doesn't want me here anymore than I want to be here."

"But emotionally . . . don't you think she's going to need someone to talk to . . . someone to help her through this?" Steven felt desperate.

She put her sunglasses back on and then looked directly at Steven. "You know what . . . she has her God. She doesn't need me for anything." And with that, the callous woman walked away, got into a red sports car, and roared from the parking lot.

Steven was stunned. He couldn't imagine things ever getting so bad between him and Stacy that he would turn his back on her if she needed him. He moved to a bench in front of the hospital and sat dumbfounded. He had taken the woman's verbal attack personally and was at a loss for what he should do.

"Figures I would find you here."

Steven turned around to see Jones walking through the electric doors.

"Ms. Porter has asked to see you."

SEVEN

Steven stood nervously outside Amber's room. He had wanted to see her, but now that the time was here, he wasn't sure what he would say. Det. Hastings emerged from her room.

"Why does she want to see me?"

"She asked about the man who found her. Asked if we knew who you were. She said she wanted to talk to you."

Steven took a deep breath and slowly let it out. He paused a moment before pushing against the heavy door.

"Prepare yourself, Mr. Levitt, she doesn't look much better than when you found her."

Steven took another deep breath and quietly went into the dimly lit room. He walked slowly to the foot of the bed and stopped. Hastings was right. Although the blood was gone, the left side of her face was horribly swollen and bruised, and a patch of her hair was replaced by a painful looking row of black stitches. But even with her wounds, Steven could tell that she was beautiful. He stared at her, imagining how she would look without her injuries. Even though her hair was a bit tangled and skewed, he could envision how her rich, espresso brown curls would perfectly frame her fair complexion and delicate features.

It's not fair that she should have to go through this.

Steven continued to stare as she lay unmoving and silent. The only noise in the room came from the buzzing machines to which she was hooked. He closed his eyes and prayed, asking God to tell him what he should say or do. When he opened his eyes and saw she was still sleeping, he decided maybe it would be better if he came back when she was stronger. He was ready to step away from the foot of the bed when he saw her stir.

She opened her right eye and blinked a couple of times as if she was trying to clear her vision. The look of fear quickly distorted her face so Steven hurried to explain why he was there. "Det. Hastings said you wanted to see me. But I can leave if you want me to."

Her voice was soft and timid. "Are you . . ." she swallowed hard, having difficulty speaking. "Are you the man who found me?"

"Yes. My name's Steven Levitt. I . . ."

He froze. He didn't know what else to say. What could he say? It took a minute for him to gather his composure. He cleared his throat and smiled. "I'm glad to hear you're going to be okay."

She swallowed hard again, wincing. "I wanted to thank you." She sighed as if those few words took all the energy she had. She closed her eye, wet her lips and then opened her right eye again. "I heard you praying for me . . . and I know you stayed with me. It meant a lot knowing I wasn't alone."

It pained him to see her strain for every word. "I just wish I could have done more. I wish I had come along sooner." He felt tears sting his eyes.

"Well . . . I just wanted to be able to thank you personally." She closed her eye with another sigh, their short conversation obviously exhausting her.

"Amber?" Steven spoke softly.

Her eye fluttered open.

"Would it be okay if I came to visit you again tomorrow?"

"That's not necessary, Mr.—"

"Steven. Please, call me Steven."

"Steven," she whispered, her energy all but spent. "That's not necessary. I'm going to be okay. I actually get to move to a normal room tomorrow."

"But I'd like to if that's . . . if that's all right with you."

She didn't have a chance to say anything before exhaustion took hold of her completely. Her eye closed, and he watched as her breathing took on a slow, steady rhythm.

Jones was waiting for him when he emerged from Amber's room. "Satisfied?" the detective asked.

"What?"

"Well, you saw her. She's going to make it. Are you satisfied now?"

Jones didn't understand. It wasn't proof Steven was looking for, not really. There was something more. Something even he wasn't sure he understood.

"I'll be back tomorrow."

Jones just shook his head as Steven walked away.

"Levitt."

Steven turned.

"We're done with your phone."

"Keep it. I already deactivated it and bought a new one."

Steven left the hospital energized. He would come back tomorrow. Her sister might've left her, but he wouldn't.

He intended to stay true to his word. She would not have to go through this alone.

Getting into his truck, Steven checked his phone. He had seven missed calls. He scrolled the list and smiled. His sister and mother had tried to call him repeatedly. His family was there for him. Unlike Amber's.

Steven took a short drive to process all that had happened in the last few hours. He was no longer a suspect, and he had been able to talk with Amber. Now he needed to have a conversation with his family but was hesitant. They would be thrilled to know he was no longer a suspect, but something in his gut told him they might not be as excited to find out he planned on spending more time with Amber.

He pulled his phone out, but before he could call his sister, Stacy's ringtone chimed.

"Hey, Stacy, what's up?"

"I just wanted to check in with you . . . see how you're doing."

"Well, you and Connor can rest easy. I'm no longer a suspect.

Amber Porter was able to describe her attackers, and I wasn't one of them." His sister was silent. That seldom was the case. "Stacy, did you hear me? I'm not a suspect. There's nothing to worry about."

"I . . . I know."

"You know? How could you know? I just found out myself a little while ago."

"Steven, don't be mad."

"Mad? Stacy, what are you talking about?"

"I read the report on Amber Porter's attack."

"You did what? You had no right to do that!" He was shocked at his sister's total disregard for Amber's privacy. "You're not her lawyer. You had no business reading her file."

"I was afraid for you. I thought you could be in serious trouble if things turned sour. Connor got me the report so I would be prepared in case charges were filed against you."

"Did Connor read it, too?"

"No. He didn't want to invade her privacy if it wasn't necessary."

"What an upstanding guy! So, he gives it to you instead so you can read all the gory details!" Steven was shouting, feeling as if he had somehow betrayed Amber.

"Steven, please. I know I jumped the gun, but I was worried when I couldn't get a hold of you. I didn't mean to be disrespectful of her feelings. I was just looking out for you. I'm sorry."

Steven gritted his teeth, wanting to unload on his sister. But he didn't. He knew she was only trying to protect him. Something he would've done in a heartbeat if the situation had been reversed.

"Did you find out anything more about her?" Stacy asked, obviously trying to change the subject.

"I got to see her."

"And?"

"She wanted to thank me. She heard me praying for her, and she said it had helped, knowing she wasn't alone."

"That's great, Steven. What about friends and family?"

"She has a sister. I saw her at the hospital, but you won't

believe what she said to me."

"Defensive, huh? Did she feel you were intruding?"

"No, the exact opposite. She was on her way to the airport. She said she was a busy woman and didn't have time to play 'nursemaid.' "

"What?"

"Yeah. You heard me. She was a real piece of work. She said she and Amber weren't really that close, and she had other things she needed to do. I couldn't believe it, Stace, her sister is lying in a hospital bed—beaten to a pulp—and she has more important things to do?"

"Steven, that's awful."

"Yeah, well, good riddance to her. That's not the kind of help Amber's going to need."

"And *you* think you know the kind of help she needs, Steven?" Stacy asked pointedly.

"No, but I want to at least try and help her."

"Steven, I know you have nothing but good intentions, but do you think that's a good idea? This woman is going to have severe emotional and psychological issues. I don't know how you're going to be able to help her with that."

"Neither do I, but I want to be around in case I can. Look, Stacy, do me a favor and call Mom. Assure her everything's going to be fine. I'll talk to her later tonight. Right now I have some things to take care of at work. I'll talk to you later. Say hello to my niece and nephew for me. Tell Jaime and Jarrod I'll be by on the weekend for a rematch."

Steven thought about how he had spent the previous Saturday wrestling with his five-year-old niece and nephew. They were twins just like him and Stacy, and Steven loved them to death. He wanted to have kids of his own someday, but he had yet to find that special someone. Right now, Levitt and Son—the construction business his father had left him—was his partner in life. That and Bo.

After a restful night's sleep, Steven felt rejuvenated and

hopeful. He had cleared his work calendar and had told Scott he would be in and out the rest of the week. Mostly out. He wanted to be able to spend as much time at the hospital as possible. Well, as much time as Amber would allow. Scott would field any calls that needed to be handled and Wendy—his personal assistant—would hold down the main office.

He'd already made one stop this morning before heading to the hospital and glanced at the gift that lay on the passenger seat next to him. Amber probably wouldn't be able to use it right away, but he was hoping it would bring her a level of comfort. His second stop was at the florist around the corner from the hospital. With a fresh bouquet and a handful of festive balloons filling his car, he smiled. He hoped the added color would make Amber's room look cheery and bright, instead of sterile and cold.

Amber had said she would be moved to a normal room, so he asked at the Information Booth at the main entrance and was told she was now on the second floor. When he stepped off the elevator, he immediately went to the nurse's station. "Hi. I'm here to see Amber Porter. Can you tell me where room two-fifty-one is?"

"It's the first door on the right, but the doctor is with her right now. You'll be able to visit as soon as he's done."

The nurse directed him to a few chairs in a small waiting area. He sat, glancing at his watch. It was awhile before he saw the doctor emerge. Just as Steven got to his feet, a man hurried from the elevator.

"I'm here to see Amber Porter! I'm Craig Bailey."

"Oh yes. She's been expecting you."

"I was out of the country when I got the call. It was a nightmare trying to get a flight."

"Well, I'm sure she'll be glad to see you." The nurse escorted him right past Steven and into Amber's room.

Steven wasn't sure what he should do. The man was obviously someone special to Amber . . . someone she was expecting to see. He immediately felt out of place.

He turned to leave but the nurse flagged him down before he

could reach the elevator. "Young man, aren't you going to wait to see your friend? I told her you were waiting."

Steven stopped. "You did?"

"Yes. You can go on in. She can have up to four visitors at a time. Just be careful not to tire her out."

The nurse returned to her station unaware of the dilemma that churned inside Steven. He really didn't belong here. It wasn't like he was her friend or anything. He stood for a minute before walking towards Amber's room. When he glanced through the small window on her door, he saw the man holding her hand between his, his head hung in prayer, Amber crying.

What am I doing? I don't belong here.

Steven took his gifts to the nurse's station. The nurse who had spoken to him earlier looked up and smiled. "I'm needed back at work," Steven explained. "If you could just make sure Amber gets these, I would appreciate it."

"Okay. But—"

Steven didn't wait for the nurse to finish. He quickly turned around and headed for the elevator before the doors could close. Alone inside, he hung his head in embarrassment. *I'm such a fool.* He had convinced himself Amber needed him, that he could protect her, that she had no one else but him.

You arrogant jerk! You're not a knight in shining armor. You're just a man that happened to be in the right place at the right time. No, actually, you weren't even that. If you had been in the right place and at the right time, none of this would have happened.

With a heavy heart, Steven headed for his job site.

Where he belonged.

EIGHT

"Hey, what are you doing back already?" Scott asked. "If I remember our conversation from yesterday correctly, you were going to be in and out. Mostly out." Scott spoke as he headed to their office trailer at the front of the construction site.

He and Steven rarely worked out of the main office. Wendy took care of everything there. Calls, appointments, paperwork. The only time Steven ever spent there was when he had a meeting with a potential client. Usually, all of his work was done directly at the site. He believed in being hands-on and wanted to be visible and available whenever decisions needed his attention. The construction project they were currently working on was a multi-million dollar office complex. One that Steven had lobbied long and hard for to win the contract. It would be the pinnacle of Levitt and Son to date.

Somehow it no longer seemed that important, at least not in light of . . .

Steven followed behind Scott into the trailer. "I just wanted to keep an open calendar, be available." Steven acted nonchalant hoping to diffuse any more questions. "So, bring me up to speed."

"Well, the cement pour on the east side finished ahead of schedule. So I was going to see if we could move up the delivery date on the bracing."

As hard as he tried, Steven wasn't able to focus on what Scott was saying. That is until he heard him mention something about skydivers doing the welding.

"What did you say?"

"I didn't think you were listening." Scott chuckled.

"I'm sorry, Scott. It's just that . . ." Steven's words drifted off as he took a seat in his chair and looked across the desk at his best friend.

"Steven, look, you're the kind of guy who feels like it's up to him to save the world. But what about you? All that happened was traumatic for you, too. Why don't you go ahead and take some real time off? Go home. Decompress. I can handle things here without you for the rest of the week. I'll make sure Wendy or I call you if anything comes up that needs your attention."

Steven thought for a moment. "No, work will be good for me. I need to get my mind on something other than . . ." he pictured Amber and how vulnerable she looked in the hospital. "I need the distraction."

"Okay," Scott said sternly, "but working twenty stories up on steel bracing and girders is not the place you should be when getting *distracted*. If you can't keep your head in the game, you're going to be a danger not only to yourself, but the crew as well. You may be the boss, but I'm still the site foreman. If I think you're being careless, I'll kick you out until you get your head together. Understood?"

Though Scott's words were firm, Steven knew his friend was just looking out for him. He couldn't let his personal issues interfere with the safety of the crew. "Understood."

Steven had done his best to stay focused. He walked the site, inspecting the work that had been completed, but Scott was right. Being on site was the wrong place to be with his mind still on Amber. Resigned to the fact that he didn't have his head in the game, Steven decided working in his office would be safer. He hammered out the bid for an up and coming project and worked on putting together a competitive proposal.

When he glanced at his watch, he was surprised to see it was already seven o'clock at night. Scott had left an hour or so ago while Steven had chosen to finish up what he was working on. He was just calling it quits when his phone rang.

"This is Steven." There was a long pause. "Hello, this is Steven Levitt." When no one answered for the second time, he said, "Look, I think we have a bad connection. Why don't you hang up and then try—"

"This is Amber, uhh . . . Amber Porter."

Steven's heart jumped into his throat as he pressed his phone closer to his ear. "Amber, I'm sorry, I didn't know it was you."

"That's okay. I just wanted to thank you for the present you left at the front desk for me. That was very thoughtful of you."

"You're welcome. I just thought you could use something to brighten your day." An awkward silence hung between them, and Steven didn't know how to fill it.

"The Bible is beautiful," Amber said. "Not many people would think to give someone a Bible."

"Well, it's always been a comfort to me when I've gone through difficult times."

Again there was silence.

"Uhh . . . I can't really see well enough right now to read it, so I just keep reciting some of my favorite verses. It's helped a little."

"Isn't there someone with you who could read it to you?"

"No, but that's okay."

Steven was surprised. *Where's that Craig fella that had burst through her door earlier?* When Steven heard what sounded like a muffled cry, he pressed the phone closer to his ear. "What is it, Amber, what's wrong?"

"I'm sorry. I'm fine. Really. I'm just . . . I'm just . . . tired."

"Have you told the nurses? I'm sure if you told them they would give you something to help you sleep."

"But I can't sleep," she said, panic rising in her voice. "Whenever I close my eyes . . . I see them . . . I hear—" Amber's crying was more pronounced.

Steven didn't know what to do or say.

"I'm sorry, Mr. Levitt," Amber said, sniffling and clearing her throat. "I was only calling to thank you for the gifts. I didn't mean to fall apart on you. I guess it's the medication. Thank you again for the Bible."

"Don't be sorry, Amber," he said. "Is there someone I can call for you, someone who could come and sit with you?"

"It's okay. I'll be fine," she said.

Steven could tell she was trying to sound stronger than she was.

"Amber, you shouldn't be alone. Let me call someone for you."

"There's no one to call, Mr. Levitt." Her words were firm. "I'll be fine, really. Good night and thank you again for everything."

Steven listened as the phone went dead. He got to his feet and paced. *Who was that Craig guy? And why wasn't he with her now?* He'd gotten the impression he was close to Amber. He had assumed he was her boyfriend or someone special by the way he was clutching her hand and praying with her. Where was he now?

Steven dialed the number for the hospital and had his call transferred to the second-floor nurses station.

"Second-floor, Dottie speaking."

"Hi, Dottie. I'm a friend of Amber Porter in room two-fifty-one. I was just wondering, how late are visiting hours?"

"Standard visiting hours are until nine o'clock."

"Thank you." Steven shoved his phone in his pocket, locked the office, and jogged to his truck.

⁂

Exhausted, Amber lay in bed unable to keep her uninjured eye open, but not wanting to fall asleep. Her nightmare waited for her in the darkness of slumber. She was terrified the two men who had done this to her would somehow find her and finish off what they had started.

She was sure they thought they had left her for dead. The bat they used on her skull had only left her unconscious, but she was certain they thought it had killed her. What if they found out she was alive and could identify them? Amber began to cry and pray. God would understand why her eye remained open.

Amber jumped at the sudden knock on her door. Who would be

coming to see her? It certainly wasn't her sister Erika, and Craig was on his way back to Mexico. Maybe there had been a shift change and it was a new nurse? But the staff always just walked in after tapping on the door. They didn't wait to be acknowledged. Straining her voice to be heard, Amber asked, "Who is it?"

The door opened slightly, and she saw Steven Levitt. "Can I come in?"

Amber cringed as she nodded, feeling horrified and embarrassed. *What have I done?* She could only imagine how desperate she must've sounded on the phone for a perfect stranger to show up at her door.

She watched as his silhouette crossed the room. Her vision was blurry and still slightly impaired, but when he stepped into the soft light cast by her bedside lamp, she was able to make out some of his more dominant features.

He was tall with broad shoulders, his dusty brown hair a little on the long side. But what drew her attention, was his piercing blue eyes, and how they stood out against his tanned complexion and the scruffiness of a five o'clock shadow. When Amber realized she was staring, she quickly looked down to where her hands fiddled with the edge of the blanket.

"Mr. Levitt, I'm—"

"Please, it's Steven."

"Steven." She cleared her throat again, doing her best to mask the pain. "I'm sorry for calling you. I know I must've sounded pretty desperate for you to come all the way down here this late at night. It was just momentary panic, but I'm doing much better now." She tried to sound convincing even if it was the furthest thing from the truth. She didn't want to be alone. She was afraid to be alone or to fall asleep. But that wasn't Steven's problem, it was hers. It was unfair of her to burden him with the reality she would have to come to grips with sooner or later. "I'm sorry I bothered you. Please go and enjoy your evening."

"It wasn't a bother, Amber." Steven picked up the Bible from the side table and reached behind him to pull a chair closer. "I thought maybe I could read to you, help you relax." She watched as Steven thumbed through the Bible. She wanted to protest, but he silenced her words when he started reading from the Psalms.

Amber closed her eyes, trying to concentrate on the verses, not the darkness. But it was no use. Tears rolled down her face, and she looked away from Steven. She knew the verses were meant to comfort her, but somehow it only exposed her weakness.

"What is it, Amber?" Steven's words were soft and gentle as if he really cared.

"It's not your problem. It's just something I'm going to have to deal with."

"But I want to help you . . . if I can."

"But you don't even know me!" she snapped, then shrank back, hating herself for sounding so rude. "I'm sorry, I don't mean to sound ungrateful. I just don't understand why you're here. I'm a complete stranger."

"Because I promised you I wouldn't leave you alone. I—"

Amber raised her hand, cutting him off. "And that brought me a great deal of comfort. But I'm okay now. The doctors and nurses are taking care of me. I'm not your responsibility."

"Then why did you call me?"

His question hit her like a slamming door. She wanted to be angry at him for being so blunt—for questioning her—when the gentlemanly thing to do was to leave, but she didn't have the energy. She wiped the tears from her cheek, trying to decide if she should answer him. Maybe if she gave him the silent treatment he would just go away. After several hushed moments, she realized he was waiting for an answer. So, she decided to tell him the truth.

"I know I'm not supposed to be afraid," she said, still not having the nerve to look him in the face. "I know God is with me, but every time I close my eyes, I see them. I feel them. I hear the crack of the bat against my skull and the ripping of my clothes. I just know if I keep my eyes closed too long, they'll come back. They'll find me and kill me. I'm exhausted. But sleep terrifies me."

There. She'd said it. As humiliating as it was to be so honest, she'd said exactly what she was feeling.

"Then this is what we're going to do," Steven said with a gentle but take charge voice. "I'm going to stay right here while you close your eyes and try to get some sleep. I'm not going to leave your side, not even for a minute. You'll be safe. No one can hurt you. Not as long as I'm here."

Amber sniffled. "But I can't ask you to do that."

"You're not. I'm volunteering."

Amber could hear the sincerity in his words but she argued anyway. "It wouldn't be fair of me to ask you to stay."

"What happened to you wasn't fair either, Amber." Steven leaned forward in the chair and took her hand in his. She flinched at his touch but didn't feel the need to pull away. "I made you a promise that I wouldn't leave you alone. I'm a man of my word." Amber could faintly see the reassuring smile on his face. "Now, close your eyes and try to get some rest. You need all the strength you can get."

His firm hand transferred the same assurance she had felt the day of the attack. She wasn't sure who Steven Levitt was or why he was here, but at the moment he was the physical embodiment of a comforting God.

Steven watched as Amber's right eye slowly closed. She stirred for only a few minutes before her chest rose and fell with slow, even breaths. While Amber slept, he studied her. He tried to imagine how she would look minus the bruising and bandages. He wondered if her teal-blue eyes would sparkle if they weren't bloodshot and dulled by fear, or how pretty her smile might look if it wasn't marred by a swollen lip. He couldn't begin to fathom the pain she must've felt when the bat slammed against her head, or how she would be able to overcome the other injuries hidden beneath the crisp white sheet that covered her.

Why her, God? Why her?

Steven found himself wondering about the person—Amber Porter. Why was her sister so unmoved by her condition? How could her friend have come and gone, leaving her alone to deal with her pain? How is it that she seemed all alone? So alone she resorted to calling a stranger? Steven didn't know what the circumstances were that surrounded Amber's situation, but he was convinced God had a purpose in bringing them together.

Amber had been asleep for about an hour when the night nurse walked in and informed Steven visiting hours were over.

"But I promised I would stay with her while she slept. She's afraid to be alone."

"I'm sorry, sir, but only family members are allowed to stay through the night."

"What's your definition of a family member?" Steven asked.

"Excuse me?"

"Well, I just assume exceptions could be made in certain situations, like if someone was engaged or—"

"Oh, I had no idea." Her demeanor quickly changing from authoritative to apologetic. "No one told me. Well, of course you can stay. I'll make a note on Ms. Porter's chart. What was your name again?"

Steven volunteered his name before he even thought about what he was doing. The nurse quietly slipped from Amber's room, leaving Steven with his deception. He chastised himself for not being clearer. Though he had never said *he* was Amber's fiancé, he'd allowed the nurse to think exactly that.

Well, what was done was done. He would explain himself in the morning, first to Amber, then to the hospital staff. But for now, Amber was asleep, and he had no intention of disturbing her. Instead, he hunched further down in the small bedside chair, trying to make himself as comfortable as possible. He closed his eyes and prayed Amber would get a full night of rest.

NINE

A cry split the silence.

Steven jumped to his feet—ready to assure Amber she was not alone—only to see that she was still asleep, held captive by her nightmare. Her face was covered with perspiration, her breathing hurried, her hand clenched at her side. Steven wanted to wake her, to pull her from her torment, but he feared his touch would only panic her further.

Instead, he chose to talk to her. "Amber, I'm right here. You're not alone. No one can hurt you. Wake up, Amber. You're having a nightmare."

Her eyelids fluttered, barely opening. When she saw him, she stiffened, fear evident in her eyes, but then her body relaxed. "You're still here."

A sigh escaped Amber's lips and her eyes closed once more. Just like that, she was sleeping once again.

A nurse hurried into the room, but Steven held up his hand. "She was having a nightmare, but she's sleeping now."

The nurse looked from Amber to him. "Okay, but if she needs anything, have her press the call button."

Steven nodded.

Once the nurse left, Steven exhaled the breath he'd been holding. He sat back down in the chair and looked at the clock on the wall. It was four in the morning. They had almost made it through the night. He stretched out his stiff back muscles knowing dawn would come soon enough.

❧❧❧❧

Amber was awake but lay with her eyes closed. She wasn't ready to face another day. Last night, her mind had played terrible tricks on her. The men from the park were back, but they were dressed in hospital scrubs, rolling her bed towards a dark, petrified forest. She tried to get the attention of the hospital staff as she rolled passed them in the corridor, but they just waved and smiled. Then a voice assured her she wasn't alone, that no one could hurt her. She saw the silhouette of a man hovering over her, but somehow she knew he wasn't there to harm her. She spoke to him, and his words of assurance lulled her back to sleep.

The sound of running water pulled Amber into the present. She opened her eyes and watched as Steven emerged from the bathroom, and crossed the room to her bedside.

It wasn't a dream. He was here.

The light of day brought to mind the sharp reality of what she had done. She had called a complete stranger so she wouldn't have to face the night alone. And this man who knew nothing about her, had come. His presence had calmed the panic and fear that had kept her awake the night before. She had gotten some much-needed sleep, but at what price? The comfort she felt from a night of rest was quickly replaced by embarrassment and humiliation.

"How are you feeling this morning?" Steven asked with a smile.

"Humiliated."

Amber tried to scoot up into a sitting position, but it was too painful. "Mr. Levitt, I can't tell you how sorry I am. I can't believe I called you last night. I was afraid and alone, and the medication they're giving me must be messing with my senses. When I saw the Bible you gave me and read the note with your phone number written inside, I overreacted."

Steven chuckled slightly. "I thought we got past the 'Mr. Levitt'. And if you think you overreacted, then have I got a story for you."

His smile was disarming. Amber didn't know what he was

talking about, but before he could say anything more, a nurse walked in.

"Good morning, Ms. Porter. How are we doing today?"

"Uuh . . . a little better I guess." She lied.

"Well, I would be to if I had such a handsome young man waiting on me." The nurse stepped past Steven and worked on Amber's I.V. "How's the pain this morning?"

"It's there."

"I have something for that." She inserted the syringe into the shunt in the line. "Your breakfast will be here soon. We had a second tray made up for your fiancé."

Amber quickly turned to Steven. He pressed his index finger to his lips and shook his head.

The nurse continued her routine, checking Amber's vitals while asking embarrassing, personal questions. Steven was kind enough to move to the far side of the room. Amber appreciated his attempt to give her some privacy.

"Okay, sweetie, I'll be back a little later," the nurse said. "Try to get some rest. The doctor will be by to see you around ten o'clock."

When the nurse left, Steven turned around and stepped closer to her bed, guilt written all over his face.

"Why does she think you're my fiancé?" Amber asked, feeling annoyed.

"That's what I was going to tell you. The nurse came in last night to kick me out because visiting hours were over. I knew I couldn't leave you . . . sooooo . . . I might've inadvertently given her the wrong impression . . . I didn't lie, but I didn't correct her either."

Amber could see that Steven was trying not to laugh by the grin on his face. "So, what did you say to give her that impression?"

Steven cringed. "I asked if a fiancé was considered immediate family."

"You didn't!"

Steven started laughing. "I never said *I* was your fiancé. She just assumed it."

Amber laid there and stared at Steven, not sure what to do or say. She should be mad at him, livid that he would be so forward. But she wasn't. She had finally gotten a few hours of sleep because he had stayed. How could she be mad? But, the nurses now thought he was her fiancé. She tried to conceal the smile that pulled at her swollen lips but couldn't. Instead, she started to laugh.

"Ouch." She pressed her hand to her tender lips as tears streamed down her face. She was laughing. Amidst everything she'd gone through, she was actually laughing, and it felt good. It took her a moment to gain her composure and wipe the tears from her cheeks. "I can't believe you let them think we were engaged."

"I didn't mean to. I knew if I didn't come up with something quick, they were going to kick me out. I didn't want you waking up and finding out you were all alone. Not after I said I would stay."

When a burly attendant came in with two breakfast trays, Amber and Steven watched silently as he set one tray on the small table that flanked the side chair, and the other on Amber's bedside tray. "Enjoy," he said, as he excused himself with a smile and a little salute.

"Well," Steven said with a grin, "no sense wasting good food." He walked over to the chair and began to inspect the food on the tray. Amber tried to push herself further up on her pillows, but pain radiated through her left side. Her ribs felt like they were on fire, and her left wrist couldn't take the pressure of the mattress. Defeated, she collapsed back against the pillows with a moan.

Steven turned around and took a step closer. "What is it? What's wrong?" he asked.

"It hurts too much, and I don't have the strength to sit up and scoot back at the same time."

"Here." Steven moved her tray out of the way and extended his muscular forearm across her bed. "Hold onto my arm, and I'll pull you up."

"I don't know. Maybe I should wait for one of the nurses."

"Well, why don't you give this a try, and if we can't get you comfortable, I'll get one of the nurses to help you."

Amber debated what she should do. Steven was nice and all, but . . .

Steven lowered his arm. "Amber, I only want to help. But if you're uncomfortable with me being here, I can leave."

The dejected look on his face saddened her. She had no reason to distrust him, and she certainly didn't want to hurt his feelings after all he'd already done. "No, it's not that." She smiled timidly. "We can try it your way."

Amber wrapped her right hand around his forearm while she braced her ribs with the other. Slowly, he pulled her up. She winced but tried not to cry. Steven pushed the buttons on the side of her bedrail, and slowly the back of the bed came up to meet her. She carefully lowered herself back against the mattress while Steven reached across her and placed a pillow under her head.

Amber stared at the front of Steven's t-shirt. She felt his breath against her hair as he adjusted the pillows behind her. His closeness was causing her senses to overreact and her heart to race. She had to convince herself she wasn't in any danger and that he was only trying to help. But the feeling of him so close to her was claustrophobic.

"There. How's that?"

"Better," she whispered.

Steven pushed her food tray back within reach, then sat down with his tray across his lap. He uncovered his food, stuck the bendy straw in his juice, and pulled the silverware from its plastic pouch.

Amber fumbled with the cellophane that covered a bowl of oatmeal. Not only were her hands shaking, but her left wrist hurt more than she expected. She tried to use her right hand, but was all thumbs. When she tried again to peel back the plastic covering, the bowl scooted farther across her tray. Exhausted from what little effort she expended, she let out a huff, rested back against the pillows, and closed her eyes. The small meal wasn't worth the energy.

When she heard the crackle of cellophane, she opened her eyes to see Steven once again hovering over her.

She flinched at his closeness, causing him to stop what he was doing.

"I was just going to help you with the plastic wrap."

She forced her fear back down. "Thank you."

He uncovered the bowl of oatmeal, pulled the tab on the cup of yogurt, and freed a straw from its wrapper before putting it in the carton of orange juice.

Amber watched as he picked up his tray from the chair, sat down, and put it back on his lap. "Would you mind if I prayed?" he asked.

Before she could answer, a nurse walked into the room and quickly crossed to the monitors at the right of her bed. "Is everything okay in here?" She glanced at Amber. "How are you feeling?"

"Fine."

"Well, your heart rate spiked just a second ago," she said, as she pressed some buttons.

"I was just trying to get comfortable," Amber explained. "Maybe I pinched the cord." She looked at the small monitor clamped on her finger. Of course, Amber knew it was Steven's nearness that had caused her heart rate to escalate.

The nurse watched the digital readout for a moment, then turned to Amber. "Well, everything seems to be okay now. Just don't try to do too much."

"Okay. Thank you for checking on me."

"No problem. But if you need any help, just give us a buzz. That's what we're here for," she said as she left.

Steven looked concerned. "Are you sure you're okay? I didn't hurt you, did I?"

"No. I'm fine. Why don't you go ahead and pray for our breakfast."

"Okay." Steven bowed his head and closed his eyes. "Dear Lord Jesus, thank You for this new day. Lord, I would ask that You help Amber in the days ahead. We know none of this has taken You by surprise, but in our humanness, we struggle to try and make sense of it all. Lord, I pray You will continue to show Amber Your strength when she is weak, Your comfort when helplessness overcomes her, and Your incredible love when fear fills her heart. Heal her body, Lord, and return joy to her soul. Bless this food to our bodies and give us a day that brings honor and glory to you. Amen."

Amber didn't know what to say. She was so overwhelmed by the compassion in Steven's words, she had to choke back tears and try to concentrate on the food in front of her. She lifted her spoon to her mouth and carefully swallowed her yogurt.

"So what's wrong with your arm?" Steven asked as he slurped the last of his orange juice.

She looked at the bruising on her left forearm and wrist, remembering the way it had been pinned to the ground by her attacker's knee. She shuddered. "It's just really sore."

"You're left-handed, aren't you?"

"How did you know?"

"Because you're having such a hard time using your right."

Amber took another spoonful of yogurt and then rested her head back against the pillows. She couldn't believe lifting a spoon could wear her out. And even though she'd thought she was hungry, everything she swallowed tasted like blood.

Steven was chowing down on his food when he looked up and stopped. "You're not finished, are you?"

"It takes too much work, and it doesn't even taste good."

"Is there anything else I could bring you? Your favorite snack or something from a favorite restaurant?"

"No. I just don't have much of an appetite."

"But you need to eat something to replenish your strength. Why don't you just concentrate on the yogurt?"

A tap on the door interrupted their conversation. Det. Hastings stood at the door. He smiled at her but eyed Steven with a look of irritation.

"I must say, Mr. Levitt, I didn't expect to see you here. In fact,

I was told Amber's fiancé had been with her all night and was having breakfast with her. You care to explain that bit of misinformation?"

Steven sat up straighter. "Well, somehow the night nurse got the impression I was Amber's fiancé. I knew she would make me leave if I corrected her, and I'd promised Amber I wouldn't leave her alone. So I went along with it."

Det. Hastings turned to Amber. "You realize they're going to find out it was a lie. Some of the other nurses already saw Mr. Levitt hanging around the hospital after you were brought in. They know he's not your fiancé."

Amber didn't know what to say, but Steven quickly spoke up. "Look, detective, this isn't Amber's fault. She's terrified to be alone. Something you should've picked up on." The agitation in Steven's voice was evident. "Maybe if you had posted a guard outside her door or had done something to ensure her safety, she wouldn't have felt the need to call me."

"Are you telling me, if I had posted someone outside Ms. Porter's door, you wouldn't be here?"

Steven looked away without answering.

"That's what I thought."

Amber watched the interaction between the detective and Steven, surprised by what seemed to be a mutual frustration they had with each other. Hastings was actually glaring at Steven, but when he turned his attention back to her, his expression softened. "I have some more photos I would like you to look at."

Instantly, Amber felt like she was going to be sick. Her face flushed hot, her hands began to shake, and her skin tingled. *I'm going to pass out.* Just the thought of having to look at what could be her attackers was causing her to fall apart. *Calm down.* She scolded herself. *You need to calm down.* She tried to take a deep breath to relax but the pain in her body made her stop short with a whimper.

"Amber, are you all right?" Det. Hastings asked. "We could do this later if you would rather, but the sooner you—"

"No. I can do it now." She didn't feel as confident as she sounded but wanted to put this behind her. If that was even possible. She took a few more breaths before she reached for the pictures.

"These guys were picked up last night. Do they look familiar at all?"

Amber held the pictures with a shaky hand but didn't look at the images until the last possible moment. She glanced at them, then sighed. "No. It's not them." She quickly handed the pictures back.

"Are you sure?" Hastings extended the photos again.

"Yes." Her answer was quick.

"Okay. I just wanted to be sure."

❧❧❧❧

Det. Hastings moved toward the door. Steven decided to follow him out. "Amber, I'm going to try and clear things up at the nurse's station. I'll be right back. Will you be okay?"

She nodded and closed her eyes.

Steven waited until the door was completely closed before talking to Hastings. "So, I guess that means you have no leads?"

"Not yet."

"What are the odds of finding the men that did this?"

"Slim."

His answer was like a punch in the gut. "There's nothing more you can do?"

"Look, Steven, we're doing everything we can. We recovered some physical evidence from the scene but I'm not optimistic. If these guys aren't in the system, there isn't much we can do."

"So you think it was random? That these guys just got up in the morning and said, 'Hey, let's go rape and kill someone today?' "

"No. It was too planned out for it to be random, but it doesn't mean they've ever been caught. Thousands of rapes go unreported every year. Some women are too afraid to come forward or feel somehow they're to blame."

"So what are you saying?"

"I'm saying, unless they do it again, and slip up, I don't think we have much of a chance of catching them."

Steven allowed that to sink in. How would Amber ever recover if the men that did this to her were never caught? "Do you think she's in danger? I mean, if they know she can identify them, do you think they'll come after her again?"

Hastings sighed. "We're in a difficult position. If we go public with a sketch and try to get more information, they'll know she's alive and can identify them. If we don't go public, we won't have much to go on." Hastings drug his hand down his face, obviously tired and frustrated. "They got away with it. Chances are they've probably already moved on."

Steven could see right through the detective's explanation. Hastings wasn't convinced Amber was out of trouble any more than he was. When Hastings turned to walk away, Steven stopped him.

"Look, could you maybe help me smooth things over with the nurses? Maybe if you vouch for me, they won't turn me out on my ear."

Hastings paused. Steven could read the expression on the detective's face. The expression that said 'you got yourself into this mess'. Hastings didn't bother to answer, he just turned around and approached the nurse's desk.

"There's been a little misunderstanding here." Hastings looked to Steven to finish the explanation.

"Yes . . . uh . . . I might have given the attending nurse the wrong impression last night," Steven said, sounding guilty as sin. "Somehow she came to the conclusion that I was engaged to Amber Porter. This is not the case . . . but we are very close."

Steven looked at Hastings to see if he was going to correct him, but he didn't. In fact, the look on his face was one of understanding. Steven turned his attention back to the nurse, hoping she was the compassionate type. "Can I ask for leniency where visitation is involved?"

The nurse clicked away on her computer, looking too busy to be bothered. "Mr. Levitt, the hospital has rules. I just follow them."

"I know, I know. But those rules are meant for the protection, privacy, and comfort of the patient. Amber has no family that can be with her right now. Do you think she should be penalized for that? She was able to sleep last night, knowing she wasn't alone." Steven thought he saw a softening in the nurse's demeanor so he continued. "Look, I know you are aware of the tragedy that put her here. Amber has been severely traumatized. That's why she's terrified to be by herself. Amber needs to know someone will be there to protect her. She needs that peace and reassurance. That's all I'm trying to give her."

The nurse shuffled some papers in front of her, looking agitated. She glanced at Hastings, obviously waiting to see if he had anything to add.

"It would be a help to the department," Hastings offered. "We are short-staffed right now so we don't have the manpower to post a guard. I can vouch for Mr. Levitt's character. His brother-in-law is the District Attorney and his sister is a prominent lawyer in the community. He's not going to cause any trouble."

Steven looked at Hastings, surprised.

"Well, Mr. Levitt," the nurse spoke. "I can't say that I appreciate the fact that my staff was deceived, but I do see your point. I will talk with her doctor and if he doesn't oppose the idea, I'll speak to the administrator and see what I can do about this evening's visitation."

She excused herself to help with another matter.

Steven turned to Hastings. "Thanks. I don't think she would've agreed if you hadn't said what you did."

"Well, the only reason I did was because of the background check I did on you yesterday. You have no record, and I don't think you would take the chance of tainting your brother-in-law's reputation just to make time with a woman. But let me tell you one thing, if you see anything or anyone that looks remotely suspicious, you call me immediately. It's not your job to play superhero and save the day. Understood?"

"Understood . . . and thanks."

TEN

Steven jumped out of the shower to answer the phone.

When nurses, attendants, and doctors had started making their rounds—poking, prodding, and asking Amber questions too personal for him to be a part of—he had decided it was a good time to go home and take care of his own personal needs.

He played with Bo and assured him he hadn't been abandoned, then called Scott and Wendy to confer about business matters. His sister had tried to call several more times last night and already this morning. He had planned on calling her and his mother once he was done getting cleaned up, but his sister once again beat him to the punch.

Wrapping a towel around his midsection, Steven grabbed his phone.

"Steven, where have you been? I've been trying to get a hold of you. You weren't home, and you didn't answer your cell."

"I was at the hospital, so I had my phone turned off."

"All night?"

"Yeah. I stayed with Amber so she wouldn't have to be alone."

"Steven, you're not going to get yourself in trouble, are you? Just because Amber cleared you as a suspect in her assault, doesn't mean the police couldn't still misinterpret your interest in her case."

"As what?"

"As someone trying to stay close to the victim in order to find out what evidence or leads the police have."

"Well, I am interested in what the police find out. Why is that wrong?"

She sighed.

"Stacy, what are you getting at?"

"They could suspect you of being a plant. Someone trying to stay on the inside to get information for someone else; someone you're protecting."

"Gee thanks, *Counselor*, you just profiled your brother as a co-conspirator."

"And that's exactly what the police will do if you keep showing up where you don't belong."

"Actually, I talked to Det. Hastings this morning. He understands I'm not a threat to Amber. And just so you know, she called *me*."

"What?"

"Last night. Amber called me because she was afraid to be alone. She just needed someone to talk to."

"But why you? You're as much a stranger to her as the men who attacked her."

"Wow," Steven felt physically assaulted. "I can't believe you just said that."

"I'm sorry, Steven, I didn't mean—"

"Look, Stacy, I had prayer with Amber and bought her a Bible as a gift. When fear got the better of her, she saw I had written my phone number in the Bible so she called me."

"So you were there all night? I thought hospitals had rules about that."

"They do. There was a miscommunication last night that allowed me to stay. When I talked to one of the nurses this morning about Amber's situation—and the fact that she had no family—the nurse said she would talk to the doctor and the administrator about Amber's extenuating circumstances. With Det. Hastings vouching for me, I'm pretty sure I'll be able to stay again tonight."

His sister started laughing. "I always knew you would take over the family business, but I swear, Steven, you could've been a top-notch lawyer. You could finesse a thirsty man out of his last drop of water."

"Yeah, but I don't like suits, and I don't like the indoors. Levitt and Son fits me just fine. I'll leave the depositions and court filings to you and Connor."

"Okay, Steven," her tone softened, "but be careful."

"Me? I have nothing to be afraid of."

"I wasn't talking about being afraid. I was talking about leading too heavily with your heart. This woman has been through a traumatic experience, one that will take her quite some time to come to terms with, if that's even possible. I just don't want to see you get hurt in the process. It might appear as if she needs you now because she doesn't have anyone, but when the time comes for her to move on and try to put this all behind her, you might end up as collateral damage."

"That's not fair, Stacy!" Steven defended, his tone reaching fever pitch. "You have no idea what you're talking about!"

"Steven, you just proved my point. You're emotionally involved with a woman you know nothing about. Come on, Steven, think about it. You saw firsthand the violence she was subjected to. Do you really think she'll be able to forget that? You're part of the situation if you like it or not. It doesn't matter that you're the one that saved her or the one trying to help her now. You're still a part of an event that she will spend the rest of her life trying to forget."

"I don't think so, Stacy. I mean, come on, she called *me*. She needed someone. There's a connection between us. I can feel it."

"Steven, I just don't want you to romanticize what happened. Yes, you have a connection with her, but it might not be as healthy as you would like."

Steven's call-waiting interrupted them. "Look, Stacy, I have to go, but don't worry. I know what I'm doing."

❧❧❧❧

Stacy hung up the phone thinking the exact opposite of her brother. He was blind when it came to matters of the heart. He refused to see the bad in people. His heart had been trampled on in the past because he chose only to look for the good in someone. She knew Steven was a very astute businessman—but somehow in the personal arena—he had been blind-sided once before, and it almost cost him his life.

ༀ

"Hi, Mom, I was just going to call you," Steven said as he switched from talking to his sister.

"What's wrong, Steven? You're using that 'I need to calm down Mother voice.' "

"Everything's fine, Mom, really. I just wanted to let you know I'll be spending more time at the hospital. So if my phone is off, that's why."

"Why would you be spending time there? Oh, Steven, you're not somehow becoming involved with that woman, are you?"

"You know what, Mom, I just had this conversation with Stacy. I'm not going to rehash it again with you!" Steven snapped, then took a breath to compose himself. "Look, Mom, I'm sorry for jumping down your throat. I'm only trying to help Amber through a difficult time, that's all. I'm sure anything more than friendship is the furthest thing from her mind right now. Like you said, she has bigger issues to deal with at the moment. I'm just trying to make it a little easier for her."

"Okay, Steven, but please be careful."

"Don't worry, Mom, everything's going to be fine."

ELEVEN

Amber was numb.

She could hear both horror and outrage in Dr. Troup's tone as he tried to explain to her what had happened. She didn't need an explanation. She didn't need to know the safeguards that were usually taken to prevent such mistakes. All she knew was the physical evidence they had gathered—the very same evidence that could identify her attackers, and let her know if she had been exposed to a litany of diseases—had been mishandled and subsequently destroyed.

"This is deplorable, Amber," Dr. Troup continued. "I won't even try to make excuses for the hospital. The technician has been fired, but I know in no way does that help your situation."

She tried to listen as Dr. Troup spoke of her options, of medications recommended to fight against the possible exposure to STD's, but she didn't hear a thing he said.

It didn't matter.

None of it mattered.

Nothing he could do or say could turn back the hands of time and erase the last seventy-two hours that changed her life forever.

❧❧❧❧

Steven was surprised to see Amber sitting in a chair by the window when he returned to the hospital.

"Hey, you must be feeling pretty good," he said as he crossed the room.

She jumped when she heard his voice, making Steven angry for not announcing himself better.

Amber didn't answer him.

"Should you be out of bed, though? You still need your rest, and your body needs plenty of time to heal."

Again, Amber didn't answer. She didn't even move her gaze from the window.

"Amber?" Steven said softly.

Finally, she blinked and her shoulders shuddered. "I'm sorry, what did you say?"

"I'm just concerned you're overdoing it."

"The doctor said I could get up and move around. I'll be going home on Friday or Saturday, so I need to get used to it."

"So soon?" Steven was surprised. He didn't want to say anything to Amber, but she certainly didn't seem stable enough to be on her own.

"Soon? I've been here since Saturday."

"I know, but you were . . . I mean you'd been . . . It just seems like you could use the extra time."

Amber stared out into the darkening horizon, struggling with the decisions she'd made. She felt like she was in a fog, her mind trying to comprehend all she'd been told. The doctor had taken his time, explaining her options in-between apologies, letting her know it was her decision to make. But in the end, when she told him what she'd decided, he seemed concerned. He again explained her options, making sure she understood in painstaking detail the ramifications of her decisions, and the urgency to start a method of treatment, but her mind was made up.

Her decision was final.

There would be no going back.

After Dr. Troup left, she tried to concentrate on the next task at hand, going home—being able to sleep in her own bed and sit in her own living room. It sounded great. But it was the thought of being alone that still terrified her.

She had always loved her privacy and her solitude. Being alone had never bothered her. She wasn't a hermit—as definitions of hermits go—but she was definitely a person who liked the quiet and seclusion of her simple life. The friendship she shared with her next door neighbor had always been enough. But now Cara was gone, and the thought of being by herself was more than she could bear.

"What are you thinking?"

Amber had forgotten Steven was even there, her mind weighed down with all she was trying to absorb. "What?" she said, even though she had heard him just fine.

"You seemed to disappear for a moment."

"I guess I was just thinking." Amber stood and slowly moved to the edge of her bed, sighing at the exertion she was expending. Carefully, she pushed herself to the center of the mattress and slid her legs under the cold, stiff sheets.

"It's okay to be afraid, you know."

Amber turned a sharp look on Steven, wanting to refute him, but she couldn't. She *was* afraid. Afraid of closing her eyes. Afraid of being outside. Afraid of what her future held.

"So you never told me, what is it that you do?" Steven asked.

Amber appreciated his willingness to change the subject, even if she didn't understand the question. "Do?"

"Yeah, you know," Steven pulled the side chair next to the bed and took a seat. "What do you do for a living?"

"I'm a photographer."

"Really? What kind of photographer?"

"Mostly weddings, engagements, and family portraits."

"You don't sound too happy about that."

"It's not that. I just aspire to more."

"More? Like what?"

Amber didn't feel like explaining her dream of becoming a serious artist. She wanted to be a photographer who traveled the world taking pictures that would speak to a generation in a positive way. There were already countless photographers that captured riveting portrayals of war, destruction, and despair. But she wanted to counter those images with pictures of hope in the face of war, communities banding together after the devastation of natural disasters, children whose smudged faces reflected joy, even in poverty. She knew it was a lofty goal, a pipe-dream as her sister had called it. But it's what she wanted to do.

"It's nothing." She brushed aside his question. "What about you? What do you do?"

"Construction."

It didn't surprise Amber. With Steven's muscular built and tanned complexion, it was obvious he spent a lot of time outdoors. "Do you like it?"

"Sure. Of course, it's the family business so I grew up knowing that's what I would be doing with my life. Besides, there weren't many job openings for superheroes when I was growing up."

Amber laughed, then winced slightly at her discomfort. "You wanted to be a superhero?"

"Yeah."

A child-like grin dimpled his cheeks, making Steven look so sincere. So handsome.

"I thought it would be fun to be a hero, you know, right the wrongs in the world."

Immediately, Amber felt a twinge of resentment. *Is that what this is about? Is that why he's hanging around? Because he has some twisted fantasy that he's a superhero? And I'm in need of saving?* "That sounds pretty noble," her tone was cold. "Is that why you were in the park? Looking for someone to save?"

"No. I gave up trying to right wrongs a long time ago."

"Why? It seems to have paid off for you this time. You could tell reporters all about how you saved 'the woman in the park.' You'd be famous. Isn't that what superhero's want, to be famous?" She did nothing to hide the belligerence in her voice.

"Yeah, well, saving people isn't all it's cracked up to be."

His answered surprise her as did his sullen demeanor and biting words.

Amber wasn't sure what to make of his change in behavior, but her conscience reminded her she knew next to nothing about Steven

Levitt. His charm and compassion had been comforting, but he was still a complete stranger. Mentally, she began to question his motives. She still didn't understand why he was spending so much time and energy on her. He certainly couldn't be attracted to her. She was bruised and swollen, dirty and soiled. Not exactly pleasing to the eye for such a handsome and charismatic man. He had to have a girlfriend, and if he did, she couldn't be happy about the time he was spending with her. Amber was sure it was pity Steven felt for her. His wannabe superhero alter ego probably saw her as a charity case or some kind of pet project he could donate a few hours to from time to time.

Hostility grew in Amber.

She didn't want anyone's pity or charity. Instead of enjoying Steven's company, she felt agitated by his presence. She listened as his tone became more upbeat and he jumped from one innocuous subject to another. The changing weather, the political climate of America, the unrest in the Middle East—and how he strongly felt the need for the U.S. to have a presence. Amber nodded, but inside she was playing her own game of twenty questions.

How old is he? Why is he here? Does he know the extent of my attack? Why would he be here if there was nothing in it for him? She went on and on, each question she posed to herself making her angrier. She was beginning to feel as if maybe she was being used. Finally, her inner struggle broke through to the surface.

"Why are you here?" she blurted out, cutting him off mid-sentence while he was talking about his favorite sports teams. She could see he was noticeably shocked by her question. Maybe he realized she was finally onto him.

"I made you a promise," he replied calmly.

"But you don't even know me. So why are you spending your time here and bringing me presents?" She waved her hand at the balloons, flowers, and Bible that decorated her bedside table. "What's in it for you? This is just some sort of ego trip for you, isn't it?" She pinned him with an angry stare.

Amber's words stung, her eyes more stormy gray than tranquil blue.

Steven looked at her and saw a different person—a person accusing him of being an opportunist, labeling his motives as manipulative and self-seeking. She jutted out her chin, daring him to say anything.

He stood, ready to walk out, figuring she no longer wanted him there. But before he did, he would set her straight. He was ready to make his point when he saw a single tear roll down her cheek. It twisted his heart, silencing his words.

He sat back down and reined in control of the adrenaline pumping through his veins. "Amber, years ago, I made a promise to a friend of mine. I went back on the promise . . . and he died. People told me it wasn't my fault, but I swore then and there I would never make a promise I couldn't keep. In the park, I promised I wouldn't leave you alone."

"But I'm not alone. I'm in a hospital."

"A hospital where you're afraid to close your eyes because of your nightmares."

"Then I'll release you from your promise—free you from your obligation," she said sharply.

"Amber, I don't feel an obligation." He paused, moved to the edge of the chair—his elbows on his knees—and let out a cleansing breath. "Somehow, I feel responsible for you." Amber tried to interrupt, but he held up his hand so he could finish. "But not in a burdensome way. The minute I found you, I felt a connection to you. I don't know what it is or how to describe it."

"Pity?" Amber snapped.

"No, I don't pity you, Amber. I feel horrible for what you're going through, but it's not pity." Steven searched again for the words that seemed to elude him. "Amber, you're all alone, and I don't think you should be. I believe God allowed me to find you so you wouldn't have to go through this all by yourself. I'm not an opportunist if that's what you're afraid of. I don't have ulterior motives to take advantage of you because you're vulnerable. I just want to see you through this. I want to be your friend. But if that's too much for you to handle, I'll leave. I don't want to make your life more complicated. I was only hoping to help you through the stretch of road you have ahead of you."

His words didn't even seem to faze her. She just sat there, her swollen features doing a good job of masking her emotions.

He waited for her to say something. *Okay . . . so I guess this is it.*

"Look, Amber, I'm sorry," Steven said. "I never meant to put more pressure on you. I only wanted to help. But I can understand where you're coming from, so I think I'm going to head out." He stood and moved towards the door. "You've still got my number. Please call me if you need anything, anything at all. Even if it is just someone to sit with you while you sleep. I really do want to help you, but only if you want it."

❧❧❧❧

Before Amber could find her voice to apologize or stop Steven from leaving, he was gone. She dropped her head back on her pillow and cried. She cried because she saw the hurt in his eyes, and she knew she was responsible for putting it there. She had obviously been transparent enough that he had guessed what she was thinking—that she questioned his intentions. She felt confused and embarrassed. What could she do now? She had insulted his character when he had done nothing to deserve it. He was the Good Samaritan, and she was the Wicked Witch of the West.

TWELVE

Steven spent the next few days at the job site, working out his frustrations. He stopped several times throughout each day to pray for Amber. It was killing him not to call or visit her, but he knew he had to let it go. It had been her choice to make, and she had obviously made it.

His daily jog no longer brought the contentment it once did. He couldn't bear using the jogging path where he had found Amber, so he altered his routine. He started jogging neighborhoods instead of going near the park. But even then—if he didn't take his thoughts captive and force himself to think of other things—pictures of Amber's bruised and beaten body would flash through his consciousness. His senses were raw and nothing seemed to help. If he could just call her, see how she was doing, he was sure he would be able to put the last week behind him. At least, that's what he kept telling himself.

It was the end of the week, and he and Bo were pounding the pavement. Steven had shown restraint and left Amber alone, but now—knowing it was Friday and she was scheduled to go home—he found himself nearing Crescent Drive. He slowed as he passed the circular street she lived on, questions ricocheting around in his head. *Is she home, yet? Does she feel safe? Is she afraid of being alone?*

Bo stopped ahead of him, his expressive eyes asking why their pace had slowed. Steven knew he needed to respect Amber's privacy, so he quickened his stride and headed home where he belonged.

He peeled off his sweaty clothes and stepped under the cascading water of a hot shower. He wished he could wash away his thoughts of Amber as quickly as he could a day of grime, but that wasn't going to happen. She consumed his thoughts and prayers. He actually found himself crying into the flow of water, surprised at the emotional toll this was having on him. But the connection he had felt with Amber was more than mere chance. He felt God had pulled them together for a reason and somehow he had blown it.

Lord, if this is Your doing, then You're going to have to help me out. I can't live with my emotions in knots like this. Either release me from this need to protect Amber or help her to see there's no reason for her to go through this alone. I know Your ways are perfect, but I'm not. I'm ready to snap, and it's up to You to help me.

Steven flipped through channels, looking for something to watch on T.V. The normal drivel did nothing to hold his interest. He reached for the ringing phone, hoping it was Amber.

"Hello?"

"Hey, Steven, it's Connor."

"Connor. What's up?" Steven said with a disappointed sigh.

"Nothing. Stacy just wanted me to check in with you. See how you're doing."

"I'm fine. And you? Have you heard anything at work?"

"A couple of murmurings about a rape in the park, but it seems the police have decided to keep the extent of the attack under their hats."

"I think they're afraid for Amber's safety. The attackers left her for dead. But if they realize she's alive and can identify them, she could be in danger. I know that was why Det. Hastings was hesitant to release a sketch."

"Well, I just wanted to let you know that your name never came up."

"Thanks, Connor. I'm glad to hear it. I wasn't worried about me as much as I was for you and Stacy."

"There's nothing to worry about, Steven. At least I don't *think* there is."

Steven heard the subtle change in his tone. "What's that supposed to mean?"

"I hear you've spent some time with the victim."

"She has a name, Connor. And if you must know, I *was* spending time with her. Past-tense."

"That's good to hear, Steven. Getting involved with this woman would not have been in your best interest."

Steven had to fight back the impulse to attack his brother-in-law's every word. "Well, now you don't need to worry. Look, Connor, I'm pretty wiped out. Can you get me a rain check with the kids for this weekend? I promised them I would come over, but I don't think I feel up to it."

"Hey, no problem. They'll be disappointed, but I'll make sure they understand. Take care, Steven. And let me know if there's anything we can do."

THIRTEEN

Amber stepped from the minivan—the name of the hospital blazoned across it—and stared at her favorite place in the whole world: her home. She clutched her 'going away bag' from the hospital with her good hand. It held her medication and the disposable items from the hospital. Of course, what she would do with the bowl she had thrown-up in was beyond her. Other than the contents of her purse that had been recovered from the scene of her attack, she had nothing personal with her. Even the clothes she wore home had been given to her by the hospital. Her clothes had been ruined and taken into evidence by the police—not that she ever wanted to see them again.

She glanced at the 'For Sale' sign in the yard next to her, her emotions quickly coming to the surface. *Cara, I miss you so much. I wish you were here right now.*

Her best friend and confidant had just moved to Texas. It had been a tearful goodbye. She and Cara had been inseparable. Even after Cara started dating Eric, and eventually got married, she still always found time to spend with Amber.

It had been a struggle for Amber not to call Cara since the attack, especially since she'd scared Steven away. Just to have someone to talk to would've made it easier for her to cope. But, she couldn't do it. With thousands of miles between them, it wouldn't be fair to Cara. Amber knew her friend would jump on a plane the second she found out. That's exactly why Amber didn't call. Cara had a new husband and a new life. She was just getting settled in

Texas, and Amber didn't want to complicate things for her. Besides, sooner or later she would need to learn how to cope on her own.

She turned the key in the front door and pushed. The door was resistant because of the ever-present pile of mail that had dropped through the mail slot and had gathered in the entryway. Amber pushed through anyway, desperate to get the door shut and locked behind her. She leaned against the door, scrambling for the lock, her breath labored. With the bolt turned, she looked at the pile of mail but didn't bother to pick it up. Her energy was gone.

Home. Her corner of the world. Her sanctuary. She closed her eyes for a moment. *You're safe. No one can hurt you here,* she assured herself as she checked the lock again then stepped into the living room.

She waited for the rich fall colors to relax her, to soothe her like they had so many times before, but they did nothing to warm the chill inside her. The brown, overstuffed couch she hunkered down in night after night when watching T.V., didn't call to her. The goldenrod linen pillows snuggled in the side chair looked cold, and the chenille orange throw over the back of the couch held no warmth. Her sanctuary felt more like a mausoleum.

She moved to the Pothos plant on the end table alongside her couch and took in its drooping, yellowed leaves. It depressed her because it mimicked the way she was feeling. Weak and withered.

She took slow, even steps to her bedroom and sat on the edge of her bed. The sunny yellow walls and whitewashed furniture did nothing to lift her spirits. She remembered the day she chose the color for her bedroom. Cara thought she was crazy. "You need something more soothing," Cara had said. "Something in a tranquil blue." But Amber would not be swayed. Morning was her favorite time of day, and what could be better than being woken up with walls that screamed "Good Morning"!

Amber didn't know how long she had sat there, staring at the floor. But when she looked up, she caught her reflection in the full-length mirror inside her closet door. She set down the hospital bag, slowly got to her feet, and stood before the mirror. Trancelike, she disrobed and stared at herself. She touched her side where her skin was yellowed and grimaced at the other discolored blotches that covered her body. She pressed her hand to her abdomen, feeling a sense of panic. But then she stepped closer and stared at her face. Much of the swelling had diminished, but her skin still had a bluish tinge to it. She took one more overall look at herself, then burst into tears. She collapsed on the bed, rolled into a ball, and pulled her striped yellow comforter over her exposed body. Finally, in the privacy of her own room, Amber allowed herself to cry at the horror she had gone through, knowing she would never be the same again.

❧❧❧❧

After Steven got off the phone with Connor, he called the hospital. He had to know.

"She was released a short time ago, Mr. Levitt."

"Do you know who took her home?" he asked. *What business is it of yours? She's not your responsibility.* His inner voice taunted him. "What? Okay, thank you." He hung up the phone dejected. Amber had allowed a hospital volunteer to drive her home instead of calling him.

It was her choice and he realized it, but it hurt just the same. He closed his eyes and revisited what little time he had spent with Amber, trying to figure out what he could've said or done to upset her. But it was his sister's words that echoed in his thoughts. It wasn't anything he had said, it was the fact that he was a part of the most horrible thing a woman would ever have to endure. Amber would never be able to look at him without remembering how they met. As much as he hated to admit it, Amber had done what was right for her. She had made her choice, and he couldn't blame her.

❧❧❧❧

A sudden noise startled Amber from her sleep. She sat up, wincing at the pain, clutching the comforter to her chest. Her eyes darted around the room. Panic intensified her breathing. It took a minute for her to realize she was home and in her own room. The pop she'd heard was her bedside lamp clicking on at the pre-set time. She tried to calm her racing heart by chanting to herself.

You're okay. You're okay. Everything is going to be okay. It took some time before she felt calm enough to get up from where she had been cowering.

Amber dragged the comforter with her to the bathroom. She removed her robe from the back of the door and carefully slipped her sore arm through the sleeve. She pulled the sash tight, then quickly loosened it against the pain. Slowly, she made her way to the kitchen. Lights had gone on automatically throughout the house—a measure she used for safety. *A lot of good that did you.*

She opened her refrigerator and was surprised she didn't even have a simple loaf of bread. Then she remembered she'd had her groceries with her when she was . . .

She slammed the door causing the refrigerator to rock. Reaching for a banana on the counter, she realized it was past its prime. She grabbed the bunch and tossed them in the trash—trash that reeked after sitting for a week. She struggled to pull the liner from the can and half carried, half dragged it to her garage and panicked when she didn't see her car.

"The mechanic!"

Amber moved as fast as her aching body would allow. She went to her office and found the mechanic's business card. She dialed while holding her breath, hoping they hadn't closed for the evening.

"Yes, this is Amber Porter," she said to the person on the phone. "I left my car on . . . yes, I realize I was supposed to pick it up but . . . Yes, I know but . . . but you still have it, don't you?" Her heart sank. "Then where can I pick it up?" She quickly jotted down a name. "And how much is that going to cost me? Yes, I will make sure you get your money."

Amber hung up the phone before the mechanic could finish. She collapsed into her chair and rested her head on her desktop blotter. "What next, Lord?" she said as she raised her head. "What more can I possibly handle at this very mo—" Before she could even finish her hypothetical question, she zeroed in on tomorrow's date on the oversized calendar. "Oh no . . . I can't Lord, I just can't."

What am I going to do?

There, in bold print was her appointment for the following day. She had an engagement photo shoot scheduled . . . at the park.

Lord, why are you doing this to me? I can't go there. You know that. What am I going to do?

Amber toiled over the thought of canceling the appointment. How could she let anyone see her like this, let alone go back to the park? But this wedding would be huge for her career. Jessica Reeves and Tony Myers both came from very prominent families. Their wedding was not going to be the typical run-of-the-mill wedding. It would be a much publicized social event. Amber had been surprised when Jessica had called to set-up the appointment. The bride-to-be explained she had seen Amber's work through a friend of a friend. Jessica said she had immediately fallen in love with Amber's unique style and her flair for the romantic. Amber had been looking forward to the photo shoot for weeks.

And now I'm going to blow it.

As she sat there wondering what to do, she noticed the blinking number on her phone. Seven missed messages. *Maybe Jessica canceled?* She quickly listened to her machine, hoping beyond hope that one of them was about the photo shoot. No such luck. Four telemarketers and three from the mechanic.

Taking a breath, she dialed the contact number she had for Jessica.

"Hi, Jessica, this is Amber Porter, the photographer."

"Oh hi, Amber, I was just talking to Tony about tomorrow."

"About that . . ." Amber spoke quickly. "Is there any way we could postpone the sitting until next week? I had an accident. I still haven't been able to get my car out of impound, and I just got out of the hospital."

"Oh my gosh! Are you all right?" Jessica asked.

"I will be. I just need a little more time before I can return to my normal routine."

"Well, of course you do. Now let me see . . ."

Amber waited, knowing Jessica must be scrolling through her calendar.

"How about next Thursday? We'll have to do it before lunch because Tony and I have some other plans, but that's really the only time we have free in our schedules."

"Perfect!"

Actually, it was far from perfect. Amber pointed to the day on her schedule blotter and noticed the two other appointments already scheduled for next Thursday. She didn't care. She would cancel the others if she had to. She just couldn't handle the thought of leaving her house, the pain of lifting a camera, or the terror of returning to the park. "Okay, let's say ten o'clock. Would that work for the two of you?"

"That's fine," Jessica said. "Should we still plan on meeting you at the park?"

"Aah . . . let's meet at my house and then we can go from there?"

"Okay, ten o'clock it is."

Amber was ready to disconnect the call when she heard Jessica say something.

"I'm sorry, Jessica, what was that?"

"Oh, I was just asking about your accident. It wasn't your fault was it?"

"No," Amber mumbled.

"Oh, that's good. But it must've been more than a fender-bender to put you in the hospital. Tell me the other person had insurance."

"I . . . I don't know."

"You mean it was a hit and run? Oh, that's just awful. Well, I hope they catch the guy."

"Yeah . . . me too." Amber could feel her stomach churn as the men's faces flashed before her eyes. "Look, Jessica, I have to go. Thank you for being so understanding. I'll see you next Thursday." Amber quickly ended the call.

She looked back at her appointment calendar to see what she

had next on her schedule. She had four sessions on Monday. *Are you kidding me? Why do I do this to myself?* Amber knew why. She thought nothing of booking several appointments on the same day so it would free up the rest of her week to take the pictures she wanted. Pictures that were artistic and had meaning.

Yeah, well, this time you've painted yourself into a corner.

First, she had a sitting to do with a couple celebrating their 50th wedding anniversary. She thought to herself for a moment. *I can handle that. I'll be doing it in studio, and it won't take more than a half-hour, forty minutes tops.* Then she had two viewings. *No problem. Just setting up pictures.* Last, she had an in-house engagement shoot. *I can do this. I'll be exhausted, but it's better than canceling.* She left the appointments for Monday on her schedule and then looked at the Thursday that now had conflicting appointments. She steeled herself to call Mrs. Bender.

"Hi, Mrs. Bender, this is Amber Porter, the photographer. I was calling about our appointment on Thursday. You see—"

"Well, I hope you're not calling to cancel. I've already told Jimmy he would be taken out of school for the day, and we would do whatever he wanted. I can't go back on my word. He would be too disappointed."

Amber could tell by the woman's tone, this wasn't going to go well. She took a deep breath. *Here goes nothing.*

"The thing is, Mrs. Bender, I've had an accident. I've just been released from the hospital and still haven't been able to get my car out of the impound yard."

"Can you still take pictures?"

"Well, I think I can, but—"

"Then I don't see how any of this is my problem. I'm sure you are a professional and won't allow a little discomfort to interfere with your work."

Amber wanted to hang up on the woman and show her how completely unprofessional she could be, but she didn't. Her pride was taking a hit, and she would not let this woman get the best of her.

"If that is how you feel, Mrs. Bender, I'm going to have to ask that we move your appointment to nine o'clock. I'm sure that won't be a problem since you already told Jimmy he would have the whole day off."

"Well, I don't understand why I have to rearrange my schedule."

"Mrs. Bender, it's either that or I will have to cancel altogether. If you would like, I can bring you a note from my trauma doctor. Maybe an x-ray of my broken ribs would help you better understand the situation I'm in."

"Well!" Mrs. Bender said with a huff. "I don't think that will be necessary."

Amber could tell the woman still wanted to add her two cents, but she wouldn't allow her the chance. "Then I will see you at nine o'clock sharp." Amber slammed the phone in its charger.

She adjusted the times on her schedule and sighed. "Nine o'clock, ten o'clock, one o'clock. How am I ever going to make it through that day?"

She had no idea, especially since her one o'clock appointment was a kid's party at one of those loud and obnoxious children's restaurants. But she didn't care. The important thing was she wouldn't have to go to the park tomorrow.

Looking at her schedule for Monday, Amber realized she still had some work to get done. She had negatives in her darkroom, ready for preparation. At least her appointments were later in the afternoon. That would give her until Monday morning if she couldn't get her act together before then.

"Help me, God. I can't lose my business, too."

Amber sighed and took a deep breath. Then, she steadied herself and headed once again to the kitchen. After a dinner of crackers with peanut butter, and a glass of water, she moved to her bedroom. Exchanging her robe for an oversized sweatshirt and sweatpants, she went to work in her darkroom.

Once inside, she locked the door. She had never used the inside lock—knowing there was never anyone to disturb her—but now she felt she had to lock herself in. Paranoia was now her constant companion—that and the Lord. How the two could co-exist at the same time, she wasn't sure, but the Lord was bigger than her. It was something He would have to figure out.

❧❧❧❧

Steven thought about Amber all day. How would she do on her own? What if she needed something? He wanted to call but realized he didn't have her number. He could go by Amber's house, see if she needed anything, but that might startle her. He sat in his office, feet on his desk, eyes staring out the window when Scott came in.

"Okay, I rescheduled the concrete pour, and I have a meeting with Frank tomorrow. I'll know better—" Scott stopped talking. He walked over to Steven's desk and dropped his clipboard on the surface.

"I heard you," Steven said without looking at Scott. "Rescheduled the pour . . . talking to Frank . . ."

"Go home, Steven. You're only getting in the way here. I'll call you if something comes up that needs your attention."

Steven didn't acknowledge him.

"Steven . . . did you hear me?"

"Yeah, I heard you, but it's not going to get any better if I go home. I'll still be thinking about her."

"Then do something about it. Call her, go by her house, send her some flowers. Just do something before you go nuts."

Steven considered Scott's suggestions, but felt anything he did would be an intrusion. If Amber had needed his help, she would've called him by now.

His sister was right. Amber would lump him in with the other horrific memories of that day, and do her best to erase them from her mind. He was part of the problem, not the solution.

Help her, Lord. Comfort and heal her. Remind her she doesn't have to go through this alone. She has You . . . and she has me. I want to be there for her, Lord. But it has to be her choice.

FOURTEEN

Amber finally came out of her darkroom, exhausted and ready to collapse. She had pushed herself to the limit. Her left wrist continued to hurt, and her ribs ached from standing so long. But, for a few hours—with her attention completely on her work—she had survived without terror accompanying her every breath.

But now it was late and the house was quiet. An extremely loud quiet. She turned on the television to help fill the room with something other than silence. When she saw a news reporter standing in front of the gazebo at the park, she froze. She reached for the remote so she could turn up the volume.

The reporter stared into the camera. "Though police have very little to go on regarding this attack, they are warning women in the area to take extra precautions. It is not clear if this was a random act or if the victim was targeted. Needless to say, caution is the watchword for the moment. This is Stan Grissom at Riverbend Park for Channel 3 News."

Amber sunk into her living room chair, as she stared at the television. *How did they find out? Did they mention my name or the fact that I'm alive?* The police had promised they wouldn't let her personal information out.

She quickly flipped through the channels to see if any other station was carrying the story, but it was too late. It was the end of the late night news. She would have to wait until morning to hear a full report.

After getting over the shock of seeing the report on television,

Amber looked in the refrigerator for something to eat. Of course, it didn't hold anything more than it had earlier that day. Normally, she would've called one of her favorite late night delivery places, but the thought of having to open the door to a stranger made her lose her appetite. She looked at the medicine bottles on the counter, with the 'take with food' symbol on them, and sighed. Looking again in her refrigerator, she discovered two sourdough heels of bread shoved in her crisper drawer. She pulled them out—knowing they were stale—but dropped them in the toaster anyway.

She leaned her body against the counter, her legs weak. She held her hand out in front of her and watched as it trembled. She pressed her palm to her forehead and felt the dampness of her warm, clammy skin.

The bread jumped from the toaster causing her to scream and grabbed her side in discomfort. Her heart was ready to pulse right out of her sweatshirt, and she had to steady herself by clutching the tile counter before she could resume what she was doing. She closed her eyes and took as deep of a cleansing breath as her injured ribs would allow.

She laid the toast on a plate and spread it haphazardly with peanut butter. She placed her medicine next to the bread and moved to the living room, then slowly lowered herself to the couch.

Lord, help me. I don't know what else to say to You.

Her prayer was short and to the point, the way an angry teen might talk to an absentee parent, because that's how she felt at the moment. God was supposed to protect her, but somehow, He'd been AWOL when she needed Him most. Where had He been when she was being dragged into the bushes? Why hadn't He protected her? Or sent Steven sooner? "Are You even there?" she shouted to the ceiling, tears running down her face. "I thought You cared? Was I wrong to believe in You all this—"

She stopped herself.

Amber knew if she questioned her relationship with God, her anger would consume her. She couldn't afford to turn her back on God. He was all she had. But she wasn't letting Him off the hook that easy. In her mind, He had some major steps to take to regain her trust.

She ate her toast without really tasting it and sipped enough water to choke down the pills that were supposed to make her feel better. She stared at the television lifelessly as an infomercial spokesman fervently explained how his latest exercise contraption worked. Laying her head against the pillow-back of the couch, she closed her eyes and drifted slowly into a restless sleep.

Amber's head snapped up and suddenly she was very awake. Her eyes darted around the room looking for what had startled her. She wanted to run—run to her bedroom, lock herself inside, hide from the noise, but she was momentarily paralyzed with fear, unable to move.

Her body was covered in perspiration and tremors shook her limbs. Her glass of water she'd been holding had spilled and saturated the cushion of the couch along with the leg of her sweatpants. Finally, she exhaled. It was just the glass of cold water that had awakened her, but it still took a moment for her to get control of her emotions. When she did, she slowly walked the distance to her bedroom, locked the door behind her, and crawled under the covers of her bed. She sobbed in earnest as she allowed overwhelming fear to consume her.

Steven slowly drove down the cul-de-sac. Lights illuminated Amber's windows while the rest of her neighborhood rested in a dark slumber. He wondered what she was doing and how she was feeling. He was concerned that it was after midnight, and she was still awake. Or, were the lights a way to keep the things that frightened her at bay?

He knew he couldn't stay long. The neighbors were obviously very observant, and though the other houses were dark and still, he couldn't take the chance of being seen creeping around once again. He pulled from the curb and waited until he got to the end of the street before he turned his headlights back on and headed home.

FIFTEEN

Distant voices filtered into Amber's consciousness. She listened carefully, trying to figure out who was talking and what they were doing in her living room. After a moment, and a few rubs of her temples, it dawned on her it was morning. She realized she had left the television on, and it was the roar of a crowded sports stadium that had awakened her from the other room.

She pulled the covers back and winced, wondering if her body would ever feel normal again. She dragged herself into the bathroom and—without looking at herself in the mirror—turned on the shower as hot as she could handle it. She stood under the cleansing flow and cried. It was as if her tears were now an involuntary reflex, something she wasn't able to control. They mingled with the hot flow of water that stung her skin.

"Why, God?" she cried aloud. "Why would You let them do that to me? What have I done to deserve this? Am I that bad of a person? Have I not loved You enough? If You didn't care what they did to me, why didn't You allow me to die? Why should I have to relive the horror day after day? What are You punishing me for?" She cried uncontrollably, hoping He was listening, because she was falling apart and it felt as if not even He could help her.

Instantly, a picture of Steven crossed the lids of her eyes. She heard the calmness of his voice promising her that he would not leave her alone, that he wanted to be there for her. Her pulse calmed ever so slightly. She turned off the water and stepped from the shower. Wrapping a towel around herself, Amber walked to the side of her bed and sat down.

Staring at the phone on the nightstand, she willed it to ring. When she saw the hospital bag that sat by the edge of the bed, she rifled through it, searching for the Bible Steven had given her. Inside the cover was his phone number. Amber held the phone for several minutes before pressing the first three numbers, then disconnected.

She put the phone back in the cradle, but in an instant, reached for it again. Dialing before she could talk herself out of it, the phone connected. Again, she pressed to end the call. Amber held the phone in her hand knowing it was a lifeline if she would only choose to use it. Closing her eyes, she debated what to do.

Steven said I could call him whenever I wanted to. But why? Why is he making himself so available? Does he feel guilty? What was he doing in the park that day anyway? Why did it seem like he was the only other person there except for the men that had—

"Why am I doing this, God? This isn't who I am. I'm normally a trusting person. I always look for the good in people. Why am I having such a hard time accepting Steven for who he is? What he's offering?"

Because he's a stranger. Just like the men who attacked me.

Amber stroked the cover of the Bible Steven had given her and remembered the prayers he had said on her behalf. He was offering her the same hope she had extended to Henry at the park last year.

Henry was a homeless man she had noticed on occasion while working with clients in the park. He was older, walked with a limp, and pushed a shopping cart loaded down with blankets and odds-n-ends. What started as a simple smile and wave, turned into small talk about the weather and his fascination with her photography. Then Amber started bringing Henry sack lunches and sitting with him to talk when no one else would give him the time of day.

After months of conversation, Amber had learned about the death of his wife, the loss of his business, and a son who had succumbed to drug addiction. Henry was not homeless because he'd given up on life, life had just dealt him more than he could handle.

When Fall winds turned into Winter chill, Amber had finally persuaded Henry to go to the homeless shelter run by her church.

With nothing more than the Bible she had given him and his shopping cart of possessions, Henry had checked into New Beginnings. Ten months later he was still there. Not as a resident but as a faculty member. He had given his life to the Lord and was now a peer counselor offering eternal hope to men who had fallen into the same trap that he had.

Amber had been a part of that. She had stepped outside her comfort zone and had allowed herself to be used by God. She had learned something about who she was as a person during that time. She didn't do crowds, or appreciate large gatherings. She was a one-on-one person. That was her strength. And God had used it to help transform someone's life.

Not knowing if God would bring another 'Henry' into her life, she'd gone back to her quiet habits of leaving a Gospel tract with her tip at a restaurant, or a small New Testament in the changing room at a department store. She was not a gregarious person with her faith. To her it had always been personal and private. Until Henry. Until God had asked her to become His hands and feet in someone's life.

Is that what Steven was trying to do for her?

The shrilling ring of the phone in the palm of her hand made Amber jump, the phone dropping to the floor. She stared at it as it continued to ring, not sure what she should to do. Picking it up, she pressed the button on the phone and brought the receiver to her ear. "Hello?" she said, timidly.

"Amber? Is that you? Are you okay?"

"Steven? How did you get my number?" Paranoia, not trust was Amber's first instinct.

"You just called me. I was in the shower and didn't get to the phone in time. So I used my callback. Are you okay?"

"Yes . . . yes, I'm okay."

"Are you sure? You don't sound so good."

She tried to shake off her fear. Steven was nice. A decent guy;

she could feel it . . . or is that just what she wanted to believe?

"Amber, are you there?"

"Yes, I'm here."

"Why did you call? Is something wrong?"

"No, nothing is wrong. I was just . . ." She felt awkward and wasn't sure what to say.

"What is it, Amber?" His tone was gentle and reassuring.

Tears fell from her eyes and trickled onto her lap. She pinched the bridge of her nose, trying to regain some emotional control. "I was just wondering . . . I mean if you weren't busy . . . because if you have other plans I completely understand. Never mind. I shouldn't—"

"Amber? Why don't you just tell me why you were calling, and then I can answer you?"

Amber exhaled. "It's just that I don't have my car back, and I need to get some groceries. I was wondering if maybe you could take me to the market, or even just up to the mini-mart around the corner. It wouldn't take long. I just need to get the basics, like bread and eggs. If you're busy though, I completely understand. In fact, I shouldn't have bothered you."

"Amber . . ."

"You probably already have plans."

"Amber . . ."

"You know what, I can figure this out on my own."

"Amber, I'll be over in twenty minutes. Can you hold on that long?"

"Sure. Yes. That would be fine. Anytime would be fine."

"Then twenty minutes it is. I'll knock twice and then ring the bell. That way you'll know it's me."

"Okay, let me give you my address."

"What?"

"My address. Do you have something to write it down with?"

"Uhh . . . sure. Yeah."

He sounded hesitant.

"Steven, are you sure you're okay with this?"

"Of course."

Amber rattled off her address and thanked him again before disconnecting the call. She sat on the edge of her bed for a few seconds before putting the phone back in the cradle, hoping she wasn't making a huge mistake.

Slowly getting up from the bed, Amber walked to her armoire and pulled out a change of clothes. Deciding on a pair of loose fitting jogging pants and a black t-shirt, she walked to the bathroom, closed the door, and locked it.

When Amber dared to look at herself in the bathroom mirror, she winced at her reflection. Turning her head slightly, her fingers probed the shaved area behind her ear with its ugly crisscross of black stitches. Instantly, Amber was back at the park, hearing the grotesque sound of the bat slamming against her skull and feeling the excruciating pain that had caused her to black out. She gripped the counter when her knees began to buckle. *Stop it. It's over. You're going to be fine.* Shaking away the memory, she reached for her hairbrush. She tried styling her hair differently—to camouflage her wound—but nothing helped. Frustrated and weak, Amber tossed her brush in the sink and leaned against the vanity for support, hating that her pain was getting the better of her.

Amber rested for a minute before tackling her makeup. She tried using her concealer stick to cover the discoloration from the bruising around her left eye and cheek, but it wasn't enough. She rummaged around in her tiny makeup drawer, looking for something more, but her collection was sparse. She'd never been much of a makeup hound like some women are, mostly because she'd inherited her mother's beautiful complexion. Her makeup regiment—when she decided to use it—consisted of a little blush, a touch of eye shadow, and a good mascara. And for those times that she stayed up too late in her darkroom and didn't want to look like a raccoon the next morning, she had her concealer. *What I wouldn't give for a good liquid foundation right about now.* Realizing her attempts to cover the bruising wasn't working, Amber applied a little mascara and blush, and called it good.

Making her bed took longer than normal. Every pull on the sheet and every tug on the blanket was accompanied by a gasp or a groan. When Amber finished, she moved to the living room and sat in the side chair. But that only lasted a few seconds before she was up on her feet, walking towards the kitchen. There, she washed the few pieces of silverware that lay on the bottom of the sink and wiped down the counters, anxiously waiting for Steven to get there.

The sudden knock on the door made her jump, even though she was expecting it. There was a second knock as she approached the door and then—as Steven had promised—the doorbell rang.

"Amber, it's me."

After hearing his muffled voice, Amber looked through the peephole and saw Steven, his arms loaded down with plastic bags. Removing the security chain, she opened the door.

"Hi," she said timidly.

"Hi," he smiled. "Where would you like these?"

"What are they?"

"Just a few groceries."

She motioned to the kitchen.

He walked around her, stumbling slightly on the pile of mail still lying on the floor.

"Sorry about that," she said, as she followed him into the kitchen where he placed the bags on the counter.

"Steven, I didn't expect you to go shopping for me. I just needed a ride to the market."

"Well, I thought this might be easier," he said, as he started to unload the groceries.

She watched him for a moment and then started putting away the items he was stacking on the counter. They worked in silence while Amber's conscience peppered her with questions and doubts. *What am I doing? He's a perfect stranger. Never mind that he's been caring and compassionate. I still know nothing about him. How stupid can I be? Letting some man I don't even know into my house. I deserve what happened to me in the park. That's what I get for being so careless.*

Her pulse raced as small pinpoints of light danced before her eyes. She held onto the counter for balance and took a deep, silent breath. *No. I don't believe that. I didn't deserve what happened to me. It wasn't my fault. And Steven's been nothing but nice.*

When the groceries were put away and the bags stowed under the kitchen sink, Steven leaned against the counter and looked at her, but she quickly looked away. Making eye contact with him seemed too personal. Like he would be able to look right through her and see the turmoil brewing deep inside.

"How are you doing?" he asked.

"Okay. I guess."

"You look good," he said softly.

She dipped her head. "You must have a pretty low opinion of what *good* looks like," she said sarcastically, her words sharper than she intended. "I'm sorry. I didn't mean to sound so rude."

"Hey, it's understandable."

Silence filled the room once again.

"Why don't I fix you some breakfast?"

"No. That's okay. I'm fine." She didn't want to give him a reason to stay.

"Well, I'm starved. Would you mind if I fix something for myself, and maybe make a little extra for you?" He reached for the refrigerator door and started pulling out some of the items they had just put away.

What could she say? He had just completely stocked her refrigerator. How could she tell him he couldn't make himself breakfast?

They worked in a comfortable silence, only talking when Steven asked her for a utensil or an ingredient. When he dished up two plates of food, he turned towards the main room and stopped, obviously looking for some place to eat.

"I don't have a dining room table," Amber offered. "I just use the coffee table."

"Works for me," Steven said as he followed her to the living room, and set the plates down.

She carefully lowered herself to the edge of the side chair while he went back to the kitchen. He returned with silverware and two glasses of orange juice.

"Let's pray," Steven said before bowing his head. Amber followed.

"Lord, thank You for this new day and for the strength You have given Amber so far. Bless this food to our bodies and help Amber in the days ahead. Amen."

Amber cut her pancakes and pushed them around the edge of her plate. She chewed on a slice of bacon, like it was a piece of beef jerky.

"It's not that bad, really. You should try it." Steven grinned as he took a forkful of pancakes, dripping with syrup.

Amber gave him a weak smile and began to eat the soggy pieces of pancakes on her plate, surprised how good they actually tasted. Steven quietly moved to the kitchen, returning with a second helping and the pitcher of orange juice. He refilled her glass before sitting down.

"Thank you."

"My pleasure."

Steven ate a couple more bites. "So, where's your car?"

"The mechanic had it towed. It's at an impound yard."

"Why did he do that?"

"I was supposed to pick it up days ago. When I didn't return his messages, he figured I had abandoned the car. So he had it towed."

"Which impound yard is it at?"

Amber thought for a moment what she had scribbled down. "Central Impound. The mechanic said it was on Washington Street."

"How about I take you to get it after breakfast?"

"You don't need to do that, Steven. You've already done enough."

"How else will you get there?"

Amber didn't have an answer.

"Then it's settled," he said with a smile.

Amber stared into her glass of juice while Steven cleared the dishes. She listened as he cleaned up the kitchen, the whole time her paranoia asking her why Steven was making himself so available. What did she know about him anyway? She thought of the way he prayed for her and the Bible he had given her. Certainly he wasn't involved in her attack. But her questioning mind continued to nudge her doubts into fears.

She walked to the kitchen just as Steven let the dishwater out of the sink.

"What were you doing at the park?" she asked him, her voice monotone.

"What?"

"The park. What were you doing there that day?"

"I was jogging with my dog. I was hoping to get our run in before the rain. Bo's an old hunting dog and needs his exercise. When he started barking and ran off the path, I assumed he was chasing an animal. I scolded him but he wouldn't give up. When I went to get him, he was hovering over . . . you. When I first saw you, I thought you were . . . uhh . . . but when I realized you were alive, I called the police and waited until they got there."

Amber remembered the way Steven had stayed with her and prayed. She hung her head, feeling horrible. To think Steven was in anyway responsible for her attack was inexcusable.

"I understand, Amber. I wouldn't trust anyone right now either. But please believe me when I say I just want to help you."

She didn't know what to say. Here she had just questioned him, putting him on the defensive, and he still wanted to help her. She walked over to the couch and sat. Resting her elbows on her knees, she buried her head in her hands. The coffee table creaked as he sat down in front of her.

"Amber, I'm not even going to pretend I know what you're going through. I only know I don't want you to have to go through it alone. I'll leave if you want me to, but I'd really like to help if you'll let me." He paused for a moment then asked, "So, how about we go get your car?"

SIXTEEN

Steven took a moment to pick up Amber's mail and toss it on the coffee table before they headed out the door. Amber stepped out onto the front porch and froze. Even through her dark sunglasses, he could see her eyes darting from one end of the street to the other, her hand clutching the wooden porch rail. Steven stood beside her as she walked rigidly down the front walk, her steps slow and unsure. He opened the passenger door for her and stood by as she reached for the door frame. He saw her wince, as she tried to pull herself up into the oversized truck. Steven instinctively reached to help her. She flinched. He immediately pulled his hand away and watched as she struggled to get comfortable.

Closing Amber's door once she was settled, Steven quickly walked around to the driver's side of his truck. Once he got into the cab he noticed how pale Amber looked and wondered if she was overdoing it. "Amber, are you going to be all right? We could do this tomorrow or even the next day."

"No, I'm fine," she answered as she stared out the passenger window.

Steven pulled away from the curb and headed towards downtown. Amber rolled the handle of her purse around in her hand and looked as if she was going to jump out of her skin. Steven decided this wasn't such a good idea. There was no way Amber was going to be able to drive home.

"Amber, I think we should do this another time. You shouldn't drive in your condition. It's not safe." Steven started to slow down.

"No!" She turned towards him. "Please, keep going. I'll be fine. It's not that far, and I will feel a lot better knowing I have my car at home."

"Are you sure?"

She just nodded and turned back towards the window.

Against his better judgment, Steven continued to the impound yard. He could see Amber's hands were shaking and perspiration beaded her forehead. He would have to do something once they got to the yard. There was no way he was going to let her get behind the wheel of a car.

ঌঌ৵৵

Amber walked into the small office at the impound yard. She waited for someone to answer the service bell while Steven made a call outside. When the attendant appeared, he stared at Amber, making her feel self-conscious. She looked down as she spoke.

"I was told my car is here."

He pushed a piece of paper in front of her. "Make, model, and license number."

With a shaky hand, she filled out the form, slid it back, and then watched as he plucked at the relic of a computer on the beat-up desk behind him. He turned to her. "I need to see some identification."

She slid her driver's license and a credit card across the small Formica counter.

He pushed back her credit card and pointed to the sign hanging to the side of the small window. "Cash Only." He stepped back to his desk and entered more information on his computer.

"Uhh . . ." she stuttered, her mind scrambling. "But I don't have two hundred dollars, at least not on me."

"Not my problem, lady. Cash only." He didn't even turn to speak to her.

Amber took a deep breath to regroup. *Don't freak out; just explain your situation.* "I'm sure you have your policies, and I understand that, but I had an accident and just got out of the hospital. Could you make an exception this one time?"

"Look, lady, rules are rules." He turned, his stare void of any sympathy. "I didn't make them."

Amber's voice rose as she clenched the counter for balance. "I understand that, but please, if you knew how difficult this is for me, I'm sure you could make an exception. If you're not willing to, I would like to speak to your supervisor."

The attendant moved back to the partition and leaned in close. "Look lady, I know your kind. You walk in here with your nose in the air and throw your high and mighty words around, then threaten to talk to my boss. Well, that crap doesn't work on me. In fact, maybe I don't have your car at all." He stepped back to his desk and stroked his keyboard. The screen went black. "Well, ain't that a shame. My computer seems to be acting up. I can't access any records if my computer is acting up. I guess you'll just have to come back on Monday, seeing as we're closed on Sundays."

"That's not fair!" Amber could barely see through the tears pooling in her eyes. She knew yelling at this guy was not the answer, so she changed her tone. "I'm sorry you think I was being rude. I just need to get my car. What if I was to leave my credit card with you—as collateral—then brought the cash in on Monday?"

"If you can come back on Monday to bring me the cash, then you can come back on Monday to pick up your car."

She let out a sob, no longer able to control her emotions.

"Amber, what is it?"

She looked up to see Steven standing in the doorway. He rushed to her side and asked again, "Amber, what's wrong?"

"I don't have the money. I can't get my car."

"What's the problem?" Steven angrily snapped at the man behind the partition.

"Look, man, I didn't mean to make her cry, but policy is policy. The sign right there says we only accept cash."

"How much?"

"Two hundred dollars."

Amber watched as Steven pulled out his wallet and rifled through it. "No, Steven, you don't need to do this." He tugged the bills from his wallet and slapped them on the counter. His jaw was clenched as he looked at the attendant. "Can you get her car now?"

The man nodded and headed for the yard.

Steven reached for Amber's elbows and drew her close. "It's all right."

Amber tensed, instantly feeling claustrophobic. Trapped. She pulled away from Steven and swiped at the tears on her face. "You didn't need to do that."

"What, the money? It was no problem."

"That's not what I was talking about."

Amber looked at Steven, then hurried outside.

❧❧❧❧

Steven felt as if he had just been slapped. Amber looked at him like he had just assaulted her. He hadn't meant anything by his actions. She looked like she was going to keel over. All he had wanted to do was offer her some support.

Patience, Steven. One step forward, two steps back. As long as you keep moving, you'll be fine. Just give her some room.

It took over half an hour before the attendant brought out a red Opal GT. "Sorry about the wait. I had a hard time locating it."

"Right. I can imagine a cherry-red sports car would be hard to find among a bunch of junk vehicles." Steven wanted to read the attendant the riot act but didn't. Causing a scene would only make Amber feel worse.

Steven looked at Amber's car. It was a classic in near perfect condition. He could only imagine how good she must look behind the wheel.

The attendant walked back inside the building, and a moment later, Amber walked out, papers in hand.

Steven stood at the bottom of the stairs, his hands in his pockets, feeling horrible. "I'm sorry, Amber. I didn't mean to upset you," he said as she slowly descended the rickety wood stairs.

"Just forget it." Her words were cold. "I'll pay back the money as soon as I can."

"I'm not worried about the money. I'm worried about you."

"I'll be fine. I just want to go home." Amber walked towards the driver's door, but Steven intercepted her. "I'll drive you home."

"Steven, I appreciate your help, but I can drive myself."

"No, you can't. You're shaky and in no condition to drive. Besides, I called my friend, and he already came and picked up my truck. You're not going to leave me stranded here, are you?"

Amber looked over at the empty spot where Steven's truck had been parked.

"Let me drive you home and then I'll leave, okay? I didn't mean to make you feel uncomfortable earlier. I was just afraid you were going to collapse or something."

Her shoulders sagged in defeat. "Fine, but can we stop by my bank first? I want to withdraw the money I owe you for the groceries and the car."

"We don't need to worry about that right now. You look tired and pale. Why don't I take you home, and we can worry about the money later?"

"Why must you argue with everything I say?" Amber barked.

"Why can't you admit you barely have enough strength to be standing, let alone driving?" Steven barked right back.

Amber knew he was right. She could barely feel her feet beneath her. All she wanted to do was get home, regardless who was driving. Without another word, she dropped her keys into Steven's hand, walked to the passenger side of her car, and slid inside.

When Steven pulled into her driveway, Amber saw Det. Hastings and Det. Jones step from a sedan parked on the street. Distracted by the two men approaching her house, she jumped at the screech of her automatic garage door as it began to roll up.

"Were you expecting them?" Steven asked as he pulled forward.

"No."

"Are you going to be okay?"

"Depends on why they're here."

Amber moved slowly down the driveway and around to her front door where the detectives were waiting. She watched as they exchanged glances with Steven. It was clear they were getting the wrong idea, but she didn't have the energy to correct them. She opened the door, the detectives and Steven silently following behind her. She jumped when Steven shut the door with a thud.

"Ms. Porter, we're sorry to disturb you at home, but we felt we needed to make you aware of something," Hastings said.

Amber braced herself against the wall.

"The local news has gotten wind of your attack, and they're reporting it."

Amber remained calm. "I saw it last night, but only part of it," she said. "Do they know it was me?"

"No. No personal information was given out. But—"

"But what?" Steven interrupted.

"It wasn't reported as a homicide."

"So, they know I'm alive," Amber mumbled as she walked to the sliding glass door and looked out over her backyard. She wrapped her arm around her waist, bracing her weak stomach. *Please don't let me be sick.*

"I apologize, Ms. Porter," Det. Hastings broke into her thoughts. "We were hoping to keep this under wraps. The park was empty the day of your attack so we assumed we would be in the clear. But someone started filming with their phone when the ambulance pulled up. It was inevitable the story would get out."

"So what's to say her name won't get out, too?" Steven snapped.

Amber turned to see Hastings was clearly agitated by Steven's interference. "Mr. Levitt, we can't guarantee anything, but we're doing the best we can."

Det. Jones crossed the living room to where Amber was standing. "We would like you to work with one of our sketch artists and come up with a composite drawing of your attackers. If we could circulate the pictures, along with your story, we might be able to get a lead on one or both of the suspects."

Amber listened to the detective but didn't respond.

"Ms. Porter, do you think you could describe the men well enough to come up with a composite?"

The men's faces flashed in her memory. She could hear the sound of their voices—the disgusting things they had said. Their faces were clear in her head. Horribly clear.

"Ms. Porter?" Det. Jones tried to get her attention.

Steven stepped towards Amber and the detective. "You know what, guys, I don't think this is a good time." Steven whispered to Amber, "You don't need to do this right now. You can wait until you feel better."

"That's true, Ms. Porter, we could wait," Det. Jones said. "But if we're dealing with someone who might try this again, you could save another woman from going through what you did."

The detective's words pierced her heart. She wanted to shout at him. *No one was there to save me, to warn me. Why should I be forced into re-creating these men on paper?* Her selfish thoughts surprised her. Of course she wanted these men caught. She would never want another woman to go through what she did. *I have to do this. Otherwise, I will never feel safe.*

It was agreed. Amber would work with a sketch artist tomorrow. She listened as Steven and the detectives talked in hushed tones. When they were gone, Steven walked over to where she was still standing by the sliding glass door. "I know this is difficult, but you're doing the right thing," Steven encouraged.

She didn't answer him.

"Hey, why don't I fix us some lunch since you didn't eat much for breakfast? What would you like to eat?"

"I'm not hungry." Her words held no feeling.

"But I'm sure you have medicine you need to take, and you shouldn't do it on an empty stomach."

Amber heard Steven walk to the kitchen and open the refrigerator. She continued to stare out through the sliding glass door, a hundred thought spinning through her mind. She noticed a spider web in the eave of the porch, a fly caught in its silky threads.

She knew exactly how it felt.

ঌ঳ঌ঳

Steven watched as Amber silently ate what he put in front of her. She tossed her pills to the back of her mouth, followed quickly by a swig of water, and a shudder. Leaning against the pillow-back of the couch, she closed her eyes—her face expressionless. Clearly, she was on auto-pilot.

Steven didn't know what to do. He couldn't leave her like this, but he felt helpless to comfort her. He walked aimlessly around her house, admiring what he assumed was her original artwork. She was very talented. Too talented to just be taking studio pictures. When he finally took a seat, she looked at him with tired eyes.

"You don't need to stay. I'll be all right."

He stared at his hands clasped in front of him. "Is there anything I can do for you? Anything I can get?"

"My life back." Instantly, her shoulders began to shake, tears breaching her eyelids. "I just want my life back."

Steven felt the sting of tears in his eyes. He wanted to go to her, to hold her. He fought with his emotions before he moved closer and slowly sat down next to her on the couch. He waited for her to respond negatively, and when she didn't, he whispered, "Amber, I wish I could. I wish I could change everything about that day, but I can't. However, I can be here for you now, so you're not alone. I know you're strong. You've proven that already. You *will* get passed this, Amber." Steven held out his hand to her. "But you don't have to do it alone."

ঌ঳ঌ঳

Amber looked at Steven's calloused fingers. She didn't understand it. How when they'd had so few encounters had Steven gained her trust and penetrated her boundaries? He made her feel safe. Unexplainably safe. She placed her hand in his. He squeezed her fingers gently, but she could feel his strength.

A strength she didn't have.

A strength she knew she would need if she was going to survive this.

SEVENTEEN

Amber heard a crack and felt her legs collapse beneath her. She struggled to stay conscious, to do something more, but her body would not cooperate. Sounds assaulted her, distorted and garbled. She could hear labored breathing—feel its foul heat against her skin. It was a nightmare. It had to be.

This can't be happening again.

She struggled to open her eyes, to free herself from the nightmare. She heard someone talking, felt them hovering beside her. When her subconscious joined with her consciousness, she swung at her attacker. Her fist connected with flesh. She swung again. It felt good to fight back.

"Amber, it's me!"

Steven had only meant to wake Amber from her nightmare. But when he moved to the couch alongside her, the first blow took him completely by surprise, catching him right in the jaw. Her arms became a torrent of commotion, her fists connecting with his shoulders and chest. He tried to get control of her arms as they swung violently. Finally, he had no recourse but to pin them against her chest. He tried to be gentle—not wanting to hurt her—but was more afraid that if he didn't stop her, she might hurt herself.

She continued to lash about, screaming at him to stop. Steven kept his tone soothing, reassuring her he wasn't going to hurt her, and that she needed to wake-up. Finally, her panic-filled eyes shot open. It took a moment for her to be able to focus on him—

confusion replacing her fear.

"Amber, it was a nightmare. You're safe. No one's hurting you." The minute it registered in her eyes that it was just a nightmare, that she was okay, he let her go.

ఊఊఊఊ

It took several minutes for Amber to catch her breath, her heart racing out of control. She recognized her home. Her living room. Steven. He sat on the edge of the couch where she was curled up. He continued to bathe her with reassuring words as his calloused thumb stroked the back of her hand.

She quickly pulled her hand away. "It was horrible," she whispered. "It was like it was happening all over again."

It took an hour or so before Amber was able to calm down. Humiliated, she shielded her eyes from Steven, unable to look at him. She wondered—when he looked at her—if he saw her as she was or as the half-naked woman he'd found lying in the park. It made her feel filthy. Exposed. Embarrassed.

If I were dead, I would be free of these feelings.

She sat by herself in the living room as dusk fell outside. Her automatic lights began to pop on, letting her know another day had slipped through her grasp. An aroma began to fill the room, stirring her senses and her stomach. She slowly walked to the kitchen, to see Steven hovering over her stove.

"What are you doing?"

"Making dinner." He smiled at her. "I hope you like pasta."

Steven's positive attitude never seemed to dim.

It angered her.

"I don't want dinner!" she snapped at him.

"But you need to eat," he said with a smile before turning his attention back to the stove top.

"No! I don't need to eat! And I don't need you telling me what to do!"

"I'm not trying to tell you what to do." His voice was soft and gentle. "I just think you would feel better if you had something to eat."

"Food is not going to make me feel better!" she shouted. "You telling me I'm going to be okay is not going to make me feel better! Nothing is going to make me feel better! Don't you get it? This feeling is never going to go away! No matter how strong I get, and no matter how quickly the bruises and the scars fade, I will never be okay! My life will never be the same!" She stormed to her bedroom and slammed the door.

❧❧❧❧

Steven took a deep breath and exhaled. He slowly counted to ten before he went and tapped on what he assumed was Amber's bedroom door.

"Leave me alone!" she hollered.

He knew that wasn't what she wanted. Not completely. She just needed some space. He walked back to the kitchen and continued to prepare dinner, all the time counseling himself on what he thought he could expect from Amber.

He realized her emotions would rollercoaster as she struggled to regain her independence. Amber was fighting off fear, anger, and humiliation. She would have highs and lows as she continued to digest all that had happened to her and how it would forever affect her future. He realized there would be times when she would allow his help and other times when she would be angry, confrontational, and verbally abusive. He was up to the challenge. He wanted to be there for her. He was confident that if Amber dug deep and drew strength from her faith, she would be able to overcome it all. She was strong and obviously a fighter. She just needed someone in her corner.

Steven finished his dinner and put his plate in the sink. He stared at the plate of pasta on the counter he had dished up for Amber, then looked at his watch. She'd stormed off over an hour ago, and he hadn't heard from her since.

He walked to the door at the end of the hall and pressed his ear against it. *She's probably sleeping. Just give her time. She'll come around.*

He returned to the kitchen and worked on the pots and pans he'd left on the stovetop. He cleaned his plate and silverware and took a sponge to the range and counter tops. He looked at his watch again and then glanced down the hall. His inner voice told him something wasn't right. He walked to Amber's door and tapped on it.

"Amber? Amber, are you awake?"

Nothing.

He slowly turned the knob and pushed the door open a few inches. He stuck his head through the opening and looked in. The bedroom was sunny and bright. And empty. He pushed the door wider and scanned the rest of the room. She wasn't there.

"Amber?" He rushed across the room to the closed door, assuming it was the master bathroom. He knocked. "Amber, are you okay?"

He tried the handle. It was locked. He pounded on the door. "Amber, open the door!" Adrenaline raced through his veins as he questioned Amber's state of mind. Steven shouted again, pounding even harder. When his pleas were met with silence, he had no choice. Steven slammed his shoulder into the door. With a loud snap, the doorframe splintered and the door flew open. He stumbled in, looking from left to right, terrified by what he saw.

Amber was lying in the empty tub, fully dressed, facing the tile wall, a razor blade on the edge of the tub. She didn't move.

Steven sunk to the side of the tub, looking for any signs of blood. Luckily, there wasn't any. He sighed. *Thank you, God.*

He reached for Amber's chin and gently turned her to face him, but she kept her eyes downcast.

"Amber, look at me?"

Slowly, she turned her piercing, dark eyes on him. "Don't worry, I didn't have the guts to do it."

"Amber, why would you even think of doing something like that?"

"Why?" she said, her voice cracking with emotion. "Because I thought dying might be easier than living."

"That's not true."

Amber was silent.

"Amber, don't let them win."

"Win? This isn't a game, Steven. This is my life."

"You're right. It is *your* life. And it's up to *you* to fight for it."

EIGHTEEN

Amber looked at her bedside clock-radio and saw it was five in the morning.

She sighed.

She had made it through another night.

She was still wearing her clothes from the day before, and vaguely remembered the events of the previous night.

Pain gnawed at her body so she went in search of her medicine. She wandered down the hall to the kitchen and pulled on the refrigerator handle. Sitting on the shelf, next to the pitcher of orange juice, was a plate of pasta. She realized it must have been the dinner Steven had made for her the night before.

She poured herself a glass of juice and shook a pill out of each of the medicine bottles sitting on her counter. After downing the meds, motion out of the corner of her eye startled her.

Steven sat up and stretched from where he was lying on the couch. She watched as he dragged his hand down the length of his stubble-covered face.

Amber walked into the living room.

He smiled. "Good morning."

"You slept here? All night?"

"Well, let's just say I *stayed* here all night. Sleeping is a matter of opinion." He stood and stretched some more.

Amber couldn't believe the lengths Steven was going to, to make her feel safe. Even after she'd yelled at him, and scared him to death, he had stayed. She moved across the room. "Steven . . . I'm sorry for last night. I know you're only trying to help. I didn't mean to scare you like that. I just wanted to make everything go away."

He looked at her with eyes of worry, not anger. "You don't have to apologize. I grew up with a sister. I can handle the yelling. Just don't pull a stunt like that again."

Her slight smile was all the agreement she could offer.

She sat in her side chair and stared at all the mail lying on the coffee table. Slowly, she began to rifle through it, stacking it in neat piles, organizing as she went.

Steven yawned and stretched some more. "I'm going to go splash some water on my face."

He disappeared down the hall and was gone just a few short minutes. When he emerged, he headed for the kitchen and began to clink pans and rifle through cupboards.

Amber walked to the kitchen and leaned on the wall. "Steven, I appreciate everything you've done for me, but you don't need to stay. I have a lot of work to get done before tomorrow. I promise I won't do anything stupid. You're free to go."

"What's tomorrow?"

"I have some appointments."

"What kind of appointments?" he asked as he scrambled half a dozen eggs in a bowl.

"I have an older couple coming to do a portrait sitting at four o'clock, viewings at five and six, then an engagement sitting at seven o'clock. I have film to develop and set-up for the showings, which will keep me busy most of the day."

"You still use film? I thought that went the way of the dinosaurs."

"I prefer film. I know it's old-fashioned, but I believe in the quality it offers."

"Yeah, but digital is instant. You know if you got a good shot or not."

"I'm a professional. I know when I've gotten a good shot," Amber said, trying not to let Steven's inquisitiveness bother her. "Like I said, I have plenty to—"

"What about your appointment with Hastings and the sketch artist? You said you would meet with them today."

Amber lowered her head, squeezed her eyes shut, and sighed. "I know. They said they would be here around one o'clock."

Steven dished up breakfast. He handed a plate to Amber, then walked to the couch. Amber followed him and sat in the side chair. He said a quick prayer before forking a mound of eggs into his mouth.

"Tell you what," he said between bites. "After breakfast, why don't you take a shower? I'll stay until you're finished, then I'll go home and get cleaned up. I'll make sure I'm back by one o'clock for moral support."

"You don't need to do that. I'll be fine. Besides, I'm sure you have other things you could be doing, like making up for all the work you've missed."

"I'm the boss and I have plenty of time on the books. Besides, I already told my foreman and office manager I would be out indefinitely."

Amber pushed the eggs around on her plate, feeling sick to her stomach. *Was it the medicine, the attack, or something else?*

"You know . . . if you keep playing with your food instead of eating it, you're going to give me an inferiority complex. I really do know my way around a kitchen. In fact, cooking is one of my hobbies."

"And I suppose rescuing battered women is your other one. Mr. Superhero to the rescue," she mumbled.

Steven tensed slightly but continued to eat.

"I'm sorry," Amber hurried to apologize. "That wasn't fair. I guess I'm just having a hard time understanding why you're doing this."

"Why is it so hard for you to believe I just want to help?" His words were soft but firm.

"I guess I'm just a cynic at heart."

Steven slowly shook his head. "No, you're not. You're just scared. I understand that, Amber. But I assure you, all I want to do is help."

Amber didn't comment, she just leaned forward and set her plate on the coffee table. "I'm sorry, but I'm just not hungry."

When Steven was done, he picked up her plate from where she'd laid it on the table and took it to the kitchen with his own. "Why don't you go take a shower while I clean up?"

Amber didn't argue. It took too much energy. She just walked to her bedroom, closed the door, and locked it. She grabbed an old dumbbell from the back of her closet, brought it into the bathroom with her, then locked the door. She looked at the weight in her hand—a makeshift weapon if she needed it. Though her heart was telling her to trust Steven, her mind was warning her never to trust again.

Steven heard the shower running and started to pray. He knew Amber's faith would help her through this. She was just grappling with all that had happened. He certainly couldn't blame her. What God had allowed was vicious and unfair. But Steven could tell she was a fighter. A survivor. She would make it through. He just wanted to help where he could and make sure she didn't give up on herself.

Steven prayed until he heard the water stop. Amber emerged from her bedroom wearing faded jeans and a flowing red blouse. She was gently drying her hair with a towel. She had reapplied her makeup to cover the bruising, but the discoloring was still visible. She actually greeted him with a half-smile. And it was the first time he saw a sparkle in her incredible teal-blue eyes.

"You look like you're feeling a bit better."

"A little."

"So, if I leave for a few hours do you think you'll be all right?"

"You can leave for the rest of the day, Steven. I'll be fine."

He ignored her suggestion. "Would you mind if I borrowed your car?"

She stopped drying her hair. "Uhhh . . ."

"That's okay," he quickly amended as he pulled his phone from his pocket. "I'll just call a cab." He started to dial.

"No. Steven, don't call a cab. That's silly. Just take my car."

He disconnected the call. "Are you sure?"

She nodded. "It's not like I was planning on going anywhere. Besides, if it wasn't for you, I wouldn't even have it."

"If you're sure?"

"I'm sure."

"Okay then. I'll go home, get cleaned up, and be back by one o'clock."

"No!" Amber's voice was abrupt and firm. "I don't want you here when I talk to the police."

"Why?"

"Because, I just don't. It's going to be hard enough, having to picture the men . . . and describe . . . I won't be able to if you're sitting here."

"But Amber—"

"Steven, please!" she shouted, crossing her arms against her chest. "I can take care of myself! I don't need you holding my hand, telling me everything is going to be all right! It's not going to be all right!" She took a breath and lowered her tone. "I'm sorry. I didn't mean to yell at you. I just need to do this by myself."

The defiance in her stance was a good thing. She was fighting. That's what she needed to do. But Steven felt a twinge of regret. He wanted Amber to be strong, but he still wanted to be there for her. "Okay, but will you at least call me when you're done, so I know you're okay?"

"I'll text you."

"I would feel better if I could hear your voice. Promise me you'll call."

She sighed. "Fine. I'll call."

NINETEEN

Amber was in her darkroom when she felt the floor vibrate. She dropped the tongs she was holding and froze. When she felt it again, she looked at her watch and realized it was already one o'clock. The vibration she was hearing was someone knocking—more like pounding—on her front door.

Quickly, she fished the last photo out of the solution tray and pinned it to the line hung across her work table. She twisted the bolt on her darkroom door and hurried to the entry way. With her heart still racing, she leaned into the door and looked out the peephole. There stood Det. Hastings, Det. Jones, and a sharply-dressed woman who looked to be in her mid-forties.

Unlatching the door, she stepped aside and allowed the trio in.

"Ms. Porter, this is Officer Mary Reynolds, our sketch artist."

Amber acknowledged the introduction and led everyone into the living room.

"Ms. Porter," the female officer said, addressing her in a soft tone, "I know this is a difficult time for you, but agreeing to do this could help us identify your attackers."

Amber nodded her understanding even as her stomach twisted and rolled. She took a seat on the couch as the woman sat down in the side chair, setting her briefcase on the floor. Amber watched as Officer Reynolds pulled out a sketchpad.

"Don't sketch artists use computer programs these days?" Amber asked.

"We do. And if you prefer, we could use that, but I like to

begin with a hand drawn sketch, especially when the witness feels confident they can provide a good description. I feel the computer programs might inadvertently lead the witness. That's just my opinion, and I know it might seem old-fashioned, but I still feel the traditional way has value."

Amber smiled to herself, knowing that was exactly what she had tried to explain to Steven about her photography. "I completely understand."

Sitting with her sketchpad poised on her lap, Officer Reynolds waited for Amber. With a cleansing breath, she closed her eyes and began to describe the men who had raped her.

Steven had showered, shaved, played with Bo in the yard for a while, and downed almost a whole pot of coffee. He turned on the television and saw the report about Amber's attack. It scared him to think the men that had intended on killing Amber were still out roaming the streets. What if they found out who she was? What if they figured out where she lived? They knew what she looked like.

His head spun with scenario after scenario. All of them horrific.

He looked at his watch for the hundredth time, waiting for his phone to ring. It was already after three o'clock. What if Amber hadn't handled the session with the sketch artist well? Having to conjure up images of her attackers and describe them in detail had to be a gruesome task. What if the detectives had left and she was spiraling? He pictured Amber laying in the bathtub, the razor blade in her hand, and decided he couldn't wait any longer for her to call.

He grabbed Amber's keys and headed for her car where it sat in his driveway. When he pulled up at Amber's house, the detectives were just walking toward their car.

"Det. Hastings?" Steven walked quicker towards the detectives. "How did Amber do?"

Hastings glanced at Det. Jones and the woman holding a briefcase. "It went well. She was able to give a very detailed description of one of her attackers. But emotionally it took its toll.

She said her schedule is too full tomorrow, so we'll start fresh again on Tuesday."

Steven could feel Jones scrutinizing him as they spoke. With a nod of his head, the detective said, "You seem to have made yourself quite a fixture around Ms. Porter. At her house . . . driving her car . . ."

"Is there a problem with that?" Steven did nothing to hide his annoyance. He was tired of the insinuations.

"No. I just hope we haven't misjudged you. You seem like a nice guy, Mr. Levitt. I would hate to find out you're an opportunist milking the role of the hero."

"You know what, Det. Jones, I don't give a rip what you think about me, but I'd appreciate you keeping your opinion to yourself. Amber needs a friend right now. She doesn't need you polluting her mind by attacking my character."

"And she's on edge," Jones shot back. "She doesn't need some lover-boy trying to make moves on her when her defenses are down."

"Why you—" Steven lunged at the detective, stopping only because Det. Hastings got between them and shoved him away.

"Cool it, Levitt!"

"Me? What about him?" Steven pointed angrily at Jones. "He's making me out to be a real tool. Amber has no family—or friends to speak of—and he's trying to intimidate me into staying away." Steven glared at Jones. "She needs someone right now. And I plan on being here as long as she'll let me."

"And it's our job to protect Ms. Porter," Jones said as he walked away, then turned back to Steven with a parting shot. "I'm not sure you're motivation is quite so pure."

Steven watched as the detectives pulled away. When he turned toward the house, he saw Amber. Clearly, she had heard the detective's accusation. Steven rushed toward her as she hurried back into the house. "Amber, wait."

❧❧❧❧

Amber had only a second to replay what the detective had said before Steven walked through the door. She crossed the living room and stood with her back to him.

Steven closed the door. "Amber . . . I don't know what you heard, but it couldn't be further from the truth. I have no intentions towards you. At least not like he's making it sound."

"I know." She turned to him, coldness in her tone and in her stare. "Who could possibly be interested in me, right? I mean, certainly not you. You saw firsthand what they did to me. No one will ever want to be with me once they know the truth."

Steven shook his head and stepped closer. "Amber, that's not what I meant."

She quickly stepped away. "Look, I have work to keep me busy the rest of the evening. There's no reason for you to be here."

"But I want to be here."

"Yeah, well, maybe I don't want you here."

Amber walked into her darkroom, slammed the door, and flipped the lock. She leaned against the door and listened. When she heard the front door close, she began to cry.

Amber screamed, sitting straight up in bed. She couldn't do it. She couldn't sleep. Her old cottage-style house had too many creaks and moans. Every creak sounded like a footfall, and every moan reminded her of her attackers.

She moved to the living room where she had left on every light. She curled up against the arm of the couch and flipped through the channels from infomercials to classic movies. She adjusted the sound to drown out other noises but muted the T.V. every time a strange sound got her attention. She tried to get comfortable and stretch out on the couch, but soon she found herself curled up in a knot.

Her ribs hurt.

Her arms hurt.

Everything hurt.

Her stomach rolled with nausea.

Was it because of her memories or was it something else?

She focused in on the wall clock across from the couch.
The numbers blurred.
Only three more hours until dawn.

TWENTY

The following morning, Amber had to drag herself from one place to another. She didn't have the energy to stand in the shower, so she'd opted to sit in what should have been a relaxing bath. But she felt too vulnerable, too exposed. After ten minutes she was out and dried off. She ate a piece of plain, white bread just so she could stay on schedule with her medicine, knowing she was going to need it. As she sipped at her water, she watched her hand shake.

She would never make it today.

There was no way.

She was utterly exhausted. She couldn't even walk from one room to the other without reaching out to the wall for balance, or bracing herself on the furniture.

What am I going to do?

At eight o'clock, she heard the slam of a car door. She looked outside and watch as Steven walked from his truck to her front door.

Why is he doing this? Why is he making this so hard on me? Doesn't he realize he's only making this more difficult? Yes, he helped with my car and he helped with my groceries, but he . . . Then it dawned on her. She owed him the two hundred dollars he paid at the impound yard and probably another fifty dollars for the groceries he had bought.

He knocked twice and rang the bell once.

"Just a minute." She hurried—as best as she could—to her home office to grab her checkbook. She didn't have the energy to rush to the door, already feeling winded. "I'll be right there," she yelled, as she slowly walked to the entryway. She opened the door, surprised that Steven looked a little worse for wear. He looked her in the eyes, then shook his head. "You didn't sleep at all last night, did you?" he asked.

"From the looks of it, neither did you."

They stood at the front door in an awkward silence.

"Can I come in?"

"Yes." She stepped aside. "I was just about to write you a check for the money I owe you."

Steven walked passed her and into the kitchen. "I told you before that isn't necessary."

"It most certainly is. I'm not going to be indebted to a complete stranger."

"Wow, I had hoped we'd gotten past the whole *stranger* thing," he said, as he pulled eggs, bread, and butter from the refrigerator.

He's doing it again. He walks in here like he owns the place, like we've been doing this for years. She stared at him, dumbfounded. Then she put it together.

"Oh, I get it now," she said, with her hands firmly planted on her hips. "Was that some sort of buy in? I guess you just figured if you loaned me money, I would feel obligated to let you hang around?" She waited for a reply but got nothing. "What are you doing?" she asked, frustrated that he seemed to have his own agenda.

"I'm making us breakfast."

"I already had breakfast."

He turned to her, looking her square in the eye. "What did you have?"

She could lie. She could tell him anything. He wouldn't know any different. "I had a piece of bread." *Why didn't I lie?*

"A piece of bread is not breakfast."

"I wasn't hungry. I just needed something to settle my stomach so I could take my medicine."

"Good. That was my next question, if you were current on your medication." He turned back to the counter and started cracking eggs into one of her ceramic bowls.

"Are you just going to ignore my question?"

"I didn't hear you ask a question. What I heard was more like an indictment. And since it was completely ludicrous, I'm not even going to dignify it with an answer. The money was a gift. If you can't accept that, then fine, pay it back. But don't make it sound like I had ulterior motives."

She could hear the hurt in his voice, and it only served to make her feel more miserable. "I'm not hungry. I'm just tired."

"Then why don't you lay down while I make breakfast. I'll wake you up when it's ready."

Amber was going to say something but stopped. There was no use arguing with him. It would just be easier to lay down, sleep for half an hour or so, write him a check, then politely tell Steven she could handle the rest of her life on her own.

Amber laid on the couch, shifting from one position to another until she was comfortable. She reached for the chenille throw from the back of the couch, pulled it up to her chin, and fell asleep to the sound of Steven humming in the kitchen and butter sizzling in the pan.

Amber could hear the sound of rattling pans. *Steven must be cleaning up his breakfast dishes.* Strange, she felt pretty rested for only getting a few minutes sleep. When the aroma of melting butter filtered into the living room, she just figured he must be having seconds. Oh well. Technically they were his groceries. If he wanted more eggs, he was welcome to them.

When Steven sat down in the side chair, she slowly opened her eyes. He was balancing a plate on his lap, some kind of sandwich clamped between his fingers. She chuckled to herself. "I guess breakfast is your favorite meal."

He grinned but didn't say anything.

Feeling a little more alert, she pushed herself up on one elbow. "Is that a grilled cheese sandwich?"

"Yep. And I have one warming in the oven for you when

you're ready to eat."

"But I told you, I don't want breakfast."

"That's good because I'm offering you lunch." His smile broadened.

Amber quickly looked at the clock. "Are you kidding me?" She slowly swiveled her feet to the floor. "Is it really two-thirty?"

"Yep," he said before taking another bite of his sandwich. Then he set his plate down and walked to the kitchen.

"Why did you let me sleep so long?"

"Because there was no reason to wake you up," he said from the kitchen, reappearing with a plate he set in front of her. "Your appointment isn't for another hour and a half, and you needed the rest. That's probably the most sleep you've gotten since leaving the hospital."

Amber couldn't argue with him because it was true.

She looked at the plate in front of her, then leaned back into the couch, and pulled her feet up under her. The grilled cheese sandwich was the perfect shade of golden brown, and next to it were three small pills. "I'm really not hungry."

"But you need to eat. You're going to be on your feet for a few hours, and you need to take your medication. Do you really want to take the chance of keeling over or throwing up in front of your clients?"

He was right. No matter how little her appetite, she needed to eat something if she hoped to keep her medication down and her nausea at bay.

She nibbled at her sandwich as Steven went to the kitchen to do the dishes. After eating just enough to help with her pills, she curled up on the couch and closed her eyes. She wasn't asleep, but she wasn't in the mood for conversation. Not when she was inwardly panicking about her upcoming appointments.

"Amber?" Steven whispered.

"Humm?" she answered, without opening her eyes.

"It's three-thirty. Did you want to get ready before your appointment?"

She opened her eyes, shocked another hour had gone by. Slowly, she got up and hurried to her bathroom. The vanity mirror pulled no punches. She quickly dabbed concealer over the worst of the bruising. Then gently ran her fingers through her hair—still trying to cover the ugliness of her stitches. *I can't believe I'm going to let people see me like this.* But what could she do? If she was strong enough to stand and hold a camera, she had to keep her appointments. Financially, she couldn't afford cancelations or the negative hit it would be to her reputation. She relied heavily on word-of-mouth referrals. This was her livelihood. She had to gut it out.

"How are you feeling?" Steven asked when she walked back into the living room.

Just then, the doorbell chimed.

Immediately, her heart began to race. She tried to take deep breaths—to control her emotions—but they turned to short, panting breaths that had her seeing stars. Amber wiped at her eyes, trying to stop the tears before they ran down her cheeks. The thought of another person seeing her in her present condition was more than she could handle. "I'm not ready for this." She turned to where Steven was sitting. "I can't do this right now."

Steven jumped to his feet. "Yes you can, Amber." He reached out with both hands and held her at arm's length. "You can do this. You just need to focus on what it is you have to do." He gave her arms a gentle squeeze. "Go dry your eyes. I'll answer the door and let them know you'll be right with them."

Amber took a second. *He's right. I've got to do this. I can't lose my business.* Without saying a word, she walked toward her bathroom to once again try to make herself look presentable.

❧❧❧❧

"Hi. Come on in. Amber is expecting you and will be out in just a moment." Steven welcomed the elderly couple in, then closed the door.

"Amber didn't tell me she had an assistant," the older woman said as she gave Steven the once over.

"Oh, I'm not her assistant; I'm just a friend. Steven," he said as he stuck out his hand. "Nice to meet you."

"Oh . . . I see."

It was obvious to Steven the woman was reading more into the title *friend* than was necessary.

The gruff looking man stuck out his hand and gave Steven a firm handshake. "Nice to meet you, Steven. I'm Harold and this is my wife, Irene."

"Nice to meet you both."

Irene took another long look around the house and then asked, "We're not early, are we? I thought our appointment was at four o'clock."

"No, you're not early. It's just that Amber—"

Before Steven could finish, Amber stepped into the room, a smile plastered on her face.

"Hello, Mr. and Mrs. Everett, it's so good to see you again."

Neither of the couple spoke; they just stared.

As much as Amber had tried, her wounds could not be concealed.

"My heavens! What happened to you?" Mrs. Everett asked as she and her husband stood gawking.

"I had a little accident. In fact, I just got my car back the other day."

"Goodness, gracious. Are you all right?"

"Yes, I'll be fine. Nothing time won't heal."

"Did they catch the person that hit you?"

Amber glanced at Steven, both of them knowing her words were a bit deceptive. "No. It was a hit and run, but enough about me." Amber quickly switched their attention. "Let's step into my studio and do what we can to preserve this special anniversary for the both of you."

Amber led them down the hall to her home studio, complete with backdrops and props. It mimicked the portrait studio Steven had seen at the local mall.

"Now . . . let's choose a few backdrops befitting a 50th

anniversary, then you can tell me if you have any preferences on how you'll be sitting."

Steven watched from the doorway as Amber immersed herself in her work. The elderly couple was putty in her hands. In a half hours' time, she had taken numerous pictures with a variety of backdrops and poses.

When they were finished, Amber scheduled a time when Mr. and Mrs. Everett could come back and preview the pictures. They handed Amber a check for the deposit, thanked her for her time, and wished her a speedy recovery.

Once the couple had left, Amber completely revamped the room into a viewing gallery. She raised the adjustable bench the Everett's had been sitting on and draped it with black velvet. Then, she arranged a variety of frames with pictures of a little girl dressed in ruffles and lace. She was adorable. The prop in the picture—of a huge number one—explained the reason for the special photo session.

Steven studied the photos as Amber put them in place, thinking each one was better than the last. The pictures that didn't fit in frames, Amber arranged in a small album. She glanced at the clock on the wall while massaging her wrist.

"You okay?" he asked.

"Yeah, it's just a little sore from taking all those pictures."

Before Steven could say much more, there was a knock at the door. Her next appointment was right on time.

Amber introduced Steven as a friend and once again gave a misleading explanation for her stitches and bruises. She quickly ushered Mrs. Langley into the studio where the woman was immediately enraptured by the mini gallery showcasing her daughter.

After many comments and decisions, Mrs. Langley decided what pictures she wanted, what size, and the quantity of each. If Steven had done the math right, he estimated the woman had spent upwards of three hundred dollars. Amber explained the payment process to the woman. Half was due today, and the remainder was to be paid when she picked up the pictures. Mrs. Langley handed Amber a check, thanking her profusely for doing such a wonderful job.

Amber escorted her out, explaining that she had another appointment. Once the woman was gone, Amber hurried back to her studio to prepare for the next viewing. She removed the pictures of the adorable toddler from each frame and replaced them with photos of a young couple.

Steven watched as Amber's steps slowed, and her complexion paled. That's when he noticed the backdrop in the pictures was Riverbend Park.

"You okay?" he asked.

"Fine," she replied, as she brushed past him and headed for the kitchen. Steven followed a few steps behind.

Amber grabbed one of the bottles of medication on the counter and reached for a glass of water. She leaned against the counter with her eyes closed and her head back. Perspiration beaded her upper lip, her cheeks flushed red. She was pushing her limits, and her body must be letting her know it.

"Amber, why don't you sit down until your other appointment shows up?"

"I'm afraid if I sit down, I won't be able to get back up."

"Then I'll help you." With a gentle hand on her shoulder, he steered her in the direction of the couch. She sunk into the oversized cushions, letting out an audible groan.

"See, doesn't that feel better?"

"Uh-huh." Amber answered with her eyes closed. She started rubbing her temple, in a slow, circular motion with her fingertips.

"Is your head hurting?"

"Yeah, I'm sure it's just eye strain."

"So it has nothing to do with the pictures taken in the park?"

❧❧☙☙

Amber didn't understand how Steven could be so intuitive. Looking at the pictures freaked her out, but it wasn't just the park. The pictures of the adorable little girl decked out in ruffles and curls had done a number on her as well. One minute she was looking at a happy couple with their whole life ahead of them, and then Bam! Amber saw the park, the shrubs, her attackers. *How am I going to be able to go back there on Thursday? I'll never make it. I'll fall apart and lose the job. And what if I can't bring myself to photographing children anymore?* She couldn't erase the pictures of the little girl from her mind. 'Children are a gift from God.' That's what she'd always been told. But what if that child . . .

"It's okay to be afraid, Amber."

Amber looked at Steven wondering how he knew what she was thinking, then realized he was just referring to the park. *If he only knew.*

"It will pass. You just have to give it time," he said.

"But almost half of the jobs I do are shot in that park. It's the ideal location for engagements and weddings. How am I going to handle going back there?"

"I guess you'll just have to cross that bridge when you get to it."

"Yeah, and that's on Thursday. And it's a big account. One I cannot afford to lose."

"Maybe you could persuade them to do it in studio."

"I don't think so. This bride knows exactly what she wants. Besides, I've already had to ask them to reschedule. Our original appointment had been for Saturday."

Before Steven could give Amber any more suggestions, the doorbell chimed, announcing her last client for the night.

It was almost eight o'clock when Amber's last appointment finally left, the sitting taking longer than usual. The couple had been great to work with, but were a little fickle when it came to poses. The groom-to-be wanted their pictures to be more traditional, whereas the bride-to-be's taste teetered somewhere between romantic and whimsical. Amber had to resort to using a tripod because her sore wrist couldn't handle the weight of the camera any longer. She had taken a record number of pictures, assuring the couple they would have plenty to choose from. When it was time for them to leave, they wished her well, and a speedy recovery.

Amber thanked them as she ushered the couple to the door, counting the seconds until she could wipe the false smile from her face and finally sit down.

TWENTY-ONE

Steven watched from the living room as Amber accompanied her last appointment to the door. He heard her secure the latch before she joined him in the living room and slowly sank into the comfort of the sofa.

"I made it. Now I don't have to see another client until Thursday."

Steven saw a hint of pride brighten Amber's expression. It was obvious she enjoyed her work, even if it wasn't her dream job.

"You did great. You should be proud of yourself. You have quite a way with people."

"It wasn't that hard. They were so distracted by my ugly appearance they pretty much tripped over themselves trying to be nice to me."

"Amber, that's not true."

"Yes it is. I look horrible, and you can't convince me otherwise."

Steven wanted to refute her, but he remained silent. *No use starting an argument.* Instead, he rested his head on the back of the chair and closed his eyes. Silence filled the room for several moments. When he opened his eyes, he found Amber staring at him with a questioning look.

"What?"

"Who are you, Steven Levitt? I mean . . . other than the fact that I know you do construction work, I really don't know anything else about you."

"What do you want to know?"

Amber shrugged her shoulders. "I don't know . . . tell me about your job, your dog, what you like to do in your spare time . . . you know . . . the normal stuff."

"Okay . . . stuff. My dog's name is Bo. He belonged to my dad until he was killed in an auto accident. That's when Bo came to live with me. My mother's name is Kathryn, I have a twin sister named Stacy, and a brother-in-law named Connor. They have five-year-old twins; Jaime and Jarrod. I took over the family business when my father died, and I enjoy anything outdoors. How's that?"

Amber smiled. "Not bad."

"What about you?" Steven asked.

"What about me?"

"You know . . . stuff." Steven grinned, using her own words. When Amber seemed hesitant to say anything, he decided to get the ball rolling.

"So, what's up between you and your sister?"

"How did you know I had a sister?" Amber asked, sharply.

"I ran into her outside the hospital. She seemed . . . well, she seemed . . . a little self-absorbed."

"Yeah, you met Erika all right." Amber rubbed her temples. "Let's just say we don't have a lot in common."

"I got the impression she doesn't have much use for God either."

Steven could tell by Amber's expression he had sized up her sister pretty well.

"What else did she have to say?" Amber asked.

Steven wasn't sure he should tell Amber how insensitive her sister had been regarding her condition. He decided it would be best if he downplayed her reaction. "Not much. She was in a rush when I talked to her, and I didn't want to be a bother."

"You don't have to sugar-coat it, Steven. I know Erika can be pretty abrasive."

He chuckled. "Abrasive is a good word." He waited to see if Amber would elaborate.

She curled up against the arm of the sofa, tucking her feet underneath her, massaging the back of her neck. "Erika and I were raised by just our father from an early age. He's a very driven man and didn't have a lot of time for us. We were told over and over again we would never amount to anything if we didn't rely on ourselves to make things happen. He didn't believe in chance, luck, faith, or failure. His philosophy was, and I quote, 'You're born to succeed in life. If you don't, you have no one to blame but yourself,' end quote."

"But you *are* a success. You're a talented photographer. You own your own business. And even if you're not exactly doing the work you dream of, you still seem to enjoy what you do. Who could ask for more?"

"My father for one." Amber took a long, exaggerated breath. "My father and I don't see eye-to-eye, and I've come to accept that. Erika on the other hand is his pride and joy. She is as driven as he is and will stop at nothing to get her way."

"What about your mom?"

Melancholy darkened Amber's expression as she sunk further into the sofa, closing her eyes momentarily, then focusing somewhere across the room. "My mother died when I was nine. She abused alcohol most of her life, and even though she gave it up, it was too late."

Amber's faraway look told Steven she was reliving a memory. So he waited quietly.

❧❧❧❧

"It was my mom who first told me about Jesus." Amber turned to Steven and smiled, but felt tears welling in her eyes. "My mother was hospitalized after falling down a flight of stairs. She was drunk at the time." Amber chanced a look at Steven, but saw no condemnation. "When my mom was released from the hospital, she knew she needed to get some help. My father accused her of overreacting. He told her she'd had an accident, not a drinking problem, but it was the eye-opener my mother needed. She checked herself into a substance abuse program."

"That had to of been hard for you," Steven said.

"It was. My father would put me in a taxi and send me to visit her alone. He said he didn't have time to visit, but I knew the real reason he didn't go. He was angry with her for admitting she had a weakness. My father and Erika never visited her, not even once. Erika was embarrassed, and on more than one occasion she was hateful enough to call our mother a falling-down drunk."

"That's a lot for a little girl to handle," Steven said, his tone soft and filled with compassion.

Amber nodded. "I hated riding in taxis by myself, but I did it because I wanted to be with my mom. I visited her every Saturday and was allowed to stay with her overnight. The center was run by a Christian organization, so all the patients were required to go to Sunday services. She would listen to the preacher's sermon and then talk to me all afternoon about his message. I began to see a change in her, but I just assumed it was because she was sober. I didn't realize it had to do with the change in her heart. One day she asked me if I understood what it was to believe in God. I kind of understood but wasn't sure."

Amber looked at Steven and smiled. "My mom became a Christian while in the program. She explained to me how she had tried for years to satisfy the emptiness inside her with alcohol and material things. But she now knew it was a part of her only God could fill. I didn't completely understand, but I was thankful to see my mom feeling so much better.

"When my mom came home from the center, she and I continued to go to church. We tried to get Erika and my dad to go, but they wouldn't. That summer, my father and Erika became more and more distant. Dad spent long hours at the office, sometimes not coming home at all, and Erika thought my mom had been brainwashed and accused her of trying to do the same thing to me.

"Erika would have huge fights with my mom, calling her names, saying she was an embarrassment to have around. My mother was crushed, but she refused to let go of her new found faith to accommodate my father and sister. As miserable as they made it for her, I could still see a difference in my mom that made her eyes bright and words soft. She never lashed out at my father or Erika, even though they said ugly things about her.

"I decided if that was the difference Jesus could make in someone's heart, I wanted to have it too. I asked my mother to pray with me so I would know I did it right."

"She must have been thrilled," Steven said with a smile.

"She was, but it didn't change things at home. We prayed for Erika and Dad all the time, hoping they would change, but they only got worse."

"What happened?"

"Mom and Dad got a divorce the following year. I went to live with my mom, and Erika stayed with my Dad. As much as I hated to see our family split up, it actually was a relief. There was no more arguing or fighting. No more listening to Erika put down my mom or calling me a brainwashed Jesus freak."

"But I thought you said your dad raised you?" Steven asked.

Amber nervously played with the fringe on the throw she had pulled over her lap, no longer able to hold back her tears.

"My mother got very ill. By the time we realized how serious it was, she was hospitalized and in need of a liver transplant." Amber coughed, clearing her throat. "I had to move back in with Dad and Erika, and was only allowed to see my mom on weekends. We talked on the phone every day until she grew too weak. In the meantime, I had to change schools from the private Christian academy my mom had enrolled me in, to the prep school my dad insisted would be better suited for me. He thought 'religion' was just a phase and once I was exposed to culture, the phase would pass."

Amber brushed a tear aside. "When my mother died, I was angry with her and God. I felt so alone. No one understood me, and my father and sister kept trying to change me. After a few months, I realized I wasn't really alone at all. My commitment to the Lord was the most precious gift my mom had left me."

Steven smiled at Amber when she glanced at him, then to the

clock. "My goodness, I've been rambling for over an hour. I'm sorry. I didn't mean to bore you with so many details."

"I'm not bored at all." Steven leaned forward in the chair, resting his elbows on his knees. "When did you take up photography?"

"That was the only positive thing about the prep school I attended. They insisted—even at an early age—that you take part in some kind of art. I was a klutz when it came to dance, and I had a horrible time with paint brushes. Then I was given a camera to experiment with. I finally found something I was good at and really enjoyed. To me, photography seemed like such a personal expression. It was how I viewed the world, the way I saw things. As long as I had the camera in focus, I couldn't be wrong. Photography became my world after that. I hung onto it all through high school and college."

"Did things ever improve at home?"

"No. Erika continued to shine in my father's eyes, and I continued to fade into the background. When I went away to college, I finally started to feel like a person of worth. I excelled in all of my classes and received several awards for achievement."

"That had to say something to your father."

"It didn't," Amber said forlornly. "He didn't think photography was a *worthy* enough profession. When I told him I was changing my major from business to photography, he cut me off."

"Cut you off?"

"Yep. He was no longer going to pay my tuition if all I was going to do was 'play around with a camera.' "

"So, did you have to drop out?"

"No. My grades were good enough to secure academic scholarships. It was tight, but I made it."

"When did you move to California?"

"Actually, I didn't move to California," Amber clarified. "I ran from New York. California is just where I landed. It's been a little more than a year."

"Did you know anyone here?"

"No. I just packed up and moved. I found this house the second week I was here. I fell in love with it and the neighborhood."

"How did you get your photography business started so quickly?"

"Cara. She was my next door neighbor. She taught pre-school and told the mothers of her students that I was a photographer with inexpensive rates. That was all the start I needed. Children's photographs led to family sittings, then weddings. I've been busy ever since."

"So, were you and Cara friends?"

"Yeah. She was great."

"Was?"

Amber sighed. "She got married last month and moved to Texas. It was hard to see her go. She was the only person I really connected with since moving here."

"What about Craig?"

Amber looked at him quizzically. "How do you know about Craig?"

Steven stammered, "I . . . I saw him with you in the hospital."

"And?"

"Well, I know it's none of my business, but . . . I guess I don't understand why he hasn't come around to see how you're doing. You seemed pretty close in the hospital. I thought maybe he was someone special."

Amber could hear what Steven *wasn't* asking. The way he stumbled over his words and fidgeted with his hands was a dead giveaway. He had assumed she and Craig had a thing. Amber almost laughed, but there was nothing humorous about her conversation with Craig or the counsel he'd given her. She'd been confused and terrified, and needed someone to help her make monumental decisions—decisions that would affect the rest of her life. *I can't explain that to Steven. I can't go there. Not right now.*

"Hey, it's none of my business," Steven said, clearly feeling awkward.

Though she could easily explain her relationship with Craig

without going into detail, Amber decided instead to have a little fun.

"You're right, Steven." She nervously twisted her hands together, acting as if she'd been caught red-handed. "Craig *is* someone special. You see . . . he left his wife to be with me. I told him it wasn't fair to Sara, and that he needed to go back to her."

She hung her head to hide the smirk on her face, but when Steven was completely silent, she chanced a look at him. His entire countenance had changed from curiosity to disbelief. The look of total disappointment in his eyes was so obvious it actually hurt. *This was a bad idea.*

"Steven, I was just—"

"Hey, it's none of my business." His words were clipped as he got up from where he was sitting and walked to the kitchen.

Amber felt horrible. Her little joke had completely backfired. She just assumed Steven would've had something more to say or would've question her behavior in light of her convictions. She figured she'd keep him on the hook for a minute or two and then tell him who Craig really was. But instead, Steven had left the room and was now fumbling around in the kitchen. Amber got up to see what he was doing and watched as he pulled a package of ground beef from the refrigerator and a pan from the cupboard.

"Steven . . ."

"No . . . like I said, it's none of my business."

"Steven . . . I was only teasing. Craig's my pastor. He was on his honeymoon when he came to visit me. I was freaking out and needed his counseling. After he met with me and prayed, I assured him I was going to be fine and told him his place was with Sara and he needed to get back to her." Amber waited for Steven to turn around and say something, but he didn't. "I'm sorry, Steven. It was just a joke—and a bad one at that."

Steven wouldn't even look at her, he just kept working at the stove.

Amber didn't think she could feel any worse than she already did.

Once again she was wrong.

TWENTY-TWO

Steven made one of his favorite meals. Homemade chili and cornbread. He dished up two bowls and carried them to the living room before tapping on Amber's bedroom door. "Dinner's ready." He didn't wait for a reply, he just went to the kitchen and grabbed the plate of cornbread and two cans of soda.

Amber had disappeared into her room after her "little joke." He'd done nothing to stop her because he was mad and needed time to cool off before talking to her.

When Amber emerged from her bedroom, she was wrapped in a plush, white robe and sat down in the living room chair.

"I'll pray," Steven said quietly. "Dear Lord, thank you for helping Amber through her business appointments. I ask that You would continue to strengthen her. Bless this food to our bodies. In Jesus' name. Amen."

❧❧☙☙

Amber held the bowl of chili, inhaling its rich aroma. "Chili is one of my favorite meals," she whispered as she stirred the meaty sauce.

"I'm glad," Steven answered as he ate.

"I had bought everything to make it *that* day, knowing a storm was predicted. It's what I do every year. Kind of my way of ushering in winter—even if it was only September. I was grumbling to myself because the bags were so heavy when . . ." she shuddered at the memory.

Steven shrugged. "Sorry, I didn't know."

"Don't be sorry. There's no way you could've possibly known." Amber took a bite of cornbread hoping Steven would engage her in conversation the way he'd always done when they ate. But he didn't. She knew it was because of her stupid joke. *What was I thinking? There's nothing remotely funny about infidelity.* Amber had thought it would be funny to watch Steven squirm. But instead, she felt horrible. He didn't deserve to be treated that way, not after all he had done for her. She continued to stir her chili but before taking a spoonful, she spoke up.

"Steven, I'm really sorry. There is no excuse for it. I purposely gave you the wrong impression regarding Craig as a joke. It was in extremely poor taste, and I can't tell you how sorry I am."

❧❧❧❧

Steven hated the silence between them, but he didn't know what to say. He had to admit, her comment about Craig going back to his wife had thrown him for a loop. But when she admitted it was just a joke, he'd found nothing funny about it. He didn't appreciate being made to feel like a fool.

He had planned on telling Amber exactly what he thought of her joke, but then she apologized. Steven still wanted to tell her how he felt, but as he watched her stir her chili and nibble at her cornbread, he decided to let it go. He didn't need to make her feel worse than she already did. She had enough tormenting her. She had eaten very little in the last few days and didn't appear to be getting any stronger. He needed to swallow his pride. Amber's health was more important than his ego.

"You really need to eat some more, Amber."

"I know. I'm trying."

She stirred her chili and took another bite before scooting back in the chair, slowly drawing her feet up underneath her. She rested her head back against the tufted cushion and closed her eyes.

Steven found himself staring at Amber as she drifted off to sleep, his anger gone. Looking past the bruises and the swelling, he was struck again by how beautiful she was. The slope of her nose, the curve of her neck, the fullness of her lips, her long lashes resting on high cheekbones—she was gorgeous.

Who do you think you're kidding? Steven scolded himself. His reaction to her joke wasn't out of shock. It was jealousy. Just thinking about her being with another man had made him jealous. *It's not just protection you're offering Amber, it's you. You want to give her you!*

Unsettled by his thoughts, Steven quietly took their dishes to the kitchen, while convincing himself anything more than a friendship with Amber would never work. After what she'd been through—what she'd endured—a relationship would be the furthest thing from her mind. Besides, he had made great strides in gaining her trust. He didn't want to do anything that would make her doubt his intentions.

Steven rinsed their dishes and put them in the dishwasher as he continued his inner struggle. He needed to keep his feelings for Amber to himself. Her safety was the most important thing at the moment, that and her recovery.

Amber was still curled up in the chair when Steven turned off the light in the kitchen and walked back into the living room.

"Amber . . . Amber." Steven gently nudged her shoulder.

Her eyes fluttered, and she jumped slightly.

"Amber, why don't you go to bed?"

❧❧❧❧

It took a moment for Amber to focus and comprehend what Steven was saying. She stood up and tried to stretch her sore muscles. When she stumbled slightly, Steven reached out to steady her.

"Are you okay?"

"Yeah. Just tired."

Steven held onto her elbow as she slowly moved across the room. The safety and comfort of his touch warmed her, made her feel things. Immediately, she hated herself for where her thoughts were leading her. Steven had been nothing but admirable, doing what he could to make her feel safe and secure. It was wrong to read anything further into his attention or confuse his protectiveness for anything more than that. She stopped. "Steven, I'll be fine tonight. You need to go home and get some rest of your own."

"I'll sleep better if I'm here. Just in case something—"

"Steven, I'll be okay."

Their eyes met and held each other. Amber quickly looked away. "Steven, please, I know you're only trying to help but you can't stay here forever. Sooner or later I need to figure out how I am going to cope on my own." She walked to the front door and waited for him to follow.

"Can I call you tomorrow to see how you're doing?"

"Sure."

"And you promise you'll call me if something frightens you or you just need someone to talk to?"

"I promise."

"Remember, you have an appointment tomorrow with Det. Hastings and—"

"I know, I know, they said they'd be here around ten o'clock." Amber could hear the strain in her voice and quickly softened her tone. "Steven, I can't thank you enough for everything you've done, but I can't keep monopolizing all your time. You have a family, a job, and a life."

Steven's look of dejection was tearing at Amber's heart. The last thing she wanted to do was hurt his feelings. "Look, Steven, why don't you plan on coming over tomorrow for dinner. I'd like to show my appreciation for all you've done. It's the least I can do."

"That's not necessary, Amber."

"But I want to." She smiled. "I make a pretty mean lasagna if I do say so myself. How about you plan on coming over around six o'clock?"

"How about I come at five and give you a hand?"

The smile on Steven's face was convincing.

"Sure."

Amber closed the door behind Steven and locked it. She turned to the shadows of her living room and had to force down the panic that immediately rose inside her. She made sure all the doors were locked, then closed her bedroom door, and quickly flipped the latch before she climbed into bed.

Lord, help me get to sleep quickly before I drive myself crazy.

❧❧☙☙

Lord, help her get the sleep she needs and drive her fears away.

Steven couldn't get Amber out of his head. He thought about what it would be like to have her as a part of his life. He had loved watching her work. She was incredible. She had made each of her clients feel comfortable and special. He tried to envision what she was like before the accident. Before fear clouded her beautiful eyes and her battered body moved with such timidity. Steven hoped he would have the chance to get to know the real Amber Porter in the days and weeks ahead.

TWENTY-THREE

Amber was up early the next morning. Actually, she wasn't sure she ever went to sleep. She saw the clock several times throughout the night and argued with her conscience whenever fear crept in. After a long, hot shower, and a piece of peanut butter toast to help keep down her meds, she spent the morning working in her studio. The clock was an unwanted distraction as she ticked off the minutes until the detectives would arrive.

When the phone rang, she hoped it might be them canceling. She wouldn't mind a day without having to relive her attack.

"Amber?"

The sound of her father's voice on the line stunned her into silence.

"Amber, are you there?"

"Hi . . . Dad." She felt like a little girl caught doing something wrong.

"Hi, yourself." His tone was authoritative. "Erika tells me you got yourself into a little scuffle. She said I should call and see how you're doing."

A little scuffle. She pressed her hand to her stomach. *Leave it to Erika to minimize anything in my life.*

"It was more than a scuffle, Dad. I was in the hospital for a week," Amber said, doing her best to mask the hurt she felt.

"Wow," he said gruffly. "That's going to be quite the hospital bill. I wouldn't be surprised if my insurance premium goes up."

"Really, Dad, that's what you're concerned about? You don't

even care that I was—"

"Now, now, now. Don't get all sassy on me. You're the one who brought up the hospital. I was just calling to see how you were doing. I guess if your attitude is any indication, you're back to your normal rebellious self."

Amber swallowed her pride and the nasty retort on the tip of her tongue. "I'll be fine, Dad." She tried not to let emotion slip into her words. She refused to have him think of her as weak.

"That's what I like to hear. Porters aren't quitters."

His voice seemed muffled for a moment before coming back on the phone. "I've got to go, Amber. I'm glad you're doing fine. When you decide to get serious about that photography career of yours, give me a call. If that's what you insist on doing with your life, I'm sure I could get you a job here in New York doing something more than taking baby pictures."

Amber clicked off the phone and set it down. Staring at the receiver, she wondered if her father had ever loved her.

She hardly had time to recover from her father's call when she heard the doorbell ring. After looking through the peephole and confirming it was the detectives, she opened the door and watched Hastings, Jones, and Reynolds file into her living room. She closed the door with a cleansing breath as she prepared herself for what would be another agonizing session.

Everyone took a seat in the living room, but Amber noticed Officer Reynolds did not immediately ready her sketchpad.

Det. Hastings cleared his throat before speaking. "Amber, we might have a lead on the men who attacked you."

Amber felt her blood run cold.

"We fed the sketch you and Officer Reynolds did on Sunday into our database and think we might have come up with a match. You said that one of the men was named Jack. Or at least that's what you thought you remembered?"

Amber nodded her head slowly.

Det. Hastings pulled out a page of headshots from the file he was holding and laid it on the coffee table in front of her. "I want you to look at these photos and tell me if you recognize any of these men?"

Amber closed her eyes and took a deep breath, then leaned forward to look at the page of photos. She studied each mugshot in the first two rows. Nothing. Then she saw him. The last photo in the third row.

It was him.

She shot to her feet and clutched her hand across her lips. Amber felt her stomach explode, bile stinging her throat. She ran to the kitchen sink, losing what little she'd eaten for breakfast. With her arm wrapped around her midsection to counter the pain, she stood at the sink, dry heaving. It felt like an eternity before her stomach settled. When the worst had passed, she turned on the water and flipped the switch for the garbage disposal.

"Are you okay, Ms. Porter?" Officer Reynolds asked in a soft tone.

Amber filled a glass with water, swished it around in her mouth, and spit into the sink. She cupped the running water with her hands and brought it up to her face. She turned off the disposal and the faucet, then reached for the dishtowel hanging from the handle of the refrigerator. She never answered Reynolds' question; she just turned and walked back to where the detectives were sitting. With her heart racing, she clutched her hands together trying to get them to stop shaking. All she succeeded in doing was to cause her sore wrist even more pain.

"I take it from your reaction, that—"

"Yes. Third row. Last photo. It's him."

Jones glanced at Hastings and then at Amber.

"What?" Amber looked back and forth between them. "What aren't you telling me?"

"We have another picture we'd like to show you. His name is Jack Morris—brother of Jay Morris. The man you just identified."

Amber took a couple deep breaths before looking at the second picture, hoping she was better able to control her stomach. She steadied herself, then opened her eyes. When she did, she found herself staring at the face of the other man she would never be able to erase from her memory. She snapped her eyes shut and nodded her head.

"So you're giving a positive identification that Jack and Jay Morris are the men who attacked you, correct?"

She nodded. "Have they done this before?"

"Not that we know of," Det. Hastings said. "Their rap sheets include theft, burglary, possession, and assault, but they've never been charged with a sexual crime. Jay did time for armed robbery and was released three weeks ago. Word is, the Morris brothers have moved up the ladder and teamed up with some real heavyweights."

"Now what?" she asked.

"We'll put out a BOLO and get a warrant for their arrests. We'll also distribute their pictures to the media and ask the public for any information that might lead to their whereabouts and arrest."

"But . . ." She took a deep breath. "They'll know it was me. They'll know I can . . . I can identify them. They'll know I'm . . . that I'm alive." Amber had a difficult time getting words passed the knot in her throat.

"Correct. They'll know the woman they attacked identified them. But they won't know who you are," Hastings was quick to clarify.

"But what if they find out? What if my name is leaked or someone at the hospital talks? What if my neighbors put it together and someone says something to the wrong person? What then?" Tears rolled down Amber's face as she got to her feet.

"Amber, we've done everything possible to protect your identity."

"You mean like pulling up in front of my house in that black sedan of yours, or walking up to my door in suits and ties? People aren't stupid, Det. Hastings. Especially nosy people. I live close to the park. I was away from my house for a week. I come back in a hospital minivan, and have all kinds of *official visitors*, and you don't think someone might put that together?" Amber was pacing, her breathing labored. She felt like she was going to hyperventilate.

Det. Jones stepped in front of her and stilled her with a gently placed hand to her upper arm. "Amber, you need to calm down. We have no reason to believe anyone in your neighborhood can identify or has identified you as the victim in this case, and the hospital staff has a confidentiality policy they must abide by. If for any reason, we discover your identity has been compromised, we will do everything in our power to ensure your safety."

Amber took a seat but didn't feel the least bit safe. She felt numb, almost paralyzed. She looked at the pictures of the two men askew on her coffee table. They were there . . . in her home, her place of safety from the outside world. She felt phantom hands clutching at her neck and invisible fingers pulling at her clothes.

Amber was startled by the ringing of a phone and jumped.

"Hastings. Yeah, we're just finishing up. Not quite yet. Give us twenty minutes." He slid his phone back into his pocket.

"Go," Amber said, her voice monotone.

"But Amber, we—"

"Just go!" she yelled. "You got what you came for."

"Amber, you're upset at the moment and I completely understand that but—"

"You understand? Really?" She was up on her feet again, staring at Hastings. "You know what it's like to have your clothes ripped away and your body beaten? You know what it's like to have a bat taken to your head or to have to listen as someone tells you the vile things they're going to do to you? Or maybe you know what it's like to lay in bed at night paralyzed by sounds you think are your attackers back to finish off what they started? Is that what you mean? Is that what you understand?"

Hastings hung his head at her dressing down, but she didn't feel the least bit regretful for her outburst.

"I'm sorry, Amber. You're right. I can't even begin to comprehend what you're going through, but I can assure you we'll do everything we can to catch these guys." Jones and Reynolds made their way towards the front door while Hastings hung back.

"You know, Amber, I really think you could benefit from some counseling. I know you said you weren't interested, but I think it would help if you were able to talk to someone about your ordeal."

He handed Amber a business card. She took it but didn't say a word.

"Call us, Amber, if you need anything—anything at all. If you hear a twig snap or a door creak. If you feel the least bit uncomfortable in any situation, we want to know, and we'll keep you up to date on any leads we get. We want to help you through this Amber, really we do."

"Then catch them before they find me."

TWENTY-FOUR

Amber paced throughout her house, not knowing what she should do or how she should feel. The police assured her she was safe. But how could they be certain?

Jack and Jay Morris . . . Morris? Do I know them from somewhere?

Amber went to her files and searched through her records. She had no clients with the last name of Morris.

The auto shop? What if one of the Morris brothers worked there? They would've known I was walking home.

She dialed the mechanic's number she had jotted down on her blotter. A gruff voice answered the phone.

"Yes . . . I'm looking for a gentleman that helped me with my car earlier this week. He said he was a professional mechanic. Would you happen to have a mechanic working there with the last name of Morris?"

"Nope. No Morris here, but we'd be happy to take a look at your car if you need some work done."

"No, thank you." She quickly hung up the phone.

Where else? Where else might I have come in contact with them?

The police were confident her attack was random, but what if it wasn't? What if it was someone she knew? Or someone who knew her? No. It couldn't be. She knew exactly what they looked like, but hadn't recognized them.

You have to stop! This isn't helping! She had to believe the police. Because if she didn't, she'd just keep twisting herself into knots. She had to try and move on with what was even a shred of her previous life.

But how could she?

Her life would never be the same. She wouldn't be able to walk in the park or down any street for that matter without wondering if she was being followed, wondering if her attackers would find her and finish what they had started. And what if she was—

Amber couldn't even finish her train of thought. It was more than she could handle. She walked to her darkroom, turned the bolt, and immersed herself in her work.

ൟൟൟൟ

Steven decided it was time he do a little multi-tasking. Because of the extra time he'd been spending with Amber, he had neglected Bo and his current building project. So, he thought he would make it up to his trusty companion by bringing him to the work site.

"Come on, Bo, we're going for a ride."

The crew gave Steven and Bo a warm welcome when they arrived. Bo pranced around in his bright yellow hard hat, acting like he was king of the hill. Everyone gave him a pat or a rub and the scraps left from their lunches. Steven talked to some of the veteran crew members before they all headed back to their work areas, then followed Scott into the office trailer.

"Everything looks great, Scott," Steven said as he plopped down in his chair, and Bo waltzed over to his doggie bed in the corner.

Scott smiled as he took a seat. "The investors are pleased. That's the important thing. They're excited to know we're on budget and on time."

Steven listened as Scott caught him up on need-to-know information. Steven, in turn, thanked Scott over and over again for being the glue that was holding the project together. But, as much as Steven wanted to be on site and listen to all the progress they'd made, he couldn't help but glance at his watch every few minutes wondering if Amber was doing okay.

"Are you seeing her again tonight?" Scott asked.

"Well, yes, but I wouldn't call it 'seeing her.' "

"Then what do you call it?"

"Making sure she's okay."

Scott took a swig of his soda. "So, is she?"

Steven sighed and thought a moment before answering. "I think she will be. She already looks a thousand percent better than when I found her. To tell you the truth, I didn't think she was going to make it."

"That bad, huh?"

"She looked horrible."

"And now?"

"Now? She's healing, but she's still weak and skittish. She's terrified her attackers are going to find out who she is and finish her off."

"Attackers? Plural?"

Steven nodded. Scott shook his head in disgust.

"How about you? How are you doing?"

Steven shrugged. "Me? I'm fine."

Scott gave him a scrutinizing look.

"What? I'm fine!" Steven noticed the defensiveness in his tone. "Hey, sorry about that. I didn't mean to snap at you."

"It's all right, I can take it. But I'm going to be straight with you. I think you're in over your head."

Steven tried to defend himself but Scott cut him off.

"I know you, Steven. You wear your heart on your sleeve. And I can tell you're in this thing way too deep. You had better watch yourself, man. This could blow up in your face."

"Look, Scott—"

"I know, I know. You have everything under control. I'm just sayin', I don't want to see you get blindsided. Not like the last time."

Steven knew Scott was referring to Jenny and the situation he'd gotten himself into his senior year of high school. But this was completely different. "I appreciate your concern, but I'll be fine."

"Okay, man." Scott got up from his desk and headed for the

door. “As long as you’re keeping your head in the game.”

Steven puttered around the site doing everything he could to pass the time. When it was four-thirty he headed home to get showered and changed before going to Amber’s. Bo sat outside the bathroom door, a look of desertion on his face. When Steven saw his dejected expression, he decided to make a call.

❧❧❧❧

Amber heard the phone ringing through the darkroom door. “Shoot!” She’d forgotten to bring it in with her, and she was right in the middle of a process. When the timer went off she left the darkroom to listen to her phone message.

“Hi, Amber, it’s Steven. I was wondering if you would be up for a little extra company tonight. Bo is getting pretty lonely in the evenings, and I was hoping I could bring him along. Give me a call when you get this message. Hope you’re doing okay. See you at five.”

Amber swung around and looked at the clock in the corner. It was almost five, and she hadn’t even thought about dinner. She moved as quickly as she could to her bedroom and retrieved the Bible from the nightstand. She found Steven’s number and dialed it.

“Hi, Steven, it’s Amber.”

“Amber, you sound winded. Is something wrong?”

“No, I’m fine, but I just got your message. I have to admit I completely lost track of time and haven’t even started on dinner.”

“That’s fine. I wanted to help anyway.”

“Are you bringing Bo?”

“Would that be okay?”

“Sure. I mean, I don’t see why not.”

“He’s very well-behaved and a great companion. I promise he won’t be a problem.”

“Then I guess I’ll see you both in a little while.”

TWENTY-FIVE

Amber rushed to the kitchen, a list of needed ingredients circling in her head. Lasagna was one of her go-to meals, but unless Steven had brought more than a pound of hamburger, she would be out of luck. She pulled the freezer basket out. *No hamburger.*

Frantic, she rummaged through her freezer, tossing foiled wrappers and bagged leftovers onto the counter. When she came across three fused together pre-fab hamburger patties in the bottom of the basket, Amber sighed with relief. She couldn't remember when she'd last had burgers—and for a second wondered about freezer burn—but she didn't have much of a choice.

They'll be fine.

She unwrapped the burgers and chiseled them apart before putting them in a frying pan of water. It was an old trick she had learned that would speed up defrosting and cook the patties at the same time.

Scouring her pantry, Amber started to panic. *I know I saw two cans of tomato sauce when I made out my grocery list.* Shifting around the things Steven had bought, she finally saw them. "Ah ha!" Pushed to the back of the cupboard were the two cans she needed, along with a package of broken lasagna noodles that looked like they'd been run over by a shopping cart.

"Great!" she huffed, frustration rising inside her.

It doesn't matter. Broken or not, they'll still layer the same. Everything will be fine. The cheese will cover it an—

"Cheese!"

It was the last straw.

Slamming the pantry door, Amber tossed the box of noodles across the kitchen and began to cry, only to have her meltdown interrupted by the ringing phone.

"Hello!" she snapped.

"Hey, it's me," Steven said. "We must have a bad connection because I can barely hear you."

For which Amber was thankful.

"Look," Steven continued. "I stopped at the market to get some dessert. Is there anything you need?"

Amber couldn't believe his timing. "Yes," she answered quickly, hoping he didn't hear the emotion in her voice. "I don't have any cheese."

"Which do you prefer, mozzarella or ricotta?"

"Both."

"Sounds good. Anything else?"

"I don't think so."

"Okay. We'll be there soon."

Amber put down the phone, dried her eyes, and picked up the box of noodles that rattled even more than before. *Oh well, they'll cook faster this way.*

Once Amber had everything underway, she took a moment to run a brush through her hair and check what was left of her makeup. The swelling of her left eye was almost completely gone, but the discoloration was still there. She reapplied concealer to the bruising and some blush to her cheeks, then stepped back and looked at herself. Each day her face was beginning to look a little more like the old Amber, even though she still felt the ugliness just below the surface. Looking in the full-length mirror and turning slightly, she pushed on her abdomen, wondering if she could feel a change. Her jeans hung looser than normal and so did her blouse, evidence of the weight she had lost in the last several days. Unfortunately, it was weight Amber didn't need to lose.

She had been teased about her size all through grade school. Teeny Weeny. Skinny Minny. Flatsy Patsy. It wasn't until her adult years that Amber had become comfortable with her petite size. Of course, that was because she had developed a serious exercise regimen that had added muscle to her small frame.

A lot of good that did me.

A scene from the park flashed in Amber's mind. The men overpowering her, pinning her raised arms under heavy knees. A hand pressed against her mouth while strong thighs straddled her hips. She'd been immobilized in a matter of seconds. Her added muscle mass had not helped in the least.

It took a minute to shake off the memory and get her act together. She was back working in the kitchen when she heard two knocks at the door and then the ring of the doorbell. The simple signal made her smile. Cautiously, Amber opened the door but only after hearing Steven's voice. When a large, black nose poked through the opening, Amber gasped, then smiled. She was about to meet her true rescuer.

Amber opened the door wide, once again seeing Steven with his arms loaded down with groceries.

"I thought you were just getting dessert and some cheese?"

"I was, but what's lasagna without garlic bread? So, I took a detour through the bakery department, just as fresh cinnamon rolls were being pulled from the oven. They smelled so good, I decided to pick some up for breakfast. While I was there I grabbed another loaf of bread. Then, knowing Bo shouldn't have lasagna, I picked up some kibble. Well, one thing led to another, and I found myself getting a little of this and a little of that. I figured it wouldn't hurt to have a few extra groceries on hand."

Amber laughed at Steven's enthusiasm as she closed the door and locked it behind him. Steven made his way to the kitchen, the yellow lab right on his heels. Amber followed the two of them, then bent to pet Bo. He whimpered lowly, causing Amber to withdraw her hand.

"I don't think he likes me," she said.

Steven turned and watched as Bo gently nudged her hand and whimpered some more.

"He's remembering what happened. Dogs have a keen sense when it comes to things like this." Steven knelt beside Bo and stroked his head. "It's okay, boy. Everything's okay now." Bo's large ebony eyes met with Steven's and then turned to Amber. He stepped closer to her and nudged her hand with his nose.

"See, he likes you. He just had to be assured you're no longer in danger."

"It's okay, Bo," Amber spoke softly. "You're a hero, you know that? You saved my life." Bo's wagging tail just about knocked him off balance. His ears perked up, and if dogs could smile, she was sure he was wearing a grin. Amber caught Steven's expression out of the corner of her eye, not sure if his smile was directed at his faithful friend or at her. Either way, it made him look even more handsome than he already did.

Bo set off to explore the rest of the house while Amber checked the progress of her meal, and Steven unloaded groceries. Amber could tell by the way Steven was watching her, he was looking for some sort of clue to how things had gone with the detectives. But she didn't want to talk about it. At least not now. Instead, she decided to make polite conversation about anything other than herself.

"Bo's a beautiful dog. Didn't you say he was a hunting dog?"

"Yeah. He belonged to my father. But when my dad died, I took Bo because I knew he was going to be too much for my mother to handle."

"When did your father die?"

"Three years ago."

"I'm sorry, Steven. That had to be hard on you. Were you close?"

"Very close. My whole family is. It was devastating at first. It's not like he had been sick or in poor health. He just left for work one morning and never came home."

"How did your mother handle it?"

"She fell apart of course. But after the initial shock wore off, she asked the typical questions people do when they lose a loved one. Why him? Why now? Why us? It was a slow process, but she knew she had to put one foot in front of the other if she was going to go on with life."

"Is she a Christian?"

"Yeah. I'm sure that's what made the difference. She argued with God for weeks, but realized that wasn't going to bring Dad back."

"What about you? Were you angry with God?" Amber asked nonchalantly, as she began to layer the casserole pan with gooey, broken noodles.

"Are you kidding me? I was enraged. My dad was the greatest. He was a good father, a wonderful husband, and the perfect grandpa. I really felt like God had screwed-up. With so many delinquent fathers out there and all the abusive husbands, I wanted to know why God had to take my dad."

"Do you feel you ever got an answer?"

"Yeah." Steven sighed before continuing. "Because sin is sin. It's a horrible disease that has plagued the earth from the beginning of time. Just because my dad was a Christian, didn't make him immune to life's tragedies. It stinks, and I don't think it's fair, but having Christ in your life doesn't give you a free pass from heartbreak, failure, or hardship. Hopefully, it just makes you strong enough to overcome those things if and when they ever happen to you."

❧❧❧❧

Amber's silence drew Steven's attention just in time to see her swipe at a tear falling from her cheek. Inwardly he groaned.

"Amber, I'm sorry. I didn't mean for that to sound like a sermon. I've had three years to deal with this—to work through my pain. But your pain is fresh, and your fear is real. I didn't mean to sound so matter-of-fact. When we sin we know there will be consequences, but to live with the consequences of someone else's sin is hard to comprehend. It doesn't seem right or fair."

"But like you said, there are no free passes in life."

Steven could hear the callousness in her tone as Amber

continued to haphazardly layer the lasagna—red sauce and meat splattering everywhere. He gently pulled on her elbow and turned her to face him. Amber stared at the floor, unwilling to meet his eyes. He placed his forefinger under her chin and tipped it so she had to look at him. "God knew we would have fears and anger in life. It's not wrong, Amber, we just have to make sure we don't let it consume or destroy us, or interfere with our relationship with God. God is angry right alongside you, Amber. Imagine how He must feel seeing the injustice in the world *He* created. It pains Him. It pains Him so much He made sure we would have an eternal escape from pain and death. But just like everything else in life, that doesn't remove the road that has to be traveled." Steven gently stroked a tear away from Amber's cheek before bringing his hand down to his side.

"Christ knew as He walked the road to the cross, He was about to face the worst pain and the darkest period of His life. But He also knew on the other side of that pain He would be returning to His Father, to His rightful place in heaven.

"So, when times get rough or incomprehensible we need to look to the cross, and if we look close enough we'll be able to see through to the other side."

❧❧

Amber looked into Steven's eyes—eyes filled with hope and compassion. She so wanted to believe what he was saying. She wanted to hold on to the trust and protection he was offering. "You make it sound so simple."

"It *is* simple to believe in God's grace and mercy," Steven said, "but sometimes it's hard to accept it for yourself. God spared your life, Amber. That was a gift, not a curse."

She wondered if that was true. Not knowing what else she would have to endure, she silently pled. *Please, God, show me mercy. I don't know how much more I can handle.*

Amber turned back to her lasagna. It would be in no way her best effort, but somehow, she didn't think Steven would mind.

❧❧

Steven watched as Amber finished the lasagna and put it in the oven. He helped with the clean-up, enjoying working side-by-side with her. While they waited for dinner to cook, he wanted to ask how her meeting had gone with Hastings but knew he needed to allow her to bring it up.

Walking into the living room, Steven noticed Bo had his nose pressed up against the glass door. He decided it would be a good time to work off some of the canine's pent up energy.

"Would you mind if I took Bo outside for a little bit? He hasn't gotten much attention or exercise lately."

"No . . . sure . . . go ahead. In fact, I probably even have a ball around here somewhere."

❧❧☙☙

Amber disappeared into her studio. She rummaged through the box of children's props and came up with a blue rubber ball. Steven and Bo were already in the backyard when she reappeared. She walked to the patio and saw Steven on his hands and knees, growling at Bo. He pushed at the big dog's face and wrestled with him like he was an overgrown puppy. Amber pulled up a chair from the patio set and watched them. She had never been much of a dog person. They always seemed like such a masculine pet. The scene she was witnessing proved her point.

Steven tussled and played with Bo a few more minutes before walking breathlessly over to where she was sitting. He looked at the rubber ball that was still in her hand, then nodded towards Bo.

"Why don't you play fetch with him for a little bit? I'm wiped out," Steven said as he collapsed into one of the patio chairs.

Amber looked at the ball, then to Bo where he was sitting in the middle of the yard, ears raised, waiting for some attention. She held her ribs as she tossed the ball over his head and watched as Bo scrambled to retrieve it. He ran back to Amber and gently dropped it at her feet, then raised his head and waited for her to do it again. This time, she only pretended to throw the ball. Bo was only fooled for a second before he turned a quick eye back on Amber and waited. She tossed the ball, causing him to bolt. He was able to catch up with it before it even reached the fringe of the lawn.

ↂↂↂↂ

Steven watched as Amber continued to throw the ball. He could tell Amber was enjoying herself, even though each throw took more exertion on her part. She was a natural with dogs, and it was obvious Bo was enjoying the extra attention. But Steven didn't want Amber to wear herself out. When Bo trotted towards Amber with the ball, Steven intercepted it. "Okay, Bo, let's show Amber some of your other skills."

Steven walked to the middle of the yard and whistled. Bo immediately ran to him, sat in front of Steven, and waited for his first command. He took Bo through a series of exercises, Bo instantly responding to each directive. When Steven was done, he gave the canine overwhelming praise. Bo proceeded to prance around the yard like he was king of the hill.

When Steven sat back down, he couldn't help but notice the smile on Amber's face. "You should do that more often."

"Do what?"

"Smile. You have an incredible smile."

Amber looked away. "It must be the new blush I'm wearing. You'd be amazed what black and blue does for the complexion."

Steven knew she was trying to deflect the compliment, but he wasn't going to let her get away with it. "But you do realize how beautiful you are, right? Bruises can't hide that."

Amber stood and walked towards the house. "I'd better check on the lasagna. I've already done my best to massacre it. I'd better not let it burn, too." She quickly walked into the house, putting distance between them.

Feeling defeated, Steven slumped forward in his chair. Bo walked over and sat in front of him, meeting him nose to nose. "I didn't handle that so well, did I?" Steven said. Bo tipped his head from side to side as if trying to understand what his master meant. Steven gave Bo a pat on the head before walking into the house. He leaned against the wall of the kitchen—his arms crossed against his chest—and watched as Amber washed a few dishes that were laying in the sink.

"Amber, I'm—"

"I see you brought stuff to make a salad," she said, cutting him off. "Why don't you start on that, and I'll get the bread ready."

Steven didn't answer, he just stepped to the refrigerator and gathered the fresh vegetables in his arms. He unloaded them on the counter next to the sink and started rinsing them.

He tried again. "I'm sorry if I made you feel uncomfortable. That wasn't my intention."

Amber fumbled with the loaf of bread wrapped in foil. "I know. I overreacted. Let's just forget it, okay."

"Forget that you overreacted or forget that you're beautiful?"

Amber smacked the knife she was wielding down on the cutting board and turned a scornful look on him. "What is it with you? I didn't invite you over for dinner so you could do a number on my ego. I wanted to thank you for all you've done. But, if you're going to continue to be so . . . so aggravating, you can go home now."

Steven threw up his hands in surrender. "Okay . . . okay. I promise not to say another word about how beautiful you are as long as you agree to let me and Bo stay for dinner."

Though Amber tried to hide her smile, Steven could see it pull at the corner of her lips. When their eyes met, she threw a damp dishcloth at his broad chest. "Just make the salad."

Steven raised his brows at Amber's reaction. If he was a psychiatrist, he would think there was something more to her playfulness. A spark of interest maybe? Steven knew they were connecting, even if Amber acted resistant. He smiled. He could wait. He would give her the time she needed to figure it out for herself.

As they worked together in the kitchen, Steven still wanted to ask about her appointment with the sketch artist. He was trying to be patient, hoping she would bring it up on her own, but it seemed obvious she didn't want to talk about it. So he would continue to wait, hoping she would eventually open up and see that he could be trusted with her fears and worries.

While Amber poured them each a glass of sparkling cider, Steven poured Bo a bowl of kibble and placed it on the floor by the coffee table. Once they both took a seat—she on the couch, he in the chair—Steven asked, "Do you mind if I pray?"

Bowing her head was Amber's only response.

When Steven had dished up his second helping of lasagna, he noticed Amber wasn't eating. She just pushed her food around on her plate, her focus clearly somewhere else.

"What are you thinking?"

Amber jumped, her fork clattering against her plate. "I'm sorry, what did you say?"

"What are you thinking? You've been staring off into space for the last ten minutes."

Amber's eyes were downcast as she dragged her fork through the sauce on her plate. "I'm thinking about moving back to New York."

"You're what?" Steven was caught completely off guard. "Why? When did you decide this? Does it have something to do with what happened this afternoon?"

Amber took a breath before looking at Steven. "My father called earlier today. He said he could get me a job in New York. I'm thinking I should consider it."

Steven stared at her, studying her body language. There was more she wasn't telling him. "What else, Amber? What happened this afternoon with the sketch artist?"

She hesitated for what felt like an eternity before she spoke. "They know who attacked me. I identified their pictures today."

"Amber, that's great. Now the police have something to go on. Everything's going to be okay."

She stood abruptly. "How can you say that? How can you say everything is going to be okay?"

Bo whimpered at the commotion as Amber marched across the living room and out into the backyard. Steven waited a few moments before joining her. When he stepped out on the patio,

Amber was leaning against the pergola, her shoulders shaking.

"Why New York?"

"Because I'm afraid to stay here." She turned to face him. "I can't sleep; I can't eat. I know they're out there, Steven, and when they find out I can identify them, they'll come looking for me. I can't stay here. I've got to get away."

"But they don't know who you are. There are over a million people in this city. Do you know what the odds are of them finding out who you are?"

She didn't answer.

Steven lowered his voice and stepped closer. "Let me help, Amber. You can come stay at my place, or I can stay here in the evenings."

"I can't ask you to do that. You can't continue to put your life on hold for me. I'm a nobody to you. A person you met by accident."

Steven stepped even closer. With the pad of his thumbs he gently brushed the tears from her cheeks. "You're not a nobody, Amber, and I don't feel we met by accident. I want to help you. I want to see you through this."

Amber couldn't control her tears. She covered her face and began to sob. She felt Steven's arms wrap around her, and without even thinking, she pressed her forehead to his chest and welcomed the strength of his embrace.

The events of the last few days flashed through her mind like a hideous strobe light. The horrifying attack, waiting for test results, the mug shots, the thought of moving to New York, the thought of being . . .

But then there was Steven.

She took a deep breath and allowed herself to feel the comfort he offered her. She felt his strength. His compassion. His concern. And she didn't know how to explain it or even comprehend it, but she felt safe. Safe with a complete stranger. Safer than she'd ever felt before.

TWENTY-SIX

After Amber had calmed down, Steven walked her back into the house. Dinner was history so they sat on the couch.

"I'm sorry for falling apart like that. I just feel so out of control right now."

"Amber, stop apologizing. There's no blueprint, no right or wrong on how to deal with what you've been through. You have nothing to be sorry for."

They sat for a moment before Steven pursued the New York thing. "So, you're really willing to give up everything you've accomplished here—on your own—and move back to New York?"

"I'm not sure what I want to do. I know it sounds like a knee-jerk reaction, but I feel so claustrophobic here. I think maybe a change of scenery would help me move on."

"Then let me help. Like I said, you could stay at my house. I have three bedrooms and three bathrooms, plenty of space for the both of us. Besides, not only would you be getting me," he said jokingly, with a roguish smile, "but you'd be getting the best watchdog in the world."

"That wouldn't work, Steven. All my stuff is here: my darkroom, my studio, my office. I can't just pick up and move to your place."

"Then let me and Bo stay here. Bo could stay with you during the day, and I could sack out here at night."

"I couldn't take Bo away from you. That wouldn't be fair."

"Fair? Are you kidding me? Bo would love to have someone to

hang out with all day."

Bo pranced over when he heard his name being mentioned, but instead of sitting by Steven, he walked to Amber and placed his head on her lap.

"See. He's already smitten by you."

❧❧❧❧

Amber let the subject drop as she cleaned up the dinner dishes, but an idea continued to roll around in her head. *Maybe getting a dog isn't such a bad idea.*

She rinsed the sink and dried her hands before joining Steven and Bo in the living room where they were watching an old movie on TV. Steven had his arms stretched across the back of the couch, and for the first time Amber noticed a large scar that ran the length of his tricep. She sat in the side chair and pulled her feet up under her.

"So, how'd you get the scar?"

Immediately, the smile on Steven's face disappeared and his arms drop to his sides. "You don't want to hear about that."

"Sure I do."

"It's a long story."

"Well, it's not like I have grand plans for the evening," Amber joked, but Steven remained quiet. She could sense his reluctance, but pursued it. "Does it have to do with your friend's death?"

"No." He shook his head and sighed. "That was a climbing accident. I know now there wasn't anything I could've done for Jeff, but I should've kept my promise. I should've stayed with him."

"So, then, how did you get that scar?"

He shrugged his shoulders. "I got into a fight my senior year of high school."

"No, come on. I want the unabridged version. You wanted me to share—to spill my guts. Now it's your turn."

❧❧❧❧

Steven stalled for a moment, not sure if he felt like rehashing the painful time in his past. But when he looked at Amber, he realized she wasn't going to take no for an answer.

Maybe some transparency will help strengthen our relationship.

"Okay, but you asked for it." He took a long swallow of his cider then started. "I was eighteen and a senior in high school. I had pretty much skated through adolescence. I had great parents, top grades, had lettered in three sports, and was dating the captain of the cheerleading squad. You would've thought I had it all, and I did."

"So what happened?"

"I was a nerd."

"Wait a minute, you just said you were a jock and dated the captain of the cheerleading squad. That in no way qualifies you as a nerd."

"Okay, so I wasn't a nerd. Maybe dull is a better word."

Amber laughed. "I find that hard to believe. Try again."

"Okay, I wasn't much of a partier. I was a part of the "in crowd", but wasn't comfortable there. How's that?"

She shrugged. "So you didn't like to party. So what?"

"But my football buddies did. They liked to go from one party to another. I went with them a lot of the times—mostly to keep them out of trouble—but it really wasn't my scene. Then, one night Jenny Conrad came over and sat with me. We'd been friends on and off since grade school, but something clicked that night. We went on our first date the very next day." Steven thought back, wondering for the umpteenth time how things could've gotten so bad.

"Jenny and I had a great time together. We liked the same kind of music, the same movies, and the same restaurants. It felt natural being with her. At least in the beginning."

"What do you mean?" Amber asked.

"Unfortunately, the more time we spent together, the more our differences came to light. There were two major obstacles in our relationship. One of those was partying. In the beginning, Jenny was content spending time with just me. Dinner for two. The movies. But the novelty of that soon wore off. She enjoyed the fast lane and wanted to get back into it. Not me. I no longer wanted to go to parties just to watch my friends get drunk, high, or hook up with someone they barely knew. It wasn't for me. I was looking to my future, what college to attend, what to major in, while all my friends were getting wasted."

Sighing, Steven thought back to when things had gotten complicated. "Jenny and I began to argue a lot. She complained we didn't go out enough and started hinting at the fact she didn't think we were going to make it."

Steven was quiet as long ago memories played in his mind. When he looked at Amber, she was staring at him with curious eyes. "What are you thinking?" he asked.

"You said there were two things you didn't agree on."

He paused. *Be vulnerable. Let Amber know the real you.* "Jenny wanted a more intimate relationship." He took a breath. "But I knew that would be a mistake."

Amber tipped her head and arched her brow. "So you're saying you didn't . . ."

He chuckled. "Don't get me wrong, I wasn't a choirboy by any stretch of the imagination. Jenny and I had our heated moments and close calls. It's just that I'd been raised in a conservative home and the respect of my parents was very important to me. I had a promising future in sports, and my parent's support and trust. I didn't want to screw things up just because I was hormonal."

He looked at Amber looking at him. "Okay, so when I put it that way I guess I do sound like a goody-two-shoes. Anyway," he continued, "one evening, Jenny broke off our regular Saturday night date. She said she needed some time to think about where we were headed. I tried not to read too much into it. I cared deeply for Jenny, but I also began to realize our differences might be too big to overcome. I struggled most of the day, trying to figure out a way I could give into what she wanted without compromising my convictions."

❧❧☙☙

Amber watched as Steven clenched his jaw and his eyes turned to pinpoints. His story had come to an abrupt stop.

"So what happened?" Amber blurted out, feeling bad the

moment she did. She could tell Steven was struggling with something, and should've let it go. "I'm sorry. You don't need to answer that."

"No . . . it's all right."

Though Steven had said it was all right, it was still several minutes before he continued.

"That night, Scott—my best friend—came over to hang out. He told me he heard about some kickin' party happening on the west end and wanted me to go with him. He tried to convince me it would help me forget about Jenny for the night. I didn't believe him for a moment, but Scott had a tendency to drink too much, and I knew he was going to that party with or without me. So, I told him the only reason I would go is to keep an eye on him, to make sure he got home safe at the end of the night.

"When we got to the party, the cars in the driveway were all high end. Vets, Porsches, custom cars. And the house was a beachfront mansion. It was obvious to me this wasn't a typical high school party. Even the mood inside was different. I mean, most parties we went to had a keg in the middle of the floor, loud music blasting through the speakers, and too many people packed into a room—half of them making out while the others were dancing. But not this party. It was like we had just walked into the Playboy Mansion. Barely dressed girls were hanging on men a lot older than our normal crowd.

"I turned to leave but Scott stopped me. I told him I didn't want any part of what was going on, but he refused to let me go. I knew something was up because Scott's demeanor changed. He wasn't his usual happy-go-lucky self. His look was serious, almost angry. That's when he told me about Jenny."

"Told you what?"

❧❧❧❧

Steven fisted his sweaty hands, his heart racing. He closed his eyes and relived the moment Scott had told him the truth.

"You can't leave, man. Jenny's here," Scott said between clenched teeth.

"What?" Steven asked, sure he had heard wrong.

"I knew if I just told you, you wouldn't believe me. That's why I brought you here. She's here, and it isn't her first time."

"Scott, what are you saying?"

"She's playing you for a fool, Steven. That girl, Tina, Jenny's been hanging with . . . this is her scene. This is what Jenny's been doing when she's with Tina."

"I don't believe you. I know we haven't been getting along lately, but she would never do this."

Steven opened his eyes and turned to Amber.

"Scott told me Jenny was a regular at that house. I tried to leave but Scott wouldn't let me. He was going to prove to me Jenny was not the person I thought she was. He explained how he had found out, how he had seen Jenny making out at one of these parties. She swore him to secrecy—said she was crazy for going out on me and that it would never happen again. He believed her . . . until the next time. Scott decided the only way I would believe him is if I saw her for myself."

Steven could still hear Scott. *"See for yourself, Steven. I bet she's already upstairs."*

"I wasn't sure what I should do. I wanted to deck Scott for making such accusations, but another part of me needed to prove he was wrong. I ran up the stairs two at a time, afraid of what I would find. When I got to the landing Tina emerged from one of the rooms, hanging all over a man twice her age. She was shocked when she saw me standing there—but she quickly recovered—her expression morphing from shock to a twisted sense of gratification. That's when I knew what Scott had said was true.

"When I asked Tina where Jenny was, she tried to ignore me. So, I got louder and started making a scene. When the man with Tina tried to interfere, I pushed him. When it looked like we were going to come to blows, Tina pointed to a room—told me she was in there. Told me I was just holding Jenny back and she was better off without me.

"The door was locked so I burst through it and found Jenny

having sex with some guy. She looked at me, her eyes made of glass. She was so stoned she didn't even know it was me."

Steven wasn't sure why he had gone into such detail. He guessed maybe, in some way, he wanted Amber to know he knew what it was like to be hurt by someone.

He flashed her an awkward smile. "So now you're asking yourself, what on earth does this have to do with the scar on my arm, right?"

She just nodded.

"As much as I hated Jenny at that moment, I couldn't leave her there. I lunged for her and tried pulling her away from the slime she was with. She was so incoherent; she was like a rag doll. She slid from the bed while the man she was with started ranting and raving about his privacy.

"I tried wrapping Jenny in a blanket when out of the corner of my eye, I saw the man coming at me. I called him some choice names and assured him the cops were going to find out about him and the other men in the house having sex with underage girls. That's when he pulled a knife."

Amber gasped. "He attacked you?"

"Yeah, he stabbed me in the arm and in the stomach."

"What happened next?"

"It was chaos. As soon as Scott heard the commotion upstairs, he called the cops. I was sure the man was going to kill me. Jenny was screaming and crying. I was bleeding and losing consciousness while I tried to defend myself. People were running through the halls, trying to get out of the house. They knew their party was over, and they wanted out before the cops arrived."

Steven leaned forward, resting his elbows on his knees. He stared at his clasped hands as he continued.

"Turns out the man who attacked me was the owner of the house. He was arrested, and I ended up in the hospital."

"What about Jenny?"

"She was arrested for prostitution. Since she was under age and it was the first time she'd ever had a run-in with the cops, she was given probation and mandated to get counseling."

"What did your parents and Stacy do?"

"They were horrified. Imagine, getting a call that your son has been picked up—at what amounted to a whorehouse—and was being hospitalized with injuries. Luckily, Scott was there and was able to explain to them what had happened while I was in surgery."

"Surgery!"

He shook his head. "When I came to, my parents were still having a hard time understanding everything that went on. They had really liked Jenny and couldn't believe she was living a double life. I had to keep assuring them the only reason I was at the house was because I was looking for Jenny, not because I was involved with what was going on there. After several conversations, they finally understood what had happened."

"What happened between you and Jenny?"

"She hated me. I went to see her after I was released from the hospital, but she could barely stand to be in the same room with me. Jenny blamed me for ruining her life and her reputation. She said I got what I deserved and never wanted to see me again."

Steven saw the look of shock on Amber's face.

"How could she say that?" Amber asked. "You were almost killed trying to save her. How could she blame you?"

"Jenny didn't want to be saved, Amber. She thought she had found an exciting new life with men, money, and drugs. Jenny never cared about me. I was just some dumb jock that thought he was in love."

"And she thought being labeled a prostitute was better?"

Steven sighed and leaned back against the couch cushions. "She was searching. Jenny was looking for something more out of life. She was just looking for it in all the wrong places."

"Had Stacy known what Jenny was doing?"

"She'd heard rumors. But Stacy liked Jenny and didn't want to see me get hurt. So she kept it to herself. That's why my sister is so protective of me. She felt responsible, realizing if she had spoken up none of it would've happened."

"So how bad were you injured?"

Steven pulled up his t-shirt to show Amber the nine-inch scar that crossed his well-defined abs. "The doctors said I was lucky no major organs were damaged. When I saw the length of the scar, I knew it had nothing to do with luck. God had protected me." Steven lowered his shirt. "Unfortunately, I was no longer in any shape to play sports. It took several months for me to recover, and since I couldn't assure college scouts I would ever be a hundred percent again, I lost any chance at an athletic scholarship."

Amber shook her head. "I don't get it. She was wrong; the man was wrong, but you were the one penalized. How was that fair?"

Steven raised an exaggerated eyebrow at her.

"I know, I know," Amber blurted out. "life's not fair, but come on. If God expects His people to want to follow Him, you would think He would do a little more to show us He cares."

"Amber, God doesn't want us to follow Him because He can wave some magic wand and make all the bad things in our world go away. He wants us to recognize we need a Savior. He wants us to accept Him for who He is, not what He can do for us. Salvation is not about a better life. It has nothing to do with superficial things like money, relationships, position, or freedom from difficulty. It's about forgiveness. Having your sins wiped from your record."

❧❧❧❧

Steven wasn't telling Amber anything she didn't already know. But she still hated it. She hated the fact that God hadn't done something more to save Steven or her. Bitterness and indignation churned inside her. She pushed herself back in the chair and flinched with pain. "Let's talk about something else," she snapped.

"Amber, I didn't tell you all this because—"

"Please, Steven, just change the subject!"

"Okay." Steven nodded, as he stroked Bo's head. "Then let's talk about my housing proposition. Bo would make a wonderful houseguest."

She turned to Bo where he was sprawled out on the floor. "Maybe I should just consider getting a dog of my own."

"You could, but Bo is already trained." Bo popped his head up, all ears at the mention of his name. "He'd be a great guard dog for you. Why go to all the trouble of finding a dog and training it, when Bo is at your disposal?"

Amber smiled at Bo. The minute he knew he had her attention, he got up and walked over to her chair. He sat in front of her and stared. If she didn't know better, she would think he was asking if he could stay. She sighed and reached out to rub his ears. "Are you sure you wouldn't mind? I mean, it's an incredible offer, but I just can't help but feel it would be selfish of me to accept. Don't you think Bo will feel like you're neglecting him?"

"I'll see him every night."

"I can't ask you to come over here every night, Steven."

"Then I'll be rude and invite myself. You wouldn't keep a man away from his best friend, would you?"

Steven's smile was so disarming, it flustered Amber. She didn't know what to say or what to do. Steven picked up the slack.

"Look, it's getting late. Why don't we call it a night?"

"Steven . . . does your family know you're spending so much time here?"

Steven looked surprised by her change of subject. "Yeah."

"And what do they think about it?"

When Steven didn't answer immediately, she could tell he was trying to formulate a polite response.

"They're concerned. Since I was considered a suspect, they think I'm going to get myself in trouble."

"You were? Why?" This was the first Amber heard that Steven had actually been considered a suspect.

Steven rolled his eyes and sheepishly explained how suspicious he had looked showing up at the hospital and again on her street.

"You did all that?" Amber couldn't believe the lengths he had gone to.

He nodded.

Steven continued to amaze her. He was kind, protective, compassionate, charming, and handsome. *Handsome?* Amber shook away her thoughts. Steven was helping her because he somehow felt responsible for her. It had nothing to do with attraction. *Could it?* No. She would have to keep reminding herself of that fact. Because the more he was around . . . the more she wanted him around.

&

Steven made sure all the doors were locked before Amber said goodnight and disappeared down the hall. He sat on the couch feeling tired and restless as he massaged Bo's ear. Bo let out a howl of a yawn and stretched out on the floor next to the couch. Steven unbuttoned his shirt and tossed it over the arm of the chair. He kicked off his shoes and pulled at his socks. He laid on the couch—resting his arms behind his head—and sighed.

I'm losing it, Lord. Every time I look into Amber's amazing eyes it's all I can do not to pull her close and let her know she is still every bit a beautiful woman. I know I can't put that pressure on her right now. It wouldn't be fair. Help me to help Amber without screwing everything up.

&

Amber slipped into a t-shirt and some flannel pants before crawling between the covers. She stared at the light on the nightstand, reached for it, but couldn't bring herself to turn it off. She would fall asleep easier with the light on, where shadows could be kept far from her.

Laying there, staring at the ceiling, Amber replayed in her mind her earlier conversation with the police. She silently prayed they would be able to find the Morris brothers. Because if they didn't, she wasn't sure how she would be able to move on.

Amber realized her attackers' control over her had not stopped that day in the park. They were controlling her even now. Her independence, her love for life, even simple things like going to the market or enjoying the outdoors was now controlled by the fear they had beaten into her. Her future was uncertain. Her business. Her personal life. They controlled it all.

It was too overwhelming to process.

Then she remembered the business card Det. Hastings had

given her. *Maybe a counselor isn't such a bad idea.* But the idea of explaining to yet another person what she had endured did not sound comforting in the least. Amber thought about Erika, wishing their relationship wasn't so estranged. She really needed another woman to talk to.

Mom, I wish you were here.

Her mom would know what to say, how to comfort her, to assure her everything was going to be okay. She would be at her side no matter what the future held. But another part of Amber was glad her mother didn't have to see her in her present condition.

Tears slid down Amber's face, wetting her ears and soaking into her pillow. It would be one of many nights she would cry herself to sleep.

TWENTY-SEVEN

After a quick shower, Amber did what she could to make herself look presentable, then followed the unmistakable aroma of bacon to the kitchen. Amber was ready to greet Steven with an obligatory 'good morning' but stopped short when she saw him working busily over the stove. Shirtless, his jeans riding low on his hips, Steven's physique rendered her speechless. His muscular back, sculpted arms, and the rich tone of his skin, easily put him in the Adonis category. But his disheveled hair, laidback manner, and his sing-song whistling of "Take Me Out To the Ballgame", spoke more of his boy-next-door charm. Oblivious to the fact that he was being observed, Amber studied Steven as he pushed scrambled eggs around in a skillet and pulled a pan of cinnamon rolls from the oven. When she realized her studying had turned to ogling, she closed her eyes, shook her undisciplined thoughts from her mind, and cleared her throat to make her presence known.

"I wondered how long you were going to just stand there." Steven gave her a devilish look over his shoulder as he spoke.

She casually crossed the kitchen and opened the refrigerator, pretending to look for something while trying to conceal the flush of embarrassment on her face. "If you knew I was standing there, why didn't you say something?"

"I thought you might be enjoying the view."

Amber was caught completely off guard by Steven's egotistical comment. He was right of course, but there was no way she was going to tell him that. She pulled the orange juice from the refrigerator and closed the door a little harder than she meant. "I was trying to come up with a polite way of telling you I'm not a fan of scrambled eggs." It was the best she could come up with on the spot.

"Well, we'll just see about that. These are not your ordinary, run-of-the-mill scrambled eggs," he said, as he tipped the pan over a plate, allowing eggs to tumble onto it. He dished up a second plate—ignoring what she had said—while Amber poured two glasses of orange juice.

"You want to eat on the patio?" she asked, averting her eyes, not wanting to get caught gawking again.

"Sure. Lead the way." Steven followed her out to where Bo was playing in the yard. Bo ambled over to Amber, pushing up against her, clearly looking for attention. She put down the juice glasses and gave him a few strokes on the head while Steven headed back into the house to get the rest of their breakfast.

When Steven returned, he had a plate stacked with the cinnamon rolls he had bought the night before, forks, a few napkins, and his shirt lapped over his shoulder. He doled everything out then stretched to pull his shirt over his head. Amber couldn't help but watch as the muscles in his abs and arms flexed. But when their eyes met as Steven poked his head through the collar of his shirt, Amber quickly looked down and fiddled with her silverware.

"I could leave it off," Steven said as he took his seat, "but my mother taught me never to come to the table without a shirt on. She said it was rude and in bad taste. I guess all those years of conditioning sunk in," Steven explained with a grin before bowing in prayer.

Amber followed along with Steven's prayer not sure who she was angrier with. Herself for getting caught staring a second time or Steven for teasing her.

Bo waited for handouts while they ate in an agonizing silence. Every time Amber wanted to say something to defend herself, she thought better of it and shoved a forkful of eggs in her mouth instead. She watched as Steven tried to suppress a smile, but after a few raised eyebrows in her direction and what she was sure was a snicker, she put down her fork and blurted out, "Okay, fine. You caught me staring. Why are you making such a big thing out of it?"

"I'm not," he said quietly, but with a grin. "I was just going to say, for someone who claims she doesn't like scrambled eggs, you sure seem to be enjoying them. In fact, it's the most I've seen you eat in days."

Amber was caught in her lie. She started to reply but her stammering caused Steven to laugh. She felt her cheeks heat up with embarrassment and agitation rise inside her. She stood to leave, but Steven took hold of her wrist, stopping her.

"I'm only teasing you, Amber. I'm just glad you're eating."

She sat back down. "Well, they do taste pretty good."

"That's because I grate cheese and bacon, and mix it all together before cooking them." Steven swallowed a scoop of eggs and chased it down with a swig of juice. "I knew you'd like them."

❧❧❧❧

Steven finished what was on his plate, but noticed Amber hadn't taken another bite. He knew his teasing was the reason for her lost appetite and hated himself for it, but the thought of her possibly being attracted to him thrilled Steven beyond belief. He knew now was not the right time to question her about her feelings, so he decided to move the conversation in a different direction.

"So, how'd you sleep last night?" he asked, as he leaned back in his chair, stretching out his legs.

"Good actually. It took a while to fall asleep, but once I did, I didn't wake up until about five o'clock. How about you?"

"Not bad. Your couch was a lot more comfortable this time."

Amber rolled her eyes. "There's no possible way you could be comfortable sleeping on that couch. It has to be at least a foot shorter than you are."

"I just stretched my feet out on the coffee table. It wasn't that bad, really."

Amber gave him a conciliatory smile as she stared at what was left of her eggs.

"Are you done with that?"

"What? Yeah." She put her fork down. "I'm done."

He reached over, took the plate, and put it on the ground for Bo. The happy retriever inhaled the leftover eggs and finished off by licking the plate until it started creeping across the patio. Steven bent down, picked it up, and gathered the rest of the plates from the table. He carried them into the kitchen and put them into the sink. Amber followed with the glasses, picking up a dishcloth.

"I thought maybe we could take a walk today?" Steven said casually, as he ran dish water in the sink.

"A walk?" Her tone was abrupt. "Why would I want to do that?"

"You have a photo shoot at the park tomorrow."

Amber swallowed hard. "I know."

"I thought maybe it would be a good idea to go today. We could take it slow—work through any issues you might have."

"I don't think I'm ready for that." Amber set down the dishcloth and went to her room.

Steven heard the door slam and sighed. *That went well.* He leaned against the counter, hating himself for how the morning had gone. He should've slowly introduced the idea of going to the park. He was only trying to protect her. Amber's first trip back to the park shouldn't be for a photo shoot. She would have a lot to process, and he didn't want her to lose clients because she had a meltdown on their dime.

Steven waited for Amber to reappear, but she didn't. He glanced at his watch, thinking it might be a good time to go home and take a shower, give Amber some space. He also had promised his sister he would check in with her. Steven walked to Amber's bedroom door and gave it a tap.

"Amber?"

No answer.

"Amber, I'm going to head out. I'm leaving Bo here. I'll bring—" before he could finish, she opened the door.

"Are you sure Bo will be okay without you?" she asked.

"Sure. He'll do fine."

Amber rocked the door back and forth. Steven could tell she had something more to say.

"You're right. I should probably go to the park before tomorrow."

Steven smiled at the determination in her eyes. "Okay . . . when?"

"I have another set of prints I need to finish. Maybe you could come back around two or three? That is if you don't have things you need to do, because if you have things to do, I totally understand. I mean, I don't want to monopo—"

"Two o'clock will be fine."

"Okay. I guess Bo and I will see you then."

TWENTY-EIGHT

Steven slowly pulled into the large circular driveway in front of his sister's house. He smiled as he walked past two bikes on the way to the front porch, one outfitted with a pink basket, the other resembling a motorcycle. Before he could ring the bell, the door flew open. With a squeal of laughter and a blur of blond hair, his niece flung herself at him, nearly toppling him over.

"Hey Jaime, how are you?" Steven knelt down so he could give his five-year-old niece a hug.

Jaime wrapped her little arms around his neck, gave him a tight squeeze, then took a step back. "I got a gold star in school today. Mrs. Andrews said I was a good listener."

"That's great, Jaime."

When Steven peered around his niece, he saw Jarrod standing by Stacy, partially hidden by the open door. "Hey, Jarrod, don't I get a hug?"

His nephew moved a little closer, his head hung low. "But I didn't get a star today. Mrs. Andrews said I have to use my indoor voice if I want to get a star."

Steven could hear the disappointment in Jarrod's voice. "That's okay. You can do it. I know you can. Now, can you come over here and give me a hug anyway?"

Jarrod's eyes lit up. He lunged toward Steven and squeezed him around the neck, then backed up, all thoughts of gold stars quickly vanished. "Can I have a piggyback ride?"

"Sure thing. Just let me talk to your mom first."

Both kids screamed in excitement as Steven stood and gave his sister a kiss on the cheek. She whispered a 'thank you' and nodded at Jarrod. "He's been moping around here ever since I picked him up from school," she said as the kids raced ahead of them. "You would've thought the class turtle had died."

"Hey, those gold stars are serious status symbols in kindergarten. And if I remember correctly, I had a sister that paraded hers around in front of me all the time," Steven smiled as he wrapped his arm around his sister's shoulders.

"And as I recall, you too had trouble remembering to use your indoor voice."

"Hey, share time was too exciting to waste on whispers."

They both laughed as they walked out onto the patio, Jarrod and Jaime waiting anxiously to play.

Stacy sat in the nearby swing, anxious to ask Steven about the last week. But she would wait until he was done playing with the kids. The time he shared with Jarrod and Jaime was too important. She wouldn't dream of interrupting.

She watched as the three of them wrestled and rolled on the grass, listening to squeals of laughter and screams of delight. In the eyes of her children, Uncle Steven could do no wrong. Stacy loved watching her brother interact with her kids, knowing he would make a great father one day. If only he could find the right woman.

Steven was pinned to the ground with both kids perched on his chest. He conceded that he had been captured, and they were too strong for him to fight back.

"Okay, kids, that's enough. Let Uncle Steven up so Mommy can visit with him for a little while." There were a few moans, but it didn't last long. Steven reached into his pocket and pulled out two pieces of taffy. The kids took the pieces of candy and ran to their mother.

"Can we have it now, Mommy?" Jaime asked.

"Okay, but only if you promise to play quietly while I talk with Uncle Steven."

They vigorously nodded their heads in agreement.

"Sit at the table and don't put the whole piece in your mouth at one time."

Stacy watched her kids quickly unwrap their treasures as Steven took a seat alongside her in the swing. She kept an eye on the kids, making sure they were being careful with their candy. As soon as she was convinced they were okay, she turned her attention to her brother and patted his leg.

"So, how are you doing these days?"

"Me? I'm fine."

"And . . ."

"Amber? She's doing okay."

Stacy looked at Steven wanting to ask a deeper question, but not sure if she should.

"What?" Steven asked, a hint of annoyance in his tone.

"You're spending a lot of time with her. Are you sure you're not in over your head?"

"Well, we're not involved if that's what you're asking."

"But do you want to be involved? That's the question." Stacy knew her brother too well. The way he was avoiding her stare was a sure sign he was trying to hide his feelings. "I knew it," she huffed, doing nothing to hide her frustration.

❧❧❧❧

"Come on, Stacy. No lectures, okay?"

His sister's agitation played out in the quick motion of the swing. Steven let her stew for a few moments before asking, "Okay, what are you thinking?"

"I'm only thinking of you, Steven. I don't want to see you get hurt again."

"I'm not going to get hurt."

"How can you be so sure of that?"

"Because."

"Come on, Steven. She has to be dealing with a roller coaster of emotions right now. She's vulnerable and fragile, and there you are a handsome, strong, compassionate guy. She has to be developing feelings for you, just like you are for her."

"So, would that be so wrong?"

Stacy leaned forward and looked at him with piercing eyes. "Steven . . . think about it. Can you really handle being in a relationship with someone that has been so brutally violated? You've waited thirty-five years to give yourself to the right woman. Do you really think she's the one?"

"Come on, Stacy, we're not talking about a proposal here. Amber's just someone I would like to get to know better."

"But I've never known you to pursue a relationship that you didn't think had potential."

"Who said I'm pursuing a relationship?" Steven got up from the swing and shoved his hands in his pockets. "You're jumping to conclusions." He stepped away and then turned around to make his point. "But even if I did pursue a relationship with her, Amber is a wonderful woman. You haven't even met her so you have no reason to be so negative."

"Steven, I'm not saying she isn't wonderful enough or good enough for you. I'm not judging her; it's her circumstances I'm worried about."

"Well, don't judge at all!" He walked to the far side of the yard where a fountain trickled into a fish pond hewn out of rock. He watched as the fish darted from beneath his shadow.

"Uncle Steven . . . why are you so sad?"

Steven looked down at Jaime standing alongside him.

"I'm not sad, Jaime, I'm just thinking."

"Are you thinking of something sad, because your face looks sad?"

The sweetness of his niece's voice was enough to soften his demeanor. "No, I was just thinking about a friend of mine. She's kind of sick right now, and I guess that makes me sad."

"What's her name?"

"Amber."

"Can we pray for her? That's what Mommy does when I'm sick, and Jesus always makes me feel better."

Steven felt a tug at his heart. *The faith of a child.* He crouched down and pulled at one of Jaime's pigtails. "You know what, Jaime, Amber would love to know you're praying for her."

"Can I meet her?" Jaime's eyes widened with excitement.

"Maybe once she feels better, okay?"

"Okay."

Jaime skipped to where Jarrod was playing in the sandbox. Steven walked back to where he'd left his sister sitting in the swing. "I'm sorry I snapped at you. I guess I would just appreciate you giving me a little credit. I haven't screwed up my life yet, and I don't plan on starting now."

"I'm sorry, too. I know you'll do the right thing, but you can't blame me for worrying. You only see the good in people, Steven. And you have the scars to prove it."

Steven leaned down and kissed her on the forehead. "I'll talk to you in a few days, okay?"

"Sure. I'll be praying for you . . . and Amber."

TWENTY-NINE

Amber diligently worked in her darkroom the remainder of the morning, Bo attentively guarding the door. The few times she had left the room to get a drink of water or go to the bathroom, Bo followed her down the hall, never letting her out of his sight. It was obvious he knew what his job was, and he was doing it quite well.

Numerous times throughout the day, Amber found herself picking up the business card Det. Hastings had left with her. She had never been a strong believer in the world of psychology. Even with her mother's death and the difficulty in her childhood, she had never felt the need to relive or rehash any of the circumstances of her past. But now . . . now she thought about the possibility of talking to another woman. The doctor couldn't possibly understand how she felt, but maybe she could help her deal with her fears and what her future might hold.

Amber picked up the card once again from where it lay on her work table. She tapped it against her desk, wondering if recounting her nightmare and discussing it with another person would actually be better than stuffing it down deep and pretending it never happened.

She turned off the light in the darkroom and nearly tripped over Bo when she opened the door. He followed her into her office where she picked up the phone. She stared at the number for quite some time before dialing.

"Dr. Stuart's office."

"Uhh . . . hello," Amber stuttered. "I'm not a patient . . . and

I'm not sure I want to be, but I was wondering if I could talk to Dr. Stuart?"

"Of course. Just one moment."

Amber had figured she would just leave her phone number, and the doctor would call her back. She wasn't prepared when she heard the soothing voice on the other end of the line.

"This is Pamela. How can I help you?"

Amber didn't know what to say.

"Hello?" The doctor tried again.

"Hi. I'm sorry. I'm not sure why I called." Amber was about to hang up when she heard the strained voice on the other end.

"Wait! Are you still there?"

Amber put the phone back to her ear. "Yes, I'm here, but I think this was a mistake. I don't want to take any more of your time." For the second time Amber was ready to hang up, but again, she heard the voice on the line and decided to listen.

"May I ask how you got my number?" the doctor asked.

"A Det. Hastings gave it to me. But as I said, I think this was a mistake."

"Maybe. But since you called, what's the harm in setting up an appointment?" The doctor's voice was calm, gentle.

"But I'm not sure you can help me."

"Then let's find out."

After giving the doctor her name and contact information, Amber hung up. She wasn't sure she had done the right thing or if she would even be able to follow through with the appointment. She got up from her desk and left her office, Bo right on her heels.

Amber took her afternoon dose of medications, just as she heard knocking at the front door. Two knocks and a ring. It was a comforting sound. When Steven stepped into the entry way, Bo charged him, almost bowling him over with his excitement.

Amber watched the two of them wrestle for a few moments. Steven looked great in a pair of casual cargo shorts and a navy polo shirt that fit him perfectly. Steven once again caught her staring. With a smile, he asked, "Ready for our walk?"

She had forgotten all about their walk. With her mind on her work and the distraction of the doctor's business card, she had completely forgotten about it. "Ah . . . yeah . . . sure. Just let me go change."

"It's pretty warm outside. You might want to put on some shorts." Steven continued to play with the oversized pup as she closed her door.

A few moments later, Amber emerged from her bedroom still wearing jeans, but now she had on an oversized hooded sweatshirt and a ball cap pulled low over her eyes. She dug around in her purse for her sunglasses and slid them over the bridge of her nose. She looked up at Steven. "Ready."

"Amber . . . you're going to bake in that. It's almost eighty degrees outside."

"I'll be fine." She stepped past him and grabbed for the doorknob.

"Amber . . ."

"I said I would be fine," she snapped as she pulled the door open.

"Amber . . ." Steven gently pushed the door closed. Reaching for her elbow, he turned her around to face him. "I know you think this will protect your identity, but you're going to draw more attention to yourself in that get-up. That is if you don't pass out from heat stroke first." Amber yanked her elbow away from Steven's hand. "Come on, Amber, I was joking. Sort of."

"Well, excuse me if I don't see the humor in my situation. Just forget it. I don't want to do this. What if someone sees me? What if they were at the park the day of the attack and they recognize me?"

"That's not going to happen. The police kept away the few spectators that were there. There's no way anyone would be able to—"

"Spectators?" Amber raised her voice.

Steven sighed. "Bad choice of words. I'm sorry."

She played with the strings dangling from her sweatshirt.

"Amber, I will be right beside you the whole time. You have

nothing to worry about. I won't leave you alone."

'I won't leave you alone.' The same words he had used when he found her. Her mind played like a filmstrip from a black and white movie. She stiffened.

"What is it? Amber . . . what's wrong?"

She looked up at him with her sunglass-covered eyes. "That's what you said to me the day you found me."

Slowly and gently, he removed the glasses that covered her water-filled eyes. "I meant it then . . . and I mean it now."

He brushed back a curl that had fallen across her forehead, his touch electrifying. For Amber, time stood still. She saw in Steven everything she needed: strength, assurance, protection. His gentle spirit and tenderness made her want to reach for him.

But she didn't.

It wouldn't be fair to him. He deserved better than . . . than her.

"Why don't you take off your sweatshirt?"

His words broke into her thoughts. "What for?"

"It's too hot outside."

After a moment, Amber finally complied. She removed her ball cap and pulled the sweatshirt over her head. She winced as she rotated her sore shoulder and carefully slipped her tender wrist through the sleeve. She pulled at the hem of her simple pink t-shirt and straightened her tussled hair. Putting her ball cap back on her head, she asked, "Is this better?"

He gave her a smile. "You look great."

Steven reached around her and pulled open the door. Bo jetted out in front of them and jumped into the back of Steven's truck. Amber stepped out into the sunshine, squinting at its brightness. She pushed her sunglasses back on her face as Steven followed her outside.

"Do you have your keys?"

She pulled them from her jeans and showed them to him before shoving them back in. They walked down the cobblestone path towards his truck, Amber scanning her surroundings. She instantly felt vulnerable being away from the safety of her home but tried to shake the feeling, determined to make this work.

The ride to the park was quiet and short. They could've walked—the park was that close—but Steven had chosen to drive, and for that she was grateful.

He pulled into the parking lot and turned off the engine. Bo jumped out and was standing in front of the truck, obviously wondering what was taking them so long. Amber sat staring through the windshield at the rolling green grass of the park. Nervously, she ran her hands up and down her thighs, trying to rid the chill in her body.

"Are you ready?"

She jumped. "No. I don't think I'll ever be ready, but I know I have to do this."

She heard the click of Steven's door closing. Slowly, she opened her own door and slid from the passenger seat. Before she could shut it, Steven was at her side. She pushed her door closed but didn't move. She couldn't.

Steven reached for her hand. She watched as his fingers intertwined with hers. "You can do this, Amber. I know it's going to be difficult, but you can do it."

Amber felt strength radiate from Steven's grasp. She inhaled a deep breath and took her first step toward the park.

They walked to the gazebo first, cutting across the grass instead of using the path. Bo ran and scampered all over the park, crisscrossing in front of them. Amber glanced towards the dense foliage that lined the jogging path. Her shoulders shuddered. Steven gave her hand a squeeze, drawing her attention back to him, his smile reassuring. Amber tried giving him a smile in return, but she was sure it probably looked more like a grimace.

They walked across one of the small bridges that spanned the stream, then climbed the steps of the gazebo and walked to the other side. Steven whistled for Bo, and the retriever responded immediately, bounding across the lawn until he was at Steven's side. Amber wrapped her arm around one of the posts and leaned her head against it with a sigh. Steven took a seat on the rail and rested her still clasped hand in his lap. She couldn't stop her fingers from trembling, but the stroking of Steven's thumb against the back of her hand reassured her she was safe.

"What are you thinking?" he whispered.

She glanced to her right. "That if anyone had been here that day, they would've seen me or heard me. I shouldn't have been in the park alone. It was stupid of me. I should've known better."

Steven sighed. "Amber, it wasn't your fault. You can't blame yourself."

She pulled her hand from his grasp, walked to the far corner of the gazebo and wrapped both arms around herself.

❧❧❧❧

Steven couldn't see Amber's eyes because of her glasses, but he didn't miss the tear running down her cheek. He got up from where he was sitting and stood beside her. He wanted to wrap his arms around her and hold her tight, but he didn't. He was there to make her feel safe. His other feelings would have to wait until she was stronger.

"So . . . is the gazebo where you take most of your pictures?" Steven tried to get her to talk.

"The gazebo, the bridges, sometimes the willow tree over there." She pointed to a large, weeping willow deeper in the park. "I sometimes use the stream, when the water is running better."

"Why don't we walk over to the willow?"

As they walked down the steps at the back of the gazebo, Steven felt Amber reach for his hand. He willingly laced his fingers with hers. She glanced his way, then steadied her gaze in front of her. He wished she wasn't wearing glasses. He would've liked to have been able to read the expression in her eyes.

Bo ran ahead of them, passing the tree and then circling back. They walked to the willow and leaned against its massive trunk. Amber was still tense, her body rigid. Her head jerked from right to left at any movement that caught her attention. Steven waited for her to work through it, but it was obvious she was getting more agitated.

"Talk about what you're thinking. Maybe that will make it

easier."

Amber huffed at him. "Nothing is going to make it easier."

"Maybe we should've brought your camera. Maybe if you were occupied doing something, you would have less time to think about other things."

"Maybe, but I doubt it. It's the smell. The eucalyptus. I remember the smell of eucalyptus. And the dirt. The smell of moist dirt. I remember my face being pushed into it. I remember digging my nails and my heels into it."

Steven watched as Amber closed her eyes, but quickly opened them again. She pulled her glasses off and turned her face towards the sun, then began shaking her head from side-to-side.

"We need to go. I can't do this." Amber quickly walked away, making a beeline for the truck. Steven caught up with her and reached for her arm. She shook off the gesture, so he let her go. "I'm sorry, Steven, I'm just not strong enough."

Steven stopped where he was. He was frustrated by her lack of determination. Amber had made it so far in life with such little help. She had to have more determination then she was displaying at the moment. He decided to change tactics.

"You're copping out. You're not even trying," he shouted after her.

She spun around. Her jawline tense with anger.

He watched as her shoulders rose and fell with her every breath. He held his ground as she approached. She looked like she was ready to spit nails. Inside, he was cheering her on. *Come on, Amber, fight. You can do this, you just need to fight.*

"How dare you?" Amber jabbed her finger at his chest. "I thought you were my friend. How dare you say such horrible things to me?" Another jab. "I *am* trying. I'm trying every day that I choose to get out of bed and continue on with life. I've been trying by doing everything that everyone tells me. I've done what the doctors have told me. I've done what the detectives have told me. They want to show me pictures, I look at pictures. They want me to see a counselor, I call a counselor. I've done what they've told me, and I've done what you've told me." Amber's finger jabbing was beginning to lose its fervor. Her voice began to break and her words were beginning to slur. She pushed at him. "I thought you were my friend." She pushed harder. "I thought you wanted to help me. I trusted you to help me and now . . . now . . ."

Steven could tell the rage she had pushed down inside her was finally coming out. She had reached her melting point. Steven stood there as she pushed and shoved and swung at him. He knew she needed to release the anger she was feeling. Hopefully, she would then be able to move forward.

After a moment, with her energy completely spent, Amber stopped her fighting and allowed her forehead to rest against his chest. Slowly, Steven encompassed her in an embrace.

"Though I walk through the valley of the shadow of death, I will fear no evil for You are with me." Steven began whispering the familiar Psalm in her ear. "Thy rod and Thy staff, they comfort me. You prepare a table for me in the presence of my enemies. You anoint my head with oil, my cup overflows." Steven felt Amber's aggression weaken. She was no longer fighting his embrace. "Goodness and mercy will follow me all the days of my life, and I will dwell in the house of the Lord forever."

By the time Steven finished, Amber was holding him as tightly as he was holding her. He rocked her back and forth, just like he had done with his niece on many occasions. Amber cried as he whispered words of assurance. She leaned against his chest, as he rested his chin atop her head. When her angry cries turned to shuddering heaves, Amber stepped away. She rubbed her fingers under her eyes before looking at Steven. "I'm sorry."

"Don't be sorry." He pushed a rogue curl back from her forehead. "Do you feel better?"

She sniffed. "A little, I guess."

"Good. Then it was worth it."

"But Steven, how am I going to work here tomorrow? How am I going to be able to concentrate on what I'm doing?"

"We're going to pray for strength, and you're going to have Bo and me here to help you."

She rolled her eyes, unconvinced.

"Bo and I are not going to let you out of our sights. We will be your eyes while you do your work. You won't have to worry that anyone else is around because we'll be here."

"How am I going to explain that to my customers?"

"You can say that I'm your assistant. You can load me down with all kinds of extra equipment and let me act as your gofer. They won't think anything of it."

"What about Bo?"

"You're a dog lover, and he likes to tag along." She rolled her eyes again, clearly unconvinced. "Amber, you're over analyzing this. They won't think anything of it."

THIRTY

Bo ran into the house ahead of them, still working off the energy he had created at the park. Amber was momentarily distracted by his excitement and realized once again the advantages of having a dog around. The thought of coming home to someone this excited to see her and love her unconditionally was beginning to sound quite appealing.

Amber headed to the couch and sunk into the oversized cushions. She perched her feet on the edge of the coffee table and allowed her head to sink back against the pillows. Steven admonished Bo to calm down, and with a snap of his fingers, Bo sat at Steven's side.

Steven took a seat on the coffee table next to Amber's feet. She stared at the ceiling for a few moments and then lowered her gaze to him. "I'm going to cancel the appointment. I can't do it." She looked away.

"What do you mean you can't do it?"

"I'll fall apart, just like I did today." She offered him a glance. "I'm sorry if I hurt you."

"Well, if we're going to apologize, then I owe you one, too."

"What do you mean?"

"I said those things on purpose. My goal was to make you mad."

Amber stared at him dumbfounded. "Why would you want to do that?"

"Because you're a fighter. I thought if I could get you to fight back, you would see how strong you really are."

Amber's chin dropped. She was speechless, but that only lasted a moment. "You said all those things to me on purpose? You *wanted* to make me mad?" She pushed herself up to a sitting position.

"Guilty."

His impish grin was not going to work on her this time.

"Guilty? That's all you have to say for yourself?" She jumped to her feet, almost bowling him over as she walked around him. "I can't believe you would do that. I could have hurt you or hurt myself for that matter."

"You were already hurting yourself." Steven got up and moved to where she was standing. "You were allowing yourself to give up."

"I was coping!"

"You weren't coping, you were hiding. Hiding inside yourself and in this house. The longer you hide from this, the harder it's going to be to move beyond it."

Amber felt affronted by Steven's tone. His raised voice and accusations made her question everything she had felt about him. Anger boiled inside her. Had she misjudged Steven? She realized she had come to depend on him for words of encouragement and dependability. Now he was being confrontational. She didn't like it. She didn't want someone to challenge her or push her beyond what she thought she could handle. He had no idea the fear she harbored, the terror she felt. He had no right to judge her. He had no concept of what she had endured.

"Get out!" She snapped at him.

"Why?" Steven stood his ground.

"Because I thought you were my friend, and obviously I was wrong."

"Why? Do you think I would be more of a friend if I let you sit day after day and watch you sink further into depression and fear? Do you think it would be better if I just stood by and watched as you canceled your appointments and ruined your career?" Steven crossed his arms defiantly against his broad chest, his unmoving stance angering her even more.

"I said get out!" She marched to the front door and yanked it open. Bo abruptly jumped to his feet clearly confused by the commotion. Amber stood by the door waiting for Steven to leave.

"No. I'm not leaving. Not until you admit you're not a quitter."

"I'm *not* a quitter. I just need more time."

"Time for what? To build on your fears? To convince yourself there is danger lurking around every corner? To persuade yourself you're to blame for somebody else's actions?"

"Time to decide what I'm going to do with my life," Amber argued.

"You need to live it. That's all there is to it. Your goals in life haven't changed. You've just experienced a bump in the road."

That was it. She had heard enough. She slammed the door and with venom running through her veins, she crossed the living room and stood toe-to-toe with Steven, mere inches from his face. When she spoke, her voice was laced with hatred.

"Your 'bump in the road' as you call it, almost cost me my life. I will forever have scars to remind me of that 'bump in the road.' " She nearly spit the words at him each time she used his chosen phrase. "That 'bump in the road' stole my most precious possession. I will never be able to present myself to my husband as pure. The one thing I held onto for twenty-seven years was taken from me."

Tears ran to the corners of her lips. She took a step back and wiped away the wetness, then continued. "You're right. I am afraid. I'm afraid because the men that did this to me are still out there. And until they are caught, no one can assure me this won't happen again. Every day I get up and try to convince myself it's going to get better. And every night when I go to bed I lay there paralyzed by fear that I'll never be safe again. When I wake up in the morning, my first reaction is to thank God I made it through another night, but my second thought is, it would've been easier if I had just died.

"Why did God leave me here to suffer? Tell me that, Steven. Then maybe I can try to understand why this happened to me. Tell me!" she shouted at him, and for the first time saw the tears that were in his eyes. "Tell me why God left me here to suffer."

"Me," Steven whispered. "God left you here for me."

His words were like a punch to the gut, expunging all the air from her lungs. Amber couldn't breathe. She couldn't comprehend what he was saying. She stood staring at him, tears pooling in her eyes.

Steven reached for her, but she quickly stepped back.

"No." Amber shook her head, taking another step back, then another, until she hit the wall. "No, that's not true."

"Yes, it is. I know it is. I knew it from the moment I saw you. I've known all along. But I didn't want to scare you or pressure you. I wanted to give you time. I still do. But please, Amber, don't give up on life. Or God. Or me."

THIRTY-ONE

Amber didn't know what to do. Steven's declaration had confused her and scared her at the same time. She softly pleaded with him to go. He finally agreed, but only when Amber promised she would call him. He left Bo with her. She knew it was his way of making sure he would be able to see her. At least one more time.

Amber sat in a fog the rest of the day. She was weary from the inside out. She thought her body had ached before, but now, the crush on her heart hurt even more.

She wrestled with her feelings for Steven. She couldn't lie. They were there, right below the surface. But she'd promised herself she would not act on those feelings. There was still so much Steven didn't know, things that would definitely have an impact on the way he felt. He was blinded by circumstance. His inner man was urging him to be a hero.

Her hero.

But it wasn't what she wanted or needed. She didn't want his affection out of pity or sympathy. She didn't want a relationship based on one person healing the other. She wanted passion and love. She wanted to fall in love and discover every nuance about it over time. She didn't want a love that found her at her worse and felt the need to spur her on. She didn't want that for her or for Steven. He was an amazing man, and he deserved a better future.

As angry as she had been with Steven earlier, she realized what he had said was true. He was being a friend by not allowing her to give up. He had antagonized her to prove she still had the instinct to fight.

The slightest grin creased her face. She realized she had a valuable friend in Steven, and she didn't want to give that up. She would have to make sure he understood their relationship was a friendship. Nothing more. One day the right woman would come along, and Steven would realize she was right. He would find someone special.

But it isn't me.

She glanced at the clock, then walked to her bedroom to get Steven's number from inside her Bible. She dialed and waited for him to answer.

"Hello. This is Steven. Please leave a message, and I'll get back to you as soon as I can."

She didn't want to leave a message so she hung up. She would just try again later. But the phone was barely back in the cradle before it started ringing.

"Amber, hi . . . sorry . . . I was outside, but left my phone on the counter." Steven was out of breath.

Now that he was on the phone, she wasn't sure what she was going to say.

"Are you all right?" Steven broke the silence.

"Yeah. I've done some thinking . . . and you're right."

Steven's hope soared. Was Amber really admitting God had brought them together? Was she telling him she had feelings for him? Like he did for her?

"I know it's late, Steven, but I wanted to call and let you know I've decided to keep my appointments for tomorrow if you're still willing to be my assistant?"

Steven's heart plummeted. Amber wasn't talking about them. She was talking about her work. It took him a moment to recover from his disappointment before he could answer. "I'll be there first thing in the morning."

Amber hung up the phone knowing she'd heard a change in

Steven's tone. She was sure he wanted to talk about *them*. Or the possibility of there being a *them*. But she wasn't ready for that. She wasn't sure if she'd ever be ready for that. At least not until she had some more answers.

She turned to see Bo stretched out on the rag rug at the foot of her bed. With his head resting on his front paws, he looked at her with soulful eyes. His eyebrows danced from side to side as if he was waiting for her to say something. She knelt beside him and stroked his head. He placed his chin in her lap and sighed. Amber smiled. "I don't know how long you'll be on loan to me, but I'm sure going to enjoy you while I can."

Amber checked all the doors in the house for the second time before closing the door to her bedroom. She pulled on her over-sized flannel pants and a comfy t-shirt, then got into bed. She patted her lush down comforter to get Bo's attention. His head bobbed up from the foot of the bed, his ears raised with interest. She patted the comforter, encouraging him to jump up on the bed. He was up and nuzzled next to her body without any more encouragement.

THIRTY-TWO

Amber lay awake in bed for over an hour the next morning. She thanked the Lord for the sleep she'd gotten, then headed to the bathroom for a quick shower. It wasn't until she stepped out into the steam and wiped at the foggy mirror that she noticed something different.

The face that stared back at her actually looked like her. It was as if the discoloration of her face had disappeared overnight. She turned her head from side to side and moved closer to the mirror. Besides the patch of hair that was missing from around her stitches, and the slightest tinge of blue here and there, she looked like her old self again.

"Thank you, Lord." Her audible praise surprised even her. For once, she was thanking God instead of asking Him why.

Her improved look improved her attitude as well. It buoyed her confidence and gave her new strength for the day.

Amber was in the kitchen when she heard Steven's familiar knock. She closed the waffle iron, then hurried to answer the door.

"Good morning." Both Amber and Bo met him at the door.

"I hope I'm not too early. I knew you had a nine o'clock appointment and thought I should get here before then. In case you wanted to talk."

"You're not too early. I was just making some breakfast." Amber avoided the obvious. She could tell Steven still wanted to talk about *them*, but she knew she couldn't do that right now. She quickly went back to the kitchen to check on her breakfast.

Steven got down on his knees and played with Bo for a few minutes before moving to the kitchen. Amber could sense his presence even though her back was to him. "I thought I would make *you* breakfast for a change."

"So, are you ready for your first appointment?" he asked.

"Yeah. I already set up the studio." She pulled the waffle from the checkered form and stacked it on the other waffles she had warming in the oven, then poured another helping of batter into the iron.

"You know, Amber, unless your appetite has doubled since yesterday, I would say you have plenty of waffles."

Amber looked at the stack of waffles in the oven. She'd been so nervous, she hadn't paid attention to what she'd been doing. "I thought maybe Bo would like a treat." She tried covering for her mistake.

"I guess one wouldn't do too much harm to his figure." Steven slipped on an oven mitt, pulled the plate of waffles from the oven, and took one from the top of the stack. While Amber doctored her own waffle, Steven tore one into small pieces for Bo and put them onto a paper plate.

Amber walked out to the patio and took a seat. Her head was bowed in prayer when she heard Steven pull out a chair and sit down. When she looked up, Steven was praying silently. She waited until he was done, wondering what his reaction would be. She couldn't help but laugh at his expression.

"Amber . . . your face."

She decided to have a little fun. "What?" she said coyly.

"Have you seen yourself?"

"Steven, don't kid."

"I'm not. You look better."

"Better than what?" She looked at him but couldn't keep a straight face.

"Okay, okay . . . you got me," Steven said.

She laughed. Steven sat back in his chair, shaking his head.

Amber could see redness begin to color his cheeks. He was actually blushing. It made her laugh all the more.

"I'm sorry. I know that wasn't fair of me, but I couldn't resist. If I hadn't known what you were talking about, the look on your face would have scared me to death. You would've thought you had seen a ghost."

"Not a ghost . . . a vision."

The corner of his eyes softened, bringing a silence to their conversation. Amber played with the condensation on her glass, forgetting her breakfast altogether. Steven's look was one of unanswered questions, but she had less than an hour before her photo shoot with Mrs. Binder. There was no way she could talk to Steven about *them*. At least not now.

They ate in a companionable silence before Amber picked up her plate and took it to the kitchen. She filled the sink with soapy water and began to clean up the mess she had created. When Steven was finished eating, he brushed up against her as he slid his plate beneath the suds. Her flesh tingled and her heart constricted. She quickly moved, putting some space between them. Steven obviously read her body language and stepped back to lean against the counter. But she could still feel his eyes watching her every move.

"So, do you think we have time to talk before your appointment gets here?"

"Sure," she answered quickly. "Follow me."

Amber led him to the closet in her studio and started pulling out various gadgets. "These are the things I'm going to need to take to the park."

"But I thought we were going to—"

"Should we take my car or your truck?" she asked abruptly, not wanting to acknowledge what he was trying to say.

Steven sighed. "Since Bo's going, I think we should take my truck. We can load your stuff in the cab, and he can ride in the bed."

"Okay. I'll lay out everything I need, and you can be loading while I meet with the Binders."

"Sure." Steven took an armful of things and walked towards

the front door.

Amber felt a twinge of guilt. She and Steven could talk later, but right now, she needed every ounce of energy to concentrate on what she had to do.

She took another look at herself in the mirror and played with her hair. If she could get it to lay just right, no one would even be able to tell she had stitches. She fussed with it for a few more minutes.

When the doorbell rang, she affixed a smile to her face and moved to answer it. Steven had come in and slipped into the kitchen for a glass of water. He smiled at her as she walked by.

"Hello, Mrs. Binder, Jimmy. How are we this morning?"

"Rushed," Mrs. Binder said with an annoyed tone.

They followed Amber into the house. When Mrs. Binder saw Steven standing in the doorway of the kitchen, she gave him a once over and offered him a look of disapproval.

"I didn't realize you were married," she said snidely.

"I'm not," Amber was quick to correct her. "Steven is just a friend."

"Well," her look of disapproval deepened. "That's none of my business."

She was clearly getting the wrong idea, so Amber tried to explain further. "Steven has been helping me since my accident."

"Well, you look perfectly fine to me. The way you made it sound, I thought it was something serious. If you didn't want to do this, you should've just said so. You didn't need to exaggerate the truth."

Amber saw Steven take a step closer, his finger raised in the air. He was ready to pounce. She quickly stepped in front of him, stopping him from interceding. "Why don't we go on into the studio and get started."

Amber arranged Jimmy on the carpeted table and pulled down a backdrop from the many that hung like curtains from the ceiling.

"No. I don't like that one. It makes Jimmy look washed out."

Amber chose another one, and again was corrected by Mrs.

Binder's sharp tone.

"Is there something special you had in mind?" Amber asked politely trying to cut to the chase.

"I guess I thought I would be dealing with someone more professional." Mrs. Binder pursed her lips. "Maybe this was a bad idea, and I should use someone else. It's just that you came so highly recommended by my friends."

Amber counted to five before answering. "Mrs. Binder, I have several more backdrops to choose from. I can show you all of them, and then you can choose."

After seeing several screens, the nasty woman made her selections. Amber began shooting pictures as the woman directed her child to smile, sit up, sit straight, look intelligent. The boy squirmed and fidgeted the whole time. Amber knew she would have to take numerous shots, just to ensure a few would turn out. She changed props and lighting throughout the sitting, but everything had to meet with Mrs. Binder's approval before she could take a single picture.

When Amber thought she had enough shots, she set her camera down. "Well, I think that's it."

"You're done?" Mrs. Binder's tone reeked of pessimism.

"Yes. I took several good shots. Why don't we step into my office so we can make an appointment for you to view them?"

"You mean I can't see them right now?"

"Well, no. I have to develop them first."

"I should've known better." With an exasperated tone, Mrs. Binder lit into Amber. "You're not even using quality equipment. The *professionals* allow you to see proofs before you even leave the studio. Are you telling me I will have to make yet another appointment to choose my pictures?"

"Yes. I explained that when you made your original appointment. I don't like to use a digital camera. It might seem a little old-fashioned to some, but I prefer to develop my pictures on quality paper and display them in quality glass frames. I feel the color is richer than what a computer monitor can display and the texture of superior paper lends to the overall look of the photos." Amber was still using a controlled tone, but she was getting firmer with each statement.

"I don't remember that at all," the woman said in a dismissing tone.

"Well, it's in my brochure. Let me show you." Amber needed to get a brochure from her office and nearly ran into Steven when she stepped into the hallway.

"Are you okay?" he whispered.

"I can handle it." She rushed to her office, picked up a brochure, and turned around to see Mrs. Binder had followed her and stood in the doorway to her office. She held onto Jimmy's hand as he whined and wriggled.

Amber kept her voice calm and polite. "See, right here, it says your pictures will be ready for viewing in a week, at which time the balance of your payment is due." Amber tried to hand the brochure to the woman, but Mrs. Binder stepped back in disgust.

"The balance? Do you really think I'm going to give you money for pictures I haven't even seen yet?"

"You agreed to pay a one hundred dollar deposit at the sitting."

"That's before I knew I wasn't going to be able to see the proofs."

Amber sighed. "Mrs. Binder, I know I explained all of this to you over the phone, and it's written right here in the brochure."

"I don't care about any brochure!" she snapped. "I will not pay you a dime until I see my pictures." Her shrilling voice rose an octave with every word.

"Is there a problem here?" Steven joined them outside her office door, his voice low and authoritative.

Mrs. Binder whirled around to face him. She darted her looks between him and Amber. "Oh, I see how it is. You lure people to your home and then use your boyfriend here to strong arm your customers into paying. Well, I am not going to be swindled by you or intimidated by some two-bit bully."

"That's it," Amber declared. "This session is over. Please

leave."

"How dare you use that tone with me!"

"You heard Amber. It's time for you to leave," Steven added.

"What about my pictures?"

"Correction. My pictures. You haven't paid a dime. Therefore, they are mine."

"Those are pictures of my son! They belong to me!"

Amber swept by the woman and Steven, on her way to her studio. Mrs. Binder followed, dragging her son behind.

Amber snapped open her camera and pulled the small yellow canister from inside it. She stretched out the amber film, pulling on it until it was completely exposed. She handed the spool of ruined film to Mrs. Binder. "There are your pictures. You are getting exactly what you paid for."

Mrs. Binder stood with her mouth gaping open while her son yanked on her arm.

"Mrs. Binder, you need to leave. If you choose not to, I will have no recourse but to call the police."

Mrs. Binder's smile was menacing, her chin jutting out in front of her. "You don't know what a big mistake you have made, young lady. Cindy has told all of our friends what a great job you did with her Sarah. I'm sure you would've received many more referrals if you had chosen to treat me with even an ounce of civility, but since you didn't, I will see to it that you don't get another referral from our club."

"I'd appreciate that," Amber answered back. "I would hate to deal with any more clients as difficult as you."

With one final huff, Mrs. Binder marched towards the front door, her son barely able to keep up. Steven walked to the door behind her, adding a few choice words of his own before slamming the door.

Amber walked to her studio, picked up the discarded film from the floor, and crushed it into a ball. She stood massaging her wrist when Steven reappeared.

"Are you all right?"

“Yeah.” She tossed the film into the trash. “She sure was a piece of work, wasn’t she?”

“I can’t believe you stayed so calm and in control. I was ready to physically throw her out within the first five minutes.”

“I’m just glad she’s gone, and I don’t need to worry about a rematch.” She supported her wrist as she glanced at her watch. “My couple should be here any minute.”

“You’re holding your wrist. Are you sure you’re okay?”

“I’ll be fine. But I’m probably going to feel like Jell-O by the time I’m finished.”

The ringing doorbell made Amber sigh. “Now for the real test.”

“I’ll get it,” Steven said. “You go ahead and get things ready.”

THIRTY-THREE

Amber heard a peel of laughter drifting from the entryway. When she turned the corner from her studio, she saw Jessica Reeves with her arms wrapped around Steven's neck.

Amber stood in shock.

"Oh my gosh, I can't believe it's you. What are you doing here, Stevie?" Jessica babbled and laughed all at the same time. "What an idiot I am. Where are my manners?" Amber watched as Jessica looped her arm through Steven's and turned to the man Amber assumed was her fiancé.

"Tony, this is Steven Levitt. Stevie, this is my fiancé, Tony Myers." Both men extended their hands to each other. "Stevie and I have known each other . . . for like . . . forever. Our dads belonged to the same club, and our moms were tennis partners for a while."

"I heard you were getting married," Steven said. "but I had no idea Amber was shooting your wedding."

As if on cue, Amber made her presence known. All eyes turned to her.

"Amber, I can't believe you're seeing Stevie. Our families have known each other for years." Jessica clung to Tony, as her eyes traveled from Amber to Steven.

"I think there's been a misunderstanding. Steven and I—"

Steven cut her off. "Amber and I weren't seeing each other last month. In fact, we've only known each other a few weeks." He stepped next to Amber and casually slipped his arm around her waist. Amber flashed him a look of bewilderment. His eyes conveyed the message—*Just play along.*

Amber excused herself to her office, completely flustered by Steven's actions. "Steven, could you come here for a moment?" she called out, then waited for him to join her. "What was that all about?" she whispered with exasperation. "I thought we were going to tell them you're my assistant."

"That's before I knew it was Jessica. There's no way she would believe I'm your assistant."

"Why not? Maybe you're working for me to make a little extra cash. That's not so unbelievable."

"Except that she knows I don't need the extra cash."

❧❧❧❧

Steven hung his head in resolve. He knew Amber would eventually find out about his financial status, but he had no idea it would be like this. "Amber, the club our dads belonged to was the Winterton Country Club." Steven waited a moment to see if the name would register with Amber. When her teal eyes turned the size of saucers, he knew she had made the connection.

"*The* Winterton Country Club," Amber repeated, staring at him in disbelief. "This family business you're the head of, it's not just some mom and pop operation, is it?"

Steven shook his head like a little boy being scolded. "I was going to tell you, Amber, but I didn't think it was that important. You sounded like you came from an affluent family yourself. I didn't think it mattered."

Amber looked stunned.

"I know this isn't what you had planned, but if you can just play along, we can get through the photo shoot without a lot of questions. How else can I explain being here, if it isn't that we are somehow involved?"

❧❧❧❧

Amber felt betrayed, lied to, trapped. Not only was she going to have to psych herself up for being at the park, now she needed to pretend she and Steven were an item. She closed her eyes and inhaled.

"I'm sorry, Amber. I don't know what else to say."

There was a slight tap on the door frame. "Hey, I hope I didn't do anything to upset you, Amber." Jessica leaned into the doorway. "It's just that Stevie and I have been friends forever."

Steven looked at Amber, his eyes asking her how she was going to let this play out.

"Don't be silly, Jessica, we were just talking about your photo shoot. I'm still a little weak from my accident, and Steven was thinking he would hang around and help me with my equipment."

Steven sighed.

Jessica looked at Amber. "I'm sorry, I completely forgot to ask about your accident. I was so surprised to see Stevie, I just kind of lost my head." Jessica gave her a once over. "How are you doing?"

"I'm fine, just working on getting my strength back."

"That's good." Jessica smiled at Amber but then turned her full attention to Steven.

Amber watched the way Jessica looked at Steven. Her gaze was slow and all encompassing. Amber felt a hint of irritation. She crossed her arms against her chest and waited for Jessica to make eye contact with her again. *My gosh, she's here with her fiancé for heaven sake, but she's staring at Steven like he's the last man on earth.* Amber glanced at Steven and realized he was looking at her, looking at Jessica. The grin on his face told Amber her body language had given her away.

"Well, I'm sure you have a busy schedule, Jessica," Amber said, "so why don't we all head to the park." She walked past Steven and Jessica, back to the living room. Tony was standing there, looking out to the patio.

"Nice dog," Tony said as he heard Amber enter the room. He looked bored and not the least bit interested in what Jessica was doing.

"Actually, he is Steven's dog." She crossed the living room and let Bo in. Bo immediately pushed himself up against Amber's leg, keeping his eye on Tony. His ears were up and his tail was stiff. When Tony bent to pet him, Bo let out a low growl. Tony quickly pulled his hand back.

"Bo, heel." Steven's firm voice boomed through the room. Bo responded immediately—sitting on his haunches—but never took his eyes off of Tony.

"Sorry about that. Bo's pretty protective of Amber." Steven called for Bo, and just like that, he pranced across the room, not a care in the world. Steven opened the front door, signaled for Bo to get in the truck, then waited for Amber in the entryway.

Tony crossed the room and joined Jessica at the front door while Amber went to grab her camera pouches from her studio. When she returned to the front entryway, Jessica and Tony were already gone.

"Got everything?" Steven asked.

She nodded as she stepped out onto the front stoop and waited for Steven to shut the door. She hesitated when he stepped off the porch.

He reached out his hand. "You'll get through this, Amber, you'll see."

Jessica and Tony waited on the sidewalk that bordered the park. Steven had circled to Amber's side of the truck and fiddled with the equipment piled in the backseat. Amber hadn't moved from the cab.

"Now that Jessica knows I'm not an assistant, do you really need all this equipment?" Steven asked, trying to get Amber's mind on something other than her surroundings.

Amber got out of the truck and looked at all the stuff Steven had loaded. "I don't need the tripod or the umbrellas."

Steven left them in the cab, grabbed the reflectors, then reached to help Amber with her camera bags.

"I've got it." She resisted, defiance in her tone.

Steven tried to ignore Amber's attitude, knowing she was doing what she had to in order to get through the shoot. But her defensive attitude was beginning to hurt.

The four of them walked toward the gazebo as Bo ran ahead.

Though Jessica was hanging all over Tony, that didn't stop her from throwing exaggerated glances Steven's way.

Ah, yes, Jessica the flirt. He remembered all too well.

Steven turned to Amber and watched as her eyes darted from one side of the park to the other. He slipped his arm around her shoulder and leaned in close to her ear. "You're doing great, Amber. You're doing just fine. No one's even here. We have the park to ourselves."

She nodded but kept looking from side to side.

Tony and Jessica climbed the steps of the gazebo and discussed how they envisioned their pictures. Well . . . Jessica discussed, Tony just shrugged his shoulders and agreed to whatever she said.

Amber fiddled with her camera, then directed Steven on how to use the reflectors to remove shadows from Jessica and Tony.

"Okay, you guys, ready to get started?" Amber tried to make her voice sound light and cheery, but Steven could hear a quiver of nervousness.

❧❧❧❧

Amber clicked away as she positioned the couple in carefree, whimsical, and romantic poses—each one executed perfectly. With Jessica's tan complexion, svelte body, and platinum locks, she could easily be a model. But it was the looks she kept casting in Steven's direction that really got Amber's attention. *What are you doing? You should be enamored by your fiancé, not trying to make face time with an old boyfriend.*

"Jessica, are you okay? You seem a little distracted?" Amber was shocked by her own behavior. Never had she purposely tried to make a client feel uncomfortable or put them on the spot. But she had to admit, watching the blond squirm was amusing and worth the break in professionalism.

"I'm not distracted. I was just thinking these pictures are going to look so blasé. I want my pictures to look different. Unique." Jessica's raised brow and cocked head told Amber she was on to her, but could dish it out as well as the next person.

"Are you kidding me?" Steven said. "You look great and your

pictures are going to be spectacular."

Amber was sure Steven had no ulterior motives by his flattering comments, but they did the trick. Jessica's attention immediately turned back to Steven.

"Well, okay, Stevie, if you think they look all right. I mean, you always did have an eye for the finer things."

Jessica's words were spoken so seductively, Amber turned to Tony, sure he would do or say something to reign in his fiancée's inappropriate behavior. But he just stood there like a block of wood. Obviously, Tony was used to it because it didn't seem to bother him in the least.

Amber continued with more pictures around the gazebo and the foot bridge she and Steven had crossed just the day before. She was about to suggest moving to the willow tree when Bo began to bark and darted towards the nearby shrubs. Amber froze, dropping her camera on the grass. She watched as Bo disappeared in the foliage, the branches of the shrubs shaking violently when a covey of doves burst from their roosting place. Bo began to howl.

Instinctively, Amber started to back away.

❧❧❧❧

Steven quickly moved to Amber's side, but when he reached for her, she gasped, snatching her hand away.

"Amber, it's me, Steven." He tried to whisper under his breath so Jessica and Tony wouldn't hear, but Amber kept backing away, her steps becoming more urgent. "Amber, everything is okay. Look at me. Everything is fine."

"What's wrong with her?" Jessica's words were more accusatory than sympathetic. "She looks like she's seen a ghost."

Steven looked from Jessica to Amber and knew he needed to do something fast before Amber had a complete meltdown. He wrapped his arms around her and tried to disguise his controlling embrace as an affectionate hug. He hung his head close to her ear and whispered, "Amber, you're fine. I'm right here. Bo went after some doves, that's all." Steven stroked her back and pressed his cheek to the top of her head. "Please . . . you need to pull yourself together before you lose it completely."

Amber stepped back and looked up at Steven. She was terrified, her eyes pleading for reassurance.

"You're fine, Amber. Everything is fine."

Just then, Bo came prancing back to Steven's side, a lizard clenched between his teeth. He hadn't caught a dove but had settled for a consolation prize. Bo had no intentions of killing the lizard—with its head and tail lashing about—he had merely captured it so he could present it as a trophy.

"See. He has a lizard," Steven whispered.

Amber stared at the dog with his prize in his mouth, then back to Steven.

"Drop it, Bo," Steven commanded. Bo immediately obeyed then whimpered as he watched his trophy skitter away.

"Are you okay, Amber?" Jessica asked, awkwardly.

Amber cleared her throat and pushed herself slightly from Steven's embrace. His hold became firmer, but her reassuring look told him she had it under control.

"I'm so sorry I scared you, Jessica. When Bo bolted like that, it reminded me of what happened to my own dog. He ran out into traffic one day and was hit by a car. I don't know what triggered that memory, but something about the way Bo took off reminded me of that horrible accident."

Jessica exhaled a physical sigh of relief. "Thank goodness. For a minute there, I thought you were some kind of whack-job. I mean, I'm sorry about your dog and all, but I thought you were going psycho on us."

Amber stepped forward to pick up the camera, but Steven beat her to it. He bent down and cradled it in his hand, pretending to examine the lens. When he stood, he leaned close to Amber. "Are you okay?" he whispered.

"Yes, but I need to get out of here."

❧❧❧❧

Amber plastered a smile on her face and turned to the couple. "Well, I've got plenty of great shots. In fact, you're going to have a hard time narrowing it down to just a few."

Amber could tell Jessica was ready to protest so she quickly went on the offense. "Jessica, have you ever thought about modeling?"

It was all the distraction she needed.

Amber was able to pull the self-absorbed woman into a conversation discussing the potential of a modeling career. Jessica completely forgot about Tony, Steven, and her very reason for being there.

Amber talked to Jessica all the way back to the parking lot. Ego was a very powerful tool.

Before they said their goodbyes, Amber told Jessica to call next week and arrange a time to view the proofs. She also gave Jessica the name of a modeling agency she had heard one of her clients mention. Amber knew nothing about the agency, but Jessica didn't need to know that. She tapped the name into her phone and told Amber she would contact her next week.

Bo jumped in the back of the truck as Steven loaded the camera equipment into the cab. Amber sat in the front seat, debating if she needed to put her spinning head between her knees. Steven got in and started the truck. He was ready to pull from the parking lot when he turned to Amber. But before he could say anything, she put up her hand.

"I don't want to hear it. I know what I did was wrong, but I had no choice. I decided to talk about something Jessica enjoyed even more than flirting with you. I figured she wouldn't pass up the chance to talk about herself and I was right. I sure hope Tony knows what he's getting himself into."

Steven laughed.

"What are you laughing at?" Amber snapped.

"You. You played her like a fiddle."

"Well, it was pretty easy considering Jessica is her own number one fan."

"Come on, she's not that bad."

Amber huffed. "Of course you *would* defend her after the way she fawned all over you." She cleared her throat, then mimicked Jessica's high-pitched tone. " 'Stevie, you always did have an eye for the finer things.' What was that all about?"

Steven laughed again. "Why Amber Porter, I do believe you're jealous."

"Jealous! Are you kidding me? I just can't believe her behavior. She was having her engagement pictures taken for heaven's sake. Is Tony blind? Like I said, I hope he knows what he's getting himself into."

Steven chuckled. "He's not blind, and he knows exactly what he's getting himself into. About twenty million dollars. I guess flirting is a small price to pay for that kind of dowry."

Amber jumped when Bo barked from the back of the truck—his doggy way of saying "What's the holdup?"

"Can we just go home now?" she asked.

As Steven pulled out from the parking lot, Amber glance one last time at the rolling hills and white gazebo. It no longer filled her with a sense of calm and peace. Instead, it morphed from the enchanting woods she had always loved to a nightmarish forest from a horror movie. She turned away. She would need to scout out a new location for outdoor pictures. She never wanted to return to the park again.

THIRTY-FOUR

Steven watched as Amber headed straight for her darkroom. Though she had plenty of time before her next appointment, Steven thought she should be spending it resting, not developing film she could take care of tomorrow.

He raised his hand to knock on the door when he heard soft crying coming from the other side. With a heavy heart, he rapped his knuckles gently against the door. "Amber, are you okay?" *How stupid. Of course she isn't okay.*

"I'll be out in a minute," she answered.

Steven could tell Amber was trying to mask the emotion in her voice, but he could still hear it. He sat on the couch and waited as a minute stretched into more than an hour. He prayed for Amber and the gamut of emotions she must be experiencing, but he also thought about how good it had felt holding Amber at the park.

Good but dangerous.

He had tried to brush his thoughts aside, but he couldn't. The feel of Amber's body pressed against his, the warmth of her breath seeping through his t-shirt—heating his chest—were intoxicating. He had stroked her back to calm her, but the slope of her spine and her gentle curves did not go unnoticed.

God, I feel like such a jerk. I would never intentionally take advantage of Amber. I wouldn't hurt her like that. But, denying the attraction I feel for her won't do any good either.

With his head down, Steven alternated between talking with God and rebuking himself.

He wasn't sure how long Amber had been watching him, but when he looked up she was leaning against the living room wall, arms crossed.

"If I hadn't seen your lips moving, I would've assumed you were asleep."

Steven panicked momentarily. Had he said anything out loud? Had Amber heard his prayer? He gave her a wry smile. If she had heard anything, he would wait for her to say something.

"I need to take some medicine," Amber said as she walked to the kitchen. "Do you want a soda?"

"Sure."

Steven heard the rattle of medication bottles and the refrigerator door open and close. Amber walked back into the living room and handed him a soda before easing herself into the side chair.

"So, do you think Jessica considers me a complete nutcase?"

Steven grinned. "No. I think you were able to recover pretty well."

"It's amazing how easy it is to lie when you're trying to save face."

"So all that stuff about a dog getting hit by a car was made up?"

"Yep."

He smiled. "Don't be so hard on yourself, Amber. You were in a tough spot."

She took a swig of her soda then cleared her throat. "So, did you and Jessica date?"

Her question came out of nowhere, and Steven couldn't help but hear the slight strain in her voice. He hid the smile that pushed at his lips. Apparently, his interactions with Jessica had bothered her. *Maybe she was jealous after all.*

"We dated for a little while," he said.

"Who broke it off?" Amber asked casually.

"I don't remember." Steven thought back to the time he'd been with Jessica. She had been very high energy, always wanting to be going somewhere or doing something, including flirting with other guys. He couldn't help but make the comparisons between her and Jenny. When he had shared his feelings with Jessica, they had both decided they would go their separate ways. "I guess it was mutual," Steven said. "We decided we wanted different things in life."

Amber nodded in understanding, then asked, "So, is your business local, or am I going to find out your company is part of a conglomerate that spans the nation and is in the *Fortune 500*?"

Steven laughed, surprised by Amber's jump in subjects. "No. You're not going to find Levitt and Son on any list of Who's Who. We haven't even branched out of the state."

"But you're also not some mom-and-pop business that works out of your house, are you?"

"No. I have an office downtown. Not that I ever use it."

"So, how many people work for you?" Amber was obviously trying to get a feel for the size of his company.

"That depends on what jobs we're doing."

Amber just stared at him.

Steven didn't know why he was being so vague. He was just afraid that if Amber found out about his wealth, it would put a strain on their relationship. He decided to change the subject altogether.

"Last night you said something about calling a counselor . . ." His comment remained open-ended, hoping Amber would pick it up.

She sighed before answering. "Yeah. I made an appointment, but I'm not sure if I'm going to keep it."

"What made you decide to call?" Steven was curious what had prompted her to change her mind.

"I don't know. I didn't think much about it when Det. Hastings gave me the card, but when I saw the doctor was a woman . . ."

Steven completely understood. Amber needed a woman to talk to. Without her mom, and with the obviously strained relationship between her and her sister, she really didn't have anyone to talk to—any female, that is. He certainly couldn't expect Amber to discuss every intimate detail with him.

"What's her name?"

"Pamela Stuart."

Steven made a mental note to do a little research on the doctor. Though he didn't want to discourage Amber from seeking professional help, he wanted to make sure Dr. Stuart wasn't some psycho-analyst that would belittle Amber's faith or discount the power of God.

"So . . . your company . . . would I call you to remodel my garage or build an entire parking garage?" Amber changed gears once again.

Steven loved her determination. "I could take you by the office and give you a detailed financial report if that would better answer your questions?"

"No, that's not necessary." She nonchalantly raised her chin, acting uninterested.

"Okay, how's this? Our yearly earnings are in the low seven figures."

❧❧☙☙

Amber's eyes widened. She got her answer. Boy, did she get her answer. Steven was way out of her league. He might be in her sister's league, but Amber had walked away from that lifestyle years ago.

She tried to suppress her disappointment, even as she scolded herself for thinking of Steven as more than just a friend.

"I need to get ready for my next appointment."

"Can I come?"

Amber sighed. "Steven, you don't want to go to Pizza Pete's with me. The place is overrun with screaming kids, loud music, and noisy arcade games."

"I know. It sounds great." He grinned and rubbed his hands together. "I haven't played skeeball for years. I'm curious to see if I've still got it."

"Got it?"

"Yeah. I was a pretty mean skeeballer when I was in high school. I would challenge anyone. If they could beat me, I'd give them twenty dollars."

"And if you could beat them?"

"They would owe me ten. I knew I would get more action that way."

"So, you were a hustler in high school?" Amber smirked.

"No, it was just a specialized business venture." He buffed his nails on the front of his shirt. "Up to the challenge?"

"What?"

"Skeeball . . . at Pizza Pete's. I bet I can beat you without even warming up."

"What's the bet?"

"The same," he said, as he got to his feet.

Amber laughed. "Isn't that a bit juvenile? Surely you can come up with a more substantial bet than that?" She feigned confidence.

He wrung his hands and paced, clearly thinking. "Okay, how's this, if you win, I have to wash your car and do your yard work for a month."

Amber pictured Steven shirtless, working in the yard. It would be a rather captivating victory.

"And if you win?" she asked.

"You have to have dinner with me . . . and my family."

Amber's smile faded. "That doesn't seem like a very fair bet." She got up and threw out her soda can.

"Why not?"

"Because. It's just not."

Amber moved down the hall to the bathroom, pretending to ready herself for her appointment, but it was just a ruse. She looked at herself in the mirror, wondering what Steven's family would see in her. From outward appearances she almost looked like her old self, but inside, she was still such a mess. Would they be able to see that? Would they be able to look into her eyes and see she was on the verge of falling apart? Would they see her as some kind of lower class citizen because of what happened to her? Or would their impression be merely pity? Amber didn't know, but she was sure she didn't want to find out.

She splashed water on her face and brushed her hair before emerging from the bathroom. Steven was waiting by the kitchen, obviously looking for an answer.

"So, do we have a bet?"

"I don't think so."

"Then I guess I win?" he said cavalierly.

"How can you win if we haven't even played?"

"Because you know I'll beat you, so I win." His tone was so narcissistic she laughed.

"I know no such thing and neither do you. I just don't like the stakes."

"So what is it you want if you win?"

"Oh, I'm fine with you doing my yard work and washing my car. But—"

Steven cut her off. "I guess you're not used to winning," he challenged. "A winner doesn't think about what he'll lose, only what he'll gain. If you're worried about losing, it must be because you're used to it."

Amber had heard enough. Her competitive nature wasn't going to stand for anymore. "That's it, Mr. Levitt, you're on! I can't wait to see you on your hands and knees. My sprinklers haven't worked since I moved in, and when I win, I will expect you to fix them."

"Deal!" Steven stuck out his hand so they could shake on it.

"Deal!" Amber took his hand and shook it firmly.

The handshake was over, yet Steven was still holding her hand. She waited for him to move, not wanting to let go herself. *What are you doing? Don't encourage him. It isn't fair.* She quickly pulled her hand away. "We'd better get going," she said, as she cleared her throat.

"Sure. We wouldn't want to keep Pizza Pete waiting."

THIRTY-FIVE

When Amber and Steven entered the arcade-style pizza place, they were met with complete chaos. It was just as Amber had expected. Loud music, children yelling, large animated figures singing from a mini-stage in the corner, and the frenzied sound of bells and buzzers.

Amber had to take a breath before going any further.

Steven, on the other hand, had the same gleam in his eyes as the children who were running from one machine to another. His smile filled his face and his head swiveled from left to right to left again, trying to take it all in.

Amber forgot about her own discomfort when she saw the little boy appear in Steven's features. She couldn't help but laugh out loud.

"What?"

"You're loving this, aren't you?"

"Are you kidding me? This is great!"

Steven was about to say something more when a frazzled woman approached Amber. "You must be the photographer. I'm Melinda Snow."

"It's nice to meet you, Mrs. Snow, I'm Amber Porter."

"We're in Party Room Three." She pointed over her shoulder as she tried talking over the yelling, screaming, and ridiculously loud music. "Most of the kids are running around until the pizza is ready. That's Ricky over there." She pointed out a little dark-haired boy in a striped t-shirt. "I would like you to get as many shots as you can of him and his friends playing. The pizza won't be ready for another fifteen minutes."

Amber nodded in agreement, knowing there was no used trying to talk over the noise.

She and Steven headed towards a brightly painted room aptly labeled "Games Galore." Steven carried Amber's extra camera over his shoulder while Amber pulled her primary camera from its bag. She approached Ricky and introduced herself. He, of course, wasn't the least bit interested. He just continued to play Mega Meteor.

Amber snapped a couple of quick pictures of Ricky and the friend he was sharing the machine with. She noticed they both had a button with the number three pinned to their shirts. As her eyes roamed around the room, she noticed that all the children had a button with a number on it. She figured this was so the kids knew which room to eat in. It would make her job a lot easier, knowing which kids were Ricky's friends.

Amber followed Ricky as he rushed from one machine to another. She took a great picture of him hanging out of a make believe jet and another in a mini race car. When he and his friends dashed to the bounce room, she positioned herself next to the netting, wanting to get some action shots. When the intercom announced pizza was being served in room three, Ricky and his friends hurried towards the room. Amber and Steven followed behind.

"How are you doing?" Steven yelled over the noise as Amber switched cameras with him.

She gave him the thumbs-up with a smile.

The kids ate pizza and drank soda, but that didn't stop them from shouting and laughing. The room pulsed with the kid's energy while Melinda—and a man Amber assumed was Mr. Snow—tried to keep order. Clicking away, she continued to take pictures of the kids as they ate, laughed, and vied for Ricky's attention.

Amber raised her voice slightly to get Melinda's attention. "Why don't you and your husband lean in next to Ricky so I can get a picture of just the three of you?"

Melinda moved to where Ricky was sitting at the head of the table. "It's only the two of us. Hank is just a friend of mine."

Amber cringed, embarrassed by her assumption. She wanted to apologize but would've had to yell over the noise and figured it was best just to let it go. She turned to Steven so she could switch cameras. "I can't believe I said that."

"Don't worry about it. It was an honest mistake," Steven encouraged.

Presents were next. There was a pile of them in the corner, and although Ricky was excited to open them, he didn't spend a lot of time on any one gift. He just kept eyeing the game room, obviously anxious to be playing again.

Though Amber's attention was mostly on Ricky, she couldn't help but notice the way Hank was manhandling Melinda. He held her close and stroked her arm, even kissed her neck. Definitely not appropriate behavior for a child's birthday party. When Hank caught her staring, he smiled. She quickly turned away, but could still feel his eyes on her.

When Ricky was done opening presents and everyone had sung happy birthday, the kids scattered once again to play. Amber watched as Melinda cut the cake and laid slices of it on superhero party plates.

"Here, let me help you," Amber offered.

"Sure." Melinda passed her plates of cake. "They might not be interested now, but they'll be back when their tokens run out."

Amber smiled, working up the courage to apologize. "Melinda, I'm sorry about what I said earlier. I didn't mean to put you on the spot like that."

"Hey, don't worry about it. It's only been Ricky and me for the last three years. He's used to it."

Amber chanced a glance at Hank. He was staring at her again. An unnerving stare. The kind that made her feel dirty. When he licked his lips and winked, she quickly looked away, having to control the urge to run. *Don't overreact! Not every man is out to get you. He's just acting like a lowlife jerk.*

ॐॐ

Steven couldn't see Hank's face, but from the angle he was standing at, it was clear Hank was looking at Amber, not Melinda. Steven's jaw tightened and his fists clenched. He walked over to Amber, purposely positioning himself between her and Hank.

"Why don't you get some more pictures of the kids playing?" he suggested.

Amber agreed and walked toward the playroom. When she nervously glanced back over her shoulder, Steven knew she was aware of Hank's unwanted attention.

Steven wanted to level the guy, or at the very least warn Melinda that she was dating a real scumbag, but Steven knew he needed to keep his cool and mind his own business. As long as Hank kept his distance from Amber, Steven wouldn't make a scene.

The kids were worn out by the time they returned to eat their cake. When Steven noticed Hank was gone, he sighed with relief. He listened as Melinda thanked Amber for her work and arranged a time when she could view the pictures. When Amber and Steven stepped from the party room, he veered them in the direction of the skeeball machine.

"We still have a bet to settle," he said, with a gleam in his eyes.

"Oh, come on, Steven. We've been here for hours. I just want to go home." She rubbed at her neck and looked wearily at the machine.

"So you're forfeiting?" he teased.

"No, I'm not forfeiting." Amber glanced at the machine and back at him again. "It's just that—"

"You're chicken!" He cut her off, then laughed. "You know you're going to lose so you're backing out."

"I am not chicken! It's just that my wrist is sore from taking all those pictures." She batted her eyes at him, but it wasn't working.

"You didn't seem to think that would be a problem when you took the bet." Steven smiled. He was not going to let her out of it that easy. "Okay, to make up for your . . . handicap, I'll use my left hand. That should level the playing field." Steven dared her to concede.

"Oh all right, but I think this is awfully childish."

"Of course it is. That's what makes it so fun."

Pulling tokens from his pocket, Steven began inserting them in the machine.

"When did you get those?" Amber asked, clearly astonished.

"I had one of the kids buy them for me. Told him he would earn an extra five dollars if he could slip them to me when you weren't looking."

"You've got to be kidding?"

"Hey, I never kid about Skeeball," he teased. When Steven pushed the plunger to release the balls, he moaned. "What cheapskates. There're only six balls. There should be nine."

"Oh, well, that does it." Amber threw up her hands in exaggerated disgust. "If the ball count is going to throw off your game, I think we need to forget about the bet right now."

"Oh, no. You're not getting off that easy. It won't throw off my game in the least. It will just give you less of a chance to score big."

"Whatever."

Steven stuck to his original statement, that he could beat Amber without practicing, but agreed she could have all the practice she needed. He stood back and watched as she got a feel for the game.

Holding the ball up to her nose, Amber would close one eye. Then, with her knees pressed together, she would bend slightly—making the fit of her jeans all that more attractive. With a slight bounce, she would take a step forward, lunge, then release the ball with a sway of her hips. It was mesmerizing to watch. Hypnotic. *Wow.*

"Steven?" Amber gave him a gentle shove. "Are you even listening to me?"

Steven felt his skin flame. He'd been so busy watching Amber's form, he hadn't heard what she'd said. "Ahh . . . sorry. I was . . . ahh, concentrating on your approach."

"Why? Am I doing something wrong?"

"Oh no, you look just fine." *More than fine.*

"Having second thoughts?"

"No second thoughts." He grinned. "But this is definitely going to be more challenging than I thought."

"Okay, but I want to practice one more round before we start."

Try as he might, Steven kept finding himself watching Amber, not the scoreboard. With her second practice round finished, and two impressive scores, she was ready to start.

"Worried?" she asked with a smile.

"Not at all. I was just planning the menu for dinner with my family."

Her smile quickly diminished but was soon replaced with defiance. "Okay, what are the rules? High score or best two out of three?"

"Your choice."

"Okay. Two out of three. You go first." She stepped aside.

"Oh no, ladies first." Steven feigned a slight bow.

"No, thank you. I would prefer to know what I have to do to win. I'm better under pressure."

"Okay with me," Steven said, as he approached the machine. He picked up the weighted ball with his left hand and tossed it lightly in the air, practicing his swing before approaching the ramp. When he bent to get into position, he immediately felt self-conscious. *What if Amber's watching me as intently as I was watching her?* The thought messed with his mind and his game. The first ball he released guttered.

Amber yipped with glee—clapping as she did. Steven gave her a disapproving look. "That's not very sportsmanlike."

"Who said I was a good sport?" Amber answered with a grin.

"Okay. Game on." With his eye on the prize, Steven released his second ball.

Bulls-eye.

"That's what I'm talking about. I just needed to find my groove."

They bantered after every ball, making Steven realize, win or lose, it would be worth it to see this playful side of Amber.

Steven's turn was over. His score, two-sixty. He stepped away from the ramp as he stretched his hands in front of him, cracking his knuckles. "Beat that."

Amber positioned herself behind the ramp and carefully performed her choreographed technique. Steven once again was captivated by her movements, her score being the furthest thing from his mind. When her turn was over, she had put up her best score yet. Two-twenty.

Lucky for him, it wasn't enough.

Steven nonchalantly approached the machine for the second turn. He readied his aim. Boom. Another bulls-eye. When he saw Amber roll her eyes, he did nothing to hold back his smile. She squirmed every time he released the ball and sighed each time she watched the scoreboard tally his points. Steven had one ball left and was already over two hundred. There was no doubt. He was going to win the bet.

Just as Steven was ready to release his last ball, Amber let out a pain-filled gasp. He sent the ball sailing without aiming, his attention on Amber as she stood holding her side.

The moment he reached for her, a grin creased her lips.

He jumped back in shock. "You tricked me!"

She looked at him, her eyelashes fluttering. "Whatever do you mean?"

"I thought you hurt yourself or something. You distracted me on purpose."

"How could I hurt myself by just standing here?" she said as she shooed him away from the ramp. "I believe your turn is over."

He stepped back from the machine, shaking his head. His score two-thirty. "Okay, missy, the gloves are off. No more mister nice guy."

"Like you were holding back," she challenged.

"We'll see, won't we?"

Amber stepped up to the machine and with precision, released each ball. When she rolled her last one, and the scoreboard flashed two-forty, she jumped and hollered with exuberance—no signs of a sore wrist, arm, or shoulder.

Steven hung his head, shaking it. "That was pure luck, and I'm here to tell you, your luck has just run out."

Amber nearly strutted in her enthusiasm. Steven had never seen her so animated and almost hated to see their little competition come to an end. He had never thrown a challenge in his life, but at the moment, he was considering it. He didn't want to do anything to diminish Amber's smile, but his prize was too valuable for him to want to give it up altogether.

He stepped in front of the machine and focused. He knew Amber would try to distract him if she could, but this time, he'd be ready for it. When he had rolled five bulls-eyes in succession, he glanced at Amber. She looked like a sulking child. Beautiful, but sulking just the same. He decided to up the ante. He turned to her with a smile. "Double or nothing," he said as he juggled the sixth ball in his hand.

"What?"

"If I get a perfect score, I win two prizes. If I miss, I lose the original bet."

"What's the second prize?"

"You'll have to wait and see."

The mischievousness in Steven's grin was captivating. Amber stood silent, taking in his handsome features while her heart beat in double-time.

"Well?" Steven asked.

Amber broke from her thoughts. *Well what? Oh yeah, double or nothing.* What could she say? There was no way she was going to win the original bet, her only chance was to accept Steven's newest challenge. "You're on."

Amber stared at Steven with defiance. She knew trying to distract him was futile. So, she stepped back, closed her eyes and held her breath. She heard the ball hit the ramp and waited for Steven's reaction. He was silent. No celebrating. *Did he actually miss?* She opened her eyes to find Steven standing directly in front of her. She looked up at him, his smile sealing her fate. He stepped aside so she could see the scoreboard. Six perfect balls.

Game over . . . or was it?

She rested her hands on her hips. She was not going to give up that easy. "I have a proposition for you," she said with steeled determination.

"Really?" He raised his brow as he lowered his voice to a husky whisper. "I really don't think this is the place for that."

"Steven!" She swatted his arm as her complexion flared.

"What? You're the one propositioning me in a public place."

"Come on, Steven, stay focused."

He laughed. "Fine, what's your proposition?"

"If I can make a bulls-eye—something I haven't been able to do yet—all bets are off. What do you say?"

Steven stroked his chin. "No yard work for me?" he asked.

"No yard work for you, and no awkward family dinner for me or whatever else it is you had up your sleeve."

"Why should I take the bet when I've already won?"

"Because I'm appealing to your sense of fairness. After all, you are a Skeeball professional."

"Fairness?" he laughed. "You mean like that little stunt you pulled to distract me? Is that the kind of fairness you're talking about?"

"Oh, come on, that's water under the bridge." Amber laughed, trying to remember the last time she'd had this much fun.

"Fine. I'll take your deal, but with one exception. We seal it with a kiss."

Steven looked as shocked as she felt. *Did he really just say that?*

It was a trick. She knew it was. He assumed she would never agree to such a stipulation and so he would win by default. Well, Amber would show him. Two could play at this game. Without warning, she pushed up to her tiptoes and pressed a quick kiss to his lips.

Steven's expression said it all. Complete and utter shock.

Why did you do that? She scolded herself while looking at her shaking hand, wishing she could take back the last three seconds. *You're such an idiot. You just don't know when to back down, do you? Are you so freakin' competitive you're willing to endanger Steven's health? Well, you can't do anything about it now. Just get this stupid game over with and get out of here.*

Amber couldn't bring herself to look at Steven, her mind spinning. She flung the ball without even caring. In her mind, she tried to recall the conversation she'd had with the doctor. He had spoken about physical relationships and precautions. But since she wasn't in a relationship, she hadn't listened to his warnings. Could that simple kiss have put Steven at risk?

The clicking of the scoreboard broke into her thoughts.

Amber swallowed hard and looked up. She'd lost.

In more ways than one.

She'd lost the game fair and square, but if she ended up losing Steven's friendship because of her carelessness, she would have no one to blame but herself.

Steven didn't gloat or pump his fists in victory. But when Amber looked at him, there was no mistaking the moony expression on his face or the flush of his cheeks. It was clear he no longer cared about the bet. It was the kiss he was fixated on.

Amber swung her camera over her shoulder, then picked up her purse from where it was propped against the machine. She pulled at the hem of her shirt and huffed. "Are you ready to go?"

"Sure," he said with a goofy smile.

As they walked towards the exit, Amber stopped. "I'm just going to use the restroom before we leave."

Amber numbly walked down the hall to the ladies' room. Leaning against the porcelain sink, she looked at herself in the mirror, needing a moment to recover from what had just happened.

She brushed her fingers across her lips, still feeling the tingling sensation from their kiss. What had she done? How could she be so irresponsible? Dr. Troup had advised her to reframe from intimate activity until her test results came back.

God, what have I done?

Her mind scrambled to recall the doctor's warnings. Was kissing considered physical? Or did he only mean sexual activity? She couldn't remember.

She closed her eyes and tried to calm herself. *It was quick. Our lips barely touched. Steven will be okay. But I can't let it happen again. I can't take that chance. Ever again!*

She ran her fingers through her hair and cleared her throat. She exited the bathroom and followed the hall towards the main room. When she turned the final corner, she ran directly into Hank, causing her to stumble backward. "I'm so sorry. I . . . I guess I wasn't paying attention to where I was going." Amber looked at Hank, but his stare was so intense, she glanced away.

"Don't be sorry, sweetheart, I'm not."

She tried to step around him, but the hall was too narrow.

"Excuse me," she said. But Hank didn't budge. Amber bumped into him for a second time, causing her camera to slide from her shoulder, knocking her purse from her hand. The contents scattered at her feet. Quickly, Amber bent to pick up the mess as Hank squatted down beside her.

"I didn't mean to make you all uptight," he said. "I was just hoping to get a chance to talk to you."

"Why? Did Melinda need more pictures?" Amber stood, holding her purse close to her chest.

"Are you kidding me? She's got enough pictures of that kid." Hank smiled, then moved a little closer. "I wanted to see if maybe we could go out sometime. Melinda and I aren't exclusive or anything, so I thought you and I could meet for drinks and see where it goes from there."

Amber fumbled with her camera strap, trying to avoid eye contact. "I don't think so."

"Why not? Are you and that other guy serious or something? I don't see a ring on your finger."

Amber began to shake. She took a step back, only to bump into the wall. She leaned against it for balance, her breathing coming in short bursts. She was going to hyperventilate if she didn't get control of herself.

"Hey, are you okay?" Hank reached for her arm.

She twisted her body, knocking his hand away. "Don't touch me!" she hollered. She knew her actions were drawing attention, but she didn't care. This time, she would be heard.

"What's your gripe? I was just—"

"Hey! What do you think you're doing?" Steven came out of nowhere and shoved Hank against the wall. He pushed his face against the plaster, wrenching his arm behind him.

"Let me go!" Hank swore as he tried to wrestle free from Steven's hold.

Steven turned to Amber while he kept Hank pinned to the wall. "Are you all right?"

She felt clammy and shaky but quickly nodded that she was okay. Hank jerked, trying to get away from Steven, but Steven held him tight. "I was just asking her out for a drink, and she got all freaked out on me. I didn't know you two were solid."

Amber realized Steven was going to hurt Hank if she didn't stop him. "I'm okay, Steven, let him go."

Steven let Hank go with a shove.

A small crowd had gathered, thinking there was going to be a fight. Just then, Melinda came around the corner. "What's going on here?" she asked, directing her question to Hank.

He ran his hand through his hair and straightened his shirt, then walked over to Melinda and draped his arm around her shoulders. "Nothing, baby. Amber had a little dizzy spell, and I just happened to be coming around the corner when she did."

Melinda studied his face and then looked at Amber. "Are you all right?" Her look held more than a question. Amber got the impression Melinda was very aware of Hank's behavior. Steven stood next to Amber and gently pulled her to his side.

He whispered, "Are you okay?"

"Yeah. Just get me out of here."

THIRTY-SIX

Steven helped Amber into his truck, then rushed around to the driver's side. Once he got in, he asked one question after another. "What happened in there? Did you really have a dizzy spell, or did he make a pass at you? If he—"

"Steven, I'm okay!" Amber hadn't meant to shout, she was just on edge. "He asked me to meet him for drinks. He didn't want to take 'no' for an answer."

"What did he do?" Steven asked as he pulled out of the parking lot.

"He didn't really do anything. I just got nervous and overreacted. I dropped my purse, and he was helping me pick things up. When I started shaking, he grabbed for me."

"He grabbed you?" Steven asked, splitting glances between her and the traffic.

"Let it go, Steven." Amber closed her eyes, willing the whole thing to go away.

They were silent the rest of the way home.

When Steven pulled to the curb in front of her house, she opened her eyes. She got out of the truck and slowly walked to the front door, Steven following behind. Amber walked into the house, passed a waiting Bo, and went directly to her room.

⁂

Steven sat on the couch, not knowing what to do. His day had gone from exhilarating to devastating in a matter of seconds. He thought about Amber's kiss and how amazing it was. Then quickly fast-forwarded to the petrified look on her face when he'd found her in the hallway with Hank.

Bo stood by, whimpering, clearly wondering why no one was showing him any attention. Steven squatted down, framing the canine's head between his hands. "Why can't life be more simple, Bo?" Steven ruffled the top of Bo's head before getting up. He walked to Amber's room, hating that he was once again talking to her through a closed door.

"Amber, you need to talk these things through. You can't just internalize them."

He was surprised when the door opened and she walked out. "I already told you. I overreacted." She walked past him with rolls of film in her hand, heading for her darkroom.

"What are you doing?"

"I have film to develop."

"Now?"

"Of course, now. Why not now?"

"I thought maybe we could talk."

"About what? How I can't even go out in public without humiliating myself?"

"Amber, you didn't do anything wrong."

"He made a pass at me, Steven. Believe it or not, it wasn't the first time a guy has hit on me, and I've never had trouble handling myself before."

"And you probably would've handled yourself just fine if I hadn't jumped in. That was my fault. I screwed up."

Amber sighed, sounding weary. "You didn't screw up, and I'm sorry I lashed out at you. You're just a convenient target right now."

"That's what friends are for."

Amber looked at him, then quickly looked away.

"What are you thinking?" He could tell she was hiding something.

"Steven . . . I . . . it was wrong of me to . . . I owe you an—"

His phone interrupted her.

"Hello? This evening? No, that's fine. What time did they say?

Okay, let's say . . . seven." Steven hung up his phone and slipped it back into his pocket. "That was my office. An appointment I had for tomorrow needs to be moved to tonight. I still have some prep work to do on the proposal." He waited for Amber to say something, but she didn't. "I should be done by eight o'clock. Do you think you can wait until then for dinner?"

"Steven, you don't need to work your schedule around me. I understand you have a life and a business to run."

"I would *like* to have dinner with you, that is unless you don't want me here?" He was pressing her for an answer. He didn't want to have dinner with her by default. He wanted her to want him to stay.

"It's not that I don't want you here, it's just that I can't expect you to—"

"Can't you just say it?" Steven asked firmly.

"Say what?"

"Do you want me here or not? It's an easy question, yes or no?"

"Of course I want you here, but—"

"Okay then," he smiled. "I'll be back around eight o'clock."

"Fine," she conceded.

"I can pick something up for dinner. What sounds good?"

"No. I'm sure with the way you've stocked my kitchen, there are plenty of groceries in there for another meal." She tossed a look at her kitchen.

"But I can—"

"Steven . . . please . . ."

"Okay." He walked to the door and reached for the handle, then turned back towards her. "You were saying something when my call interrupted you."

"It can wait until you get back."

"Okay. See you at eight."

Steven hated to leave. He felt like Amber wanted to talk about something important and—after the kiss they shared—he hoped it would be about them. But the conversation would have to wait until he got back. It was definitely one he didn't want to rush.

He made sure Amber locked the door behind him before he walked away. He could hear Bo whimpering through the closed door, obviously confused why he kept getting left behind. *Don't worry, boy, I think you and I are going to be around for a while.*

ಘಘಘಘ

Amber paced around the living room, nervous energy racing through her body. She had just told Steven she wanted him around, once again giving him the wrong impression. *What am I doing? I can't even think about starting something with him.* Even though Steven had admitted having feelings for her, he had no idea how uncertain her future was. His feelings were based on what he knew, but there was so much he still didn't know.

Rummaging through the freezer, Amber looked to see what she could make for dinner. When Bo whimpered, she let him outside so he could play for a little while. She watched—from inside the house—as he ran around looking for anything he could chase. After a few minutes, she let him in, made sure the door was securely locked, then headed for her darkroom where she could get lost in her work.

ಘಘಘಘ

Steven rushed home to shower and change his clothes, his thoughts never leaving Amber. He got to his office early so he could gather the information necessary for the meeting and have a chance to catch up with Wendy on the day to day business. Wendy had been his father's assistant before his death and a longtime family friend. She knew the inner workings of Levitt and Son like the back of her hand. So, when the shift of power had moved to Steven, Wendy's knowledge and help had been invaluable.

When Wendy poked her head inside his office, Steven glanced at his watch, surprised it was already after six. "Unless you need me for anything else, I'm going to call it a night."

"Thanks for everything, Wendy."

"You're welcome, Steven. It was good having you back in the office, even if it was only for a few hours." She turned to leave.

"Hey, Wendy, I know you've been putting in extra hours since I haven't been around, and I wanted you to know how much I appreciate it. Without yours and Scott's help, I wouldn't be able to keep this business running."

"I think that's a slight exaggeration." Wendy smiled. "But thanks anyway."

Wendy left so Steven returned to his work. Only a few minutes had passed when there was a tap at the door and Wendy slipped back into his office, a question on her face.

"What?"

"Aren't you going to tell me about her?" Wendy asked as she sat down across from him.

Steven was a little surprised. He had been vague when he told Wendy he would be spending time away from the office. He leaned back in his chair and laced his hands behind his head. "Okay, who told you? Mom or Scott?"

"Your mother . . . but only because she's worried about you." Wendy's expression revealed her concern.

"So what did she tell you?" Steven asked.

"Well," Wendy kneaded her hands in her lap, "she didn't tell me too much, just that you had been at the park when a young woman was hurt and you've been helping her out."

"And she's worried?" Steven pumped Wendy for more information. "Why?"

"She didn't say exactly, but I got the feeling she's worried that maybe . . . well, that she . . . . she thought . . ."

"She doesn't think Amber is good enough for me. Is that it?"

Wendy cringed. "Well, she didn't exactly put it like that."

"So, exactly how did she put it?" Steven was irritated his mother doubted his judgment.

"Oh, Steven, please don't put me between you and your mother. I've known you both too long to want a few misguided words to cause a riff between us, or you two, for that matter. Your mother is genuinely concerned for you. Doesn't that matter, even a little?"

Steven didn't want to argue with Wendy. He would take this up with his mother later.

"So, why don't you tell me about her?" Wendy encouraged. "You can let me know what you see in her that your mother might not understand."

Steven balanced his chin on the tips of his forefingers, his heart beating in double time. "Well, her name is Amber. She's in her late twenties, has brown hair, amazing teal-blue eyes, and a beautiful smile. She's an incredible photographer and is originally from New York."

"And?" Wendy asked with a smile.

"And what?"

"Come on, Steven, you've dated beautiful women before. What makes Amber different?"

Steven thought for a moment, but words eluded him and adjectives seemed empty. "I just feel this connection between us," he finally said, "but it's hard to put into words. Amber's strong, loves the Lord, and is very talented, but she doesn't have much of a support system. She was pretty independent before her accident, but shouldn't be alone right now. Amber needs someone to remind her she's stronger than she feels."

"And you're that someone?"

"I'd like to be. And just for the record, we're not dating. I'm just being a friend during a difficult time."

"So, her accident, was it serious?"

"Yes." Steven chose not to elaborate. "But she's getting better."

"Well, she sounds wonderful, Steven, and I'm sure once your mother gets the chance to meet her, she'll see what you see."

Steven thought of the bet he'd won, hoping Amber wouldn't back out. Once his mother and Stacy saw how wonderful she was, they would better understand his feelings for her.

Wendy stood. "Well, I won't keep you any longer. The Kingsley's should be here in about ten minutes. I'll see you later, and I can't wait to meet Amber."

ᘛᘛᘚᘚ

Amber glanced at the clock on her worktable, realizing Steven had already been gone a couple hours. When she got to a stopping point, she pulled off her gloves and decided to call it a day. She stepped from her darkroom and nearly stumbled over Bo.

"I'm sorry, Bo, I didn't see you there." He scampered to his feet and wagged his tail feverishly, not the least bit offended. He trotted beside her as she walked to the kitchen.

The darkness outside her kitchen window kindled Amber's fear. She couldn't see anything, but that didn't mean someone wasn't outside watching her. *I refuse to live in fear. I'm safe. The Morris brothers have no idea who I am or where I live.* She took a deep, cleansing breath, washed her hands, and pulled the defrosted chicken from its wrapper.

She would make Steven a special dinner as a buffer to what she had to say. She needed to tell him the truth before tomorrow. The whole truth. He needed to understand things were much more complicated than he knew.

THIRTY-SEVEN

The familiar knock brought a smile to Amber's face but anxiousness to her soul. Bo ran to the front door, barking, ready to defend and guard her. But when he heard Steven's voice through the mail slot he began to dance around.

Amber took one more look at herself in the hall mirror before opening the door. She had purposely dressed for the occasion. Not to entice Steven, but to show him she could overcome all that had happened to her. She wanted to exude confidence. She wanted him to see a strong, independent woman; not the fragile, scared-of-her-own-shadow basket case he'd felt responsible for these last two weeks. She had to convince him she was going to be okay without him.

Even if she had no such assurance for herself.

❧❧☙☙

"Wow!" Steven said, unable to move, his mouth hanging open. Amber looked stunning. The black halter-style dress she wore draped her petite body perfectly. Its sheer material hung near her ankles and seemed to float as she moved. She smiled timidly and took a step back.

"You look beautiful, Amber," Steven said, closing the door behind him.

He couldn't take his eyes off of her. Her tousled curls fell to her shoulders, framing her face. Her teal blue eyes were vibrant, replacing the fear he was accustom to seeing. She wore a hint of makeup, adding sparkle to her complexion. Amber looked transformed—like a new woman. Steven realized he was staring but didn't have words. "Wow!"

"Uh, I think you already said that." Amber smiled as she turned towards the kitchen. "Dinner is ready. I hope you're hungry."

"Hungry . . . yeah . . . sure."

Amber walked to the kitchen, but it took Steven a moment to catch up with her . . . and his senses. He glanced at the living room and saw the coffee table set for two.

Amber removed two sizzling plates from the oven, set them on the stovetop, then reached for two baked potatoes and quickly tossed them on the counter.

"Let me help," Steven offered.

"No. I've got this. Just go sit down." She shooed him from the kitchen, looking nervous.

He wandered to the living room and slid down between the couch and the coffee table, his long legs sticking out the other side.

Amber walked into the room holding the two plates with hot pads. Setting the plate on the trivet in front of him, she cautioned, "This is hot so be careful."

"Is this Chicken Cordon Bleu?" Steven asked with excitement.

"Yes," she said as she set the second plate down. "It's one of my few specialties."

"That's incredible. Chicken Cordon Bleu is one of my favorites." Amber smiled, then disappeared into the kitchen. When she returned, she carried two long-stemmed glasses of something bubbly. She set them down, then carefully lowered herself to Steven's right.

"I hope ginger ale is okay," she said.

"Are you kidding me, this looks amazing. But what's the special occasion?" he asked.

Amber fumbled with her linen napkin as she spoke. "I wanted to thank you for all you've done for me over these last few weeks. I know I haven't been the easiest person to deal with—and for that I'm sorry—but I did want you to know, I'm convinced I wouldn't have made it this far without your help."

Steven could hear the emotion in Amber's words, causing his own throat to tighten. He reached out for her hand and clasped it in his. It wasn't the first time he'd held her hand. But this time, it was different. Before, he had wanted to make her feel safe and protected. This time, he was hoping she could sense his other feelings as well. The ones that went beyond friendship.

"Can I pray for us?" Steven asked, putting the emphasis on *us*.

She nodded.

They ate in silence, Steven's thoughts pinging in so many directions it made his head spin. He wanted more than anything to tell Amber how he felt.

To lay it all on the line.

To finally talk about *them*.

But he didn't want to rush her. She had planned this dinner for a reason. She'd said it was her way of thanking him for all he'd done, but he couldn't help but think it was more than that. She had dressed up—like they were on a date. Was this her subtle way of letting him know she was ready for their relationship to take the next step?

Steven played mediator between his heart and his head as he devoured the succulent chicken and steaming baked potato. As long as there was food in his mouth he couldn't say something stupid.

But the silence was killing him, and his plate was empty.

"Everything tasted great," he finally said.

"I'm glad you liked it. After all the meals you've made for me, I thought it was only fair I fix you something nice—nicer than crushed lasagna noodles, that is."

❧❧☙☙

Amber drug her fork through her potato, feeling like she was going to be sick. This was a mistake. There was no way she could have this conversation with Steven. Not now. She had no definitive answers. But what was she going to do? The whole reason she'd dressed up tonight was to prove to him she was fine. She was healed. She was ready to move on. If she didn't tell him something, the whole night would look like a come on.

Frustrated, Amber stood and picked up her plate. Steven tried getting up but was having a hard time from where he was pinned between the couch and table.

"No," Amber said. "You just sit. You've been waiting on me hand and foot. I've got this." She took their plates into the kitchen and set them in the sink. When she heard the patio door open, she turned to see Bo bound out the door, Steven behind him. She took a deep breath, needing the time to regroup.

You told him it was a thank you dinner, and he believed you. Don't make a bigger deal out of this than it is. Just leave well enough alone and get through the rest of the night. In a few more days, you'll have your answers and can talk to him then.

She spooned strawberries into the puffed pastries she'd baked earlier and placed a scoop of ice cream on the side. Carefully, she carried the bowls to the patio, but when she opened the door, her steps faltered.

It was dark outside.

Deep shadows painted the backyard.

Night sounds taunted her.

Steven turned, smiling. But when his eyes locked with hers, his lips straightened and his forehead creased. He crossed the patio in two strides and took the bowls from her shaking hands. "Why don't we eat inside," he whispered.

He had read her mind, sensed her fear. Like he had done so many times before.

Steven called for Bo, and once the dog pranced inside, he locked the door behind them. Amber curled up on the couch, pulling her feet underneath her while Steven sat in the side chair.

"This tastes great," he said in-between bites.

"I'm glad you like it."

With her appetite gone, Amber sat staring at her dessert, trying to work up the courage to talk to Steven. But she didn't know how to start.

"That was great, Amber. Thanks."

She watched as Steven leaned forward to put his bowl on the

coffee table. She got up and reached for it.

"Here, I'll take it."

Walking into the kitchen, Amber wanted to scream. Everything was out of kilter between them. The silence was back, and she didn't know how to break it. She mentally beat herself up while puttering around the kitchen, rinsing dishes, and putting things away. Amber was stalling but didn't know what to do next. Whining out of frustration, she turned around to see Steven in the doorway, holding their glasses.

"I thought I'd help out."

He took a step closer, reached around her, and gently placed the glasses in the sink. Amber heard the clink of glass hitting porcelain and waited for Steven to take a step back, but he didn't move.

He just stood there.

Only inches separating them.

So close she could feel his breath on her forehead. She tried to say something, but Steven pressed his finger to her lips.

"Don't say anything."

"But Steven . . ."

Steven framed her face with his warm, sturdy hands and leaned in for a kiss. He was only a breath away when she whispered, "Steven, don't." She turned her head aside. "Please don't."

Steven was crushed. She could see it in his expression. And it was all her fault.

"Amber, I don't understand. I thought . . . I mean the kiss earlier at the arcade, the fancy dinner, that dress. I just thought . . . I'm sorry, Amber," he said, taking a step back. "I didn't mean to pressure you."

"No. Don't be. It's my fault. I handled this all wrong."

"What do you mean? Handled what?"

This is your chance. Just tell him.

"I care for you, Steven, really I do, but this is so much more complicated than 'you like me and I like you.' "

"But it doesn't have to be." He brought her hand up to his lips and pressed a kiss to her wrist.

Amber shuddered. She wanted nothing more than to have Steven in her life, but there was so much he didn't know.

"If it's the bet you're worried about, we don't have to have dinner with my family right away. I'll run you a tab," he tried to tease.

"It's not that, Steven."

"Then what?"

She looked at him. "This isn't fair to you. You deserve someone different . . . someone without complications."

"But, Amber . . ." He reached for her other hand, but she gently pulled away.

She walked to the far side of the living room and stared into the darkened backyard, shuttering when a chill raced up her spine. She stood there for what felt like an eternity, trying to organize her thoughts.

"Amber, talk to me," Steven pleaded, standing close behind her.

Brushing a tear from her cheek, she sighed, "I have nightmares," she said softly as if it was a secret she didn't want to reveal. "I can remember what it felt like, how they sounded, what they did. What if those nightmares and those feelings never go away?" She kept her back to Steven, too humiliated to face him.

He moved closer still, gently wrapping his arms around her. She tensed, but he didn't let go.

"We'll take things slow, Amber. I promise. We can do this. I know we can."

She wanted to believe him. More than anything, she wanted to stay in Steven's embrace and forget about everything that had happened in the last two weeks. But she couldn't forget about her attack or the choices she had made. They were the right choices. But now they would affect Steven.

"Amber, say something."

She turned to face him. "Steven, I—"

Bo whimpered and wormed his way between them. He was

feeling ignored and wanted some attention. Steven squatted down next to Bo, so Amber quickly moved to the couch, putting some space between them.

"You're supposed to protect her from other people, not me," Steven teased Bo. "If you're going to keep running interference and cut in on my moves, you might be relieved of your duties."

Amber appreciated the lighter mood Steven was trying to create and his willingness to give her some space. That's why her feelings for him continued to grow. He was always so patient and kind. Gentle and compassionate. She was lying to herself if she thought they could remain friends without something more developing.

Steven got up from where he'd been stroking Bo, and sat next to Amber on the couch. "You were saying something before we were so rudely interrupted."

Tell him!

After all, that was what tonight was all about. But she just couldn't bring herself to verbalize it. Having to say it out loud would make it too much of a reality. *I'll know more in a few days. I'll have this conversation with him then.*

"Tell me about your family." Amber decided to do a complete one-eighty.

"What?" Steven said, clearly surprised. "That's a little out of left field."

"Well, if I'm going to have to meet them, it would be nice to know what I'm up against."

Steven laughed. "They're my family, not a firing squad. Besides, you have nothing to worry about. They're going to love you."

Amber doubted she would ever have to find out, but for now, it was a safe conversation that took the focus off of her.

"So, tell me about your mother."

❧❧❧❧

Steven let his head fall back against the couch. He sighed as he searched to find the right words to describe the most important woman in his life. "She's incredible. Maybe a little over-protective, but other than that, she's a wonderful woman." Steven's tone grew reflective. "My dad was really an over-the-top kind of guy. 'Bigger is better.' 'Only the best will do.' Mom was the grounded one. She made sure Stacy and I appreciated the simpler things in life. We had chores to do and had to earn our allowance. If there was something we really wanted, we had to work extra for it. Nothing was ever simply handed to us.

"Of course, my father bought us stuff all the time. He was gone on business a lot and would always come back from a trip with toys for Stacy and me. My mom would never discourage my father's show of affection, but she would always make a point of having us pick out an older toy we no longer played with and donate it to a children's shelter. She tempered my father's extravagance."

"She sounds amazing, and your father sounds pretty great, too."

"He was." Steven paused, remembering better times. "He instilled confidence in us. He never allowed us to settle for second best. He had a way of challenging us to be the best we could be without being domineering.

"Once, when I was in junior high, I had a swim meet I was a shoo-in to win. But I lost. The competition completely blew me out of the water. Pun intended," he laughed. "But it was my own fault. I had gotten so prideful about my abilities I thought I could blow off practice and still win.

"But, instead of my father giving me the 'you get what you deserve' speech, he sat down next to me and gave me a firm hug. He asked me why I thought I'd lost. When I admitted it was my own fault, that I hadn't practiced, he smiled at me and said, 'Even if you didn't win, you learned something. That makes you a winner in my book.' "

"Wow. My father could've taken lessons from him," Amber mumbled.

Steven felt a pang of guilt. Amber had already told him about the struggles she'd had growing up, and here he was going on and on—bragging about his perfect parents.

"I'm sorry, Steven, I didn't mean to interrupt," Amber said. "So, tell me about your sister. Is it true twins share a keen sense of awareness?"

"You mean if you were to slug me, would Stacy feel it?"

Amber's eyes danced with mischief as she drew her fist back. "Can I?"

He laughed, reaching for her fist and bringing it to rest on his lap, gently stroking the back of her hand. "Not so much the physical, but the emotional."

"What do you mean?"

"When Stacy and Connor—that's her husband—were having difficulties early on in their marriage, I would find myself praying for her all the time and calling her at odd hours. Whenever I called, she would be in tears. There was just something inside me that knew she was struggling. We've always been there for each other that way."

"Does she feel it too, when you're struggling?"

"Yeah."

"Then she must be pretty upset you've chosen to spend time with me."

"Not upset . . . maybe a little concerned. She realizes you have a difficult road ahead of you."

Amber's shoulders stiffened as she sat up a little straighter and pulled her hand away from his. "I guess you've told her everything."

"Not really. I mean, she knows the circumstances surrounding your case because of Connor."

"I don't understand." Amber shifted on the couch. "Why would her husband know anything about my case? Is he a cop?"

"No." Steven took a deep breath, hoping Amber didn't overreact. "Connor is the District Attorney."

"Wait a minute, you're telling me your brother-in-law is the District Attorney?"

He nodded.

"Oh," Amber groaned as she sunk back against the couch cushions. "So he read about my case? He saw in black and white all the disgusting details?"

"No, not exactly."

"What do you mean, 'not exactly'?"

Steven sighed. "Stacy's a lawyer. When she found out I had been questioned as a possible suspect in your assault, she got a hold of the police report of your attack. Just in case I needed representation."

Amber paled.

"She was only doing it to protect me, in case the police tried to build a case. I'm sorry, Amber, she wasn't trying to invade your privacy. She just got ahead of herself."

Amber shook her head. "That's it. You can't expect me to meet them now. They know everything about me. Everything that was done to me. All of it in explicit detail."

"Not *them*, Amber, just Stacy. Connor didn't read the report."

"And you don't think your sister told your mother what a horrible person I am?"

"You're not a horrible person, Amber. A horrible thing happened to you. There's a difference."

❧❧☙☙

Amber sat forward, her head resting in the palms of her hands. His sister had probably seen in vivid detail the photos that had been taken of her. The photos that showed all she had endured. *Oh my gosh . . . she probably knows about the tests. That settled it.*

"The bet's off, Steven." Abruptly, Amber got to her feet and stepped around the coffee table. "I have no interest in being paraded around in front of your family as someone to be pitied."

"That's not the way it is, Amber, and you know it!" Steven followed after her as she headed for the front door, his raised voice causing Bo to jump to attention.

"I don't care how it is!" Amber snapped. "Your sister thought she was doing what she needed to protect you. Well, I'm doing what I need to protect myself." Amber unlocked the deadbolt on the door and swung it open.

Steven stared at her. "Is this your way of asking me to leave?"

"I think it's only best, Steven. You have a strong respect for your family—and I think that's great—but I don't share that same respect for them at the moment."

He stared at her in disbelief, obviously waiting for her to change her mind. But that wasn't going to happen. This was the perfect excuse she needed to end her relationship with him. No matter how gut-wrenching it felt to tell him goodbye, she had to do it. It was for his own good.

"Steven, this just isn't going to work. We were only fooling ourselves to think it could."

"Amber, you're not being—"

"Stop!" she raised her hand, cutting him off. "I appreciate everything you've done for me—and I know I could never thank you enough—but I think this is where we need to part company. I've got to figure out where I go from here, and it's something I have to do on my own." She turned toward the living room. "Come on, Bo!" She snapped her fingers. "It's time for you to go home, too."

THIRTY-EIGHT

Stacy had been up most the night, an uneasiness keeping her awake. She had called her mom to make sure she was okay and had repeatedly checked in on the kids. When she realized the disquieting feelings she'd been having had to do with Steven, she had reached for the phone to call him. Connor had encouraged her to wait until morning. "No sense waking him in the middle of the night if nothing is wrong," he had said. So, Stacy had spent the rest of the night watching her bedside clock tick off the hours until dawn.

She waited until the kids were off to school so she could talk without being interrupted. She speed-dialed Steven's cell number and his house phone, but both went straight to voicemail. She called his office, then Scott's cell number, and finally Wendy's extension. Neither Scott nor Wendy had heard from Steven yet today. Stacy made light conversation with them both, not wanting to cause them alarm. But, with every message she left over the next several hours, her worry slowly turned to anger. Finally, she gave Steven an ultimatum. If he didn't call her back—and soon—she would hunt him down, even if it meant embarrassing him at Amber Porter's house. She waited another twenty minutes, but that's all the patience she had.

If Mohammed won't go to the mountain . . . Stacy grabbed her car keys and headed for Steven's. She would start there.

❧❧❧❧

Heavy knocking on the front door caused Bo to bolt from where he'd been sitting alongside Steven's chair. He ran to the entryway—whimpering and whining—waiting for Steven to get up and answer the door. But Steven didn't move from his chair overlooking the balcony.

He already knew who it was.

Glancing at the front door, he confirmed it was his sister, from the silhouette in the beveled glass. It would be only a matter of seconds before she would use her own key to let herself in.

Sure enough, Steven heard the deadbolt turn and watched as Stacy stepped inside. She patted Bo's head, showing him some affection, but her eyes were focused solely on him. She descended the steps that led to the living room. Steven turned his attention back toward the sliding glass door without saying a word.

"You didn't answer your phone. Either one," she said quietly.

"Most people would take that as a hint."

"What happened?"

Steven turned steely eyes on her. "*You're* what happened."

"What?"

"Amber found out you read the police report. So, she broke it off with me and asked me to leave."

"Was there anything to break off?" Stacy asked in her analytical way.

"We were getting there," Steven said as he got to his feet and pulled at the sliding glass door. He stepped out onto the patio into the cool of the early afternoon air. He wore baggy sweats, no shirt, and nothing on his feet; but it wasn't the weather that made him cold.

He had been cold all night.

From within.

Stacy followed him out onto the patio. "I'm not sure I understand," she said, in a tone much more civil than the phone messages she'd left.

"Amber had fixed a nice dinner, said it was a thank you for the last few weeks. She was all dressed up, and I think she was finally going to admit her feelings for me went deeper than just gratitude. But Amber was concerned how much my family knew about her situation and if it was going to be a problem." Steven turned to his sister. "I couldn't lie to her. So I told Amber you had read the police report in case charges were filed against me."

"Now she's embarrassed," Stacy acknowledged.

"Wouldn't you be? She was already struggling with a sense of inferiority. Then, she finds out you know all the graphic details of her attack. It was too much for her to handle."

"I'm sorry, Steven. I had no idea you two would become so involved. I was only looking out for you."

He sighed, as he leaned over the wrought-iron railing that surrounded the patio, his gaze far off in the distance.

"What are you going to do?" Stacy asked softly.

"What can I do? I can't tell her that her feelings are unfounded."

"Just give her time, Steven. I'm sure she'll come around."

"And if she doesn't?"

"Then it wasn't meant to be."

Steven didn't acknowledge his sister's simplistic advice to his complex problem. Her logical personality only saw things in black or white, pros or cons, innocent or guilty. She would never understand all that Amber had gone through or the obstacles that were sure to complicate her future.

He listened as his sister saw her way out.

Steven sat, not really thinking, only feeling. Feeling a loss that no one could possibly understand. He barely understood it himself.

Lord, I don't know where to go from here. I was sure it was You who brought Amber and me together. I don't want to disrespect her wishes or minimize the way she's feeling, but I can't help but think this is wrong.

I was meant to be with her.

I know I was.

Help me to know what to do.

THIRTY-NINE

"Hi, Amber. It's Steven. I just wanted to make sure you're okay. Please call me if you need anything. Anything at all. I'm praying for you."

Here it was Monday, and Steven was still leaving messages—the same he'd left for the last three days.

It had been four days since she'd asked him to leave. Four long, exhausting days. And in that time, she hadn't gotten any sleep. Every noise outside, every creak or groan from her old house, sent panic racing through her. Were the Morris brothers at her door? A reporter? The police? Someone trying to break in?

Then, on Friday, her big day to prove to herself she was taking control of her life and didn't need anyone's help, she experienced one meltdown after another.

First, she had tried driving herself to her follow-up appointment with Dr. Troup. She only got as far as the corner stop sign before her hands froze on the steering wheel and her feet refused to move. She felt exposed. Vulnerable. Paranoid. It had taken her a good fifteen minutes to get her car turned around and back into her garage.

But that was only the tip of the iceberg.

When she had called Dr. Troup to cancel her appointment, he had arranged for a volunteer from a women's crisis center to pick her up instead. Marilyn—an older woman with caring maternal instincts—immediately put Amber at ease. But the minute Amber saw Dr. Troup she lost it again.

Even though he was kind and compassionate, it didn't matter. The sterile examination room felt like it was closing in on her. The paper vest and sheet that exposed more of her body than it covered, and the explicit questions Dr. Troup asked as he poked and prodded her, not to mention all the information he dispensed without hardly taking a breath was all too much.

By the time Marilyn drove her home, Amber had reached her limit. She headed straight for her bathroom and heaved until she was doubled over in pain. Of course, then she was near hysteria wondering if she was emotionally ill or if it was a sign of things to come.

For the last two days, whenever Amber felt like she was losing control, she would curl up on the couch, a pillow tucked tightly against her chest. She tried to stay calm, to breathe deep, and pray, but her mind spun like a kaleidoscope of fractured thoughts and conversations. Just when she would piece information together and convince herself everything was going to be okay, the tumbler would turn, scrambling her thoughts and causing her to panic all over again.

Over and over she heard Dr. Troup's warnings and precautions. His apologies for the labs incompetence. The explanation for the different courses of treatment he recommended. The list of facts and statistics he quoted, thinking it would better help her understand her situation, when in fact, all it did was confuse her even more.

Every time it got to be too much, she would close her eyes and recall her time with Pastor Craig. The prayers he prayed. The scriptures he read. The counsel he gave.

Even though she was deeply conflicted, and lashed out at God hourly for the anguish He was putting her through, she knew what she believed. And knew her decision to decline the morning-after pill had been the right thing to do.

She had always believed in the sanctity of life and knew children were a gift from God—no matter the circumstances surrounding their conception. Her convictions were being put to the test—a test she thought was incredibly unfair—but in the end, she knew what was right. Beliefs took on a whole new meaning when the choice was yours to make, and the crisis affected you, but it didn't change the facts. Life was life. And if she *was* pregnant, it was her child and she was his mother. It was up to her to protect him.

She had left the doctor's office still not knowing if she was pregnant or if she would be plagued with any of a multitude of communicable diseases, HIV included. They needed to wait for tests results, and she would need to give another blood sample on Monday to confirm conception.

Dr. Troup had tried to explain to her what HCG levels were and the nature of the test, but she couldn't grasp it. Not really. Instead, she had come home and spent hours on Google reading everything she could about a hormone called *human chorionic gonadotropin* or HCG. The test was straightforward enough. If she was pregnant, her HCG levels would multiply every forty-eight to seventy-two hours.

Monday was finally here. Dr. Troup assured her today's test would be conclusive, and it was the reason he had waited as long as he did. He had explained to her about false positives and other errors that could happen if tests were done prematurely. Because of the mishandling of her other tests, he had decided to err on the side of caution and time rather than inconclusiveness.

Today, she would have some answers.

It will either be over or just beginning.

The rap on the door made Amber jump, even though she was expecting it. When she looked through the peephole, she was surprised to see a twenty-something woman alongside Marilyn—the women's center volunteer.

"Good morning, Amber," Marilyn said, her voice carrying a calming lilt. "This is Patricia. She's going to be drawing your blood sample for Dr. Troup."

"I don't understand. I thought you were picking me up and taking me to the lab."

"That had been the plan, but Dr. Troup contacted me last night and asked me to arrange for a mobile technician to accompany me. He realized how hard Friday's appointment had been for you and didn't want you to have to navigate another emotional outing."

Amber stepped away from the door, letting both women in. She quickly locked it behind them, then turned to speak. "Are you sure? Will the test be just as accurate? I don't want to do anything—"

"Amber," Marilyn laid a reassuring hand on her shoulder, "the test will be just as accurate. I assure you, everything will be fine."

Amber just nodded, afraid to speak. She led them into the living room. "Is this okay?" she asked, pointing to the couch.

"Wherever you're comfortable," Patricia said with a smile.

Amber sat down on the couch and waited for Patricia to take a seat next to her. Patricia pulled out the few items she would need from her kit and made quick work of drawing Amber's blood. In a matter of seconds, she was pressing a cotton ball to the puncture site and wrapping a length of bandage around Amber's arm.

"All done," Patricia said, as she gathered her equipment and got to her feet.

"Patricia, would you mind waiting for me outside?" Marilyn asked. "I would like to talk to Amber for just a minute."

The technician smiled and made a quick exit.

Marilyn turned to Amber and reached for her hand. Giving it a gentle squeeze, she looked at her, concern etched into her face. "I don't mean to pry, but I've been working with women affected by violence for years, and I can tell you're not faring so well."

Amber just hung her head.

"You need to talk to someone who understands. I know a wonderful doctor who works with women who've been sexually abused." Marilyn pressed a business card into Amber's hand. "Call her. She can help."

Amber locked the door behind Marilyn, then looked at the card in her hand. *Dr. Pamela Stuart.*

What were the odds?

Amber walked back to the living room and curled up against the arm of the couch. She had closed her eyes for only a second before her phone began to ring. Amber let the answering machine pick it up and listened as Pastor Craig left a message.

"Hi, Amber. Sara and I just got back. We wanted to check in with you and see how you're doing. Unfortunately, Sara came down with a bug our last night on the ship and is sick as a dog. We won't be able to visit for a few days, but would like to hear from you and see if there is anything we can do for you. Call anytime. We're praying for you, Amber."

Amber waited for Craig to hang-up, then replayed the message. She couldn't help but feel sorry for him. His words were comforting and heartfelt, but she could also sense his awkwardness. He was a young man with a new bride. He didn't need to deal with her . . . situation. He'd been there when she needed him most. She couldn't ask for more.

Amber scrolled through her phone directory until she found the number for the church. It would be easier to leave a voicemail for Craig than to talk with him directly. She keyed in his extension and left a message, trying to sound upbeat.

"Hi, Pastor Craig. I'm sorry to hear Sara is under the weather. I hope you were able to enjoy the rest of your trip. I'm doing much better. In fact, I'm thinking of spending some time in New York with my family. I'll touch base with you later. Thank you for coming to the hospital when you did. You don't know how much that meant to me."

Amber hung up the phone, knowing she intentionally gave Craig the wrong impression. *It's not exactly a lie. New York is still a possibility.* She just didn't want to burden him with her troubles.

She didn't want to burden anyone.

Needing a distraction until Dr. Troup called, Amber decided she'd spent enough time slumped on the couch. She needed to stay active. Busy. Or the afternoon would drag on forever.

Since she was way ahead of schedule developing her film, Amber thought about calling a few clients to see if they wanted to move up their viewing appointments. But when a vision of Jessica Reeves popped into her head, she decided against it. Amber didn't have the energy to see anyone, least of all Jessica Reeves. She knew the woman would ask a hundred questions about her and Steven, but Amber didn't have the strength or the composure to answer them.

Instead, she turned her attention to her house.

Amber cleaned out her pantry cupboard, and with a damp cloth, she wiped down every baseboard throughout the house. She took apart every light fixture—cleaning not only the globes but the bulbs, as well.

Hearing the snap of the mail slot on her door, she jumped. Even though it was an everyday occurrence—and usually around the same time—the sound always startled her and rattled her nerves.

As she bent to scoop up the mail, she saw a pink envelope with familiar handwriting. Cara! She hurried to the couch, excited to hear from her friend.

Her excitement soon turned to disappointment.

Hi Amber,

You're never going to believe it. We're headed to Dubai! The person Eric was replacing in Texas has had some sort of family emergency and needs to come back to the states. Eric has been asked to take his position. Can you believe it? Our heads are still spinning. First, Texas, and now Dubai. I know you were planning on visiting as soon as we got settled, and I hope you still will. You will just have to postpone your trip a month or two and get your passport in order. Eric has already said he will pay the difference in your airfare, and we won't take no for an answer. The fine line details are still being ironed out, but we should be gone by the end of the month.

I know I've said in the past I refuse to be tied to the electronic trappings of this world, but now I don't see that I have a choice. Being in a different country is definitely a game changer. So, once we get to Dubai I will set up an email account and learn how to text, and Skype, and all those other impersonal ways of communicating. I will contact you by one of these crazy methods once we are settled.

Amber read the rest of Cara's letter before refolding it and stuffing it back into the pink envelope. She had wavered in telling Cara about what had happened. She had been waiting until Cara had a permanent address. Now, Amber decided not to tell her at all. With Cara so far away, it would serve no purpose. Her friend was starting a new life of excitement, adventure, and love. Amber refused to put a damper on it.

With a heavy heart, Amber walked to her office and plopped the stack of mail on her desk. Seeing Dr. Stuart's business card tucked into her blotter, she picked it up. The time of her appointment was scribbled in the top right-hand corner, an appointment she'd planned on canceling. Then she pulled from her pocket the card Marilyn had handed her. It had to be a God thing. There were thousands of doctors in the city. Yet, the only referrals she'd received was for the same doctor. *I have to do something. I can't become a prisoner in my own home.*

But she had already failed once when trying to leave the house alone. Quite frankly, she didn't think she'd be able to do it again.

It was four o'clock when Amber heard her phone ring. She was curled up asleep on the couch, a dust rag in her hand. She waited for the machine to pick up, then listened.

"Amber, this is Dr. Troup. I have your test re—"

Amber scrambled to reach the phone. "Dr. Troup, I'm here."

"I'm glad I caught you." His voice sounded warm and comforting. "Your tests were negative. Amber, you're not pregnant."

Instantly, she burst into uncontrollable sobbing. *Thank you, God. Thank you, God,* she repeated silently in her mind. She took a deep breath. The first emotional deep breath she'd taken in weeks.

"Amber, I have your other results as well."

Immediately the air was snatched from her lungs, realizing there was still more that could derail her future. "I'm listening," she said, squeezing her eyes shut, preparing for a fatal blow.

"Amber, I need to remind you that even a negative result now, could still result in a positive test in the future."

"But the tests were negative? All of them?" She held her breath, hoping he would simply say yes.

"Your tests are clear *at this time*. But remember, you must undergo HIV testing in three months and again in six months."

"Yes, I remember. But other than HIV, everything else was clear?"

"Yes, Amber. I'm happy to be able to tell you all your tests came back negative."

She couldn't speak. She couldn't breathe, all she could do was thank God.

FORTY

You can do this. Don't give up now.

The walk from her car to the professional office building was almost more than Amber could bear. She had parked in a large parking structure where the echoes from slamming car doors, the chirping of tires and alarms, and the faint chatter of random voices had her on sensory overload. She was sure she was going to be sick.

Amber had struggled last night, her emotions swinging like a giant pendulum. One minute she was praising God, relieved she wasn't pregnant, only for the pendulum to make a sweeping arc to her current reality—the possibility of being HIV positive.

The last two weeks had nearly destroyed her. How on earth would she survive the next six month with uncertainty hovering over her like a misty fog? It was an intangible force with the ability to consume her. To suffocate. To paralyze. She had to do something.

That was why today was so important.

She realized the only way she would get through the next six months was with help. Help and singular determination. So, she had decided . . .

She would go to the doctors.

She would do it on her own.

She would survive.

But, by the time she'd made it into Dr. Stuart's office complex, Amber was covered in perspiration, had her purse clutched to her chest, and was doing all she could to see past the pinpricks of light dancing before her eyes. Slowly, she crossed the lobby to the bank of elevators where she scanned the directory for Dr. Stuart's name. When the elevator doors opened, Amber stepped inside and pushed the button that would take her to the fourth floor. But, just as the doors were beginning to close, two men in business suits rushed to catch the elevator. As they stepped in, she quickly stepped out, saying she'd forgotten something in her car.

Amber waited for another elevator, several coming and going before she had the nerve to step inside one. When she finally committed to the next elevator, Amber quickly pushed the button that would close the doors, then pressed the number four. After a few deep breaths, the doors opened, and she walked towards the reception desk in front of her.

She had to clear her throat several times before she could even give the receptionist her name. Amber expected to take a seat in the front office area and wait to be seen, but the portly woman immediately got to her feet and reached for Amber's hand.

"Welcome, Amber. I'm Jeanette. I know this is your first visit with Dr. Stuart, and you're probably nervous. But let me assure you, you have nothing to be nervous about. Dr. Stuart is a wonderful woman with years of experience, but it's her compassion and gift of listening that puts her at the top of her field."

Though Jeanette sounded reassuring, Amber's cynicism jabbed at her. *She's paid to say that.*

Jeanette casually moved from behind her desk and immediately escorted Amber to Dr. Stuart's office. With a light tap, she knocked on the door as she pushed it open.

To say Amber was surprised would be an understatement. She had envisioned a stereotypical doctor's office, complete with large desk, floor-to-ceiling bookcases, and a couch where she would be expected to lie down and bare her soul. But that's not what she saw. Instead, two loveseats sat opposite each other, with a beautiful pine coffee table between them. Table lamps gave off a peaceful glow, and soft music played in the background. Amber felt like she was in someone's living room.

Dr. Stuart approached her with an outstretched hand. "Amber, I'm so glad you decided to come."

Dr. Stuart acted as if she was expecting an old friend instead of a psycho patient. She wore tailored pink slacks and a silk crème blouse, but her shoes had been kicked off alongside her desk. The blazer that obviously went with her slacks lay across the back of one of the loveseats.

"Thank you, Jeanette," Dr. Stuart said, as the receptionist stepped back, closing the door as she went.

"I've got hot water for tea, and coffee brewing. What would you like?" Dr. Stuart's tone was warm and welcoming.

"Tea would be fine."

"I have a whole selection there on the table. Go ahead and pick what you'd like while I get some hot water."

Dr. Stuart walked unhurriedly to an antique buffet filled with teapots and cups. She placed two cups on a tray, along with some scones, and carried it to the coffee table.

Amber sat on the edge of one of the loveseats as she looked through her choices of tea. Blackberry sounded as good as any. Dr. Stuart sat opposite her and poured Amber a steaming cup of water.

"Ooh, blackberry, my favorite," Dr. Stuart, said as she plucked her own tea bag from the basket and poured herself some hot water.

Amber sat dunking her tea bag over and over again, not knowing what to do next. Dr. Stuart placed a scone on a plate before relaxing back against the loveseat's cushion. Amber took a few sips of her tea waiting for the doctor to say something.

"Amber, I would like you to call me Pam, and I also want you to know first and foremost, I'm here as your friend." Dr. Stuart sipped at her tea, allowing her words to sink in.

Amber waited for Dr. Stuart to grab a clipboard or steno pad. She assumed the doctor would perch granny glasses on the end of her nose and tell Amber to lie down, but it never happened. Dr. Stuart just finished her scone, then gently placed her teacup on the table.

"Amber, I would like our time together to be a time when you can express whatever it is you're feeling. No doubt you have kept many of your feelings bottled up from your loved ones because they are too painful to talk about. I understand that. Just as you wouldn't share the most intimate moments of a physical relationship with family members or friends, neither would you want to share the difficult details that are probably plaguing both your waking and sleeping hours.

"When you talk to me, I want you to feel as if you're talking to an extension of yourself. Think of me as your mirror image. I'm not here to judge you or tell you your feelings are wrong. I am here to help you work through your emotions and see if we can find a way to help you overcome your fears. Some victims even feel guilty, like they are somehow to blame for what happened to them. But I am here to tell you that's simply not true."

Amber nodded but wasn't sure where she should start.

Dr. Stuart filled her teacup again, then asked. "Would it be easier for you if I asked you some questions?"

"Yes, I think so," Amber answered timidly as she put her teacup down. "I really don't know where to start or what to say. I know I need help. I thought talking to a woman would somehow make it easier. But, now I'm not so sure."

"Do you have any other women in your life, Amber?"

"No, not really. My mother died several years ago, and my sister and I don't have a close relationship. My best friend just got married and moved to Texas. I know if I was to call Cara, and tell her what happened, she would be on the next plane out. But, that's not fair to her. She's starting an exciting new chapter in her life. I don't want to be a burden to her. Especially since there's nothing she can do."

"What about other friends, Amber?"

Amber hung her head. "I really haven't taken the time to make other friends. Since moving to California, I've put all my energy into my work. Cara was my neighbor, and we just kind of clicked from day one. So, I guess I didn't see the need to reach out to others."

"Do you go to church, or are you involved with any other organizations or clubs?"

Amber nodded. "I go to church. But the congregation is rather large. I tried getting plugged into some of the women's events, but even those numbered in the hundreds. I'm just not a big group kind of person. I guess I should've looked around for a smaller church, but I really liked the pastor's style of preaching. I just haven't taken the time to get to know the people."

"So, you haven't spoken to anyone about your attack?"

"No. At least not a woman."

"So, there's a man in your life?"

Steven's image quickly filled Amber's thoughts. His captivating smile, his tender eyes, his warm embrace . . . and the quick way she dismissed him days ago. "Not really. I mean there was, but not now."

"Not since you were attacked?"

"No . . . I mean yes. I mean, I didn't know him before the attack. He wasn't a friend . . . not that he was an enemy . . . I just mean . . ."

Amber had to stop. Taking a deep breath, she closed her eyes and tried to organize her thoughts. "Steven found me in the park, after the attack. He's the one who called the police. Didn't Det. Hastings tell you any of this?" Amber snapped, feeling frustrated.

"Amber, Det. Hastings only told me you had suffered a sexual assault and that he'd given you my card."

"Oh. I thought he would've given you my file or something."

"No. I only know your name is Amber Porter, and that Det. Hastings was concerned for your well-being. Whatever I learn, I will learn from you. I'm not here to look at a report summary and give you a recommendation. I'm here to listen to you and hopefully be able to help you process this painful and confusing time."

Amber felt guilty for the way she had lashed out at Det. Hastings. She hadn't been very nice to him, and now she found out he was genuinely concerned.

"So, tell me about Steven," Dr. Stuart asked, gently getting them back on track.

Amber didn't know what to say. She didn't even know how to explain what she and Steven had. Or didn't have.

"Remember, Amber, think of me as an extension of yourself. Verbalize your feelings for Steven."

"I don't know how I feel about him, or maybe I do. But I don't think I should have those feelings."

"Why not?"

"Because he deserves so much more."

"More than what?"

"More than I can offer him."

"What can't you offer him that another woman could?" Dr. Stuart pressed gently.

Amber swallowed hard, her gaze dropping to her lap. "Purity." Tears trickled down her face.

Dr. Stuart reached for a tissue box from under the loveseat, set it on the table, then extended a tissue to Amber. Quietly, she asked, "Amber, are you a virgin?"

"I was." Her tears continued to flow.

Dr. Stuart got up from where she was sitting and sat down next to Amber. She wrapped her arm around her shoulders and held her close. "Amber, your virginity is something you have to give away. It's not something that can be taken from you. You didn't consent to intimacy, you were attacked. Violated. When the time comes for *you* to consent to intimacy that's when you will be consummating a relationship. That's when you will be giving yourself to a man."

Amber cried from deep within her soul, Dr. Stuart holding her the whole time.

"Amber, what you're feeling along with fear and pain is grief. You're grieving what you feel you've lost. You probably fantasized—as most women do—what your first intimate encounter would be like. A romantic evening. The man of your dreams. The perfect setting. Instead of love, and the feeling of someone completing you, you were violated and brutalized."

Amber sniffed, trying to regain her composure. "I just feel if I had been paying attention, I would have seen them coming. I could have reacted, run, or done something, but instead, I just stood there begging them to leave me alone."

"And do you think if you had reacted differently they would have left you alone?"

Amber thought back at how she had tried to run, tried to fight back. The Morris brothers were large men, much stronger than her, and they had even armed themselves with a bat. Their actions had been planned. She realized for the first time maybe she wasn't to blame.

"I guess there wasn't anything I could've done."

Dr. Stuart smiled. "So . . . tell me about Steven," she said as she moved back to the loveseat opposite Amber and refilled her teacup.

Amber hesitated, took a deep breath, then continued. "He was out jogging with his dog when he found me." Amber remembered how she had felt when Steven assured her with soft words. "He prayed with me and held my hand. He assured me he wouldn't leave me alone."

"Did he make you feel safe?"

"Yes. Even though I lay there beaten and exposed, I didn't want to be alone. I squeezed his hand to let him know I could hear him. I didn't want him to go."

"What did he do?"

"He stayed. Although it got him into serious trouble."

"How so?"

"The police didn't understand his interest in me, so they considered him a suspect. Steven was questioned and everything. But he wouldn't let that discourage him. He helped me get back on my feet, adjust to home life. He even helped me with my job."

Dr. Stuart was quiet, waiting for Amber to continue. She didn't push, she just waited.

Amber sat up straight. "I don't want to complicate his life. I found out Steven comes from an affluent family. I'm sure they don't appreciate his involvement with me."

"And how does Steven feel?" Dr. Stuart asked.

The beat of Amber's heart was so strong, she ached inside. Steven had admitted his feelings for her, feelings Amber wanted to return but knew she shouldn't. She felt inferior enough already although Steven had never made her feel that way. His family would never accept her. And she would never put Steven in the position where he would have to choose.

"Amber, do you think you're protecting Steven . . . or yourself?"

Though Amber could've taken Dr. Stuart's question as an accusation, she didn't. Instead of getting mad, she thought about what the doctor was asking.

Amber slumped back against the loveseat, wishing it would swallow her up. She realized her rejection of Steven was two-fold. Emotionally, she was protecting herself from being rejected by Steven's family—the same rejection she had felt from her father and sister. But in her heart of hearts, she knew it was Steven she wanted to protect above all else. He was a wonderful man who deserved the very best in life, not a woman who was wound so tight she could have a psychotic break at any moment. Or a woman with a potentially fatal virus.

Amber hoped—no, prayed over time she'd be able to get past the paranoia that currently played with her psyche. But what if she never did? There was no guarantee she would ever be able to process her emotions like a normal person again. And what about intimacy? Would she ever be able to have a physical relationship? Or express love of any kind? What if she never got past the fear? What if she only grew more neurotic? What if her test results came back positive?

Steven deserved so much more than she could offer. And if she really cared for him, she would do the right thing.

Keep him at a distance.

FORTY-ONE

Steven set his phone down on his desk. His mother had called to check on him. When he told her she had nothing to worry about since Amber had given him his walking papers last week, she was strangely quiet. He thought his mother would be thrilled to know Amber no longer wanted him around, but she didn't seem overjoyed by the news, just pensive. Steven decided he would never understand women.

It was break time when Scott walked into the trailer juggling a package of donuts, a breakfast burrito, and a supersized drink. He plopped down in the chair across from Steven, tossing him the package of gems.

"Why don't you just go over and see her, take her lunch or something," Scott suggested. "She might have asked you to leave, but that doesn't mean she would turn you away if you showed up on her doorstep."

Steven thought a moment while eating the package of donuts. *Maybe she would at least talk to me, and I could see for myself how she's doing.*

"You're right, Scott. I wouldn't even have to stay. I could just drop it off."

Steven felt encouraged.

Lunch would be the perfect excuse to see Amber.

❧❧❧❧

"Amber," Dr. Stuart's tone was soft and non-intrusive, "have you and Steven shared any intimate moments?"

Memories flashed in her head. Steven holding her hand, comforting her during her photo shoot at the park, helping her fight off nightmares. She also thought about their kiss in the arcade. *That wasn't a real kiss.* And the way Steven had tried to kiss her in the kitchen.

"Amber?"

She sighed. "Yes. But not how you mean. He's held me, comforted me as a friend. We shared a kiss. But only once."

"How did it make you feel?"

Amber pressed her eyes closed. *It doesn't matter how I feel. Or how Steven thinks he feels.* "Can we not talk about Steven?"

"We don't have to," Dr. Stuart said as she sipped her tea.

After several minutes of silence, Dr. Stuart asked, "Amber, were you conscious during your attack?"

She didn't want to talk about that either.

"Amber, remember, I'm here to help you, not to pry or make you feel uncomfortable. But, you need to process your feelings, not bottle them up inside. You need to talk through them. I want to help you, but you have to trust me."

Amber looked at Dr. Stuart. *You have to trust someone. You need help if you're going to get through this without going crazy.* "I trust you."

Dr. Stuart smiled. "I'm glad. I really do want to help you." She pushed herself forward to the edge of the loveseat, her hands clasped together. "Amber, women are very tactile creatures. The human touch is very important to us. A simple stroke of an arm, an embrace, the way a man presses his hand to the small of the back when he guides a woman through a room, those touches are very important to us. Without exchanging words, we feel a connection. We're invested emotionally. That's why it usually takes women longer to get over a break-up. We sometimes remember those touches, those feelings, long after a relationship has ended.

"That's why it's common for women who've suffered a physical attack to be afraid of intimacy. Afraid the physical touch of a man, even a man she loves, will trigger memories of their attack.

Amber, could that be why you're pushing Steven away?"

She nodded. *But it's so much more than that.*

"Have you talked about this with Steven?"

"Kind of. I mean, I tried to."

"And how did he respond?"

"He understood. He said we could take things slow."

"But you're still afraid?"

Tears ran down Amber's cheeks. "It's not just because I'm afraid of intimacy. I know Steven would never hurt me. But . . ." Amber felt like she was going to be sick just thinking about it.

"Amber, what is it?"

"I could be infected with HIV!" Amber shouted. "There, I said it! I won't know for another six months if I'm infected. And I refuse to expose Steven."

"But Amber," Dr. Stuart used a calming tone, "there's medicine for that. Are you sure your doctor doesn't have you on some form of exposure medication?"

"I refused it." Amber wrapped her arms around her stomach and began to rock. "I refused it because of the side effects." She watched as Dr. Stuart's demeanor changed.

"Amber, are you pregnant?" she asked softly.

"No. Thank God. But I didn't know that at the time." Amber felt like she was going to jump out of her skin. Her heart was racing. Her skin tingling. She stood—no longer able to sit calmly—and started to pace. Back and forth. Back and forth. Back and forth.

The room felt smaller the more Amber paced. She was winded, her breathing labored, and she was beginning to feel light-headed.

"Amber, I need you to calm down." Dr. Stuart walked to where she was leaning against the wall. "I'm afraid if you don't manage your breathing, you're going to pass out."

Amber didn't think she'd be able to sit still but didn't want to pass out either. With an arm wrapped around her waist, Dr. Stuart walked her back over to the loveseat and sat down beside her. "Breathe with me, Amber."

Amber followed Dr. Stuart's rhythmic breathing. It was several minutes before she gained control of her emotions.

"Can you explain to me how you're feeling but still remain calm?" Dr. Stuart asked.

Amber took a few more calming breaths as she tried to organize her thoughts.

"When I was in the hospital, my lab work was contaminated. So, as a precaution, Dr. Troup wanted to put me on some form of exposure medication. He talked about a three-pill regimen being the most effective, but then said something about fetal bone problems."

Amber looked at Dr. Stuart and could tell what she was thinking. "I refused the morning-after pill. I couldn't destroy a life. Not like that."

Dr. Stuart nodded in understanding.

"So, Dr. Troup recommended a two-pill regimen. But, when he was done explaining all the adverse side effects, he let me know there was a very strong chance we had already missed the window of opportunity and that the treatment wouldn't even work."

Amber swiped at the tears running down her neck. After taking a few deep breaths to compose herself, she continued.

"I was confused, angry, and a part of me didn't even care because I would never have my life back. Nothing the doctor could do or say would make the hurt or the memories go away. In the end, I refused all treatment. I told the doctor I would only take pain meds and antibiotics. But nothing that would put a baby at risk. I figured God had allowed this to happen to me. He could take care of the fallout."

"When did you find out you weren't pregnant?"

"Yesterday."

"And how do you feel about that?"

Amber started crying again. "Relieved. Extremely relieved. But if God knew I wasn't pregnant, why didn't He somehow encourage me to take the exposure medication? Why did He allow someone to screw up my tests? Now it's too late, and I feel like I'm living with a ticking time bomb. When I made the decision to decline treatment, I was thinking of me and a possible baby. There was no one else in the picture. But now there's Steven. I care for him. I really do. And I know he cares for me. But I can't . . . no, I won't ruin his life because of the choices I made."

"But you haven't discussed this with Steven?"

"No."

"Do you think that's fair?"

"I resent that. Nothing about any of this is fair."

"But Amber, from what you've said, Steven has given you so much these past few weeks. He's made you feel safe. Encouraged you to keep going. Provided you a shoulder to cry on. He's been a friend during a very low period in your life. But you rejected him without explaining why. He'll think it's his fault. That he did something wrong or he crossed some sort of line. Do you think that's fair?"

"But I know what he will do," Amber defended. "I know what he will say. He'll tell me it doesn't matter. But it matters to me. I would rather bruise his ego and hurt his feelings than destroy his future."

"Okay, Amber," Dr. Stuart leaned back against the loveseat's cushions. "I understand your feelings, really I do. But would you mind if we did an exercise?"

"An exercise?"

"Amber, I want you to pretend you've been given a clean bill of health. Would you still be hesitant to start a relationship with Steven?"

"But I can't pretend. It's all I think about."

"Please," Dr. Stuart's tone was soft, yet encouraging. "Just try."

Amber got up from where she was sitting and walked over to the floor-to-ceiling windows. She pressed her cheek against the cool glass and closed her eyes. Instantly Steven's handsome face appeared. The way he laughed at the arcade. His smile when he played fetch with Bo. The look in his eyes when he leaned in to kiss her. Amber twisted her hands and felt heat seep into her complexion. "It scares me." She paced some more. "I'm embarrassed." Her eyes stung, tears wetting her cheeks. "What if I can't have . . . what if I never want . . ."

"Sexual contact?" Dr. Stuart finished for her.

"Yes." Amber sat down, glad she hadn't had to say it herself.

"Do you think that's what Steven wants? A sexual relationship?"

"No!" Amber was horrified she had given Dr. Stuart that impression of Steven. "He's been nothing but a gentleman. We've shared a few moments that could've led to more, but he's never even suggested . . ."

"But you think it might lead there?"

"No. He would never do that." Amber wasn't making herself clear. "Steven and I are both . . . I mean, our convictions wouldn't allow . . . Not that it couldn't happen . . . I guess if . . ."

Dr. Stuart smiled compassionately. "I understand, Amber. What you're saying is you and Steven share conservative values."

"Yes." Amber let out a sigh of relief.

"Amber, I want you to close your eyes and think of Steven. I want you to be honest with yourself. Tell yourself how you feel."

Amber closed her eyes and saw Steven. She'd missed him terribly the last few days. She missed his words of encouragement, his humor, and the smell of his cologne. She missed his arms around her, the way he made her feel safe and protected, and how he assured her everything was going to be okay. Even the way they could be in the same room, not saying a word, but still feel connected.

She loved him.

Amber had known for some time that's what she'd felt for Steven, but had tried to deny it, even to herself. At a time when she thought she wouldn't even be able to survive, she had found love.

But at what cost to him?

Even if they were to make it past the very real obstacles in front of them, how would they ever explain how they met? How would Steven feel if his friends or business associates found out the woman he was seeing had been raped? Twice. When people found out, would they look at her differently? Look at *them* differently?

It was true, she wanted to protect herself from people's open scrutiny—Steven's family's scrutiny. But Amber wanted to protect Steven so much more. And no matter how much that hurt him, hurt her, that is what she had to do.

ॐ

Steven left the construction trailer only to realize he didn't have his truck. He'd loaned it to one of the crewmen so he could pick up some supplies. He scaled the steps of the trailer. "Scott, give me your keys. Brian has my truck."

Scott tossed him his keys with a smile. "Okay, but just remember, I'm stuck here if you two make up, so don't leave me hanging here all night."

Steven smiled at the thought as he headed out the door, energized by Scott's suggestion. Bringing Amber lunch would be his way of showing he cared. No pressure. He would give her as much space as she needed. Steven just wanted her to know he wasn't mad. He was still there.

If she needed him.

He went to his favorite deli and had two chicken croissant sandwiches made. He added two sodas, two bags of bar-b-que chips, and four double chocolate chunk cookies to his order before leaving. Glancing at his watch, he quickly headed to her house, knowing it was already past lunch.

When he pulled up in front of her house, Steven's heart quickened. His feelings for Amber were so strong, so consuming, it had been sheer self-control that had kept him away this long. Steven had told himself he wouldn't pressure her. *Liar*. There was no use trying to hide his feelings. Amber needed to know how much he cared. She wasn't someone he would forget over time.

Steven reached the door, gave it his signature knock, and waited. No answer. He repeated his knock a second time. Still nothing. Steven leaned down and pushed open the mail slot. "Amber, it's me, Steven." He waited for a reply as he looked at what he could see of the living room. There was no commotion, no sound. *Why wasn't she answering?*

Steven crossed the yard and circled around to the back of the house. Setting their lunch down, he hoisted himself over the fence and landed in the backyard. He peered through the garage window and saw that Amber's car was gone.

Steven sat on the back stoop, dejected. It was obvious Amber had gotten over the fear that had kept her close to home. She really didn't need him any longer. Amber was moving on with her life.

Steven felt expendable.

❧❧❧❧

Amber pulled into her garage, noticing the strange truck parked in front of her house. She quickly hit the button to close the garage door, but it didn't budge.

"Come on you piece of junk." Amber pressed the button repeatedly before it finally started to roll down—groaning as it did. When it was completely shut, she sighed. *Safe. I'm home safe.* It was a milestone. Amber was proud she had made her first solo outing but was also emotionally exhausted from her session with Dr. Stuart. Now, all she wanted to do was grab a bite to eat and lay down. Slinging her purse over her shoulder, Amber walked around the front of her car. When she saw a shadow fall across the window of the back garage door, she jumped.

Amber watched as someone twisted the doorknob from side to side. She backed away, not knowing what to do. Groping around in the dark, Amber grabbed an old tripod leaning against a utility cupboard. As the person began to shake the door, she raised the tripod over her head. *That doors too old. It's not going to hold.* When the door finally gave way, Amber watched as a booted foot crossed the threshold.

She lunged.

❧❧❧❧

Steven only had a split second to react.

He heard a cry in the shadows of the garage, and when he turned, he saw Amber coming towards him, something raised over her head. Instinctively, he protected himself with his forearm, the jolt from the impact causing him to stumble backward. When he saw Amber pulling back to swing again, he shouted, "Amber, stop! It's me!"

Steven wrestled to get the object she was wielding out of her hand. Amber swung her arms and shrieked like a feral animal. She was in a complete frenzy.

Steven grabbed her wrist. "Amber, stop! You need to stop!"

Finally, his shouting broke through her survival mode. When they locked eyes, she collapsed against him.

"Steven, I'm sorry. I'm so sorry."

He held her tight, rocking her in his arms as she sobbed. "No. It's my fault. I didn't mean to scare you. It's my fault." Steven cradled her head against him as she held onto him for dear life. They stood in the darkness of the garage, Steven furious with himself for making such a stupid mistake.

Finally, her breathing began to slow.

"You doing okay?" he asked.

She nodded, her head still buried against his chest.

Steven picked up Amber's keys from the garage floor without relinquishing his hold on her. Leading her into the house, Steven lowered her to the edge the couch and hunched down in front of her. "Amber, I am so sorry," he said as he massaged her knees, trying to soothe her frayed nerves. Amber sat with her chin pressed to her chest, her eyes closed.

"Amber, I don't know what to say. I didn't mean to frighten you like that." Steven whispered his umpteenth apology, feeling he would never be able to convey just how horrible he felt. "I came over to bring you lunch. When you didn't answer the door, I got nervous. I went around to the backyard to see if your car was in the garage. When I heard you pull in, I knocked on the door, but you must not have heard me. I tried the door and could see the lock wasn't catching, so I just gave it a shove. I didn't even think about how it would seem to you."

She nodded again.

"Say something, Amber. I feel just awful."

Amber looked at him with eyes that were red and glassy. "It's okay, Steven. I just need a minute."

"Let me get you some water." Steven went to the kitchen to get Amber some water. When he returned, he knelt down and offered her the glass. Amber reached for it with shaking hands, took a few sips, then handed it back to him. He set it on the coffee table, never taking his eyes off of her.

"Steven, what are you doing here?"

Obviously, she hadn't heard him earlier. "I was bringing you lunch."

"Why?"

Steven paused. He wanted to tell her he loved her, and no matter what the obstacles, they could make it work. But he was afraid now was not the time. "Amber, I just want to be with you."

"Steven, this isn't going to work."

"Why?"

ॐॐ

Amber's shoulders slumped. He was patiently waiting for an answer, an answer she wasn't sure she could give.

"Please, talk to me," he said softly but with persistence.

She took a breath and let it out slowly. This was going to be one of the hardest things she would ever have to do.

"Steven, I'm grateful for all you've done for me, really I am. And I know I wouldn't have made it this far without your help and encouragement, but . . ."

"But what?"

"What I feel for you is gratitude. I'm grateful. But that's all it is."

ॐॐ

Steven sat on the coffee table stunned. It took him a moment to respond. "But what about the other night? You made me dinner and looked . . . incredible. I thought . . . maybe . . ."

"Steven, I could never thank you enough for all you've done for me. But these last few days apart have helped me sort out my feelings."

"And?"

"I think it would be best if we didn't see each other anymore."

At first, Steven was stunned. Heartbroken. But his shock quickly turned to frustration. He got up and paced the living room, his hands on his hips. No way was he going to let her off that easy. "I don't believe you." He turned to her, defiance in his stance.

Amber looked at him confused. "I don't care if you believe me or not. It's true."

"I don't think so," he said, his jaw set and his shoulders squared. "I think you're afraid—afraid of admitting your true feelings." Steven stood in front of Amber, daring her to refute him.

"Well, you're wrong." She maneuvered around him as she got to her feet.

"I can't believe you're doing this." Steven's tone was no longer one of compassion or a need to understand. He was angry and had no intention of hiding it.

"Doing what? I'm admitting to you how I feel."

❧❧❧❧❧

Amber was beyond frustrated. She assumed Steven would be hurt, but never expected he would be combative, or that he would make this even harder than it already was.

"No, you're not." He stepped within inches of her and reached for her forearms. "Look at me and tell me you have no feelings for me."

Amber inhaled her resolve. Slowly, she allowed her eyes to meet his. She stared only at his black pupils and willed herself not to look anywhere else. "Steven, I can't say that I don't have feelings for you . . . that would be a lie. Of course I do. You helped me through the lowest period of my life. But that's it. Yes, I kissed you, and yes, I thought maybe there could be something more, but I was confused. Please don't make this more difficult than it is. I know I've hurt you and I'm sorry." Amber lowered her eyes, knowing her determination was weakening. Seeing the hurt in Steven's slumped shoulders hurt her more than her own broken heart.

❧❧❧❧❧❧

Steven didn't know what to believe. Her eyes had been piercing when she spoke, but he still couldn't shake what he thought had been a clear attraction between them.

It was a moment before he said anything before he conceded. He cupped Amber's face in his hands and gently tipped it up so he could see her eyes once more. "I won't push you, but I know how I feel. If you change your mind . . . I'll be waiting."

FORTY-TWO

Jeanette, Dr. Stuart's receptionist, once again welcomed Amber with a warm smile.

"It's so nice to see you again, Amber. Has it already been a week?" Jeanette got up from her desk and walked her to Dr. Stuart's office. She opened the door and motioned Amber in. "Doctor, can I get you anything before I leave?" she asked.

"No. We're fine, Jeanette. Thank you."

"Amber, come have a seat," Dr. Stuart encouraged, as she poured some tea and sat opposite her. When she extended a teacup to Amber, she politely declined, choosing instead to curl up against the arm of the loveseat and stare out the large floor-to-ceiling windows. Amber could feel Dr. Stuart watching her, knowing she was going to ask how she was feeling. The problem was, Amber really didn't know.

"You look tired, but I think it's more emotional than physical."

Amber nodded.

"What happened?"

Amber reflected over the last week. How she had sent Steven away and had cried herself to sleep almost every night since. Amber had lied to him. But it had been the only way. He would get over it. And after enough time, he would get over her.

Then, Det. Hastings had paid her a visit, letting her know there'd been another attack. The M.O. was the same as the Morris brothers, but this time, their victim had not survived. They were murderers. Now, more than ever, the police were scouring the city looking for the Morris brothers before they could strike again. Hastings had started calling her daily, just to keep her in the loop, assuring her they were doing everything they could. But it was his visit on Sunday—along with Det. Jones—that had finally taken its toll.

Twice she had reached for the phone, wanting to apologize to Steven, to beg him to come back, but she didn't. He hadn't called or tried to stop by. He must've finally realized he was better off without her.

Once again, she was on her own.

"Amber?" Dr. Stuart's words were quiet. "You were going to tell me about your week."

Amber flinched, realizing she hadn't said a word to the doctor. It had all been in her mind.

"Do you want to tell me what happened?"

"The police," she said, coldly. "They think they're trying to find me. "

"Who's they?"

"The men who attacked me. The police think they're trying to find me. To eliminate me. No witnesses."

Amber felt like she was talking in a tunnel. Her words seemed to echo in her head, repeating over and over again. *No witnesses . . . witnesses . . . witnesses . . . eliminate . . . eliminate . . .*

"Talk to me, Amber. How are you feeling?"

"I'm trying not to."

❧❧❧❧

Dr. Stuart recognized the signs. Amber was in a very dangerous place. She was on the edge. If she wasn't willing to fight, wasn't willing to address her feelings and move forward, she would self-destruct.

"Amber, let's talk through this."

She was silent.

Dr. Stuart moved to the loveseat where Amber was sitting and reached for her hand. It was cold. Frail. "You haven't said anything about Steven."

She sat trance-like.

"Amber, you need to talk to me." Dr. Stuart stroked her hand, trying to convey assurance and security.

Her tone was pensive. "Steven was at my house when I got home last week. I didn't know it was him. I fought him off, thinking he was an intruder. I could've hurt him. I asked him to leave me alone."

"Does he know about the events of this week?"

"No."

"Amber, he needs—"

"He needs to move on!" Amber snapped. "He honored my feelings and has stayed away. I'm not going to confuse him by calling him back to deal with my messes. I'm not going to involve him again."

Dr. Stuart saw the look of loss in Amber's eyes. She had lost Steven by pushing him away, and now was losing her willingness to fight. Her posture, her demeanor, her speech—even-keeled and unexpressive. She was giving up.

"Amber, you shouldn't be alone right now."

"I'm not. They have me under surveillance. I'm now a *project* of the police department."

Dr. Stuart could see that Amber was in the midst of an emotional breakdown, she just didn't know it. She was closing herself off.

"Amber, you have to remain strong. You can't give up."

"I'm too tired to fight."

"But you have to."

Amber bolted from her seat and paced like a caged animal. She wrapped her arms around herself—a stance of defensiveness. "I can't. It's too much. I can't sleep at night. I can't function during the day. My nightmares are worse than ever. I'm feeling paranoid."

"About what?"

"I have men—complete strangers—lurking around my house, telling me what I can and cannot do. I know they're there to protect me, but I feel intimidated. Cornered. I've tried to talk to them, thinking if I got to know them I would feel more relaxed, but then my imagination runs wild. I have nightmares about them attacking me in the middle of the night or holding me against my will. I can't do this anymore! I'm losing it. I can't fight it any longer." Amber's voiced was raised, tears running down her face.

Dr. Stuart was relieved to see Amber finally show some emotion. It was anger, but, at least, it was something. "Amber, you *are* fighting. Look at you. You're angry. That's a good sign. That's your subconscious telling you not to give up."

"But I can't do it anymore. I don't have the strength."

Amber collapsed into Dr. Stuart's arms. Her body as fragile as her mind. Dr. Stuart held her for some time. It was a breakthrough. Small but significant.

FORTY-THREE

Stacy walked to where Steven was leaning over some plans on his drafting table. The straggly beard he was growing did little to disguise the gauntness of his face. She knew he'd heard her walk in, but he kept his attention on his work. She leaned in to give him a kiss on the cheek.

"This is interesting," she said, scuffing at his beard.

She watched him as he worked, waiting for him to say something.

"What do you want, Stacy?" he finally asked, obviously bothered by the interruption.

"The kids miss you. You haven't been by in weeks."

"Sorry. I wouldn't be very good company right now."

"Steven, you've got to let this go."

"I have, Stacy. I wasn't given a choice. Amber dismissed me, remember?" Steven's words were biting.

"Why don't you come over tonight? We could have pizza. The kids would love to see you."

"Not tonight, Stacy."

"Then when?"

"I don't know when!" His words were loud and abrupt. He apologized immediately.

"Steven, this isn't fair. I know you've had a hard time of it, but it's not fair that you're taking it out on us. Mom is worried about you, Jarrod and Jaime don't understand why you're not around, and Connor and I are concerned."

"I'm sorry, Stacy. I have to work through this on my own. I don't need any hand-holding right now."

Stacy paced when she got home, caught between ethics and concern for Steven. Going to her home office, she took the report from her desk drawer. Stacy would pay Amber a visit. It wasn't the smartest thing to do, but it couldn't make matters any worse than they already were.

A short time later, Stacy pulled up in front of Amber's house, took a deep breath, and rehearsed what she wanted to say before heading to her door.

All of Stacy's composure disappeared when a man in jeans and a t-shirt answered the door.

"Can I help you?" The man's voice was low, controlled.

"I-I-I was looking for Amber Porter," Stacy sputtered.

"She's occupied at the moment. Can I give her a message?"

"No. No message." Stacy quickly retreated to her car. With little time to process what had just happened before she was expected at her next appointment, Stacy was sure of one thing. She was angry.

No. Beyond Angry.

After picking up the kids from school, taking them to the dentist, then spending way too much time at the grocery store, Stacy was finally home. But, it wasn't until she and Connor, were setting up dinner on the patio and watching the kids run around in the backyard, that Stacy had decided to confess what she had done, and what she'd found out.

"I did something today that I probably shouldn't have," she said to Connor.

Her husband looked at her with a raised eyebrow. "Really?"

"But before you butt in and reprimand me, let me tell you what I found out."

"Go ahead," Connor said. "I'm listening."

"I went to see Steven today, and he was a total wreck. So, I decided to pay Amber Porter a visit."

"You did what?"

Connor glared at her in complete shock. Exactly as she had expected.

"I know. I know. But Steven was so upset. I thought maybe if I could talk to her, I could help somehow."

"Help? How did you think talking with Amber Porter would help?"

"It doesn't matter, Connor. When I got there, some guy answered the door. He said she was "occupied." Can you believe that? Here Steven is ripping his heart out over her, and this Amber person is already shacking up with some other guy."

"Uncle Steven!" the kids yelled gleefully as they came in from the yard.

Stacy turned around, horrified to see Steven standing just a few feet behind her. "Steven! I can ex—"

He didn't give her a chance to explain, he just turned and ran towards the front door.

Stacy watched as her husband hurried after Steven, but he was already in his truck, screeching from the driveway. Connor ran back into the house, grabbed his phone and dialed. "Son of a—" Connor quickly edited himself. "Steven's not picking up. You know where he's headed, don't you?"

"Well, maybe if he sees for himself that Amber's not the person he thought she—"

"Stacy, he's a cop."

"What?"

"The guy at Amber Porter's house. He's a cop."

"I don't understand?"

"I've been keeping tabs on the Amber Porter case. I didn't tell you because I didn't want you to get involved. Things have escalated. The Morris brothers attacked another woman. But, unlike Amber, she didn't make it."

Stacy had a hard time comprehending what Connor was getting at.

"Since Amber can identify them, she's now under twenty-four-hour surveillance until the Morris brothers are caught. Her life is in danger, Stacy, and now Steven is going to step right back in the middle of it."

❧❧❧❧

Steven jumped from his truck and bounded up Amber's front steps. He pounded on the door, waiting only a second before pounding again. When a man answered the door, Steven lost control. He lunged at him, only to be spun around and thrown to the floor. With a knee jammed into his back, Steven looked to see another man with a gun pointed at him.

"Steven!" Amber cried out.

"Ms. Porter, you know this man?"

"Yes, now let him go."

The guy on top of him got to his feet.

It took Steven a minute to refill his lungs with the air that had been knocked from them. As he stood, he glimpsed the badge on the man's belt. "Amber, what's going on here?"

Before she could answer, a phone rang. The cop who had taken him down reached into his pocket and put his phone to his ear. "Yeah. I got it. Understood."

When the cop hung up, he looked at the other man. "That was the D.A.," he said, slipping the phone back into his pocket. "He was warning us that we might have a problem. Seems some guy is on his way over here, and he could be trouble." The man glared at Steven.

"Steven, what are you doing here?" Amber asked.

He stepped towards Amber horrified by what he saw. She looked awful. Gone was the sparkle in her eyes, and the glow of her skin. Her eyes were sunken, her skin pallid, her clothes disheveled.

"Amber, what's wrong? What are they doing here?" He threw a look over his shoulder.

"Steven, you need to go." She stepped away, but he reached for her.

"No. Not until you tell me what's going on."

"You heard the lady, now let's go." One of the cops took a hold of Steven's elbow, but he yanked his arm free. It only took a second for the cop to wrench Steven's arm behind his back and shove him up against the wall.

"Leave him alone!" Amber yelled at the men, then looked at Steven. "What are you doing here?" she asked again.

"I want to know what's going on."

Amber sighed in what sounded like utter exhaustion before turning towards the hall and heading to her bedroom.

Steven followed after her.

"You need to leave!" one of the men yelled. "Now!"

Amber spoke up but didn't turn around. "He's a friend, okay, so just leave him alone."

When she walked into her bedroom, Steven followed, closed the door quietly behind him, and waited for her to explain.

Instead, she curled up on her bed, lifeless, looking like a little girl, afraid and alone.

"Amber, what's happened?"

She was quiet.

Steven moved to the bed and lowered himself to her side. He stroked at the unmanaged curls that fell across her forehead.

"It happened again."

"What?" Steven was horrified, his eyes scrutinizing Amber.

"Another woman was attacked and died. Hastings thinks they might be after me."

When Steven realized it wasn't Amber that had been attacked, he took a deep breath and asked, "Why didn't you call me?"

"Because I'm not your responsibility."

❧❧❧❧

Amber lay with her eyes closed as Steven gently stroked her hand. His touch was soft and gentle, lulling her to sleep. Amber hadn't slept in days, and as much as she hated herself for it, she wanted Steven to stay—needed him to stay. It was wrong to involve him again, but she didn't fight it. Amber didn't have the strength. All she wanted to do was fall asleep and never wake up again.

FORTY-FOUR

Steven was awakened by a soft whimper.

Amber had been sleeping for hours. But, in an instant, she was crying and screaming, tossing her head about, while the rest of her body lay paralyzed.

Steven moved from the over-stuffed chair in the corner of Amber's room, to her bedside. "Amber, wake up. You're all right." He was trying to wake her when the two cops barged in from the other room. Steven raised his hand to stop them. "It's just a nightmare. I've got it handled."

They didn't move. It was obvious they still didn't trust him, even though Hastings had given him permission to stay.

"Look, I'm not going to do anything to hurt her, okay?" Steven turned his attention back to Amber. "Wake up, sweetheart." He sat on the edge of the bed. "Come on, you need to wake up." Gently, he placed his hand on her forearm.

Amber screamed, snatching her arm away, her eyes opening for the first time. She sat up straight, panting.

"It's okay. You were having a nightmare."

Amber locked eyes on Steven, then threw her arms around his neck, clinging to him as she cried. He held her close, rocking her, assuring her she was going to be okay. Steven made eye contact with the cops, and they quietly slipped from the room.

When Amber finally calmed down, Steven pulled away slightly, not wanting to take advantage of the situation. When he tried to stand, Amber grasped his hand. "Please don't go."

It was all he needed to hear. "Move over," he whispered.

Amber moved slightly, giving Steven enough room to stretch out beside her. He leaned against the headboard and pulled Amber to his chest. Wrapping his arms around her, he held her close and prayed. Soon, Amber's breathing slowed, and he felt her limbs relax. She had fallen back to sleep. Steven continued to hold her close but felt guilty. This is where he wanted to be.

But not like this.

⁂

Amber was dreaming, and for once it wasn't a nightmare. She was with Steven. He was holding her close, watching an old movie, eating popcorn. No bad guys hunting her down. No police invading her home. Just the two of them. It felt so normal. So real.

When Amber opened her eyes, dawn was just beginning to break, and she realized it hadn't completely been a dream. Steven *was* holding her. And because he was there, she'd been able to get the sleep that had eluded her for days. She closed her eyes, wanting nothing more than to disappear into her dream.

When Amber stirred, an hour later, she realized it was time for her dream to come to an end. Slowly, she moved from Steven's embrace and pushed herself to a sitting position.

"Good morning," Steven said, as he smiled and stretched his arms overhead.

"Morning."

The sun washed the room with light and the harsh reality of the previous night's sleeping arrangements. "Sorry, I guess I kind of crashed last night."

"Don't apologize. It was sleep you obviously needed."

"Yeah, I guess I did." Amber finger-combed her tangled hair and wiped the sleep from her eyes.

"Amber, why didn't you tell me everything that was going on?"

"Like I said last night, I'm not your responsibility."

"You're right! You're not my responsibility!" Steven snapped.

"But that doesn't mean I just stop caring. You should've—"

A knock at the door made Amber jump, then scramble to her feet. *The police. Great! Now they're going to assume Steven spent the night.* She tugged at her shirt and tried to smooth the wrinkles from her clothes. She could feel the scorching heat of embarrassment on her face.

"Amber, we didn't do anything wrong," Steven said, as he moved to the edge of the bed.

She crossed the room and answered the door. Det. Cooper—one of the men on duty—looked at her, then glanced over her shoulder. "I just wanted to make sure you were okay."

"I'm fine," she said, feeling the need to explain her situation. "It was a long night, and Steven—"

"Hey, I'm just making sure you're okay," he interrupted. "What you do in your own house is your business."

"But that's what I'm telling you, we weren't doing anything."

Steven now stood beside her, pulling the door open a little wider. "Look, Amber fell asleep, and I didn't want to disturb her. She finally got some much-needed rest."

"I'm the protection detail, not the babysitter," Det. Cooper said flippantly.

Steven took a step forward. "Watch your mouth!"

Amber stepped in front of Steven, acting as a buffer.

"Hey, Cooper, get in here," the other cop yelled from the living room. "Hastings is on the phone. Says we've got a problem."

Amber and Steven followed the detective into the living room.

Cooper asked, "What is it, Armstrong?"

Officer Armstrong—a uniform cop pulled in to help with Amber's detail—was flipping through the television channels, looking for something. He stopped at the local news. Cursed. Then continued talking on the phone. "No. I missed the report. Yeah. I'll tell her. Yeah. Don't I know it." He tossed the phone on the couch, clearly agitated.

"What's wrong?" Cooper asked.

Armstrong took a deep breath before speaking. "The press is

reporting that there's a serial rapist at large." He turned to Amber. "There's no easy way to say this, but, one of the local news stations has identified you as the first victim."

"What!?" Steven flared. "How'd that happen?"

"Hastings' thinks a disgruntled hospital employee might have tipped off the media. We just picked him up for questioning. We've also contacted the local news agency about pulling any further reports or face charges of interfering with an ongoing police investigation."

"Great. So you question the guy, and the news drops the story. How is that going to help Amber?"

"Look", Cooper inserted himself into the conversation. "It doesn't matter how it happened, what matters is how we deal with it."

Amber ran her hand through her hair, her heart racing. "I need to take a shower." She turned and hurried down the hall.

"Amber, wait."

Steven caught up with her, but she didn't turn around.

"Amber."

Plastering on what she hoped was a convincing smile, she turned to face him.

"It's going to be okay," he reached for her, giving her arm a gentle squeeze.

"I know," she tried to sound upbeat. "But I still need a shower."

Amber ran the water hard and hot as she got undressed. Her jeans slipped easily from her waist due to her continued weight loss, but she had a hard time unbuttoning her shirt because her hands wouldn't stop shaking. She stepped into the steady stream of water, hoping it would soothe her and chase away the chill.

I don't know if I can take much more, Lord. Just when I feel hopeful, She thought of how good it had felt to have Steven back at her side, *something else happens. Now I'm more confused than ever. How long will I have to live with the what ifs? Maybe the police are wrong. Maybe the Morris brothers have no intentions of finding me.*

But if they do, I'm putting people around me in danger.

Amber's mind spun out of control. She sunk to the corner of the tub and cried as the water hit her in the face. She knew her sobbing would be drowned out by the sound of the water, so Amber allowed herself the freedom.

After getting her emotions under control, she stepped from the bathroom and quickly pulled on a different pair of jeans and a t-shirt. She was slipping on her warmest sweatshirt when there was a knock at the door.

"Amber, it's me. Are you descent?" Steven asked.

"No, but I'm dressed," she said dryly.

Steven walked into the room. "Humor, that's a good sign."

Amber stepped into the bathroom to brush out her dripping hair. Steven was sitting on the corner of her bed when she reappeared.

"How are you doing?"

"Fine."

"Fine?" Steven asked again.

She ignored him as she grabbed a pair of socks from her dresser and stood struggling to pull them on. After taking a few bad hops, Steven stood and offered his arm for balance.

"Thanks."

With her socks on and both feet planted firmly on the ground, Steven slipped his arms around her waist and asked, "So, where do we go from here?"

"I'm not sure. You're the one who keeps showing up." She gave him a quick smile as she rested her hands on his biceps.

"If I remember correctly, you're the one who asked me to stay."

Steven brushed her cheek with the back of his hand. "Amber, you're so cold."

She closed her eyes as she leaned into his touch. "I just can't seem to get warm."

"I think I can help with that." Steven pulled her close and wrapped her in his arms. With her ear pressed against his chest, she could hear his beating heart. It was strong, like Steven. Amber sunk into his embrace, never wanting to let go.

"So, did you get a chance to talk with Det. Cooper and Ofc. Armstrong?" she asked.

"I guess you could call it that. They threatened me with jail time if I got in their way, and I told them my brother was the D.A. and I would have their badges if they screwed up."

"Steven," she looked up into his eyes. "Why would you say something like that?"

"Because Det. Cooper seems too cocky for his own good." He held her tighter. "I want him to know I'll be watching him."

"And I don't want you to do anything that's going to get you in trouble. Or worst yet, hurt." She rested her head against his chest. "Promise me."

He chuckled. "I promise."

She sighed, soaking in his strength. This is where she wanted to be. This is where she felt safe. Steven had the power to make her forget about everything. But, voices from the other room reminded her of the grim reality.

Her identity had been exposed.

Her safety compromised.

They needed to find out what the next step would be.

Amber held Steven's hand as they walked into the living room. Hastings and Jones had arrived. When Hastings saw Steven, he gave him a knowing glance and a handshake. "Good to see you again, Levitt."

Amber and Steven exchanged surprised glances at Hastings' warm reception. They took a seat in the living room as the detective relayed what information they now had, and what their plan of action would be.

Everyone listened as he spoke of a safe house at an undisclosed location, the steps they would take to transport her, and the continued surveillance they would have on the house. Amber listened but had an idea of her own.

"I think I should stay here."

Everyone turned to Amber, her words catching them completely off guard.

Hastings shook his head immediately. "It's not safe. There are too many variables."

"I want this to be over with. The only way you're going to catch the Morris brothers is to allow them to find me."

Steven was perched on the arm of the chair she was sitting in. He squeezed her hand and squatted down beside her. "But Amber, like Det. Hastings said it's not safe."

"Only if they mess up," she said as she eyed the cops staring at her.

FORTY-FIVE

It took some debating, some strategy, and a few stipulations, but it was settled. Amber would stay home. That meant their plan of action had to be clear and concise. There could be no room for error.

Steven sat on the couch next to Amber while the detectives began to formulate their plan. She leaned into him, her feet curled underneath her, her head resting on his shoulder.

"You hungry?" he asked.

"Not really."

"But you need to eat. You've lost too much weight."

"I'm fine."

Hastings obviously overheard their quiet conversation. "Armstrong," he barked. "Go get us some food. No Mexican though. I'm already drinking Pepto Bismol for dessert these days."

"So, how's work going?" Steven asked. "We really didn't get much of a chance to talk yesterday. It must be hard getting anything done with those guys around." He nodded towards the discussion happening across the room.

Amber didn't say anything right away because she knew Steven would be disappointed with her answer.

"Did Jessica like the engagement shots?" he asked, with genuine interest.

Amber shifted her weight, rolling her head from Steven's shoulder to the back of the couch. Clearing her throat, she answered. "Steven, I gave it up."

"You what?"

"I canceled the rest of my appointments and sent the proofs and negatives to my customers. I didn't explain why. I just said I was unable to fulfill my end of the contractual agreement. I apologized for my unprofessionalism and refunded their deposits."

"Amber, why?"

"Because I just can't handle it right now."

"But you're going to pick it back up after this is all over, right?"

Amber looked at Steven, not believing it would ever be over. "Let's just wait and see what happens."

❧❧❧❧

A sinking feeling settled in Steven's gut. *She doesn't think she's going to make it out of this.* A knot formed in his throat preventing him from responding. Instead, he pulled her close, holding her a little tighter than he had before.

Over lunch, Hastings had discussed his plan to secure the empty house next to Amber's for a command post. But after a few inquiries, Hastings had discovered the house had already sold. So, he and the other men started formulating Plan B while Steven watched Amber push her food around on her plate.

After lunch, Steven watched as Amber wandered around her house, moving in and out of her office and studio. She was restless. Anxious. But without her job to focus on, it was obvious Amber didn't know how to expel her nervous energy. Steven wanted to do something to distract her. He smiled to himself when he came up with what he thought was the perfect idea.

It took a little time, as Steven casually gathered things from around the house. As long as Amber didn't seek refuge in her bedroom, he'd be able to surprise her.

Steven noticed Det. Cooper watching him like a hawk and knew it was only a matter of time before he was cornered.

"What are you up to, Levitt?" Det. Cooper asked, confronting him in the hall not five minutes later.

"I'm just trying to create a diversion for Amber, a distraction from all this . . . this stuff." He waved his hand in the direction of the other cops.

Cooper stood toe to toe with Steven as he spoke under his breath. "Just as long as you stay out of our way. As far as I'm concerned you're a liability. I don't know why Hastings hasn't kicked your butt out of here already. But, if you make my job harder, I'll see to it that you're gone."

"What is your problem?" Steven asked, taking a step back.

"We were doing just fine until you showed up. You're a complication."

All of a sudden it clicked. Steven put two and two together and came up with his answer. Cooper was attracted to Amber. Steven didn't think, he just responded. "You're nothing more than a—" Steven took a swing at Cooper. He was able to hit his mark, but Cooper was fast with a return punch. Their scuffle brought everyone into the hall. Hastings and Jones broke up the two men, taking a few shots themselves.

Amber immediately rushed to Steven as he wiped the blood from under his nose. "Are you all right?" she asked.

"Yeah. I'm fine," Steven replied, feeling anything but.

She turned to Cooper. "What the heck do you think you're doing?" she snapped.

"He swung at me first," Cooper said, licking the blood from the corner of his mouth.

"That's because I got in the way of your plan," Steven yelled as he surged forward.

Hastings pushed Steven against the wall, stopping him from taking another swing.

"Plan?" Amber asked. "Steven, what are you talking about? What plan?"

"Yeah, Levitt, what are you talking about?" Hastings' words were controlled but the set of his jaw belied his agitation.

Steven turned his attention to Amber. "Detective Cooper—*mister serve and protect*—wants you for himself. I'm sure he thought you'd be an easy mark under the circumstances."

"You're an idiot, Levitt." Cooper laughed in disgust.

"That's enough! Both of you!" Hastings yelled. "I am not going to play recess monitor to your adolescent behavior. Cooper, if you can't keep your head in the game, you're out of here."

"No problem," Cooper snapped, then walked away.

"Levitt," Hastings turned his attention to Steven. "You're on thin ice. If you're going to make our job harder, I'll have you arrested for interfering with a police investigation. Got it?"

"Got it." Steven was still hot but knew the consequences if he said anything more.

"Amber, you okay?" Hastings asked, softening his tone.

"I'm fine."

She looked at Steven as she gently wiped at the blood between his nose and lip. "Come on, let's get you washed up."

ꕥꕥꕥꕥ

When Amber pushed open her bedroom door she was surprised by the transformation in her room. "What's all this?" Across her bed lay the checkered blanket from her studio props. She stepped into the room as her eyes darted from the food spread out on the blanket, to the two chairs facing the television set, then to the bowl of popcorn that sat on the bedside table.

"Dinner and a movie," Steven said. "I thought it was about time we go on our first date. I wish it could be an elegant restaurant and a Broadway musical, but—"

"But nothing," she said, choking back her emotions. "It's perfect." Amber walked over to her bed and knelt on the corner.

"I took a chance on peanut butter and jelly," he smiled. "It's not very fancy, but I thought you could use the protein. Besides, I'm a simple man. I like simple things."

She watched as Steven walked to the other side of the bed and sat down, careful not to knock anything over.

"It's wonderful," Amber whispered.

"No." He reached across the bed and squeezed her hand. "You're wonderful, and you deserve so much more than what you've gotten." He let go of her hand and picked up the napkin by his plate, wiping at the blood under his nose.

"Here, let me." Amber reached across and with Steven's napkin, wiped at the blood on his lip and the smudge on his cheek. "There." She wadded up the napkin and threw it in the bedside trash can.

"Thanks."

"You're welcome."

"When this is over, I plan on making up for lost time. I figure we have about fifteen to twenty dates to make up for."

Amber smiled. "What if I decide to play hard to get?"

"You already have." He leaned over and gave her a gentle kiss, wincing as he brought his hand up to his swollen lip.

Amber laughed.

"You know he's interested in you," Steven said.

It was more of a statement than a question. But Amber knew Steven was referring to Det. Cooper. "I know."

Steven's brow lowered and his jaw clenched in anger. "You know? How? Has he tried anything?"

"Of course not. I can just tell. I *can* still read the signs, you know."

"Okay, but I think you should tell Det. Hastings this guy is trouble. I don't want him—"

"Let it go, Steven." She placed her hand on top of his. "Det. Cooper has been every bit the professional. Don't let your scuffle with him ruin all this." She looked at the blanket, food, popcorn.

Steven sighed, then proceeded to pour her a glass of soda.

"So, what would your mother do if she knew you were going around picking fights?" Amber couldn't help but tease.

"It wouldn't be my mother I would have to worry about. Stacy's the one who would read me the riot act." Steven took a bite of his sandwich while Amber sipped on her Coke. "It was Stacy who came by here," Steven said a few minutes later after taking a swig of his soda.

"Here?" Amber asked. "When? Why?"

"She was trying to be my advocate. The lawyer in her thought if she talked to you, she could plead my case. But when one of the cops answered the door, Stacy jumped to the wrong conclusion."

"But you came over here to see if it was true?" Amber accused more than questioned, feeling offended and defensive.

"No, I panicked. I knew you would never let someone into your house. Especially a man. I thought the Morris brothers had found you and I freaked. I know you had your reasons for asking me to stay away. And I was willing to give you the time you needed to sort them out. But the thought of you being in danger, or even worst. I just reacted."

Amber picked at her sandwich and nibbled on a few chips. The mood had definitely shifted from carefree to uncomfortable. She still had so much to tell Steven, things he deserved to know.

"Steven, I owe you an apology."

He shrugged and smiled. "No, you don't."

"Yes, I do. I didn't want to hurt you but there was so much you don't know. And I—"

"It doesn't matter, Amber," he cut her off. "None of it matters. I'm here now, and I have no intentions of leaving. It's going to take more than a room full of goons to get me to—"

"But it does matter, Steven! I thought I was pregnant!"

She watched as his smile thinned to an expression of anxiousness or fear, she wasn't sure which, but she'd finally gotten his full attention.

"But you aren't?" he asked softly.

"No. But there could still be other complications."

Reaching for her hand, he held on tight. "Amber, just tell me you're okay."

Amber explained to Steven everything she had bottled up inside her for the last several weeks. She started by telling him about the technician mishandling her lab work at the hospital and subsequently getting fired.

"Is that who Hastings is questioning? Is that who leaked your name to the press?"

"I think so." She went on to tell him how she had struggled with the possibility of being pregnant, and that she had refused exposure medication because she'd felt overwhelmed and angry at God. And now, because of her self-destructive decision, there was still the possibility she could test positive for HIV.

"I felt like I was crawling with disease, Steven, that's why I kept pushing you away. As much as I wanted you in my life, I refused to jeopardize your health or your future. I was falling in love with you, but you didn't deserve being faced with the problems I was dealing with. I decided I'd rather have you hate me than put you in a position to choose. So I chose for you. I asked you to leave." She exhaled, her eyes downcast.

Steven stood and walked around to the other side of the bed. He sat down next to her and lifted his finger to her chin. He tipped her head up but didn't say anything until Amber looked at him.

When she met his eyes, he looked so serious. "Only one thing you said concerns me."

"I won't know for at least six months. If it hasn't presented itself by—"

"That's not what concerns me," he said, as he gently stroked her cheek with his thumb. "You said you were falling in love with me. Past-tense. Tell me how you feel right now."

She closed her eyes, her heart beating so fast, she was afraid she was going to pass out. Her mind raced ahead, trying to play out how all of this was going to end.

"Amber." Steven cupped her jaw. "Look at me."

She opened her eyes.

"Answer me. Right now. This very moment. Can you say you're still falling in love with me?"

Tears trailed down her face. "Yes."

❧❧❧❧

Steven pulled Amber into his arms and pressed a firm kiss to her lips. He wanted to deepen it. He wanted to have that intimate connection with Amber. But, he didn't want to frighten her or ask more of her than she felt she could give. Just holding her like this, knowing how Amber felt, it would be enough.

For now.

FORTY-SIX

Amber blinked a few times before it finally registered it was morning. She looked at Steven, half sitting half lying against the headboard, his head cocked in an awkward position, his clothes crumpled, his hair eschew. Smiling, a surge of emotion raced through her. She had finally told Steven everything and had admitted she was falling in love with him. And for the second night in a row, Steven hadn't left her side. He'd held her through another night of terrifying dreams, calming her with words of comfort, doing his best to assure her everything would be all right.

But, just like the morning before, she battled a twinge of awkwardness, knowing the cops in the other room were judging her and Steven's behavior.

I don't care! She mentally stomped her foot. *I've gotten more sleep in the last two nights than I did all last week. For once in my life, I'm not going to let what other people think about me matter.*

Her survival hinged on not falling apart, on not collapsing under the mental oppression pressing in on her. Steven was the only person who could counterbalance the terror that crept up on her when she closed her eyes at night. She refused to be made to feel guilty by his presence. He had every right to be here. And now, more than ever, she couldn't imagine going through this without him by her side.

Slowly, Amber slipped from bed doing her best not to disturb Steven. He stirred but didn't wake. She closed the bathroom door behind her, brushed her teeth, and ran a comb through her hair. She was going to change her clothes but thought better of it. *Okay, so maybe I do care what people think. If I'm wearing the same clothes I did last night maybe they won't jump to the wrong conclusion.*

When she stepped from the bathroom, Steven was sitting on the edge of the bed, elbows on his knees, rubbing the back of his head. When he saw her, he stood. With sleepy eyes and a yawn, he stretched his long arms over his head. "Good morning, Beautiful," he smiled.

"Good morning," she answered back, feeling her face erupt in a heated blush.

"Would you mind if I used your shower?"

"Not at all. There are fresh towels in the cupboard under the sink. Left side. There's also some hotel soaps and shampoos in the left-hand drawer. My stuff is pretty girly. Unless you don't mind smelling like vanilla and lavender?" she teased.

"Actually, those have recently become two of my favorite scents," he said, as he smiled and placed a quick kiss on her forehead before disappearing into the bathroom.

Steven's smile did things to her that Amber just couldn't explain. It exuded strength and protection, the glint in his eyes assured her everything was going to be okay. She closed her eyes imagining this is what it would feel like to be married and wake up every day with your best friend at your side. For a second, Amber felt normal. That is until she walked into the living room and saw Det. Jones folding a blanket at the foot of her couch.

When Amber turned to the kitchen, she saw Det. Cooper staring out the window. She stood beside him and watched as her new neighbor talked with a man in a gray jumpsuit, a moving van sticking out of her driveway. The woman looked to be about her age; blonde, average size. Amber immediately thought of Cara, wondering how she was doing. Amber didn't realize she was daydreaming until Cooper abruptly pulled the shade down, startling her.

"You need to be careful around windows," he instructed.

"Sorry," she said quietly, then stepped to the refrigerator and reached for a carton of eggs.

"No. I'm the one who needs to apologize," Cooper said as he leaned on the counter. "I'm sorry for the tension I caused."

"It's okay." She set the eggs on the counter. "I appreciate everything everyone is doing. I know you guys are under a lot of pressure."

"You're being too gracious. I acted like a grade-A jackass."

"I agree," she said matter-of-factly, but with a smirk. "Now that we have that settled, how about some to eat?"

There was still a degree of tension in the room as Cooper, Armstrong, and Steven ate breakfast. But Amber realized this was the new normal. It would be too much for her to expect anything other than stress and strain.

When everyone was done eating, Armstrong left to do surveillance while Cooper hovered over his computer, doing whatever it was he did.

Amber was just finishing the dishes when Steven walked into the kitchen, his phone pressed to his ear. After a few sentences, she realized he was talking to his sister. Steven had been ignoring Stacy's calls, so Amber was glad to see he was finally talking things out. What she didn't expect was for Steven to extend the phone to her.

"Amber, my sister would like to talk to you."

She quickly shook her head.

Pressing the mute button, Steven explained. "She feels horrible and would like a chance to apologize."

"That's not necessary." Amber turned to the countertops and feverishly wiped them down with a dishtowel.

"Amber, please."

"I told you, it's not necessary."

"But it would mean a lot to me if you would talk to her."

Amber groaned. Tossing the dishtowel on the counter, she turned to Steven. Again, he extended the phone. Amber conceded and hesitantly raised it to her ear. "Hello."

"Amber, I know you don't know me, but I owe you a huge

apology."

"Like I told Steven, that's really not necessary," Amber replied.

"Yes. Yes, it is. I had no right to say what I did. I know I hurt both you and Steven."

"I'm sorry this is so difficult for you and your family," Amber blurted out, wanting to reassure Steven's sister she would never do anything to hurt her brother. "And I wish for your sakes Steven had never gotten involved. But you need to know, I wouldn't have made it this far without him. He's been incredible. Please don't be mad at Steven." Amber heard nothing but silence—and was ready to hand the phone back—when she heard a quiet sigh.

"Amber, we're not mad, and I'm not at all surprised Steven is there. I've come to realize he cares a great deal for you and it would be foolish for us to think we could convince him to stay away." Stacy sighed. "I just wanted to call to apologize and let you know we're looking forward to meeting you. When your current situation is . . . resolved, we'll have you over for an official family dinner."

Amber was shocked, not knowing what to say.

"Amber?"

"Ye-yes, I'm here."

"I'm sorry. I didn't mean to put you on the spot like that."

"No. No, it's all right. I think I'd like that . . . to meet you, that is."

Amber handed the phone back to Steven.

He spoke to his sister for a few minutes before hanging up.

"She sounds nice," Amber offered.

"She is when she's not being over-protective."

"Your family's worried about you, Steven. That's not being over-protective, that's love."

FORTY-SEVEN

Days came and went.

Amber watched as Hastings did little to hide his frustration. He ranted day in and day out that something wasn't adding up. The Morris brothers had chanced a second attack before falling off the map. It wasn't the typical M.O. for predators. Something wasn't right.

Cooper, Jones, and Armstrong had become regular fixtures at the house as they rotated duties between following leads, neighborhood surveillance, and keeping an eye on Amber. And even though Amber insisted Steven return to work, he was back every night just in time for dinner, most times bringing Bo with him. Steven and Cooper had been able to put their differences aside and—along with Jones and Armstrong—were forming a pretty impressive friendship.

Jones and Cooper were watching a hockey game and Amber was trying to read a book when a knock at the door put everybody on high alert.

The two men jumped to their feet, but it was Cooper who approached the door, his weapon pressed against the side of his thigh. He looked through the peephole, then took a step back. He whispered to Amber, "It's your new neighbor. Go ahead and see what she wants."

Cooper stepped back into the hallway. Amber waited for the woman to knock again before slowly opening the door.

"Hi. I'm sorry to bother you. I'm your new neighbor." The

woman smiled, pointing to the house on the left.

"Yes, I've seen you working in your yard."

"My name is Emily." She extended her hand to Amber.

Amber shook hands with the woman and introduced herself before even thinking about it. She cringed at her mistake, but Emily didn't skip a beat.

"I hate to be a bother, but I'm in the middle of making some cookies, and I don't have any baking soda. I thought I'd bought all my staples on my last trip to the grocery store, but I guess baking soda didn't make the list. Do you have any I could borrow?"

"Sure." Amber glanced over her shoulder, uncertain if she should let the woman in or not. Cooper nodded his approval so Amber stepped back and welcomed Emily inside.

"Oh, I'm sorry, I didn't mean to barge in on you while you had company," Emily said, as she followed Amber into the living room.

Amber wasn't sure what to say so she looked at Cooper to bail her out.

"We're not company." Cooper extended his hand. "Hi, the name's Coop. I'm Amber's brother, and this is my friend Jerry. Don't mind us we're just crashing here for a little while." Cooper nonchalantly walked back to the living room and sat down.

Emily followed Amber to the kitchen and smiled when she handed her the box of soda. "Thank you. You're a lifesaver. Or should I say a cookie saver?" Emily giggled.

"No problem," Amber answered nervously, feeling like she was going to do or say something to screw things up. When the conversation stalled, she tried to think of a benign subject to talk about. "So, do you like gardening?" Amber asked.

"Yes, but I'm not very good at it."

"I wouldn't say that. Your front yard looks beautiful."

"Well, it's easy when you buy blooming flowers from the nursery. Just don't ask me to plant bulbs or seeds." She giggled again.

Emily had a bubbly personality, reminding Amber of Cara.

"So, where are you from?" Amber asked.

Emily froze, then glanced at the box she was nervously fiddling with. "Well, thanks again for the baking soda," she said, ignoring Amber's question completely. "I'll bring it right back."

"No hurry." Amber followed Emily to the front door, unable to overlook the drastic change in her neighbor's behavior. "Emily . . . are you all right?"

"Yes. Yes, I'm fine."

Amber thought Emily sounded rather skittish. "Are you sure?"

Emily stared at the box in her hand, fidgeting some more before answering Amber. "I guess I'm a little jittery. I just left my husband, and being on my own is harder than I thought it would be."

Amber stood straighter. "Emily, I'm sorry. I didn't mean to pry."

"No. It's not your fault."

Amber was at a loss for words.

"It's okay. Really." Emily placed a reassuring hand on Amber's arm.

"Is there a chance you'll get back together again?" Amber asked.

Emily let out a huff. "I hope not. I'm not sure I could survive it."

Again, Amber didn't know what to say.

"I left my husband because he used me as a punching bag," Emily said abruptly. "I didn't find out what a violent temper he had until after we were married. When I realized he wasn't going to change, I left. I'm lucky I got out when I did. I think he would've killed me if I'd stayed around much longer."

Amber couldn't hide her shock. "Emily, I'm so sorry. I'm . . . I mean . . ."

"Wow, did I just dump on you, or what?" Emily chuckled, nervously. "Sorry about that. My therapist tells me I need to talk about it more, not hide from the truth. She assures me I have nothing to be ashamed of. Of course, that's easy for her to say, she doesn't have to look at the horrified expressions on people's faces when I tell them."

Amber watched a tear trail down Emily's cheek even though she was smiling.

"I didn't mean to unload on you. It's just that I haven't had anyone to talk to. I don't have any family and it's been kind of hard figuring out what I needed to do and then having enough guts to do it. My shrink says I need to take back control, instead of being controlled."

Instantly, Amber felt a bond with Emily. "I know how you feel," she absentmindedly blurted out.

"You do?" Emily said, sounding surprised.

"Well, sort of. I was never married, but I know what it's like to be afraid of a man."

"How did you handle it?"

"I almost didn't. I guess I'm just too stubborn to give up."

"And they say *we're* the weaker sex." Emily let out a nervous laugh and changed the subject. "Well, thanks again for the baking soda, and for the conversation. It's nice having someone to talk to. I hope we can do it again real soon."

"I look forward to it."

Steven and Bo were right on time. Dinner was almost on the table and Amber was bursting with energy. She couldn't wait to tell him about her conversation with Emily. Even though Cooper had cautioned Amber about her new found friendship, she had felt a connection. It was immediate. Emily needed someone to talk to, something Amber needed as well.

Steven greeted Amber with a warm hug and whispered in her ear. "Hey, Beautiful."

Amber immediately felt heat scorch her cheeks and her heart flutter. When she stepped away from Steven, he studied her for a moment.

"Were you out in the sun today?" he asked. "It looks like you might've gotten a little too much."

She slapped at his arm playfully, knowing he was teasing her for blushing. "No. But you'll never guess what happened today?"

Steven shot a look at Cooper. "A break?"

"No such luck." He shrugged as he took his dinner plate and moved to the living room.

Steven turned his attention back to Amber.

"I met the woman who moved in next door. She's really nice."

"How'd you do that?"

"She came over to borrow some baking soda. We just seemed to hit it off."

"That's great Amber, but how did you explain these clowns?"

She laughed. "Meet my brother, Coop, and his friend Jerry."

❧❧☙☙

Steven was glad to have dinner over with so he could have Amber all to himself. It was the time of night he looked forward to every day.

With their only light coming from the television screen, they curled up together on her bed, him leaning against the headboard, Amber leaning against him. They flipped through their cable choices and finally agreed on a romantic comedy.

At times, Steven felt a twinge of guilt concerning the routine he and Amber had settled into. He was sure his family would never approve of their cozy arrangement, but he'd been careful never to allow their situation to escalate further than holding each other close and a few gently placed kisses.

Besides, it wasn't like they would let things get too out of hand, not with the watchdogs camped out in the other room. Steven had made it clear to the men—on more than one occasion—that there wasn't anything physical going on between him and Amber. The men shrugged it off as if it was information they didn't need to know, but Steven wanted to make it very clear he and Amber were not in a physical relationship. Steven didn't care what the men thought of him, but he didn't want to do anything to make them think less of Amber.

"You seem pretty excited about meeting this neighbor of yours," Steven said once the movie started.

“It was weird. It was like I was drawn to her. When she told me why she left her husband, I felt an immediate bond.”

“Why? What happened?”

“He beat her.”

“She told you that?” Steven asked, surprised a perfect stranger would divulge something so private.

“Yeah. I was surprised, too, but she has no family and her therapist encouraged her to talk to someone. I can tell she’s still afraid.”

They watched the movie for a while, but concern ate at Steven. Finally, he asked, “You didn’t tell her anything about your situation, did you?”

“No. But I told her I could relate to how she was feeling.”

Steven slowly stroked Amber’s arm, trying to choose his words wisely. “You need to be careful, Amber, you don’t want to say too much to her.”

“I know, but I totally understand how she’s feeling. Except the person that hurt her was her own husband.” Amber sighed. “I just don’t get it, Steven. How can a person go from loving someone one day and hurting them so badly the next?”

“Because they don’t know what love is. If they don’t know the Lord, then it’s not love they’re feeling. It could be chemistry, or attraction, or lust, but none of those things come with any kind of commitment. When the chemistry wears off or the attraction grows old, resentment sets in. Some people walk away, others lash out.”

“So, what makes you such an expert? Is there something you’re not telling me?” Amber looked up at Steven, with a teasing smile.

“Just an observation.”

“Oh really.” Amber teased Steven, and the two bantered for a few minutes more. But when they turned their attention back to the movie, they realized the two main characters were in quite a clench. They watched the scene in awkward silence as the intensity heightened. When it became obvious why the film had gotten its “R” rating, Steven clicked the remote. “Okay, I think that’s enough of that.”

The screen went black.

Steven wasn't sure what was worse. Watching the explicit scene on TV or lying next to Amber—in the darkness—with his own thoughts taking form. It took only a moment for him to realize he couldn't handle either.

He got up from the bed and crossed to the bathroom in silence. He switched on the light and closed the door behind him. Splashing cold water on his face, he hung his head over the sink, feeling like an over-sexed teenager. He would never do anything to hurt Amber—that included putting moves on her in her vulnerable state—but that didn't mean he didn't find her alluring and incredibly desirable. And with that attraction came impulses.

It was a moment before Steven got his feelings under control. When he emerged from the bathroom, he used the stream of light cast from the vanity to cross the room. He pulled the two chairs from the corner of the room and placed them end to end. He sat on one and stretched his legs out on the other.

"I think it would be best if we call it a night. I'll be right here if you need me."

❧❧❧❧

Amber debated saying anything, but she had to know. She stared at the ceiling, the light from the bathroom casting shadows above her. "So, which one was it: chemistry, attraction, or lust?"

"You left out love," Steven answered back from the corner.

"Is that what it was?" Amber held her breath, waiting for his answer.

"Honestly?"

"Yeah."

"Lust is what I was feeling. Love is what made me stop."

Amber lay awake most the night, replaying Steven's declaration a hundred times over in her mind. When morning came, he didn't say anything about the night before, leaving Amber to wonder if she'd dreamt the whole thing. But when he left for work, he pressed his lips to her ear and whispered, "I love you."

It had not been a dream.

FORTY-EIGHT

Amber knew everyone was getting restless. Days had turned into weeks without any new leads. Hastings and his team were agitated, and even Steven began to show signs of exhaustion.

A knock on the door had Cooper on his feet and in the entryway. He signaled to Amber it was okay for her to answer the door while he slipped out of sight.

Emily stood on the porch with a brand new box of baking soda and a clay pot of pansies. "Here you go." She handed both items to Amber. "I'm sorry it took me so long. I meant to bring it over every time I came asking for advice, but I kept forgetting. So, here's a new box and a little thank you to compensate for my tardiness."

Amber took a step back, allowing Emily to stand in the entryway. "That really wasn't necessary, but thank you," Amber said, as she took the box and accepted the flowers. "They're beautiful."

"I wish I could say they came from my garden, but I'd be lying," Emily giggled.

Amber wanted to invite Emily in. Share a cup of tea. Like two normal people. But just like the other times she had come over seeking advice, the entryway was as far as Emily was allowed to go. Amber had already given her tips on the best dry cleaner in town, the pros and cons of a lawn service, and what satellite company had the best prices. Now, here they stood once again, the prolonged silence becoming the third party in their conversation.

"Well, I'd better go," Emily blurted out. "Thanks again,

Amber. Maybe someday we can do lunch."

"I'd like that."

Amber closed the door with a sigh, wishing she didn't have to act so cautiously.

"I'm sorry, Amber," Cooper said, his tone compassionate. "Next time she comes over, you can invite her in. We'll just make ourselves scarce in your office."

"She asked me to lunch."

"You know you can't do that," he said apologetically.

"Yeah, I know."

When Hastings walked in with Jones a few hours later, Amber could tell he wasn't in a good mood. She listened and watched as he paced the living room, informing Cooper and Armstrong that their superiors were questioning the manpower being used on a case that had run cold.

"We haven't had a fresh lead on the Morris brothers in weeks," he said as he rubbed his jaw. "I don't know how much longer they're going to let us be here."

Amber didn't want to hear any more. She hated the tension and frustration that was almost palatable, knowing she was the reason for it. "Do you think it would be okay if I sat on the patio? I could really use some fresh air." Amber had expected to be told no. Other than her counseling sessions, she hadn't been allowed to go anywhere, but the look on Cooper's face said he understood her need for escape.

"Sure. Just stay close to the house."

"That won't be a problem. It's a small yard." Amber said sarcastically.

After sliding the glass door closed behind her, she took a seat on one of the patio chairs and pulled her knees up close to her chest. Amber allowed the light breeze to dance across her face and inhaled the crisp, fresh air. Studying the fluttering leaves on a sapling, she listened to the birds call to each other from branches above her. Everything seemed so peaceful. If she just stayed out here and didn't go back inside, she could almost convince herself it was just another ordinary day.

Amber turned her eyes heavenward and began to have a silent conversation with God—asking for strength, courage, and guidance. She knew He was with her and that He had a plan, but wasn't sure she would be able to sit by and wait for that plan to unfold. Amber wanted closure from all that had happened, but would never have it if they didn't find her attackers.

Amber hadn't told Steven she was once again contemplating moving back to New York—at least until the Morris brothers were caught. Amber knew it was a decision she would have to make on her own; a decision made all the more excruciating because of her feelings for Steven. *Maybe Steven would come with—*

"Hey, neighbor."

Amber was startled from her thoughts. She looked up to see Emily poking her head over their shared fence.

"I'm sorry, I didn't mean to make you jump."

"It's okay. I guess I was kind of zoning." Amber walked to the fence line.

"Your backyard is beautiful. And here you tried convincing me you knew nothing about gardening."

"All this was here when I moved in," Amber said as she looked around her own yard. "The only thing I've done is add water and an occasional fertilizer spike."

Emily was craning her neck, taking it all in. "What is that shrub over there?" she asked, pointing to the far side of the yard.

"I have no idea."

"Mind if I take a closer look?" Emily asked, with genuine interest.

Amber glanced at the glass door leading to the house. Cooper had warned her about too much contact, but he had also said she could invite Emily in the next time she came by. *Front door, backyard, what's the difference?* "Of course," Amber said, "come on over." She reached for one of the large pickets of the fence and swung it to the side, creating an opening big enough to slip through.

"Wow, that's nifty," Emily said with surprise.

"My best friend use to live in your house. We would use this pass-through all the time. I never got around to nailing it shut."

Emily mumbled something about convenience.

"What?" Amber asked.

"Oh, nothing." Emily looked to Amber's left as she stepped through the fence. "Are those daylilies?"

At the sound of ripping material, Amber stuck out her hands. "Wait!" She tried to stop Emily, but it was too late. "Shoot! I'm sorry. I should've warned you. There's a loose nail in the fence."

Emily cursed under her breath as she inspected the tear in her blouse.

"Cara and I had gotten used to dodging it. I'm sorry. I completely forgot about it."

"That's okay." Emily quickly shrugged it off. "I didn't like this blouse much anyway." She smiled at Amber as she crossed the yard to the lilies she'd been admiring.

❧❧☙☙

Hastings caught movement out of the corner of his eye. He pulled his weapon as he rushed to the glass doors and saw Amber talking to another woman. "Who's that and how'd she get into the backyard?"

Cooper hurried to the window, then sighed. "That's the woman I told you about. She's the one who bought the house next door. She and Amber have kind of hit it off."

"The Emily Johnson you ran a check on?"

"Yeah. The one with the abusive husband. Said she moved here from Tucson to start over."

"Does it all check out?" Hastings persisted.

"Yeah. I got her full name from the realtor who sold her the house. They had a copy of her driver's license on file. I know someone on the Tucson P.D. so I gave him a call to see if any police reports had been filed by her. He came up empty, but that doesn't mean much. A lot of women don't go to the police. They just up and leave when they've had enough."

"Nothing else?"

"No. Nothing out of the ordinary."

"Well, be careful. I don't want Amber getting too relaxed around other people. She might let her defenses down."

ര്ര്ക്ക്

Amber and Emily visited in the backyard for over an hour. Emily opened up about her volatile marriage, injecting nervous humor here and there, keeping the mood light. Amber could tell humor was Emily's coping mechanism. Her way of lessening the sting of painful memories.

"When he took a baseball bat to my head, and I landed in the hospital, I knew it was over. I knew he would never stop, and I would have to leave."

Amber shuddered. She heard the crack of the bat her attackers had used on her. It was a sound she would never forget.

"Amber, are you okay?"

"Yeah," she answered though she felt far from okay.

"It happened to you, didn't it?" Emily questioned.

"Yeah," she answered somberly.

Emily leaned forward and squeezed her hand. "You're the woman who was attacked in the park, aren't you?" she whispered.

Amber didn't answer. Her omission as good as a yes.

"I thought so, but I didn't want to say anything."

Amber glanced towards her living room where Hastings was still meeting with the other guys. When she turned back, Emily's eyes flicked from the glass door to her.

"He's not your brother, is he?"

"Why do you say that?" Amber asked defensively.

"Because he has cop written all over him," Emily answered in a matter-of-fact tone.

Amber knew she'd messed up but didn't know what to do about it.

"Don't worry, Amber, I'm not going to rat you out to any reporters if that's what you're thinking. I know how horrible it is, everyone knowing your business. When I finally decided to press charges, the police treated me like it was all my fault; like I had provoked my husband. They asked me questions about our sex life and how many other sexual partners I'd had. Like I was some kind of whore. I felt like *I* was the one on trial. That's why I left. I decided I wasn't going to get any help from the cops, so I dropped the charges and left Tucson."

Amber hung her head, nervously pulling at the frayed threads on the hem of her jeans.

"Is that how they treated you? Like you were the bad guy?"

"No," Amber quickly corrected Emily. "They've been great. Very respectful."

"But I bet they've tried to hit on you. Pulled the whole serve and protect routine when all they really wanted was—"

"No!" Amber cut her off, not appreciating Emily's cynicism. "Like I said, they've been nothing but respectful. Besides, I'm seeing someone."

"I'm sorry, Amber. I didn't mean to get so indignant. It's just that my experience with the cops was almost worse than my husband's abuse." Emily's eyes glistened. "I'm glad things have been different for you and that you have someone taking care of you. I wish there'd been someone for me when I was going through it."

"Look," Amber was feeling like she'd already said too much. "I'm really not supposed to be talking about this."

"Sure. No problem." Emily changed the subject just that quick. "So tell me about this "someone" you're seeing," she said with air quotes. "It must be the hunky guy with the wavy blonde hair I've seen coming and going."

Amber grinned.

"So, do you love him?"

Amber was surprised how easily Emily talked about such private matters. She stood, deciding it was time to put an end to their conversation. "I should really get back inside."

"I'm sorry. I did it again," Emily apologized. "I didn't mean to get so personal. I have no buffer."

Emily stood and leaned forward, surprising Amber with a hug.

"Thanks for everything, Amber. It's been nice having someone to talk to. I finally feel like I'm going to make it. Thanks for being such a good listener. You'll never know how helpful it's been talking with you."

Emily embraced Amber again before walking back through the swinging slat on the fence.

Amber felt guilty giving Emily the brush-off. *She just wanted someone to talk to. You of all people should understand that.* Amber sighed. *I'll make it up to her next time.*

FORTY-NINE

Steven placed several cartons of Chinese food on the kitchen counter before they could fall out of his arms. When he saw Hastings sitting in the living room—looking intent—he knew something was wrong.

"What? What is it? Where's Amber?" Steven panicked.

"She's in the other room. She's fine," the detective answered.

"Then what is it?"

Hastings rubbed his jaw and stood, then walked over to where Steven was standing. "If we have nothing new by next Friday, the captain is pulling us out."

"What!" Steven was appalled.

"Look," Cooper chimed in. "We feel the same way. We know there's something more here. We can feel it." Cooper put a reassuring hand on Steven's shoulder. "The captain can tell us what to do when we're on the clock, but he can't tell us what *not* to do in our off hours. Armstrong has a wife and kid at home, but Jones and I don't. We've decided to sack out here at night. If anything new happens, we'll be on it and make sure the captain reopens the case."

"Reopens? You mean he wants to close Amber's case?" Steven looked at Hastings for confirmation.

"I'm doing all I can, Steven, but we just don't have the resources to continue twenty-four-hour surveillance—not when the captain thinks the Morris brothers have moved on."

"Does Amber know?" Steven asked, feeling completely dejected.

"Yeah. We talked to her this afternoon." Hastings said.

Steven glared at the men, knowing it wasn't their fault, but wanting to be angry at someone. He walked down the hall to Amber's room and gave the door a knock.

"Amber, it's me. Can I come in?"

"Yeah."

She was lying on her bed—staring at the ceiling—her bare feet perched on her headboard. Steven walked over and sat on the edge of the bed, wrapping her hand in his.

"How are you doing?"

"Okay." She continued to stare at the ceiling.

"What are you thinking?"

"That this will never be over," she said pragmatically. "That all this time being a prisoner in my own home was for nothing. A complete waste of time."

Steven wanted to refute her, but he couldn't. He didn't have any answers. He leaned over her, his chest resting against hers. He played with the curls that lay across her forehead.

"Do you really feel these last few weeks have been a *complete* waste?" His lips were dangerously close to hers. He wanted to kiss her, but he didn't. Instead, he trailed his finger across her lips. The look she gave him was the reaction he had hoped for. "I enjoyed our dinners and late night movies, didn't you?"

❧❧☙☙

Amber reflected on the evenings she'd spent with Steven. Their feelings for each other were intense. Sometimes too intense. They hadn't done anything improper, but she was sure the only reason they'd maintain control so far was because of the men that sat in the other room. And the fact that they had never closed the door when they were alone.

"I've enjoyed them too, Steven, but we can't keep living this way."

"Then let's get married," he said abruptly.

It was the last thing Amber had expected him to say, and it made her angry. "That's not funny, Steven." She pushed him away and got to her feet. She plopped down in the chair on the far side of the room and crossed her arms firm against her chest.

"I wasn't trying to be funny," Steven said as he moved to where she was sitting.

"But you can't be serious."

Steven crouched down in front of her, his hands on her knees, his eyes locked on hers. "I've never been more serious about anything in my life. I love you, Amber, and I want to marry you."

He was serious.

Amber could see it in his piercing eyes. But she was confused. She loved Steven and wanted to be with him, but her life held such uncertainty. She couldn't even think about involving him in it permanently. He had a family that loved him. A family he had overlooked since he'd been with her.

She was being selfish, only thinking of herself. Amber had chosen to ignore the obvious obstacles and red flags in their relationship because she wanted Steven's kisses and his tender caresses. He made her feel like a woman, not a victim. The warmth of his body somehow blocked out her fear and made her believe—if only for a few hours each night—that everything would be all right. But she hadn't been fair to him. While he gave of himself freely, Amber had nothing to offer him in return, because she still didn't know what the future held.

"Steven, I don't think we should talk about this right now." She tried to move away, but he wouldn't let her.

"I think it's the perfect time to talk about it. If we got married I could take you far away from here until the police figured things out."

"Is that how you want to spend the rest of your life? Running? I don't even want to live my life right now. I'm certainly not going to subject you to it."

"Don't do this to us, Amber. We've already been through all this. I love you, and I know you love me." She watched as his eyes became glassy with unshed tears. "Don't trash everything we could have together."

The hurt in Steven's eyes caused Amber to crumble. She threw her arms around his neck and held him tight. "I'm scared, Steven," she cried. "Really scared."

"I know. So am I." He held her close, stroking her back, lulling her with gentle words. "But we're going to make it, Amber. You have to believe that."

FIFTY

Another week went by with no leads. Hastings, Cooper, and Jones were planning their next steps—steps that would have to be taken on their own time.

Steven was being persistent about getting married, but Amber continued to avoid the subject. As much as she believed Steven's feelings for her were genuine, Amber still felt apprehensive. She kept asking herself, would the intensity and the passion they felt now be there when their lives went back to normal? And what if normal never came?

Amber loved Steven. She didn't question that. But she was afraid marriage was rushing it. Taking a step back to gain some much-needed perspective, Amber had made a decision. Until she was done being tested and the Morris brothers were out of the picture, the subject of marriage was off the table.

She was eating on the patio, her mind racing, when Emily poked her head through the fence. This had become a daily routine. One Amber readily welcomed. Emily could still get a little forward at times, but her chatty personality helped Amber take her mind off of her own situation.

"Hi, Emily."

"Hey, Amber, how you doing?" She came over and joined her on the patio.

"Fine."

"That sounded real convincing." Emily said sarcastically.

"I guess I'm a little distracted."

"Did he ask you to marry him again?" Emily said giggling.

"No."

"Then what is it?" Emily persisted.

Amber lowered her voice. "They're closing my case. They no longer feel I'm in danger. Well, Hastings' *superiors'* no longer feel I'm in danger."

"Wow. That should make you feel better."

"It should, but it doesn't."

"But it's good news for us. We can finally go shopping and out to lunch and all the other things normal people do."

"Steven wants me to move in with him."

"What?" Emily snapped, sounding angry.

"He doesn't think I'm safe here. If I move and we eventually get married, I'll have a different identity and different location. I can start a different life. One with him."

"He doesn't get it, does he?" Emily sneered, disgusted.

"What?"

"He thinks if you change your name and move away everything is going to magically be better. Moving in with him is not going to make you forget what happened. Him playing the doting husband is not going to be the cure-all for the way you feel."

Amber knew Emily would be disappointed if she moved away, but she hadn't expected her to be so belligerent.

"You're not going to do it, are you?" Emily crossed her arms against her chest. "You're not going to run away?"

"I wouldn't be running away, Emily," Amber said firmly. "But I have to start somewhere."

"Great!" Emily jumped to her feet. "I finally find someone I can talk to, someone who understands me, and now you're going to just pick up and leave. Thanks a lot, Amber! Thanks for nothing!"

Emily stormed off as Amber sat too stunned to move.

❧❧❧❧

Emily slammed the back door as she calculated the ramifications of Amber moving. "She can't move! Not yet!" Emily swore, hurling a coffee mug across the kitchen, watching as it shattered against the wall.

"This place is a dive."

She spun around to see Mannie skulking in the corner.

"What are you doing here?" she shot back.

"Relax, Delia. Oh, I'm sorry, I mean *Emily*. You haven't checked in for a while. I'm just seeing how you're doing." Mannie looked around the house with disgust.

"What if someone saw you? You could've blown everything," Delia said, scolding him in a whispered tone.

"No one saw me." He looked at her—scrutinized her. "What's wrong? You didn't screw up, did you?"

"Me . . . I don't screw up. Its guys like you who can't keep your pants zipped that screw things up."

"Hey, *I* didn't do anything!" He pointed one of his chunky fingers at himself, then turned it on her "So don't *you* vent that feminist woman crap on me!"

"Just shut up, Mannie, and listen. We're going to have to act fast. The police are closing the case."

"That's good. No more cops."

"No. That's bad. She's thinking of moving."

"Then you better do something before she does," Mannie sneered.

Delia glared at him. She hated having anyone telling her what to do, especially Mannie. She would have to figure out a way to take care of Amber all by herself.

FIFTY-ONE

Delia had stewed all night. If Amber moved before she could act, everything would be ruined, her reputation for getting the job done would be trashed, and she would have to find herself a nice beach shack somewhere in South America where she could start over.

Delia knew she needed to get a better feel for the layout of Amber's house. So, she decided to pay Amber a visit with the excuse of apologizing. With a plate full of cookies and a plan, Delia left her house and headed for Amber's front door.

Amber saw Emily coming up the front walk, so she headed to her door. Cooper and Jones were on their last twenty-four-hour shift and had their paraphernalia everywhere. Quickly, they packed up their things and moved it all to Amber's office, Jones staying out of sight.

Emily presented the plate of cookies to Amber. "I wanted to apologize for the other day."

Amber took the plate, touched by Emily's good intentions. "It's okay."

"No. It's not okay. I totally blew up at you. It was rude and selfish, and I was only thinking of myself."

Amber waved Emily into the house as she offered the plate of cookies to Cooper. "You remember my brother," she said to Emily, keeping up appearances for Cooper's sake. She had never told him that Emily had figured out they were cops. She didn't feel like getting reprimanded for something that wouldn't matter in the long run.

He grabbed two cookies, thanked Emily, and headed into the other room.

"Your place is really nice, Amber." Emily's eyes roamed around the room. "Is it two bedrooms or three?"

"Three. Well, a small three. I think one of the rooms used to be the utility/laundry room, but the previous owners installed hook-ups out in the garage and turned the room into a nursery. I use it for my office, and the other spare room for my studio."

ঌঌ৵৵

Delia quickly memorized the layout of the house.

"You know, maybe I should replace my back door with glass doors, like you have?" Delia crossed the room and gave the door a tug. She slid her hand over the handle and bent down to look at the lock.

"Lose something?"

Delia was startled by the masculine voice as one of the cops crossed the living room to where she was standing. She gave him a once-over, enjoying the scenery, except for the accusation in his eyes. She had to think fast.

"I was thinking about adding sliding doors like these, but wondered how safe they are." Delia gave the door another tug. "What do you think?" She gave the cop her most intriguing smile.

"I'd invest in an alarm system regardless. Especially since you live alone." His answer was civil but matter-of-fact.

Emily smiled and stepped around the unfriendly cop. "Amber, did you say your bedroom has a walk-in closet?"

"Yeah. You want to see it?"

"Sure."

The cop walked ahead of them and closed the door to one of the bedrooms. *Something to hide?* Delia smiled at him seductively as she brushed past.

Amber showed her how her closet had been extended by claiming a corner of the garage. Delia was only half listening to her, paying more attention to the layout of Amber's bedroom and the original, not so sturdy windows.

Delia wasn't sure how long the cop had been standing in the doorway when she finally saw him. He was studying her every move.

"Let me guess, you're thinking of replacing your windows, too?" He asked as he stared her down.

~~~

Amber looked at Cooper with a frown. His rude behavior was embarrassing and uncalled for. It was still her house after all.

She and Emily walked back to the front door where they spent a couple minutes talking. After saying their goodbyes, Amber marched to where Cooper was standing by the kitchen, watching Emily walk away.

"You want to tell me why you were being so rude?" Amber asked, as he glanced out the kitchen window one more time, then turned to her.

"She was snooping around, and I didn't like it."

"Emily wasn't snooping. She was just trying to get some decorating ideas. You know, not everyone is a criminal."

"Yeah. Whatever," he said as he walked out of the kitchen. "I'll be in the other room if you need me. I have a few things I want to check out."

Steven and Amber curled up to watch a Disney classic. A peasant girl dancing with a beast was a lot safer than getting caught up in another romantic comedy. Especially when it turned out to be more romantic than comedy.

Amber watched Steven watch the movie and realized he really wasn't watching it at all. He was quieter than normal, distracted even. He'd had a hushed conversation with Cooper while she had been washing the dinner dishes. And since then, he seemed to be somewhere far away.

"What are you thinking?" she finally asked.

"Nothing."
~~~

"Then why are you so quiet?"

"I'm watching the movie."

"Really?" Amber grabbed the remote from him and pressed pause. "Then what just happened?"

He stuttered and Amber laughed. "Ha! I caught you. You weren't even watching the movie. Now tell me, what has you so distracted?"

With a mischievous smile, Steven grabbed her by the shoulders and pulled her down on his lap. His eyes danced as he stared down at her. "I was wondering why you haven't accepted my proposal."

Amber looked up at him and ran her finger across the perpetual stubble on his jaw. "Steven, you know why. I told you, I want all this behind us and a clean bill of health. Besides, I haven't even met your family yet."

"You can meet them at the wedding." He grinned.

Cooper clicked away at his computer but was getting nowhere. So far, Emily Johnson—Tucson resident—still checked out. He split the blinds on the window of Amber's office and peered out towards Emily's backyard. He was staring at nothing in particular when something caught his eye. A shadow disappearing alongside Emily's house.

Cooper jumped into action, signaling Jones to back him up. Steven must've heard the commotion because he came rushing out of Amber's room. "What's wrong?" he asked.

"It's probably nothing. Just stay with Amber."

Cooper drew his weapon and silently slipped into the backyard. He edged his way to the fence separating Amber and Emily's yard and shimmied through the loose board in the fence. Emily's house was almost completely dark. The only illumination was the bluish glow from a television screen. Cooper watched and waited. He crept closer when he heard conversation coming from inside. He heard both a male and female voice but couldn't make out what was being said. When he risked looking inside an open window, he was shocked. *Emily moved in weeks ago. Why is the living room still filled with boxes?*

Cooper waited a few more minutes, trying to decipher what was being said. Then he realized what he was hearing wasn't a conversation at all but two people hot and heavy in the throes of passion. *Well, it seems she's rebounding nicely. Didn't waste much time, did you, Emily?*

Cooper quietly made his way back to where Jones was watching his six and motioned him to head to the house.

"So what was it?" Steven asked as Cooper slid the door shut.

"It seems Emily has a—" Cooper turned to see Amber clutched to Steven's side, looking terrified. He thought twice about the disparaging comment he was going to say. "Aah . . . I saw someone in Emily's yard and overreacted."

Amber gasped. "Is she okay? Did you talk to her?"

"No, I didn't talk to her, but she's fine."

"How do you know if you didn't talk to her? What if the person you saw was her husband? What if he found her and she's in danger? Or hurt?"

"I said she was fine, Amber. Just let it go."

Amber scowled at him. "How can I let it go? She told me the horrible things her husband did to her. You need to check. You need to make sure she's okay."

"She was having sex, Amber!" he snapped. "I could hear them. Both of them. And believe me, she was enjoying it just as much as he was."

Amber sunk into the chair, clearly shocked. Cooper immediately regretted being so crude. "Amber, I'm sorry. I shouldn't have said that."

"But it doesn't make sense. She didn't say anything to me about seeing another man."

"Maybe she just met him," Jones added.

"Well, if they just met, they certainly wouldn't be . . . so physical."

"You don't know that, Amber. In fact, you don't know much about Emily at all," Cooper said as he took a seat on the couch.

"Maybe Emily isn't who you think she is."

"What do you mean?" Amber was clearly puzzled.

"I know you said she was from Tucson, and that she left a violent husband, but has she said anything else?" Cooper asked intently.

"Like what?"

"Other family? What she does for a living? She's home all the time. Does Emily work out of her home?"

"I don't know. She said something about computer work." Amber paused. "I think Emily is a computer analyst of some kind. I didn't ask her much more about it because I'm so illiterate when it comes to computers."

"What about family?"

"She doesn't have any."

"And this husband of hers, did she ever give you a name? Or say anything about filing for divorce?"

Amber closed her eyes, reviewing their conversations. "Emily never said his name but did say she hadn't filed for divorce yet. Emily didn't want to take the chance of her husband finding out where she was." Amber bit her bottom lip, all of a sudden looking nervous.

"What else, Amber?" Cooper pressed.

"What do you mean?"

"You're thinking something. What is it?"

Amber looked at Cooper and then at Jones. "Emily said she went to the police and filed a report but was treated so badly, she dropped the charges. Emily said they treated her like a criminal instead of a victim. That's why she decided to run."

Cooper flinched. That was lie number one. He'd already checked to see if Emily had filed a report. Even if the charges had been dropped there would've been a record of it. He didn't say anything because he didn't want to alarm Amber or Steven. But it was clear, Emily was lying about something. Now he needed to find out why?

❧❧❧❧

Amber thought back over the dozens of conversations she'd had with Emily. She realized they never really talked about much more than Emily's abuse and Amber's attack. Amber didn't want Cooper and Jones to know she had breached the subject, let alone that Emily had figured out they were the police. She was sure Cooper was overreacting and didn't want to do anything that would fracture her relationship with Emily.

"So, Emily never said anything to you about hooking up with someone since moving here?" Cooper asked.

"No. But maybe Emily didn't want me to know she was seeing someone when she wasn't even divorced," Amber said defensively.

"So, did she say why she hasn't bothered to unpack yet?"

"What?"

"I could see into her living room. It's filled with boxes but no furniture. Emily moved in three weeks ago. Don't you think if she worked out of her home, she would've had time to put things away by now?"

Amber remembered a conversation Emily had with her just a few days ago. She talked about wanting to get a new sofa because her old one was too big for her living room. Amber just assumed Emily had already set up her house.

"Look, Amber, I don't want to overreact or anything, but do me a favor. I don't want you having Emily over to the house or even in the backyard while we're gone, okay? Let me do a little more checking, see if I can find out a little bit more about her."

"What are you thinking?" Steven pressed the issue.

"I don't know. It's probably nothing. But I'd feel better if I got a few more answers."

FIFTY-TWO

Cooper and Jones said their goodbyes to her and Steven in the morning. Amber was surprised she felt so emotional. She realized even though their relationship had started under adverse conditions, the four of them had actually become friends.

"Now, remember what I said about Emily," Cooper reminded.

"I will. Though I don't see what the big deal is. So she didn't tell me about a boyfriend. Maybe it was a one-night stand, or she was afraid I'd be too judgmental."

"Humor me, okay? I'll be by tonight anyway. I'll let you know if I find out anything."

Amber watched as Steven walked Cooper and Jones to the front door and locked it behind them. For the first time in a very long time, she and Steven were alone—something Amber was acutely aware of. She nervously straightened things around the living room until Steven took her by the hand and led her over to the couch and sat down next to her.

"I'm glad we finally have some time to ourselves," he said as he squeezed her hand. "I have something for you."

Amber watched as Steven pulled something from his pants pocket. She gasped when she saw the small black velvet box in his hand.

Steven lowered himself to one knee, then flipped open the little box, exposing an exquisite vintage diamond ring. Amber only saw it for a moment before tears blurred her vision.

"I've thought about this moment for days and wanted to woo

you with the most romantic speech. But I couldn't find the words to tell you how I feel. All I know is, I want to spend the rest of my life with you. I want to share my popcorn with you at the movies. I want to drape my jacket over your shoulders on a date when I tell you it's chilly outside, but you insist it's too warm for a coat. I promise not to squeeze the toothpaste from the middle or put the toilet paper roll in backward. I won't leave my clothes on the bathroom floor and will never purposely embarrass you in public. I'll teach you all my Skeeball tricks if you teach me about aperture settings and shutter speeds.

"Amber, I want to wake up with you in my arms every morning, and I want your lips to be the last thing I taste at night. I don't know any other way to say it. I love you, Amber, and I want to marry you. Please say yes."

Amber swiped at the tears running down her cheeks. She was not prepared for this.

At all.

Steven closed the box and set it aside. He held both of Amber's hands to his chest as he spoke. "Amber, I don't need you to protect me. I know what I want, and I want you. Nothing's going to change that."

"How can you be so sure, Steven?" she said, her bottom lip quivering. "What about my tests?"

"No matter what they say, it's not going to change the way I feel about you. About us. Even if you test positive, HIV is no longer considered an immediate death sentence. We'll get through it, no matter what."

"But what about children?"

"If we can't have our own biological children, we'll adopt. We could make a real difference in the life of a child, or two, or seven," he said, with growing excitement.

"But what happens when your friends find out who it is you're seeing? It's been in the papers and on the news. You're dating a rape victim, Steven, someone who's had degrading things done to her by other men. How can that not change things?"

"Because I love you."

He framed her face and looked at her deeply. "I won't pressure you, Amber, because I want you to be as sure about this as I am."

"What if I can't be sure?"

"Do you love me, Amber?"

She squeezed her eyes shut and lowered her head. "You know that I do, but it's just not that easy." She tried to move away, but he wouldn't let her go.

"Yes, it is. It's just that easy."

Steven wrapped her in his arms, her tears wetting the front of his shirt. She drank in his strength, pleading with God to make this one prayer come true. When she looked up into Steven's amazing blue eyes, he pressed his lips to hers. There was only one word to describe his kiss.

Love.

FIFTY-THREE

Nothing could ruin the day for Amber. She was putting her faith in God, knowing He would protect Steven and their future together. When Steven had slipped the beautiful engagement ring on her finger, she nearly danced from one window to the next, watching the way it sparkled and glimmered in the light.

Steven finally reined her in and pulled her close. He contained her with his arms and held her with his eyes. His kiss was soft, gentle, but soon hinted at the desire stirring inside him.

Amber returned Steven's affection, wanting nothing more than to banish from her mind the nightmares and worries that threaten to take her joy away.

Steven pulled back, resting his forehead against hers. "Are you okay?" Steven whispered.

She nodded, not trusting herself to speak.

Framing her face with his hands, Steven lightly pressed a kiss to each of her eyelids, causing her heart to race. He nuzzled her earlobe and explored her neck with his lips. Steven touched her like no man had. Everything with him would be new. Different. Her fear of intimacy was just that. A fear. Something she would need to put behind her. But, in that instant, as Steven's fingers grazed the tender scaring behind her ear, Amber flinched. She felt the bat, she saw frenzied eyes, she smelled the musty earth.

Steven took a step back, but Amber held onto him. "I'm okay." She looked at him through the mist covering her eyes, ready to apologize for breaking the mood.

"But I'm not." He paced across the room, running his fingers through his wavy hair, taking deep cleansing breaths. "Okay, I can't let that happen again. I'm not that strong."

Amber realized Steven hadn't pulled away because of her reaction, but because of his own impulses. "I'm sorry. You're right. We need to take things slow."

"So, when can we set the date?" he blurted out.

"What?" Amber was completely confused. "I just said we should take things slow."

"Well, yeah. But I have to know how much stamina I need to build up."

Shocked at his candidness, Amber reached for the pillow on the chair and threw it at him.

He laughed and tossed the pillow back at her. "Hey, I'm only being truthful."

They teased and kissed, hugged and cuddled the next few hours. Even though Amber agreed to wear Steven's ring, she refused to set a wedding date. They could talk about a future together, but she wouldn't plan for it until she was more certain of what lay ahead.

Steven busied himself with lunch while Amber stared out the patio door. When she turned around, she caught Steven staring at her.

"What are you thinking?" he asked, as he set down their sandwich plates on the coffee table.

"I just don't get it. Why didn't Emily tell me she had a boyfriend? I mean, I told her about you."

"And what did you tell her?" He bounced his brow and grinned.

"Never mind." She hated the way Steven could so easily make her blush. She tried to hide her grin, but nothing could diminish the permanent smile on her face.

She sat down next to him and listened as he prayed for them and their future. Then watched as he ate his sandwich with gusto while she just played with hers.

"Amber, if you don't start doing more with your food than playing with it, you're going to wither away to nothing. Is that fair to me? I'll have nothing to hold on to when we're making out."

It was clear Steven intended to keep her cheeks red and her heart racing the rest of the day. He turned his attention back to his lunch, but only for a few minutes.

"So, do you think we'll be able to get it in before the end of the year?" he asked between bites.

"What?"

"Our wedding."

"Steven, I said I wasn't going to set a date until after this whole mess was over, and we know more about the health risks."

"I didn't agree to that. Yes, I want this all behind us, but I'm not going to make it a prerequisite. Just tell me, how long do you think it will take for you to pull it all together?"

"I don't know. I've never planned a wedding before."

"Give me a ballpark. One week? Three weeks? Three months?"

"Steven," she laughed. "I really don't know."

"Okay, then give me an outline. Big? Small? Daytime? Nighttime?"

Amber leaned back against the couch cushions and closed her eyes. She had never really thought about her own wedding though she'd photographed quite a few. But there was one in particular that stuck out in her memory.

"There's a small church downtown that's incredible. It was built in the early 1900s. All brick with amazing stained-glass windows."

"You mean the one on Ninth and Willow?"

"Yeah, you know it?"

"Of course. The architectural detail is incredible. It's one of my favorite buildings in the city."

"Well, I photographed an evening wedding there last year. It was amazing. The way the church backlit the windows . . . I can't even begin to describe the colors. It was incredible. And huge antique candelabras basked the altar in an ethereal glow. It was very romantic."

"Sounds perfect," Steven smiled.

"But it's pretty small."

"I think a small, evening wedding would be nice. And no reception. I mean, unless you have your heart set on one."

"No. I don't need one but what about your mother? Won't she be disappointed if you don't have a big wedding and reception?"

Steven put his plate down and leaned back to join Amber in the comfort of the cushions. "No, she knows me better than that. I've never been one for big parties. Besides, I never understood why a couple that's just gotten married would subject themselves to that kind of torture."

"Torture? A reception isn't *that* bad."

"Are you kidding me? Spending hours having dinner with family and making polite conversation with friends is the last thing I want to do on my wedding night. If you know what I mean," Steven chuckled.

Amber didn't see the humor in Steven's remark. It only heightened her anxiety. One of her biggest fears was how she would respond to intimacy, and Steven's comment only served to emphasize his obvious anticipation.

"I was only teasing, Amber," Steven whispered as he pulled her to his side. "We're going to have the rest of our lives to share intimate moments. We'll just take our time. Having you in my arms, all to myself, night after night, is going to be a gift in itself. Everything else will fall into place. Trust me, Amber. We're going to be fine."

She nodded, not wanting Steven to doubt that she trusted him. But God would have to do a work in her to free her from the fears that haunted her.

Closing her eyes, Amber tried pushing the negativity from her mind and decided instead to think of the details that would make their wedding special. She saw no reason for it to take months to plan. If they had a small, intimate setting, it would limit the guest list and the time needed for preparations. She would be completely satisfied with Steven, herself, and Craig officiating. But knew that wasn't realistic.

Amber thought about her father and sister, knowing she would have to call them, dreading the conversations that would transpire. Her father would have something negative to say, even though Steven was from a good family and quite successful in his own right. Erika would be cynical, probably saying something snarky about Amber's inexperience with men. Her sister would belittle her naivety and blame it on her faith in God.

Amber didn't want to hear what they had to say. She didn't want to listen as they questioned Steven's intentions. He was far too good for that. Amber sat quietly, her thoughts ricocheting from one insecurity to another.

When Steven got up and reached for her plate, she realized she had checked out. "I can get those," she said.

"I've got it." Steven continued to stack their dishes. "I thought maybe you had fallen asleep. You were so quiet."

"No, just thinking."

"About eloping?" Steven said with a playful smile.

"Is that what you'd like to do?" Amber hadn't even thought about eloping. It certainly would make things simpler. But, there was a part of her that wanted to get married in a church. There was just something about it that made it seem so much more . . . solemn.

"Nah . . . I thought about it, but my mother and Stacy would never let me live it down if I got married without them being there."

Steven walked to the kitchen just as his cell phone began to ring. He set the plates down on the counter and reached into his pocket, answering his phone as he walked back into the living room.

"Hey, Stace, what's up?"

Amber saw the color drain from Steven's face. He massaged his brow and swallowed hard. "What happened?"

Amber watched his demeanor and knew whatever his sister was telling him wasn't good. Steven listened and nodded. "Okay. I'll call you back in a minute." He disconnected the call and slid his phone back into his pocket.

"Steven, what's wrong?"

"It's my mom. She's been taken to the hospital with chest pains."

"Oh no, Steven, what happened?"

"They're not sure yet. Stacy is going to drop the kids off with Rosa and get to the hospital." He looked at her. "I really need to be there."

"Of course you do."

"Let me call Cooper, tell him you're going to be here alone."

She jumped from the couch and stopped him. "Steven, I'll be fine. Just go."

"But you shouldn't be here alone."

Steven looked overwhelmed.

"Cooper said he would be coming over this evening anyway. He'll be here soon enough. Just go."

"Are you sure you feel okay about being alone?"

Amber could see the anxiety in his eyes. "I'm positive." She squeezed his arm to be more reassuring. "You need to go." Reaching up, she gave him a gentle kiss.

Steven nodded. He pulled his phone from his pocket once again and called his sister back to get some more information. Amber was finishing up in the kitchen when she noticed Emily pulling out of her driveway and away from the house. She had a flickering thought but quickly dismissed it.

Steven slipped his phone into his pocket and hurried towards the door. He gave Amber another kiss and started to rattle off a list of instructions.

"I'll be fine, Steven. Now go."

Amber said a silent prayer for Steven, Stacy, and their mom, as she watched him pull away from the curb. She knew from experience how difficult it was to watch as your mother's health declined. She didn't want Steven to go through that same pain.

Amber busied herself around the house, waiting for some kind of news from Steven. When it finally came, she was relieved to hear his mother was doing okay, and that Steven had been able to see her. She was scheduled to have an angioplasty in the morning; so Amber encouraged Steven to stay with his mother and his family.

"You're sure you're okay?"

"I'm fine, Steven. You need to stay there."

"Okay, but as soon as visiting hours are over, I'll come home. I'll call to let you know when I'm on my way. And Amber . . . I love you."

"I love you, too."

When Amber hung up the phone, she caught herself staring at Emily's house, curiosity getting the better of her. Why hadn't Emily unpacked, but made it sound like she did? And if she was seeing someone, why hadn't Emily told her?

Amber stepped into the backyard as the sun began to sink below the tree line. Her curiosity drew her to the fence that separated the two houses. Knowing Emily wasn't there, Amber pushed on the loose picket and watched it swing. She shouldn't even be considering what she was thinking, but couldn't help wondering what Emily was hiding from her and why?

Amber carefully stepped through the passageway to Emily's backyard. She stood by the fence for a few moments, feeling awkward, like an intruder. She was spying on her friend and it didn't feel right. *If we're friends, why did she lie to me?* After easing her conscience, Amber moved closer to Emily's house.

It was getting dark fast, and with the cover of dusk, Amber got a little bolder. She peered into the window of one of the bedrooms and was surprised to see a mattress tossed on the floor and a small plastic storage tote being used as a nightstand. *Why hasn't she at least fixed up her bedroom?* Then Amber looked through the back door straight through to the living room. Boxes were lined up against the wall just like Cooper said. *I don't get it. Where's the couch Emily said was too big?*

Amber moved along the outside wall to another bedroom window, but couldn't see in. Even though the shades weren't closed tight, they were closed enough, only letting faint stripes of light filter through. Amber was ready to give up when the shadow of a figure move by the window. She covered her mouth to smother her scream and dropped down against the side of the building. With her heart racing out of control, she questioned her senses. *Did I imagine it?* It could've been Emily, but Amber would've heard the electric garage door if she had come home. What if Emily's *friend* was still in the house?

Just then, Amber heard the muffled ringing of a telephone, then realized it was hers. She had left the sliding door open and could hear the distant sound. If she raced to answer the phone the person inside Emily's house might hear her. But if she took her time, the message machine would pick it up. *Please don't let it be Steven. He'll go crazy if I don't pick up the phone.*

Slowly, Amber got up from where she was crouched against the house and started toward the fence. When she was only a few steps from the loose picket, Amber heard Emily's back door open. She froze, not knowing what to do, hoping the shadows from the large elm tree were giving her some much-needed camouflage.

Amber waited for what felt like an eternity, knowing she was going to get caught. How would she explain to Emily what she was doing in her backyard? Amber heard the door close and waited—waited to see if the person was outside or had gone back into the house. Hearing only the brush of wind stirring the leaves, she cautiously moved towards the fence.

She swung the picket out of the way but before she could step through, a hand came across her mouth and clamped it shut. Amber clawed at a hairy forearm as it jerked her against a hard body and dragged her back across the yard towards Emily's house.

Her mind spun out of control. She pictured the park, the rain, the jogging path. Then she saw the backyard, the elm tree, the moving boxes. Amber struggled but it was no use. The man dragging her was twice her size, leaving her powerless to do anything. When he slammed the door shut behind them, Amber lashed about more, trying to break free. When she heard a click next to her ear, she froze. The man had a gun pointed directly at her.

"Sweetheart, you just made our job a whole lot easier."

FIFTY-FOUR

Cooper knew something was wrong. He could feel it. Clenching the photo of Emily in his hand, he dialed Steven's cell. *She was under our noses the whole time.*

"Steven, where's Amber?" Cooper asked.

"At home, why?"

"You mean you're not with her?" Cooper's words were sharp.

"No. I'm at the hospital. My mother—" Steven stopped midsentence. "What's wrong, Cooper?"

"It's Emily. She's a hired gun out of Chicago."

Steven yelled, "She's what?"

"It's a long story. Look, I called the house but Amber didn't answer."

"I don't understand."

"Steven, I think Amber might be in trouble. I'm on my way there now."

"I'll meet you there," Steven said, sounding panicked.

"No! This is a police matter. If Amber is in some sort of trouble, you'll only make matters worse. We have to find out what we're dealing with first."

"You already know what you're dealing with. A hired killer."

Cooper could hear the panic in Steven's tone. He didn't blame him, but he couldn't let Steven end up in the middle of what could be a very volatile situation. "I'll call you as soon as I know something, but until then, I need you to stay away from Amber's house."

ᘛᘚ

Steven collapsed into a chair, fighting off the sick feeling threatening to explode within him.

"Steven what's wrong?" Stacy moved to his side.

"It's Amber." He stood and paced like a caged animal. "Her neighbor, the one she's been making friends with, she's . . . Cooper said . . . she's a hired gun out of Chicago." Steven looked at his sister, not even comprehending it himself. He began to back away from Stacy. "I've got to go. Cooper called the house and no one answered. Pray Stacy. Pray nothing's happened to Amber."

"I will, Steven. But please . . . please be careful."

He ran down the corridor to the stairwell and was in a full sprint by the time he reached the hospital parking lot.

ᘛᘚ

The man flung Amber on the bed, slamming her head against the wall. Dazed momentarily, she waited for the room to stop spinning before righting herself to a sitting position.

The huge man filled the doorway, his gun trained on her. "I knew Delia would screw up. She waited too long and now look what happened."

"Who's Delia?" Amber asked, confused.

"Oh, I'm sorry, she's Emily to you. You know, your new best bud." His tone smug and vile.

Amber heard what he was saying but had a hard time believing it. "Who are you?" she asked, her voice sounding a little more controlled.

"Someone you don't want to know," he sneered.

"I don't understand."

"Our boy Jack, you know . . . your little boyfriend from the park. Well, we need him. He has some valuable information from his cellmate that he was supposed to pass on to us when he got out of the slammer. Unfortunately, he and his idiot brother couldn't keep their pants up long enough to stay out of trouble. We can't let the cops get to him before we get the information we need. You, on the other hand, are disposable."

He stood at the foot of the mattress, his eyes raking over Amber, making her feel sick. Glancing at the clock on the side table, she knew Cooper would be at the house any minute. She needed to buy more time. "You can't kill me. The police already know about Emily." Amber bluffed—trying to sound convincing. "The reason they pulled out was to force her to make a move." The man looked like he believed her, but only for a moment.

"You're lying. They never would've left you alone if they knew who Delia was."

The moan of the garage door got both of their attention. With the man distracted, Amber pushed to her feet and was going to run, but the man swung back around, the gun once again on her. "Don't try anything, or I'll kill you right now."

Amber sunk back to the mattress as the man stepped out into the hallway. She heard the door to the garage open and Emily's voice as she walked down the hallway. "What are you still doing here, Mannie? Someone will see you."

"We had a little intruder," Mannie said, nodding towards the bedroom.

When Emily saw Amber sitting on the bed, the woman's face twisted in anger. "What are you doing here?"

"I thought I was visiting a friend," Amber spit out, fueled by her own anger. "Who are you?"

"The name's Delia. Not that it matters. Unfortunately, you won't be around much longer."

Delia turned to Mannie. "What's going on?"

"She says the cops know who you are," Mannie answered, but kept his eyes trained on Amber.

The woman glared at her. "Really?" she said with a devilish grin. "Then how is it you're here and no one has come looking for you?"

"They're setting you up," Amber said assuredly.

"She's bluffing," Delia said as she dropped the bag of groceries on the counter.

Amber heard Delia's hurried footsteps as she crossed to the

living room, then back to the bedroom doorway. "Their cars aren't out front. Not even the boyfriend's." She turned to Amber. "Where's Steven?"

"He left right after you. He was told to watch where you went and to see if you were meeting with anyone." Amber tried to sound confident though inside she was convinced she would never see Steven again.

Delia glared at Amber, clearly trying to read her. "I don't believe you." The woman ran her fingers through her hair then turned to Mannie. "We can't kill her here. We have to stick to the plan."

"But what if she's telling the truth? What if they do know about you? We need to get this over with and get out of here fast."

"Shut up, Mannie!" she hollered. "I need to think."

Delia walked from the room while Mannie followed her, blathering on, the two ending up in a shouting match. It was obvious to Amber that Delia was running the show and didn't appreciate Mannie's interference.

With Mannie's back turned, Amber looked around frantically for anything she could use as a weapon. Then, she remembered scenes from old B-rated movies. The criminals always had a gun stashed under their pillows.

That's the movies. This is real life, and they are real killers.

Unable to think of a better idea, Amber began to search the pillows that were haphazardly tossed against the wall, while keeping her eye on Mannie. She felt under each of them.

Nothing.

She felt along the wall the mattress was pushed up against.

Nothing.

She knew it was a long shot but kept searching. When she ran her hand around the edges of the mattress, her hand brushed against metal.

Bingo.

ॐॐ

Hastings and Jones joined Cooper and the SWAT team at the

command post set up down the alley from Amber's house. The SWAT team had been practicing some tactical training at an abandoned warehouse when they got the call. They were on scene and briefed in less than an hour.

With the assumption that Delia had Amber—and was probably watching the front of the house expecting Steven to return—Cooper snuck through Amber's backyard and into her house. He reported back that nothing looked disturbed or out of place. The only thing that wasn't right was the back door standing wide open, and Amber nowhere in sight.

The dreaded thought everyone was thinking, but no one wanted to verbalize, was the realization that Amber could already be dead. Delia had had plenty of time to eliminate her. But they didn't know that for sure so they would treat it as a possible hostage situation.

Cooper called Steven. "I need to ask you a few questions. Where are you?"

"I'm on my way to Amber's, but I got caught behind a huge accident on the interchange. I'm about six blocks away."

Cooper could hear the panic in Steven's voice and knew he was a cannon just waiting to go off. "You can't go to Amber's."

"Just try to stop me," Steven argued.

"Steven, don't be stupid. You'll only be endangering Amber further. This is a police matter and an unpredictable one at that."

"Amber might be a "matter" to you, but she's everything to me. I need to be there."

Cooper sighed, knowing he wouldn't be able to stop him. "Fine. We've set up a command post east of Amber's house in the back alley. You can meet us there. But I still need to ask you a few questions. I need to construct a timeline. When was the last time you saw or spoke with Amber?"

❧❧❧❧

Steven looked at his phone and checked what time Stacy had called him. "I probably left about five minutes after getting my sister's call."

"Did you talk to Amber since?"

"Yes. I called to let her know my mother was scheduled for surgery in the morning."

"What time was that?"

Still stuck in traffic, Steven checked his outgoing calls. "Over an hour ago." Plenty of time for his world to come crashing down around him. "This is my fault. I shouldn't have left Amber alone."

When Steven arrived at the command post, Cooper tried to console him.

"Steven, we're dealing with professionals. Even if you had been with Amber when everything went down, you wouldn't have been able to stop them. You just would've ended up dead."

It was little consolation to Steven.

He had broken his promise.

He'd left her alone.

History was repeating itself.

Steven watched and listened as Cooper turned his attention back to Hastings, and the instructions he was giving.

"There's a possibility Delia's working with an accomplice. We're going to try and confirm that before we make entry. Here's a picture of Amber," Hastings passed around. "We need to make sure she doesn't get caught in the crossfire."

After obtaining a map of Delia's house, Hastings assigned everyone a task or a location of entry. Steven watched as the SWAT team pointman quietly entered Emily/Delia's backyard.

❧❧❧❧

The pistol Amber had found was small. Compact enough to slip into her back pocket. Thankfully her recent weight loss allowed for the extra room in her jeans. Luckily, it didn't make much of an impression, or so she hoped.

"We've got to get her out of here, that's all there is to it." Amber heard Delia say before she stalked back into the bedroom and stared at her with a look of pure hatred. "You're tougher than I gave you credit for." Delia's words were blunt, without feeling. "I thought you would've been begging and pleading by now."

Amber couldn't believe how much Delia's demeanor had changed. Gone was the sweet, talkative neighbor, only to be replaced by a woman who looked callous. Vindictive. Heartless.

"Is that what you want? For me to beg and plead?" Amber's words were fueled by anger. "Would that work? Would that buy me my life or just make you feel more powerful? I tried begging and pleading once. It got me nowhere."

"Well what do you know, the goody-two-shoes has a mouth," Delia retorted.

"Why are you doing this? Why won't you just let me go?" Amber questioned. "You could be thousands of miles away from here before anyone finds out who you are."

"Because I was sent to do a job, and that's what I'm going to do. This is just a minor setback."

Delia knelt down on the bed next to Amber and pressed her gun against Amber's neck. "Where's Steven? And this time, I want the truth."

Amber swallowed. "He's at the hospital."

"Why?"

"His mother was taken there today. She's having surgery."

"When did you talk to him last?"

"When he left the house. But I heard my phone ring when I was in the backyard. I'm sure it had to be him. He's probably on his way here right now, wondering why I didn't answer."

"Okay, this is what you're going to do." Delia pulled out her own phone and held it out to Amber. "You're going to call Steven and tell him you're doing fine and that his place is with his mother. And don't try any tricks, because if you do, I swear to you, you'll be dead before he hangs up. Then I'll find Steven and cut him up into little pieces."

Amber's biggest fear had become reality. Steven was in danger because of her. "But he'll know it's not my cell phone number." Amber was only bluffing. Steven didn't even know her cell phone number. He'd never used it.

"Then I guess you'll have to tell him something convincing."

Delia pushed the gun into Amber's neck to make her point.

"Why?" Mannie questioned. "Just blow her away and let's get out of here. We've been here too long, and the plan is already ruined. We need to get out of here while we can."

"No! No! No! I was sent to do a job you idiot, and that's what I'm going to do!"

She shoved the phone at Amber again. "Now call."

With shaky hands Amber dialed, knowing she wouldn't be able to tip Steven off, not with Delia so close.

Not with his life in danger.

FIFTY-FIVE

Steven's phone rang. He looked at the caller ID. Unidentified. "What if it's Amber? What should I do?" He looked at Hastings who was standing beside him.

"Listen," Hastings said in a calm tone. "Listen for any clues she might try to give you. Chances are someone will be listening in, so don't say anything that would put Amber on the spot. It will only put her in more danger. So just listen."

If Steven didn't hurry and answer his phone, it would roll over to voicemail. So, he touched the screen and tried to sound calm while coming up with a plan of his own. "Hello."

Tears sprung to Amber's eyes. "Hi, Steven, it's Amber." She concentrated hard to ensure her voice sounded normal.

"Hey, Amber, is everything all right?" Steven coughed and hacked.

Amber looked at Delia, knowing she heard Steven's question. "Yes, I'm fine. I just thought I'd see how your mother was doing?"

"She's fine . . . but they won't let me see her because of this stupid cold I have."

Amber's heart raced. Steven was acting strange. He didn't have a cold, and he had already told her he'd been in to see his mother. Maybe he knew she was in trouble.

"I'll be home in about an hour if that's okay?" Steven said. "Stacy asked me to pick up the kids from her friend's house and take them over to Rosa."

But the kids were already with Rosa.

Now Amber was sure Steven knew something was wrong. She had to think fast, had to think of something to say.

"I did that yard work I talked about today," she blurted out.

Delia squeezed Amber's arm, telling her to hurry up.

"You did?"

"Yeah. Not much, because it was getting dark. But it felt good to be out of the house."

"Good. But you're in the house now, aren't you?"

"Yes. I promise. I'm in the house now."

"Okay. Then I guess I'll see you in about an hour."

"Okay." Amber could feel the emotion inside her clawing to the surface. "Steven?"

"Yes?"

"I love you."

"I love you, too, Amber. I'll be home in no time."

Amber canceled the call and tossed the phone on the bed. Delia snatched it up.

"You were supposed to tell him to stay at the hospital."

"I'm sorry. I got confused."

"What was all that garbage about gardening?"

"I had told Steven I wanted to do some yard work. I figured I had to tell him something before he asked me what I was doing."

Delia looked unconvinced.

Amber knew she had to do something to avoid more questions so she began to sob and cry uncontrollably. "I did the best I could. I was terrified. I rambled but Steven is used to that. What more do you want from me?" Amber acted as if she was an emotional wreck, and it worked.

Delia got up from the bed and walked over to Mannie. "Get her ready to move."

"Why? Just do it here."

"Are you that stupid, Mannie? We can't leave her here. We need to make it look like her attackers found her. We're sticking to the plan. We'll take her back to her place, toss some things around, mess her up a little, and shoot her with the gun that has Morris' fingerprints on it. We'll leave the gun at the scene and bingo, we hold all the cards. Once Morris knows he's wanted for two murders, he'll do whatever we say."

✥✥✥✥

Steven waited with Cooper and Hastings alongside the command post vehicle, his heart racing so fast, he was sure he was going to pass out.

Jones walked over to where the group was standing. "The phone Amber used was a burner phone. We got nothing."

"I figured as much," Hastings said, "but we had to make sure."

Just then, the SWAT team pointman hurried out of Amber's backyard and over to where they stood. "I was able to identify three voices," he said. "Two females and a male."

Three? God, no! Steven begged. *Please don't let it be one of the Morris brothers.*

"It has to be one of the brothers," Hastings said.

"I don't think so," the pointman corrected. "From what I could hear, they plan on taking Amber back to her house, killing her, and framing one of the Morris brothers with the murder. So unless one brother flipped on the other, whoever's in there is an unknown. Either way, we've got to act fast if we're going to get someone inside Amber's place before they move."

Immediately, Cooper grabbed for a Kevlar vest and slipped it over his head while talking to Hastings. "Let me get inside," he said, as he snaked his earpiece through the vest. "Send two men around front. I'll let them in. I know the layout of the house and the best vantage points. Delia—and whoever's with her—will probably bring Amber through the backyard. When they do, see if someone can take them down while they're outside. If not, we'll be inside waiting for a clean shot. Between the three of us, and the element of surprise, we should be able to take them out."

"But what about Amber?" Steven asked. "She'll be in the middle of all of it."

Cooper put a reassuring hand on Steven's shoulder and looked him straight in the eyes. "I won't let anything happen to Amber. I'll get her out, Steven, I promise."

Hastings nodded his approval, and everyone jumped into action. Steven watched as Cooper quickly scaled the fence and disappeared into the shadows.

Steven paced. Anxiety coursing through his body. He knew Cooper and the other men would do everything they could to ensure Amber's safety, but what if something went wrong? What if something happened to Amber . . . No! *I can't think like that. I won't think like that. Amber's a survivor. A fighter. She'll get through this.*

She just has to.

Steven prayed feverishly.

❧❧❧❧

Mannie pulled Amber to her feet and swung her around. He reached for her hands and drew them behind her, taping her wrists together. She thought for sure he would see the gun shoved into her pocket, but luckily her untucked blouse covered it. Of course with her hands taped behind her back, there wasn't much chance of her using the gun. Amber had tried to position her hands so there would be a gap. If she could work free of the bindings she might be able to get away.

Mannie stuffed a gag in her mouth and led her to the back door. Delia joined them, holding a baggie with a gun in it. "See this? We have Morris' fingerprints on this gun." Delia moved closer to Amber and whispered, "You remember Jack, don't you?"

Amber's memory pulled her back to the park and to one of the men who had raped her and left her for dead.

"Did you enjoy your little rendezvous with him? Because he sure enjoyed being with you. He told us all about it." Delia ran her finger down the length of Amber's arm, causing her body to shudder. "He told us how soft your skin was and how you begged for him to stop. He said it turned him on."

Amber knew what Delia was doing, and even though she tried to fight it, it was working. Amber felt weak and afraid. Her emotions caused her body to shake, and her mind was numbed by fear. She tried pushing through the memories of that day, needing to keep her wits about her—to keep looking for a way of escape. She tried to block out Delia's words, but the woman continued to taunt her with graphic details that only her attacker would know.

"I'm surprised Steven even looks at you, knowing how dirty you are," Delia laughed, sounding wicked and hideous. "Do you think he's jealous of Jack and Jay because they've already had you?"

Amber's stomach lurched, the taste of bile saturating the gag in her mouth. *Don't listen to her. Stay strong. Concentrate on your hands.* Amber knew she had to get her hands free if she was going to have any chance at all.

"It's clear," Mannie said as he stood at the back door.

Delia pushed ahead of them and slowly walked towards the fence. She slipped through the opening and slowly approached Amber's house, then signaled Mannie to follow. When Mannie pushed the picket aside, Amber saw the stray nail that had caused her and Cara to tear so many shirts and blouses. Mannie gave her a shove.

Please, God. Let it catch the tape.

When Amber stepped through the picket, she felt the nail catch on the duct tape around her hands. Stumbling, the fence rattled, muffling the tearing sound of the tape. She fell to her knees with a groan. Delia's head snapped around, training a deadly stare on Amber.

Mannie stepped through the fence after her, not noticing the nail that tugged at his jacket. He yanked on Amber's elbow, pulling her to her feet. "Watch what you're doing," he whispered, the stench from his breath assaulting her.

Amber got to her feet and tested her tethers. The tape ripped a little more when she applied counter-pressure, making a raspy sound. Luckily, Mannie hadn't heard it. She would have to work slowly. Take her time.

Time she didn't have.

ô°ô°ô°ô°

Cooper was positioned inside the house. He chose the best vantage point, knowing he would only have one shot at taking Delia out. He listened to the transmissions between the SWAT team leader and his men as they watched Delia, Amber, and an unidentified man cross the backyard. They weren't able to get a bead on Delia because she darted inside the house so quickly, and they couldn't get a clean shot of the man holding Amber without endangering her.

"It's up to you, Cooper," he heard whispered in his earpiece. "Amber's gagged. Hands behind her back. The man with her is six foot. Sturdy. Both he and Delia have guns."

Cooper's heart pulsed with the transmission. He knew what he had to do. *God, don't let me screw it up.* He prayed for the first time in his life.

Two SWAT members had moved stealthily through the front door as Amber was led through the backyard. They took up positions on either side of the hall as Cooper crouched in the kitchen out of sight, listening as the two discussed their plan.

"Now what?" the man asked.

"Rough her up," Delia said, sounding cold and callous. "And Mannie, make it look convincing."

Mannie. They had a name. Cooper heard the blow. Heard Amber's muffled cry. But he couldn't do anything. He had to wait. Wait for the right time. He swore, hating that Amber was being assaulted and there was nothing he could do. *Hang in there, Amber. I'll get you out. Just hang on.*

ô°ô°ô°ô°

Amber was knocked off balance by the power of Mannie's blow. He looked at her, hunger glistening in his eyes. Amber was terrified. She had to get her hands free and get to the gun before Mannie found it.

He came towards her again, grabbing the back of her neck, drawing her closer. He pressed hard, violent kisses against her lips, and licked at the blood trickling from the gash he had opened on her cheek.

Amber squirmed as his hands roamed up and down her body. She felt the tape give a little more. Her hands would soon be free. But until then, she would have to put up with Mannie's abuse and wait for the perfect time to act.

He pushed her to the couch, smothering her with his massive body. Straddling Amber, Mannie yanked her blouse open, buttons scattering, exposing her white camisole.

৵৵৵৵

Cooper listened feeling ill. He wasn't sure where Delia was positioned. He couldn't take any chances in case she had a gun sighted on Amber. She would shoot to kill. That was her job. He hated himself for allowing Amber to be hurt, but he had no choice. He had to wait until he had a clean shot.

৵৵৵৵

Tears ran down Amber's face. She had to detach herself from what Mannie was doing and ignored the pain. Her mind focused on one thing. Freeing her hands, which were now pinned underneath her. *Help me, God.*

Amber glimpsed Delia watching with strange amusement. It was obvious she enjoyed Mannie's show of force. She pulled on a latex glove and removed the revolver from its bag. Amber knew she was almost out of time, but Mannie's aggressive frenzy made it difficult for her to move.

৵৵৵৵

Delia aimed the gun, but not at Amber. Instead, she pointed the barrel at Mannie, toying with the idea of getting rid of him, too. He was her nemesis, and she was tired of him showing up whenever she had a job to do. Delia hated herself for being weak around him. They always ended up in bed, and it angered her that he could manipulate her so easily. She would love to put a bullet in his head, but knew that would ruin the plan. No, for appearance sake, it would have to look as if Morris found Amber and finished off what he had already started.

Delia watched as Mannie tugged at Amber's jeans, pulling on

the button that held them closed, caught up in the fervor of his actions.

"That's enough, Mannie," Delia commanded. She would show him who was in control. She would make him stop before he was able to get what he wanted.

"Just a few more minutes. You said you wanted her roughed up," Mannie pleaded fervently.

"Yeah, roughed up, not sexed up."

"Leave me alone, Delia. I want something out of this, too."

"I said get off?"

Mannie turned to her.

Delia knew the second Mannie realized she was pointing the gun at him.

He froze. "What do you think you're doing?"

"Get. Off. Her."

❧❧❧❧

Amber felt the snap of the tape.

She was free.

It was now or never.

In a split second, she pulled the gun from her jeans pocket, worked her arm from underneath her, and pushed the gun against Mannie's chest. His eyes bulged with shock an instant before she pulled the trigger.

A volley of gunfire ensued.

FIFTY-SIX

"Targets neutralized!" Cooper radioed, as he rushed the couch, his weapon drawn. A quick glance at Delia was enough for him to know she was dead. With his gun trained on Mannie, he pushed the coffee table out of the way and shoved the man's lifeless body face down on the floor, and off of Amber.

A SWAT member immediately saw to Mannie while Cooper turned to Amber. He nearly collapsed when he saw Amber's chest covered in blood, her eyes wide with panic. He dropped alongside her, sitting on the edge of the couch. "I need a medic over here!" Cooper hollered, unable to mask the emotion in his voice. He pulled the gag from Amber's mouth as he scanned her chest and torso. "Where are you hit, Amber?" She was crying hysterically, her body convulsing. "Come on, Amber, talk to me. Where are you hit?" He ran his hand over her body.

"I'm not."

"But, Amber . . ."

Slowly, she pulled her hand from alongside her body. She was holding a pistol. Amber looked at Cooper, then at the gun in her hand. "I shot him."

Cooper looked over at Mannie where he lay on his back. A bullet hole dead center in his chest.

EMS was on the scene immediately, but Cooper waved them off, at least for a moment, while he took the gun from Amber's clenched fist. Cooper turned to see Hastings breach the doorway. "She's all right. Tell Steven, she's okay," Cooper yelled over the chaos.

Hastings crossed the living room while pulling his phone up to his ear. Cooper listened as Hastings tried to reassure Steven.

"She's all right, Steven. Amber's fine. Cooper's with her now. No, you can't come in. It's chaos in here, and we have some things that need to be cleared up. No, it's a crime scene, Steven. I promise you, Cooper will bring her out in a minute. Yes, I'm sure she's all right. She's a little banged up, but considering what could've happened, she faired pretty well. Look, I need to go. She'll be out in a minute. I know, Steven, I know. Just give us a few minutes."

In a show of emotion and relief, Cooper pulled Amber against his chest and held her tight. "I thought we'd lost you."

"I'm okay," she stuttered, pulling back and looking into his eyes. "You were right. Emily wasn't who she said she was. I'm sorry I didn't listen."

"Hey, no apologies. You're alive. That's all that matters." He looked her over, seeing the gash on her cheek, some swelling, the blood on her wrists, and her clothes torn and unfastened. "Are you sure you're okay?"

"Yes. I'm sure." She nodded.

Cooper watched as Hastings took in the rest of the scene and talked to the other two shooters. Delia and her accomplice were dead. But Cooper knew this wasn't over yet. They needed to act fast if they were going to follow Delia's trail back to the Morris brothers and whoever was calling the shots.

Cooper watched as Amber felt the welt on her face. She winced. He cringed.

"Does it look that bad?" she asked, wincing again as she touched it.

"Not too bad." He pulled her hand away. "But we need someone to take a look at it."

"Where's Steven?"

"He's outside waiting."

Amber tried to get to her feet but lost her balance. Cooper reached out to steady her and eased her back down to the edge of the couch. "That's it." He signaled for the medic. "I need you over here. She needs to be checked out."

"No. I'm fine. Really," Amber said. "Just a little shaky." The medic knelt in front of her, ready to take over. "Please, Cooper, I just want to see Steven."

Cooper conceded when he saw a fresh tear slip down her cheek. He helped Amber across the living room, shielding her from the carnage. The order on Delia had been shoot to kill. All three men had done just that.

When Cooper and Amber stepped through the doorway, Steven sprinted across the yard. Cooper watched the two embrace.

He was envious of Steven.

Amber was a special woman.

❧❧❧❧

Amber pulled Steven close and held on tight.

He pulled back slightly. "Amber, there's so much blood. Are you sure you're all right?"

"Yes. It's not mine. Just hold me, Steven. Just hold me."

Steven caressed her back, his touch calming. His words soothing. Amber finally let out the breath she was holding. When she looked up at Steven, he reached towards the gash on her cheek, but Amber stopped him, knowing her blood could be infected. "Don't Steven, don't get it on you." She forced a smile. "I'm sure it looks worse than it feels." Amber pressed her face to his chest and felt his arms tighten around her. "Thank you, God," she whispered.

She was safe.

Steven was safe.

It was over.

"You knew, didn't you? You knew something was wrong when I called you," Amber said, as Steven walked her out of the yard and to the command post.

He nodded. "Cooper called me. He had figured out who Emily really was. Unfortunately, it was too late. When he called your house and no one answered, he knew something was wrong."

"But you sounded so normal. Other than the fact that nothing you said made sense."

"When you called me, Hastings warned that someone might be listening. So, I said things that would sound normal to someone else, but strange to you."

"You did a great job. Saying you had a cold and that you needed to get the kids to Rosa was perfect. I knew you were onto something."

"You were giving me hints about where you were, too, weren't you?" Steven asked brushing her hair back from the gash.

"Yeah. I couldn't be sure you knew where I was. I wanted you to know I had been outside, but was now inside the house. I was hoping you'd be able to put it together."

"You did great," he said, as he leaned against the SWAT vehicle and pulled her close. She flinched when Steven's hand grazed a knot on the back of her head. "Wow," he looked into her eyes. "How'd you get that?"

"I hit it against the wall."

Cooper walked up to Amber and Steven. Clearly he had heard their exchange. "She needs to be looked at by a doctor, Steven. Maybe you can be more persuasive than I was."

"I'm fine."

Steven shook his head. "Come on, Amber, you have a gash on your cheek, a cut on your jaw, a bad bump on the back of your head, and those are only the things I can see. I'm taking you to the hospital."

"But, Stev—"

"It's not up for debate. You're going." His look was stern, his eyes full of concern.

"Okay, but I'm not staying overnight." She looked from Steven to Cooper.

"That will be up to the doctor. Either way, you can't come back here," Cooper said. "It's going to take a while for CSU to process the scene, and until then, it will be off limits. Even to you."

"That's fine," Steven said. "She'll come home with me."

Cooper reached into the back of the SWAT vehicle and pulled

out a t-shirt with the word POLICE emblazoned across the back. "Here." He handed it to Amber. "The blood on your shirt looks pretty scary, you might want to put this on."

She reached out and gave Cooper a hug. "Thank you. You saved my life."

He smiled. "It was my pleasure."

ꕥꕥꕥꕥ

Steven told Hastings he was taking Amber to the hospital. Hastings agreed her physical condition was the priority and said he would catch up with them later to take Amber's statement.

Amber climbed into his truck and he reached across to make sure her seatbelt was fastened. Once he got inside, she curled up close to the center console and reached across for his hand. He held onto it tight. She closed her eyes with a sigh.

"You're sure you're all right?" he asked.

"I'm sure."

"I'd feel better if you stayed awake, at least until a doctor has a chance to check you out."

"Then talk to me."

Steven contemplated what would be a safe subject, but before he could say anything, Amber whispered, "I thought she was my friend. I believed she genuinely cared about me, about what I was going through."

Amber's voice held no emotion, and her words began to run together. Steven feared she might be going into shock. He needed to keep her talking until they got to the hospital.

"Amber, you can't blame yourself. Emily, I mean, Delia, was a professional with a job to do. She befriended you and pretended to be a victim so you would drop your defenses. I'm just thankful Cooper was suspicious enough to keep digging. If he hadn't put it together, tonight would've ended . . ." Steven took a breath. "I don't even want to think of what would've happened."

Amber was too quiet. Steven glanced down at her and saw she was staring trance-like out the front window. "Amber, what are you thinking?"

"I just killed a man, Steven. I'm a murderer."

"No. That's not true. You were defending yourself. He's responsible for his own death." Steven had to tap down the emotion building inside him before he could continue. "I shouldn't have left you alone. If I had been there none of this would've happened."

"Steven," she looked up at him, "it's not your fault. It's no one's fault." She curled up in a ball, resting her head on the console between them. "I'm just glad it's finally over."

Steven stared straight ahead, the events of the last few hours running through his mind. From the moment he'd seen Amber emerge from the house, he'd been thanking God for keeping her safe.

He could only pray this was the end of it.

"Amber, we're here." Steven gently nudged Amber to a sitting position. "Just give me a second, and I'll help you out." He hurried around the front of the truck as Amber pushed the passenger door open. Before he could get to her, Amber slid from the seat, her knees buckling beneath her. Steven caught her by the elbow just in time, preventing her from going down. "Amber, are you okay?"

"Yeah. Sure." She looked at her surroundings, seemingly confused and disoriented.

"Amber, do you know where you are?"

She looked at him for a second and then glanced around. "The hospital."

"Do you remember why you're here?"

She grinned slightly. "Because you're a worry wart, and I have a small bump on my head." She took a step back from the open door, swaying.

"That's it. I'm not taking any chances of you doing a face plant in the parking lot." In one quick motion, he swung her up into his arms.

"Steven, I can walk. It will just take me a second to get my bearings."

"Humor me."

She looked at him like she was going to balk, then leaned against his chest, weariness trumping stubbornness.

When the electric doors of the hospital opened, Steven walked directly to the admissions desk. "She's a patient of Dr. Troup. Is he here?"

The nurse looked at Amber's face and the blood still visible on her arms then reached for the phone. "Yes, let me page him. You can take her to exam area three on the right."

Steven helped Amber onto the exam table. "Are you doing okay?"

"Yes, I just want to get out of these clothes."

She had only removed the POLICE shirt before Dr. Troup brushed the privacy curtain aside and gasped. "What the— Amber, what happened?"

"I'm fine, Dr. Troup, really. I just have a few minor bumps and scrapes."

The doctor looked at Amber's camisole, then to Steven, obviously waiting for some sort of explanation.

"The blood belongs to the other guy," Steven clarified. "But I think Amber might have a concussion. She has a nice size knot on the back of her head, and she's a little disoriented."

Dr. Troup slid the privacy curtain back around, reached for disposable gloves, and started his examination. He cleaned up the gashes on Amber's cheek and chin, then probed the back of her head. She flinched and moaned each time he made contact with the bump.

"You know, it doesn't hurt when you're not poking at it," she finally said, in a bristled tone.

He apologized but continued his examination. He checked her eyes, her reflexes, and asked a few questions. Then studied the cuts on her wrists, before taking a step back. "Amber, I would feel better if you were admitted. Just for observation."

"No. I'm fine. Really I am. I'm just a little banged up."

He looked unconvinced.

"Please, Dr. Troup, just let me go home and take a nice hot

bath. I just want to put this all behind me."

He peppered her with questions as he gathered supplies and set them on a tray. He spoke as he worked on her injuries. "You probably have a mild concussion, but since you never lost consciousness and don't feel nauseous, I'll let you go home. But not without supervision."

Amber sighed with obvious relief.

"Don't worry, Doc, I'm not letting her out of my sight," Steven said.

Dr. Troup looked at Steven. "It wouldn't be a bad idea if you woke her every hour or so, checked her eyes, asked her a few basic questions."

"No problem." Steven smiled.

The doctor applied some salve to her wrists and wrapped them with gauze. "I'm going to close the cut on your chin with skin adhesive. It will minimize any scarring." He put two butterfly bandages on her cheek, then took a step back. "So, this guy . . . was he your attacker?"

"No," Amber answered softly.

"It's a long story, Doc," Steven chimed in. "But the police are sure they're going to have this case wrapped up soon."

"Well, see that they do," he said while discarding his gloves. "I don't think this little lady can take much more." Dr. Troup reached out and shook Amber's hand. "You're a very courageous young woman, Amber. You've been through a lot. I hope things begin to look up for you."

She looked at Steven and smiled. "They already have."

FIFTY-SEVEN

With Steven's hands around her waist, Amber braced herself on his shoulders then slid off the exam table. His fingers traced the placket of her blouse where the buttons had been ripped off.

She captured his hand in hers and whispered. "It's all right, Steven. Nothing happened."

"I still don't understand; how did you end up at Emily's?"

"It was my own fault. I went poking around in her backyard after you left. I kept thinking about what Cooper said, and I didn't want to believe Emily had lied to me." Fresh tears fell from her eyes. "When I realized Emily wasn't who she said she was, it was too late. That Mannie guy saw me and dragged me back into Emily's house. He was going to kill me. I was sure of it."

The emotion in Amber's voice escalated. Steven pulled her to his chest and held her tight—swaying back and forth—shushing her cries. "It's all right, Amber. It's going to be all right."

"Can we go home now?" she asked, exhausted.

"Yes. We can. Except, I was wondering . . ."

"Wondering what?" She looked up at him.

"I know this isn't the most ideal situation, but would you mind if we went upstairs and saw my mother? My sister is most likely still there, and they're probably beside themselves with worry."

Amber pulled away from him. "I can't meet them looking like this," she said quietly, as she looked at her blood soaked camisole and her torn shirt stripped of its buttons. "And I'm not going to wear that POLICE shirt either."

"Just a minute. Wait here."

Steven quickly left the exam area, leaving Amber dumbfounded. He returned a few minutes later holding a bright blue t-shirt. "Here, you can put this on."

"Where did you get that?"

"From one of the nurses, I told her our situation and asked if she had any extra clothes in her locker."

"And what exactly is our *situation*?" Amber said, feeling mildly irritated.

"I told her the woman I love, the one I just asked to marry me, was going to be meeting my family for the very first time. I explained that naturally you wanted to make a good first impression and didn't think you would be able to do that while wearing a blood-soaked shirt. She was more than happy to help."

"Steven, I completely understand you wanting to check in on your mom. I get that. And by all means, you should. But can't we do the introductions in a day or two? Maybe once she's home and rested, and I don't look like this?" She swept her hands in front of her.

Steven reached for her hands and pulled them to his chest. "Amber, I know the doctors told me my mother is going to be fine, but after tonight, I don't want to take any chances. I want you to meet her—and give her a chance to meet you—before she goes into surgery."

Amber didn't know what to do. She was emotionally and physically exhausted and was beginning to feel every bruise and abrasion. But one look into Steven's eyes told her how important this was to him.

"You know what," Steven shook his head, "we don't have to do this right now." He turned to pull the curtain aside, but Amber tugged him back around.

"No. You're right. Let's do this. I would love to meet your mother," Amber smiled at him, "and your sister."

"Are you sure?"

"Very sure." Amber took the shirt from Steven. "Turn around

so I can change."

"You don't have to do this, Amber. Not if you don't want to."

Amber slipped her tattered blouse off and playfully tossed it at him. "Turn around already or I'll tell your mother you were less than gentlemanly."

Steven stepped around the curtain to wait. It took her a few minutes to wash off the blood that had soaked through her shirt and what was left on her arms. When she slid the curtain back a few seconds later with the bright colored t-shirt on, Steven smiled. "You look great."

"You are such a liar." She lightheartedly punched him in the arm. "I look horrible." But she forced a smile, even though she felt dizzy and horribly jittery.

Steven looked at her intently. "Never mind. You're exhausted. I shouldn't have even asked. I can run up there real quick and see how Mom is doing and let Stacy know you're okay."

"No, I want to Steven, really I do. But do you think this is a good time? I mean, this could be uncomfortable for your mother. Will she feel awkward meeting me while she's in the hospital? I don't want her to feel put on the spot."

"Amber, you were nearly killed tonight. If anyone has a right to feel put on the spot, it's you. Which is why I'm taking you home. We can do this in a day or two."

"Would you stop already! You're giving me an inferiority complex. Just make sure your mom is up to a visit, okay?"

"I'll ask her. I know she won't mind, but even if she does, you can at least meet Stacy."

"Okay," Amber said timidly.

Steven reached for her hand and guided her towards the elevator.

Amber stood outside Mrs. Levitt's hospital room, waiting for Steven. He had slipped into his mother's room to see how she was doing and if she felt up to having visitors. He hadn't been in the room but a couple minutes when a doctor walked up to her and smiled.

"I'm Dr. Tomlin. Are you family of Mrs. Levitt?"

"No. I'm just a friend. Her son is in with her now."

"Well, I'll just be a moment," he smiled, as he pushed the door open.

Steven stepped out into the hallway, a beautiful woman at his side. She had sparkling blue eyes and dark blonde hair. Just like Steven.

"Amber, this is Stacy." Steven stepped closer to Amber and wrapped his arm around her waist. "Stacy, this is Amber."

Amber extended her hand, but Stacy opened her arms and stepped forward, tears in her eyes. She hugged Amber with genuine affection. "It's so nice to finally meet you." She took a step back. "I wish Connor was still here. He just left to go relieve Rosa of babysitting duty." Stacy looked at the bandages on Amber's wrists and forehead. "Are you okay?"

"I'm fine." Amber nervously rubbed her arms and crossed them in front of her chest. "It looks worse than it is."

Stacy reached for Amber's left hand and smiled. She turned to Steven. "Grandma's ring."

Steven nodded.

Stacy smiled at Amber and gave her hand a squeeze. "I know you've been through an incredibly difficult time, and you and Steven met under the most adverse of circumstances, but I want to assure you none of that matters to us. Steven is a wonderful man with a solid head on his shoulders. We know he cares for you very, very, much. You're an incredible woman, Amber. You have to be to have touched Steven the way you have. We look forward to having you in our family."

Amber was overwhelmed. She had to swallow the knot in her throat before she could say anything. "Thank you, Stacy. That . . . that means a lot to me." Amber wanted to say so much more but was afraid she'd fall apart. She didn't want Steven's mother's first impression of her to be that of a blubbering mess.

Stacy stepped forward and gave her another hug, then turned to Steven and gave him a hug as well. "I can't believe you're actually going to get married. Mom will be so excited."

"Yeah, well, it's not going to be a crazy wedding like yours."

"Why do you say that?"

"Because we want something small. Besides . . . there's no way I'm going to wait a year like you did."

Stacy looked ready to comment when the doctor stepped out into the hallway. Amber watched as Steven and Stacy looked at him expectantly.

"Your mother's doing fine. Do either of you have any questions regarding tomorrow?"

Steven looked at Stacy, then to the doctor. "No. I think we're fine."

"Okay." The doctor smiled, then shook each of their hands. "I'll see you tomorrow."

"So, where were we?" Stacy said with a grin. "Oh, that's right, we were talking about your mega wedding."

Steven held up his hand with a smile. "That can wait until later. Right now I want to make sure Mom still feels up to visitors." He turned to Amber. "You're sure you're feeling okay?"

She rested against the wall and smiled. "I'm fine."

Steven slipped into the hospital room leaving Stacy and Amber in the hallway.

"Should you be standing?" Stacy asked. "Let me get you a chair."

"No. I'm fine. Really."

Amber pushed her hair behind her ear and nervously twisted her hands together. Stacy reached forward and gently grasped both her hands. Amber met Stacy's eyes.

"Don't worry, Amber. We love you already."

Just then, before Amber could even respond, Steven stepped quietly from his mother's hospital room. "Come on in." He pushed the door open wide. Stacy walked ahead of them while Steven held Amber close to his side.

Amber was intimidated from the moment she saw Mrs. Levitt. She was sitting up in the hospital bed, hair perfectly coiffed, wearing a quilted blue bed jacket. She looked almost regal. She glanced at Amber, a coy smile on her face.

"Mom," Steven started the introduction, "this is Amber."

Amber stepped forward. Mrs. Levitt lifted her delicate hand, and Amber gently took hold of it.

"It's a pleasure to finally meet you, Amber. I guess with my recent health issues and your own situation, it's not a complete surprise we should meet in a hospital room."

Amber didn't know what to say, so she only smiled. Mrs. Levitt looked at her bandaged wrists and then at her face.

"Stacy told me there had been an emergency. Are you okay?"

"I will be," Amber answered nervously.

Mrs. Levitt zoned in on the ring on Amber's finger and glanced from it to her son. "Steven, can I assume from the ring on Amber's finger that there's going to be a wedding?"

"Yes, Mom, there is. And if Amber will consent to it, I'm hoping it will be before the end of the year."

"Isn't that rushing things a bit, Steven? That's quite an undertaking to accomplish in just two months."

"Well, it's not for you to worry about, Mom. You need to concentrate on your health right now."

"I'm not worried about it, Steven, I'm just being practical. A wedding takes a lot of time and preparation."

Amber was beginning to feel awkward. Mrs. Levitt was being nothing but polite, but it was obvious she was hesitant about the prospect of a wedding. Was it really the preparations she was concerned about or the fact that her son was engaged to a woman he barely knew?

"Amber, what do you think?" Mrs. Levitt asked.

"I'm not sure," she said timidly. "I really haven't had much time to think about it with everything else that has been happening."

"But surely you must have an idea of what you want? Every little girl dreams of her own wedding day."

Steven slipped a reassuring hand around Amber's waist and answered on her behalf. "Mom, Amber's had a very traumatic day. I don't think this is the best time to talk about all of this. Besides, you need your rest."

Amber looked at Steven, silently thanking him for coming to her rescue. He gave her a wink and a gentle squeeze. "I think we're going to go now," he said. "Stacy and I will be back in the morning before your surgery." Steven leaned over and gave his mother a kiss on the forehead.

Stacy stepped forward and squeezed her mother's hand. "I'll just walk Steven and Amber out, and then I'll be back."

"Amber," Mrs. Levitt turned her attention to her. "Would you mind staying for a moment? I would like to speak to you alone. If I may?"

Steven spoke up. "I don't think that's such a good idea, Mom. You have no idea what Amber's been through today. She needs to go home and get some rest, just like you should be doing right now." Steven cocked his head and raised his eyebrow.

"Now, don't you give me that look, Steven David Levitt. I just want to talk to Amber privately for a moment. I don't think that's asking too much. After all, she is going to be part of the family."

Steven gave Amber a knowing look. She knew he was leaving the decision up to her. Amber nodded in response. Steven leaned close to her ear. "I'll be right outside. You don't have to stay if she says anything out of line, understand?"

Amber nodded again, knowing this was something she had to do. If Mrs. Levitt was going to tell her how she felt . . . how she really felt, Amber would prefer Steven and Stacy not hear it. She was their mother after all, and Amber didn't want to interfere with Steven's relationship with her.

Amber watched as the large hospital room door swung closed, mentally preparing herself for an awkward conversation with Mrs. Levitt. She would undoubtedly list the numerous reasons she and Steven shouldn't get married. Any self-respecting mother would.

Amber lowered herself into the chair next to Mrs. Levitt's bed, knowing she didn't feel strong enough to take a reprimand standing up. She could feel Mrs. Levitt's eyes on her, and after a long, slow breath, Amber finally brought her eyes up to meet hers.

"Thank you for allowing me this time," Mrs. Levitt said with a polite smile.

"You're welcome," Amber said nervously.

"Amber, I would like to be completely honest with you, if I may."

Mrs. Levitt was asking Amber's permission to voice her disdain. There was little Amber could do but allow it, so she nodded.

"I wasn't thrilled when I found out Steven was attracted to you. I felt you, well . . . your situation and how you met wasn't a healthy one. Steven is a wonderful, caring man, and I felt he was confusing his need to protect you for feelings of another kind—feelings that should develop over time, not as a result of tragedy or a promise he made in a moment of panic." Mrs. Levitt took a moment to take a long cleansing breath before she continued.

"Then I saw a change in Steven once you asked him to stay away. I realized then I was wrong. Steven's love for you was coming from his heart, not from an obligation or a need to protect you. I know my son, Amber. He's very stubborn and very decisive. He loves you, and no one is going to tell him any different."

Mrs. Levitt reached for Amber's hand yet focused on her eyes. "I can also tell a little something about you."

"About me?" Amber whispered, nervously. "I don't understand."

Mrs. Levitt grinned. "I know what you did. What you were sacrificing by telling Steven to stay away. You love my son. You love him so much, you were willing to give him up."

Amber looked at the woman, amazed by her keen sense of perception.

"You wonder how I know that?" Mrs. Levitt asked.

Amber nodded.

"Because . . . I did the same thing with Steven's father."

Amber was sure she was missing something. "I don't think I understand," Amber spoke softly.

Mrs. Levitt settled back against her pillows, sighing. "When David and I were dating—David was Steven's father—his mother didn't think I was a suitable choice for him. You see, the Levitt family was very affluent, very established in the community. Whereas, my family was part of the working-class. We didn't come from the wrong side of the tracks, mind you, but we were certainly several rungs lower than the Levitts when it came to the social ladder.

"Anyway, David and I had been seeing each other for several months when I overheard some guys, friends of David's, talking. They were weighing in regarding our relationship. They thought he was lowering his standards by dating me. They said some rude things about my father and even talked about how David had gone toe-to-toe with his dad, defending our relationship.

"I was horrified. I was so in love with David, I had never even considered how our different social classes could be a problem for him, or should I say, for his family."

Amber sat amazed as Mrs. Levitt shared such a personal story.

"Well, I decided to break it off with David. It was the hardest thing I had ever done, but I was convinced it was the right thing to do—for David's sake. I cried for days. He would come by to see me, but I would refuse. I even stopped going to school, feigning illness."

Mrs. Levitt looked towards the window, silently staring at nothing. Amber could tell she was caught somewhere between telling her story and reliving moments from her past. Amber waited patiently for her to continue. Finally, Mrs. Levitt broke from her daydream and smiled at Amber.

"You see, Amber, I know how you feel. I know what it's like to love someone so much you're willing to hurt them and yourself."

"How long were you and David apart?" Amber asked inquisitively.

"It was a month before he came to my house and threatened to break down the door if I wouldn't let him in. David convinced me that night that he would never let me go. That he was determined to make me his wife."

"How did you get along with your mother-in-law?" Amber asked, inadvertently voicing her own concern.

"She tried to convince David to change his mind right up to the night before the wedding. We had been married five years when she finally realized I was very much a part of David's life, and she was only weakening her relationship with her son. My relationship with my mother-in-law grew stronger each year. She apologized to me on more than one occasion for causing me such grief."

Mrs. Levitt turned piercing eyes on Amber, eyes that spoke her heart. "I don't want to make that same mistake, Amber. I don't want to put Steven in a situation to choose because I most definitely will lose. And you Amber, you've been through so much already. I don't want to make your life an ongoing struggle. You deserve peace and happiness."

Mrs. Levitt sat up straight as if making a noble announcement. "Welcome to the family, Amber. I look forward to getting to know the wonderful woman who stole the heart of my Steven."

Amber was wiping a stray tear from her eye when she stepped from the hospital room. Steven surged forward, anger in his eyes.

"What did she say, Amber? Why didn't you just leave?"

Amber chuckled. "I didn't need to, Steven. Your mother was wonderful. She was honest with me. She's an amazing woman."

FIFTY-EIGHT

Amber stood near the railing, overlooking the city. The view from Steven's patio was spectacular, but all Amber could think about were the shots that rang out. The way Mannie had collapsed against her chest. Her shirt sopping up his blood. She was beginning to assimilate all that had happened. She couldn't shake the numbness in her body.

I killed a man.

That makes me a murderer.

Bo seemed to sense her anxiety. Whimpering, he moved closer to her. Amber bent down and stroked his forehead. "I feel lousy, too. But it will be all right." *At least that's what everyone keeps telling me.* "I just wish I could believe it."

Amber half listened as Steven carried on a hushed phone conversation with Cooper. She could hear him speaking, but not what was being said. As much as she appreciated everything Hastings, Cooper, and Jones had done for her, she had a hard time believing them when they tried to assure her everything was going to be okay. How could they say that? Her life would never be normal again.

Steven walked up from behind and wrapped his arms around her. She tensed, then allowed her shoulders to relax and her head to fall back against his chest. Steven didn't spoil the moment with conversation, for which she was glad. He just held her in his arms.

After a few moments of silence, Steven asked, "How's your head feeling?"

"It's throbbing."

"Cooper and Hastings should be here any minute. Are you going to feel up to talking with them?"

"I don't think I have a choice," Amber said softly.

They gently swayed in the late night breeze, ignoring everything but the peace and quiet surrounding them. "Why can't every moment feel like this?" Amber wondered out loud. "I just want to be able to close my eyes and block out everything, but I can't."

"This will all be over soon, then we can concentrate on us," Steven said, then pressed a kiss to the top of her head.

"I just want to take a nice hot bath and pretend today never happened."

"I know. After they leave you can—"

As if on cue, the doorbell rang.

Amber sighed.

Steven slipped away to answer the door—Bo in step alongside of him.

Taking a deep, cleansing breath, Amber walked into the living room. Steven stood with Hastings and Cooper, all eyes on her. She crossed to the couch and sat. Steven took a seat next to her, immediately reaching for her hand and holding it tight. Hastings and Cooper sat in the chairs flanking the coffee table.

"So," Steven asked, "what now?"

Hastings directed his attention to Amber. "We've been in contact with the FBI, and we now know we are dealing with something far bigger than we expected."

Amber stiffened. "I don't understand."

Hastings continued. "Delia and Mannie worked for the Ferrelli family."

"*The* Ferrelli family out of Chicago? The ones who are always in the news?" Steven asked.

"One and the same. I can't go into all the details with you, but the Feds are hoping this is the break they've been waiting for. The piece of the puzzle that will finally connect a known assassin to the kingpin who's been calling the shots for years. But, in order to do that, they're going to have to move slow and methodical. Even though the FBI knows all the players involved, they don't know what the connection is with the Morris brothers. With Delia and Mannie dead, and the Morris brothers in the wind, the Feds don't have anyone to strike a bargain with. Somehow, they need to find the thread that connects Delia to Ferelli. Once they have that, they'll be able to bust his organization wide open. Without that thread, Ferelli can deny everything and say Delia was acting independently or directly for the Morris boys."

"But that's not true," Amber interrupted. "Mannie said Jack Morris had information they needed."

"He told you that?" Hastings asked, nearly coming up out of his chair. "What else did he say?"

"He said that Jack Morris' cellmate in prison had information, information he passed to Jack when he knew Jack was being released."

"Did he say what kind of information?"

"No. Just that they couldn't let the police pick up Jack before they got what they wanted. After they had the information, they planned on framing Jack for my murder." Amber shuddered at her own words. "Mannie made it sound like it was their way of keeping him loyal."

"Did he or Delia use any names?"

"No. Just that they were going to make it look like Jack assaulted and killed me. The gun had Jack Morris' fingerprints on it. That's why they didn't kill me at Emily's, I mean Delia's." Amber was still having a hard time accepting Delia's deception. "She kept saying they had to stick to the plan."

Cooper smiled. "Lucky for us they did. Otherwise, we never would've made it in time."

"I don't understand," Steven said. "Why would Mannie tell Amber about their plans? Wasn't he taking a huge risk shooting his mouth off like that?"

Hastings cleared his throat, wringing his hands. "Delia had a reputation for getting the job done. Mannie figured he was talking to a dead person."

Amber shuddered at the realization of his words. Steven draped his arm around her, pulling her closer to himself.

"Okay, Amber," Hastings said. "We need you to tell us what happened from the time you left the house. Walk us through everything. Everything Mannie and Delia said and did, no matter how insignificant you might think it is."

Amber explained in detail everything that happened—from Mannie grabbing her in the backyard to her grasping at straws and coming up with the gun under the mattress.

Hastings just shook his head. "Sounds like Delia might have been a little paranoid."

Amber sighed. "Thank God she was. Otherwise . . ."

Steven squeezed her hand. "Let's not think about that."

"So what happened next?" Cooper asked.

"Delia came home. She and Mannie argued over what they should do with me. Mannie wanted to kill me there and get out. But like I said, Delia kept insisting they stick with the plan. Once I knew what that was, the nail in the fence was all I could think of."

"What nail?" Hastings asked.

"There's a loose nail in the fence where we pass through. I can't tell you how many blouses Cara and I ruined because of that nail. I knew if I could get it to catch on the tape around my wrists, I would be able to get free. Thankfully, it worked. I knew then that I had a chance. But once we were in my house, everything started happening so fast. Mannie hit me a couple times, then threw me down on the couch."

The longer Amber spoke the more detached she felt. It was the only way she could continue. By focusing on the details, not her feelings.

"When Delia raised her gun, I knew I was out of time. I pulled the gun from my pocket, pointed it at Mannie, and squeezed the trigger. After that, I'm not really sure what happened. There was a lot of gunshots and shouting and . . ."

"That's okay, Amber. Cooper can fill us in from there," Hastings said.

Everyone sat in silence while Hastings finished with his notes. Then he asked, "Is there anything else, Amber?"

"It was my fault. I talked to Emily about my attack. When she told me about her abusive husband and being fearful of being found, I wanted her to know I completely understood. I realize now it was all a lie. A lie so I would open up to her. But Cooper told me not to talk about it, and I did. I'm sorry." Amber couldn't hold back the tears. "I'm sorry I didn't listen."

"Hey, it's not your fault," Hastings was quick to reassure her. "Delia used your emotional need of wanting to talk to someone. She painted a picture of a situation you could relate to, what you'd been through. It was a tactical move to get you to open up. To feel safe."

"And that's just it. I did feel safe talking to her. She sounded so convincing. I never would've thought of Emily as anything but another victim. That is until some of the things Cooper found out made me question my conversations with her."

"Amber, you can't blame yourself," Cooper said. "Delia knew what she was doing. She manipulated you. But you've got to know, Delia would've gotten to you if you had spoken to her or not. You were the target. She didn't need to gain your trust to complete her mission. In fact, you opening up to her and catching her in a lie is what really saved your life. You outsmarted a professional assassin, Amber. Not many people can say that."

Everyone was quiet again as they took in the events of the last several hours. Cooper scooted forward in the chair and looked intently at Amber. "How's the cut?"

"Stings a little."

"I'm sorry I couldn't react sooner. It was killing me not to be able to stop him, but I had to wait for the right opportunity."

"I know." Amber gave him a reassuring smile. "You did what you had to do."

"Okay." Hastings and Cooper stood up. "We need to get this info to the FBI. We'll keep you informed as things progress."

Steven got up to walk them out while Bo stayed at Amber's side.

Pulling her feet up under her, Amber asked, "When can I get some of my things?" She had nothing but the clothes on her back, such as they were.

Hastings turned to answer. "We're not sure. CSU is still on the scene, and until we hear back from Chicago, we have to assume others might be watching your place. This could take a while. It depends on how many agencies and players get involved. But we will let you know as soon as we can."

Amber didn't have the energy to argue.

FIFTY-NINE

Amber curled up in the corner of the couch and closed her eyes. Next thing she knew, Steven was laying a blanket over her and tucking it up under her chin.

"I need to take a bath," she said without opening her eyes.

"You can. But since you're already laying down, why don't you go ahead and rest first while I make us a late dinner."

Amber heard Steven walk away. She wanted so badly to get up and wash the events of the night off of her, but her body would not obey. She was powerless against her exhaustion. Giving in, Amber allowed the security of the blanket to swallow her up. Bo whimpered at her and paced in front of the couch. With what little strength Amber had, she patted her hip. It was all the encouragement Bo needed. He jumped up on the foot of the couch, nestled his body close to hers, and perched his head atop her ankles.

Amber wasn't sure how long she'd been asleep when she felt something brush against her eyes. When she opened them, Steven was sitting alongside her on the couch, his fingers pushing back a stray hair from her face.

She rubbed her eyes and stretched her body. Bo stretched too, sniffing the aroma coming from the tray in Steven's hands. When Amber looked around the room, it was cast in a burnished glow from a few lamps scattered around the large living space.

"Smells good," Amber said, as she pushed herself to a sitting position. "What time is it?"

"A little after midnight."

Steven slid the tray over Amber's legs and nudged Bo off the couch so he could sit next to her.

"Aren't you going to eat?" she asked, as she inhaled the smell of parmesan cheese and marinara sauce.

"I already did."

"Why didn't you wake me?"

"Because you needed your sleep, and I knew I would have to wake you eventually."

Amber picked up the single rose Steven had laid on the tray and brought it up to her nose. She inhaled the beauty of it and smiled.

Steven said a prayer of thanks for Amber's protection and God's provisions. He prayed for all those involved, that they would be able to bring closure to the case, and that he and Amber would be able to look to the future.

When Steven was done, Amber kept her head bowed and silently added her own thanks. She realized, though she had experienced pain, horror, and scars that would last a lifetime, God had indeed spared her life. When she finally looked up, Steven was staring at her.

"You okay?" he asked.

"Yeah. Just trying to keep things in perspective."

Steven watched as she ate. When Amber finally pushed her plate away, she looked at him. "Did I do okay?"

He smiled. "I would've preferred you ate a little more, but it's a start."

The doorbell chimed, making Amber jump and Bo bark as he ran to the front door. Amber looked at Steven as he got to his feet. She quickly clutched his hand, not wanting him to leave her.

"It's probably Stacy. I asked her to come over." Steven walked to the door while Amber nervously pushed her hair behind her ear and tried to make herself look more presentable.

Steven walked in with Stacy who was loaded down with several shopping bags, all from a fancy downtown boutique.

"What's all that?" Amber asked.

"I had Stacy do a little shopping for you since your house isn't accessible," Steven said.

"*Some* shopping?" Amber was surprised. "That looks like more than just a few things."

"Well, I guess I did kind of go a little overboard," Stacy said with a smile.

"But it's so late. You can't tell me Jolee's is open at this hour?"

"My friend is the owner. I called in a favor."

Steven reached for one of the bags, but Stacy slapped his hand. "Don't get nosy. Some of these things are personal, you know."

Amber wasn't sure because of the ambient light, but she could swear Steven was blushing. He looked at her and smiled, then turned to his sister.

"Why don't you take this stuff into Amber's room, and you two can go through everything together?"

Amber smiled at Stacy, hoping the awkwardness she was feeling didn't show.

Stacy smiled at her knowingly, reading her like a book. "Actually," Stacy looked at Steven, "I really need to get home. Amber can go through these things by herself." Stacy turned her attention back to Amber. "I wasn't sure of your size so a few things I bought in duplicate. I can return whatever doesn't fit."

"Thank you, Stacy. I don't know what to say."

"You're welcome, Amber. It was fun. Will I see you tomorrow at the hospital?"

"Ahh . . ." Amber didn't know what to say. Steven quickly fielded the question for her.

"Amber can't, Stacy. She needs to keep a low profile for a few more days, and get some rest, but I'll be there. What time?"

"Surgery is at eight o'clock. I told Mom I'd be there by seven."

"Then I'll see you at seven." He placed a light kiss on Stacy's cheek. "And thanks."

"You're very welcome."

While Steven walked his sister to the door, Amber peeked

inside the large shopping bags. She was rummaging around inside one of the bags when Steven returned.

"Here, I'll take those to your room for you, that way you can look through everything privately." He gathered the numerous bags and headed down the hall.

Amber followed Steven to the room she would be using while staying at his place. He set the bags on the bed, and she immediately started poking around inside them.

Steven chuckled. "Curiosity is getting the better of you."

"I just want to find something I can sleep in so I can take a bath."

Steven pulled her into an embrace. "Are you sure you're feeling okay? It worries me to think of you drifting off while in the tub."

"How about I come say goodnight when I'm done?"

"Okay, but if you're not out in an hour, I'm coming in to check on you, so use plenty of bubbles."

Amber felt her complexion heat up.

Steven placed a tender kiss on her cheek and closed the door behind him when he left.

Amber pulled things from the bags, pleasantly surprised that Stacy had much the same taste as she did. Stacy had bought a little of everything, from underpants and bras, to yoga pants and t-shirts. She had even thought to buy body wash and bubble bath in a lovely flowery scent.

Gathering up a pair of satiny pajama shorts with its matching tank-top, and a pair of panties, Amber walked into her own private bathroom.

She turned the ornate faucet handles until she had the right temperature, then poured a good dollop of bubble bath under the stream of water. Sitting on the edge of the tub, Amber admired the beautiful bathroom—its décor and its colors. Everything about Steven's house was striking. The rooms were spacious and open, the furnishing masculine, but not overpowering, much like Steven.

She looked down at her engagement ring and smiled. She was

hopeful—hopeful all the chaos in her life would soon be over. She wanted a future with Steven, minus the police, the Morris brothers, and the pain and fear that continued to plague her.

Lord, please bring an end to all of this. I want to be normal again. I don't want to live behind closed doors, afraid to go anywhere. I want to live life to the fullest. I know now Steven was a gift You sent to help me, to show me unconditional love, and to keep me from falling away from You. I'm thankful, really I am. But I just want it all to be over.

Amber continued her conversation with God while she tried to enjoy the luxury of a soothing bath. She washed and rinsed her body several times, still feeling the weight of Mannie on her chest. *Make it go away, Lord.*

Amber dressed in her new things, but the chilly air raised gooseflesh on her arms and legs. She grabbed the guest robe from the back of the bathroom door and wrapped it around her. Its plush terry fabric warmed her where her outfit did not. Walking to the living room, Amber found the room silent and dark. Seeing a light from the end of the hall, she followed it.

Steven was stretched out on his bed, wearing only flannel pajama pants, Bo curled up at his feet. Steven looked up from his Bible when he saw her standing in the doorway.

"Feel any better?" he asked, as he slowly closed the book and set it on the nightstand.

Amber nodded.

She hesitated for a moment before crossing the room, ignoring the little warning bell going off in her head. She shouldn't be there. The moment felt too intimate. Steven was only half-dressed, and she wore very little under her robe. *But I just want to be next to him, to feel the safety of being in his arms.* Amber slowly walked to the edge of the bed while Steven scooted over to give her room to sit. Hitching herself onto the edge of the mattress, Steven reached for her hand.

Silently, Amber laid down next to him and pressed her back to his chest. He draped his arm around her and held her close. She closed her eyes, trying to calm her racing heart.

"You okay?" he asked.

"I will be."

Amber's thoughts ricocheted around in her mind like a ballistic pinball machine. She knew her feelings were getting out of control—went beyond the limits of appropriate behavior—but she didn't care. She wanted to replace her nightmares with true intimacy, her torture with passion. Amber wanted Steven to erase everything the Morris brothers had done to her. She wanted to know what it felt like to give herself to someone in love, instead of having a part of her soul ripped away.

Amber turned to face Steven, his lips dangerously close to hers. She reached up and gently touched her fingers to his lips, then curled her hand around his neck and pulled him closer. She closed her eyes, feeling the press of his lips against hers. Soft. Gentle. *This is what it's supposed to be like.*

In an instant, a flash of Jack Morris crushing himself against her filled Amber's senses. *No! Go away!* She kissed Steven. Passionately. Trying to erase the gruesome image.

It vanished.

See. I just need to replace those horrible memories with something better. I need new memories. Good memories.

With her head nestled against Steven's chest, Amber stroked his bicep—feeling his strength—when a vision of Jay Morris tugging at her clothes materialized.

No!

She needed Steven to make the image go away. "Closer, Steven. I need you closer," Amber whispered. When she pressed her body into his, Steven pulled away, putting distance between them.

"I'm sorry, Amber," he said, as he pushed himself back against the headboard, his hands raking through his hair. "I can't do this."

What was I thinking? Completely appalled with her actions, Amber quickly got to her feet and backed away from Steven's bed. "I'm sorry," she whispered—tears flooding her eyes—then turned and hurried down the darkened hallway.

"Amber, wait." Steven caught up with her in the living room. "Amber, please . . ." He grabbed for her arm. She stopped, her head in her hands.

"I'm so sorry, Steven," she cried. "I knew the moment I saw you, I should've turned around and walked away, but I didn't. I wanted this, Steven. I wanted you. Even though I knew it was wrong. I thought I could replace the images in my mind with new ones. I wanted to be the one in control. I wanted to feel as if I had a choice, that I was making the decisions." Her cries turned to sobs. "I wanted to give myself away, not have something taken from me."

Steven wrapped her in his arms. "It's okay, Amber. It's okay." He held her tight, stroking her back.

"I can't believe I acted like that. I'm so embarrassed."

"Amber, it's as much my fault as it is yours," Steven said as he held her head to his chest. "I should've stopped things before they even started. You're vulnerable. I should've taken control, and I didn't."

They held each other for several minutes. Once Amber felt as if she'd regained her composure, she pulled back and dried her eyes. Steven tipped her chin up, but she quickly looked away.

"Hey," Steven framed her face with gentle hands. "Look at me, Amber."

She looked up at him, feeling mortified and ashamed.

"I love you, Amber, and we *are* going to get past this. We *are* going to make our own memories. Beautiful memories. We just have to wait until the time is right."

She started crying all over again.

"Come on, Amber," he wrapped her in his arms, her head press against his chest. He held her until her sobs turned to stuttered sighs, then led her back to the guest room, Bo following. "I'll be in to check on you periodically, okay?"

She nodded.

"Bo will stay with you, and I'll be right down the hall. All you need to do is holler, and I'll be right here, okay?"

"I'll be fine." Amber rose up on her toes to give him one last simple kiss goodnight. “I love you, Steven.”

“I love you, too, Amber.”

SIXTY

Amber heard jingling as she emerged from a foggy sleep. She glanced at the side of the bed and saw Bo itching his ear, causing the dog tags on his collar to clink together.

It was morning.

Amber remembered Steven gently nudging her awake throughout the night, checking her eyes, but other than that, she'd slept without nightmares or worries.

She sat up and stretched—feeling the aches from the night before and the thudding of her endless headache—when she noticed the tray perched on the dresser. She walked over to it while Bo stood, wagging his tail for attention. She picked up a note that was leaning against a vase with a single yellow rose.

Good morning, Beautiful-
I've gone to the hospital. I'll call you when Mom is out of surgery. The house alarm is on, so stay inside until I get home. Enjoy breakfast. I love you.

Steven

She lingered over the note for several moments before turning her attention to the tray of goodies in front of her. Sighing, she carried the tray to the bed and allowed Bo to jump up next to her. His obedience was tested, but he behaved himself just fine, never once reaching for her food. But when offered, he helped Amber polish off the toasted bagel and cream cheese and lapped at the leftover milk in her cereal.

Amber rifled through the bags of clothes Stacy had bought the night before and started separating things out. There were only a few items that needed to be returned. Everything else either fit perfectly or was a style that lent to a loose-fitting look.

She slipped on the pricey underthings Stacy had picked out, cringing with every price tag she snipped. Even a simple white t-shirt had a hefty price tag. *Sheesh. It's cotton for goodness sake.* She pulled on a broomstick skirt in variegated hues of orange and red, the tag boasting a hundred percent raw silk. It was obvious Stacy had expensive taste.

After getting dressed, Amber wandered around Steven's house, looking at personal pictures and the things that made Steven's home uniquely his. She felt a little strange, as if she was eavesdropping on his life, but loved getting to know him this way.

He had pictures of his niece and nephew on a shelf, next to a ragged old stuffed bear. He had his mother and father's wedding picture on top of the sofa table, next to an antique camera that looked to be perfectly restored. The picture of Stacy with a man—Amber assumed was her husband—was on a shelf next to a stack of law books.

But not everything was as proper and formal as the living room. Steven had several shelves in his office that were devoted to baseball card collections and souvenir balls. There was a picture of Steven as a child in a baseball uniform, smiling without his front teeth and a picture of him in his teen years, wrestling with his dad.

It was obvious to Amber, everywhere she turned, that family was important to Steven. Although he had fine collectibles and expensive furnishings, it appeared his most prized possession was his family.

The phone rang.

Amber followed the sound of the ring to Steven's desk. "Hello?"

"Amber, it's me. Mom's out of surgery and doing just fine."

"That's great, Steven." Not only was Amber relieved to hear his mother was doing well, but just hearing Steven's voice brought its own sense of relief. "How are you and Stacy doing?"

"We're fine. How's your head this morning?"

"Better than I thought it would be."

"Amber, I have a huge favor to ask you. How would you like to do some babysitting?" He paused for a minute and then explained. "Stacy wants to stay at the hospital, but Rosa's feeling a little under the weather, and Connor has some urgent business to attend to. How would you feel about watching Jaime and Jarrod? They're really good kids, and I will make them promise to be on their best behavior. I know it's asking a lot, but I thought it might be a welcome distraction."

"Are you sure it's safe? Them being here with me?"

"My security system is state-of-the-art. Believe me, I wouldn't have left you alone otherwise."

Amber paused to think a moment. She'd never really babysat before, though she didn't see why she couldn't. Jaime and Jarrod were kids, not toddlers. They would probably entertain themselves.

"If you don't feel up to it, I completely understand," Steven said.

"No. I would love to meet them. As long as you think I can handle it. You know them better than I do."

"Like I said, they're really good kids. You won't have any problem with them."

"Okay. When?"

"I'll bring them by in about thirty or forty minutes. I'll pick up something for lunch while I'm at it, so you don't have to worry about fixing them anything to eat. Are you sure you feel up to this?"

"Sure. Like you said, it will be a good distraction."

"I love you, Amber."

"I love you, too, Steven. And assure Stacy that I'm looking forward to this. I don't want her to worry about me or the kids."

"I will. I'll see you in a little bit."

Steven arrived about forty minutes later. His nephew raced passed Amber straight for Bo. She met Steven in the entryway where his niece had a death grip on his forearm. Steven was juggling three bags of fast food in one hand, so she quickly took them from him and carried them to the kitchen counter.

"Jarrod," Steven said with a hint of sternness, "where are you manners?"

The little boy hung his head and walked quietly back to where Steven and Amber were standing.

"Amber, the speed demon here is Jarrod," Steven said, as he ruffled his nephew's hair, "and this little princess is Jaime." He gave Jaime a squeeze on the shoulder. "Jamie and Jarrod, this is Miss Porter."

"But you can call me Amber," she quickly corrected.

Jarrod put out his hand like a little gentleman, but Jaime ducked behind Steven's arm.

"She's a little shy around strangers."

Amber bent down eye level with Jaime. "Then I guess we'll have to do something about that."

Jaime stole a glance at Amber and smiled.

"Okay," Steven clapped and rubbed his hands together. "I brought food for lunch. The kids know where to find their favorite videos, and their toys are in the hall cupboard. And what's the rule?" he asked, as he looked from Jarrod to Jaime.

The kids chimed together: "Before you can take out one toy, you have to put the other one back."

"Good," Steven said, obviously proud of his niece and nephew. "I need to get back to the hospital. Jarrod, Jaime, you behave yourselves for Amber. Remember what I told you." Steven put Jaime's hand in Amber's and placed a kiss on both their cheeks. "I'll see you later." He winked at Amber.

Jarrod and Jaime disappeared down the hall. Jarrod came back with a portable garage full of race cars while Jaime carried a simple book. She took Amber's hand and led her to the couch. Jaime crawled up next to her and placed the book on Amber's lap.

"This one is my favorite."

The little girl looked up at Amber with crystal blue eyes much like Steven's, her smile enchanting. Amber felt honored the little girl was willing to give her a chance.

Amber opened the book across both their laps and started, "Once upon a time . . ."

SIXTY-ONE

Jaime and Jarrod warmed up to Amber instantly. They had lunch together, then laughed and played as the day went on. Jarrod spent time playing with Bo while Jaime asked Amber a hundred questions. She wanted to know her favorite color, favorite ice cream, favorite flower, and which she liked better, summer or Christmas.

"Are you still sick?" Jaime asked Amber, as she placed another book in her lap. "Mommy and I have been praying for you at night. Uncle Steven said I could meet you when you got better. So, are you better?"

Amber was stunned, tears welling in her eyes. "I think I am."

"But you still have bangdages on."

Amber laughed at Jaime's pronunciation. "Yes I do, but I am feeling much better. I'm sure it's because of your thoughtful prayers."

"I'm glad." Jaime beamed.

When they had finished their third book, Jaime crawled up into Amber's lap and put her hands to Amber's cheeks. "Are you and Uncle Steven going to get married?"

Amber kissed her little hands. "Would that be all right with you?"

"Can I wear a pretty dress?"

"The prettiest dress in the world."

"Oh, no," Jaime said, her eyes growing big, her expression priceless. "The bride has to wear the only prettiest dress, but I can wear a pretty dress, too."

The two of them were laughing and giggling when Steven walked in. Jarrod and Bo ran to greet him.

"Sounds like someone's having a good time."

Jaime squealed and ran to greet Steven as well. "I get to wear a pretty dress. Amber's dress will be prettier because it's supposed to be, but that's okay because she said I can throw flowers. Is that okay, Uncle Steven? Can I throw flowers?"

Steven looked at Amber, an adorable smile on his face. "Making wedding arrangements without me?"

"Maybe just a few." Amber grinned.

Steven pulled Amber close and spoke so only she could hear. "Well, then, if you're starting to plan the wedding, I guess I can start planning the honeymoon." His grin was devilish, sending a chill through her body.

She and Steven played with the kids until they were worn out. When Stacy arrived, she found the four of them in the den, in front of the television watching *Finding Nemo*. Amber and Steven were sitting together, Jaime lying across their laps. Jarrod was sprawled out on the floor, Bo using him as a pillow.

Stacy whispered, "I can't tell who wore out whom."

"It was close, but I think Amber and I won," Steven answered, reaching for the remote. As soon as the T.V. clicked off, Jarrod came to life.

"Hey, I was watching that." He stretched and yawned.

"Well, unless your eyelids are see-through, you haven't seen the last twenty minutes," Steven said, tossing a pillow at Jarrod.

Jaime rubbed at her eyes. When she saw her mom, she burst from the couch and hugged her. "Mommy, Mommy, Amber said I could wear a pretty dress and throw flowers. Can I Mommy, can I?"

Stacy picked up her daughter full of energy. "How could I say no? You'll make the prettiest flower girl ever."

Jaime hugged her mom. "I get to play dress-up for reals."

"You sure do. And you know what else you get to do?" Stacy asked with an over-animated expression. "You get to clean up your things and get your shoes and socks on."

Both kids moaned, but did as they were told.

"Can't you stay for a little while, Stacy?" Amber asked.

Stacy smiled. "I wish I could, but I need to get home. Connor's making dinner for me and the kids, and then I'm going back to the hospital to sit with Mom for a little while. Hey," Stacy smiled and looked at them both. "Why don't you and Steven come over for dinner? When Connor cooks he has no sense of portion control. He makes enough to feed an army."

Steven looked at Amber for an answer.

"I don't know. Do you think it would be okay?" She looked at Steven, knowing she'd been told by Det. Hastings to stay put.

"I'll call Hastings and see what he says." Steven got up from the couch to make the call.

"So, you're planning the wedding?" Stacy asked Amber.

"Not officially. But I would like Jarrod and Jaime to be in it. If that's okay with you?"

"Like I could tell Jaime otherwise," she laughed, then glanced at Amber. "That skirt looks wonderful on you. I knew it would be your color."

"Thank you, Stacy. In fact, thank you for everything. The bubble bath was much appreciated. And I'll pay you back as soon as—"

"You *will* not. I enjoyed every minute of shopping for you, and Jolee gave me everything at cost."

"Then let me at least reimburse you for that."

"Nope. You more than paid for it with your babysitting today."

When Steven walked back into the room he said, "Hastings gave the okay. Of course, I'm sure Connor being the D.A. had something to do with that."

Jaime grabbed Amber's hand. "I can show you my room, and my playhouse, and we can have a tea party and a puppet show."

"Jaime, Amber's coming over for dinner, sweetheart, not for the weekend," Stacy laughed.

Jaime crossed her arms and frowned.

"None of that, missy. You had Amber all day."

Jaime uncrossed her arms and looked at Amber with her beautiful blue eyes. "Can I still show you my room? If I make it fastest?" she whispered.

"Of course." Amber smiled and squatted down to give Jaime a hug.

Amber excused herself so she could freshen up, then grabbed the bag of clothes that needed to be returned. When she walked back into the living room, Stacy and the kids had already left, and Steven was waiting for her by the front door. "Ready?" he asked.

Amber nodded, then cautiously walked outside.

"So, did you have a good time with the kids today?" Steven asked as he pulled from the driveway.

"I did. I was nervous at first, but they're so well-behaved and loveable. Jaime is such a cutie, and Jarrod—he's going to be a heartbreaker when he grows up."

Steven glanced over at her and smiled. "Talk about a heartbreaker, I didn't tell you how beautiful you look in that outfit."

Amber played with the folds of her skirt. "Stacy has good taste."

"It runs in the family." He gave her a wink.

When they pulled up to Stacy and Connor's house, Amber's mouth dropped open. House was not a fitting word. A mansion was more like it, or hacienda to be exact. Large arches wrapped in vibrant bougainvillea plants greeted them, along with terracotta tile, and an old-world fountain at the center of the cobblestone circular driveway.

"Steven, it's breathtaking."

He chuckled. "But you should've seen the place when Stacy and Connor bought it. It was a mess. The wood floors were rotting and the tiles were chipped and broken. I thought they were crazy. But Stacy has always loved Spanish architecture. Plus, the house had quite a history, including being used as a movie set in the forties. Stacy spent five years restoring it, between work, marriage, and having kids. They've lived here for three years now."

Steven and Amber were just walking up to the large wooden door when it opened wide. A good-looking man with salt-and-pepper hair stood there in black slacks and the sleeves of his silk dress shirt rolled up to his elbows.

"Hey, Steven." The man shook his hand, then pulled him in for a hug. "Glad you could come."

"Hey, Connor."

After Steven made the obligatory introductions, Connor shook Amber's hand and smiled. "It's nice to finally meet you."

Amber smiled in return, not quite sure what to say. She felt incredibly nervous. After all, Connor was the District Attorney. Even without a tie on and his sleeves rolled up, he looked distinguished and authoritative.

Connor led them to the patio where the aroma from the barbecue permeated the air.

The kids were playing in the yard and ran over to meet Steven and Amber like they hadn't seen them in days. Jaime immediately took Amber's hand and started leading her back into the house.

"Come see my room, and then we can play dolls." Jaime had Amber halfway to the circular staircase before Stacy interceded.

"You can show Amber your room, but then she needs to come back downstairs. You played with her all day, Jaime. Now it's time for the grown-ups to get a chance to talk."

Jaime gave what was obviously her trademark pout, but was careful not to talk back. She continued to lead Amber up the stairs.

Steven watched Connor as he worked the grill. When Connor was done seasoning the steaks and burgers, he leaned back against the wrought iron rail of the patio and grinned at Steven.

"You humanitarian, you."

"What's that supposed to mean?" Steven was clueless at Connor's obscure remark.

"She's gorgeous. I can see why the attraction."

Steven understood what Connor was getting at, but still got defensive. "Well, she didn't quite look like that when I found her."

Connor immediately backpedaled. "Hey, Steven, I'm sorry. I didn't mean anything by it. It's just that Amber is quite a stunner."

Steven realized he'd jumped at Connor needlessly. "I know. I didn't mean to snap at you."

Connor stepped back to the grill. "I hear that things have gotten a little complicated. That other agencies are involved, and they're trying to go after the big fish."

"Yep."

"And you proposed?"

"Yep."

"And you've thought this through?"

Connor was almost ten years older than Stacy and Steven. Though he was married to Steven's sister, he had a tendency to treat Steven like a son in his father's absence.

"You don't approve?" Steven wanted to know what Connor thought.

"It's not for me to approve or not. I just want to make sure you're not jumping into something too soon."

Steven thought a moment before he spoke. "I've prayed about this, Connor, and I know it's what I want, what God wants for me. Amber is everything I could ever want in a woman. She's smart, talented, and most importantly, she loves the Lord."

"And she's beautiful," Connor added with a laugh. "Come on, Steven, be honest with yourself."

"Okay, Connor," Steven chuckled, "you're right. Amber's incredibly beautiful . . . both inside and out."

❧❧❧❧

Amber stood in the doorway overhearing the short exchange between Steven and his brother-in-law. She hadn't meant to eavesdrop, it just sort of happened. But she got the distinct feeling Connor had reservations about her and Steven's relationship. Steven didn't seem bothered by it, but it played at Amber's insecurities.

Dinner was finished in a hurry, and once again, Amber was on babysitting detail. Connor had received an urgent call and needed to go back to the office, and Amber encouraged Steven to go with

Stacy to visit his mother. Steven had questioned leaving her, but Stacy assured him Amber would be just as safe in their house—with their security system—as she had been in his.

The kids were thrilled, and Amber had to admit, playing with Steven's niece and nephew kept her mind off of the Morris brothers, the FBI, and all the other insanity plaguing her life at the moment.

Jaime and Jarrod did their best to compete for Amber's attention once the adults had left. By the time she put them to bed, she had played cars with Jarrod—building a superhighway out of Hot Wheel tracks—and had read just about every Disney storybook that graced Jaime's bookshelf. They moaned and groaned like all kids their age did when told it was bedtime, but they went through the routine of brushing their teeth and dressing for bed without argument or complaint.

Amber had just gotten them into bed when she heard someone at the front door. Slowly, she descended the stairs expecting to see Stacy and Steven but was surprised to see Connor instead. He tossed his briefcase on one of the two leather couches flanking the fireplace, took off his jacket, then glanced her way.

"Hey, Amber. I see you ended up on night duty." He smiled as he loosened his tie and collapsed on the couch. "Did the kids behave themselves?"

"They were great. They're really wonderful kids."

A proud smile filled Connor's face.

Amber stood behind the couch directly opposite him, feeling awkward and out of place. Connor obviously sensed her anxiousness.

"Amber, I know you overheard my conversation with Steven, and I think you might have gotten the wrong impression."

Wow, he's definitely a straight shooter. Amber nervously played with the nail-head trim on the couch she was leaning against. "No. I think I understood what you were saying." She tried to sound bold and self-assured. "You're worried Steven's making a mistake."

"Not a mistake, Amber, just that he might be taking things a bit too fast." Connor leaned forward, resting his elbows on his knees.

"I've known Steven for quite a few years. He's a levelheaded guy. But, I would be shirking my responsibilities as his brother if I didn't ask him the hard questions."

"I understand," she said quietly.

"What about you, Amber? Are you sure you're not just reacting to your situation, looking for Steven to give you stability during an unstable time?"

Amber wanted to get defensive, but when she looked at Connor, his expression told her he meant no disrespect. She sighed heavily and took a moment to think. "I tried pushing Steven away for that very reason. I had never been in love before and didn't know if what I was feeling was a reaction or an emotion."

"And now?" Connor asked diligently.

"I love Steven." A tear ran down her cheek that she quickly brushed away. "I'm sorry I'm not what you and Stacy, or his mother would've wanted for him, but I promise you, I do love him."

The front door rattled open. Stacy and Steven walk into the living room carrying on a conversation before they saw Connor and Amber. Amber quickly turned away, trying to dry her eyes before Steven saw her.

"Hey," Stacy leaned over the back of the couch and placed a kiss on her husband's cheek. "I didn't expect you to be home yet."

Steven walked over to Amber. He squinted and looked at her long and hard. "Is something wrong?" he whispered.

She shook her head and smiled.

"Actually," Connor spoke up. "Amber and I were just enjoying a little conversation." He looked at her with a genuine smile. "You're getting a great woman, Steven. I'm happy for you both."

SIXTY-TWO

After weeks of being sequestered at Steven's, Amber's case had been officially closed. With the information Mannie had carelessly divulged to Amber—combined with a story fabricated by the FBI—the word on the streets was the Morris brothers were ready to roll on their Chicago connections. This not only flushed out the terrified Morris brothers—desperate to cut a deal in exchange for protection—but it caused the Ferelli contingency to misstep. In a matter of days, the FBI had their connection between the Ferelli Family, the Morris brothers, and Delia and Mannie. No one knew it was Mannie's conversation with Amber that had helped them put the pieces together. To those involved, she was just an unfortunate victim of a gruesome assault.

But, the best news Amber had received was that neither Jack nor Jay Morris had tested positive for the HIV virus.

Amber had been given a clean bill of health.

And to Steven's delight, she had agreed to a December wedding.

It had been an emotional Thanksgiving for Amber, Steven, and his family. Not only had they celebrated the fact that Amber was safe, healthy, and they all had a wedding to look forward to, but they also had rejoiced that Steven's mother had recovered from surgery without complications. Her only complaint in the last few weeks was not being able to help Amber with the wedding plans.

Steven had stood his ground, explaining to his mom they wanted a small, intimate wedding, not the elaborate affair she most likely would've orchestrated. And, since they only had three weeks to plan, she conceded, offering her love and support instead.

Amber had done the right thing and called her father and sister, letting them know she was engaged and the date of their upcoming wedding. Her father explained he would be out of the country at an international business symposium, and Erika was expected to hold down the fort in his absence. Amber was more than gracious as she listened to their excuses, feeling a sense of relief they wouldn't be there to dampen her and Steven's special day. Amber knew she needed to mend fences with her father and sister, but her wedding day was not the time or place for that. Amber let them know she would miss them, and that she and Steven would make plans to visit New York after the first of the year.

Amber had talked to Cara several times in the last few weeks. Their first conversation had lasted three hours and was filled with equal parts joy and sorrow. Amber let Cara know she was engaged, getting married, and was the happiest she'd ever been. Then she went on to explain the circumstances in which she and Steven had met.

Cara had felt horrible Amber had gone through so much and had never called for help. But Amber was quick to point out, if Cara had come to take care of her after the attack, Amber never would've been given the chance to fall in love with Steven.

Cara had her own news to share. A baby due next summer. Unfortunately, because of a few health concerns, she would be unable to attend the wedding. But Amber assured Cara she completely understood and would touch base with her after the honeymoon.

The day was quickly approaching. Only two days until Amber would become Mrs. Steven David Levitt. She stood in front of a wall of mirrors having her final dress fitting, Stacy at her side, her future sister-in-law getting her first look at the dress Amber had picked out.

Amber had found the dress at an antique store in the old

downtown district. She had walked past the store—after dropping the deposit off at the church—and saw it hanging in a glass showcase.

The sweetheart neckline was a bit daring, but the sheer lace overlay gave it a modest, romantic feel. The long, tapered sleeves were also fashioned from lace with six tiny pearl buttons at the cuff. The A-line skirt was the most gorgeous shade of champagne silk, and from the amount of material pooled at the bottom of the showcase, Amber assumed it had a sizable train.

It was the most beautiful dress she'd ever seen. But since it was a true antique, it came with an impressive price tag. Amber hadn't planned on spending that kind of money for her wedding dress, but she just couldn't seem to take her eyes off of it.

After admiring it for several minutes, an elderly store clerk asked Amber if she would like to take a closer look. The woman carefully removed the dress from the glass case and watched as Amber inspected every button and every seam. The back of the dress was just as beautiful as the front. The sheer lace bodice plunged to the waist with over thirty pearl buttons fastening it shut.

After close inspection, Amber deemed the dress in perfect condition. All the pearl buttons were accounted for, and the silk lining was still intact with only the slightest hint of yellowing from age.

The minute Amber slipped it on, she knew it was the only dress for her. The sales clerk helped with the row of buttons that started at Amber's hips and stopped just below her neckline, the whole time oohing and aahing at Amber's reflection. Though the dress was a bit long, Amber knew the right pair of heels would make it the perfect length.

The older woman pinched an inch of material on either side of Amber's waist, showing her some alterations would be in order if the dress was to fit the way it was intended. Amber wasn't sure she wanted to chance altering it, but the elderly woman gave her the name of a woman who was a professional and assured Amber the seamstress would do a wonderful job. "Besides," the sales clerk had added, "you have too cute of a figure not to accentuate it." Amber smiled, remembering the way the old woman's little gray eyebrows danced up and down.

Now, just a few days before the wedding, Amber stood in front of Stacy and Jaime, wearing the perfectly fitted dress. The vintage looking t strap heels Amber had found were the perfect complement to the overall look, and the five-foot train of flowing silk lay beautifully behind her.

"Amber, it's beautiful." Stacy looked on with approval.

Jaime stepped forward and gently touched the dress. She looked at Amber in wonderment. "Aunt Amber, you look like a princess."

"Do you think Steven will like it?" Amber asked Stacy as she turned to see the back of her dress.

"Are you kidding me? You're going to make him cry," Stacy said laughing.

The dressmaker held the delicate piece of scalloped lace she had fashioned into a veil and fastened the clip to Amber's hair. She billowed the material until it laid gracefully across Amber's shoulders and down the length of the train.

Amber admired her reflection for a few moments more before taking off the dress and carefully slipping it into the garment bag.

"Okay, now your turn."

While Amber waited for Stacy and Jaime to change, she turned to the seamstress—a measuring tape draped around her shoulders. "Thank you, Irene, for everything. I still can't believe you were able to do my alterations, create my veil, and make two dresses in such a short amount of time. You truly are a miracle worker."

"Oh, sweetheart, I was glad to do it. You and your future family were a joy to work with. That Jaime is a real darling."

Amber watched as Jaime and Stacy emerged from the fitting room wearing dresses Irene had designed to follow the same lines as her wedding dress.

"Oh, Jaime, I have never seen a prettier dress on a prettier girl." Amber bent down and kissed her niece-to-be. "I must be the luckiest bride in the world to have you as my flower girl."

Jaime beamed, turning from side-to-side watching her dress twirl around her.

"Stacy, you look stunning. What do you think?"

"It's gorgeous. I really love the color."

"Well, I thought cranberry was an appropriate choice with the wedding only a week before Christmas."

Amber waited until Stacy and Jaime had changed back into their street clothes before saying goodbye. She declined going out for coffee, having one more errand to run before meeting Steven at her house to finish packing her things. She needed to pick up their wedding announcements at the printer's. Since she and Steven had personally called the few people who would be attending the wedding, there wasn't a need for invitations. The announcements were a gift of sorts for Steven's mother. Though she'd been supportive regarding their decision to have a small wedding—of just family and a few close friends—Steven knew she was still disappointed. So, Amber and Steven decided to have announcements printed up so she could send them to all her friends. She'd been over-the-moon when she found out and had immediately gone to work on a list that numbered over two hundred.

The clerk at the printer's handed Amber two boxes and a copy of the announcement for her to see. Amber smiled when she looked at the black and white picture of Steven holding her tight while they both laughed uncontrollably. They had both agreed it was the perfect picture because it represented the joy they had found with each other. It had also been the last photoshoot Amber had done at her house before packing up her studio and moving everything to Steven's office building downtown. When she got back from the honeymoon, she would set up her new studio in the office space down the hall from Steven. She was excited about the new venture and already had a few appointments set-up in the weeks ahead. It wouldn't be the same as working out of her house, but being so close to Steven gave her the courage she needed to make a fresh start.

Though Amber had been back to her house several times to pack up, she'd never gone alone or spent the night.

She just couldn't.

Though the company hired to restore the house did a superb job removing all evidence of what had happened, Amber's memories were not so easily erased. After spending a week at Steven's, they had decided it would be best for her to move in with Stacy and Connor until after the wedding. Not only for appearance's sake but because they were becoming way too comfortable around each other late at night. Knowing they were getting married in just a few weeks was a little more tempting than they could handle.

Though Amber had been concerned about moving in with Stacy and Connor, she knew it was the right thing to do. She soon found out not only did she fit in, but she found the chaos of the family setting incredibly energizing. Her world, previous to the attack, had been quiet and structured, an environment she thrived on. Or so she thought. But the activities of a bustling family that consisted of soccer practices, ballet recitals, women's bible study, and a litany list of other things had a new energy she found herself craving. It made her realize how much she wanted to have a family, something she wanted to get started on right away.

Amber still suffered from night terrors, and needed someone to hold onto in crowds, but was happier than she ever thought possible. She only wished her mother had lived long enough to see the joy she'd found with Steven.

Amber pulled into her driveway and sighed. Steven was supposed to meet her and help go through the rest of her things. Glancing at her watch, Amber realized she was a few minutes early. She looked at her house. Really looked at it.

I can do this. Steven will be here any minute.

Amber pressed the button for her garage door and pulled inside. Getting out of her car, she ignored the twinge of fear that poked at her senses. Looking at the odds-n-ends stacked in the corner, she needed to decide what was junk and what would go with her. Sorting the items into two separate piles, Amber was down on her knees, looking through a box of old dishes, when she heard a noise.

"Excuse me?"

A man's voice startled her from behind. When Amber turned, she saw a stranger standing in her driveway. Her heart immediately began to race, and her hands were shaking.

"I'm sorry, I didn't mean to startle you, but I was wondering if you could help me out?"

Amber didn't answer. She just backed away from her car and closer to the house door, waiting for him to explain himself.

"I was supposed to meet a realtor to see the house next door. She's not here yet, and my cell phone is dead. Could I use your phone to call her and see if maybe I wrote down the wrong time?"

Amber still didn't answer him. She just continued to walk backward towards the door, unable to speak, trying to figure out what she should do.

"Well, here . . ." He began to move towards her, his extended hand holding onto something.

"Stop!" she hollered.

He stopped.

"Now, please, just go."

"But this is her business card." He continued towards Amber. "If I could just—"

"Get out!" she yelled as she stumbled on a rolled up pile of garden hose.

"Here, let me help you." He stepped forward.

Amber felt like she was going to hyperventilate. *Who is this man, and why is he being so persistent? He's after me.* She started to cry. *He was sent to kill me.*

The man stood in her garage, just staring at her when a commotion behind him forced him to turn around.

Amber watched as Steven pounced on the man and threw him up against her car. "What did you do to her?"

The man held up his hands in surrender. "Nothing, man. I asked to use her phone, and she went all schizo on me."

"Leave. Now. Or I'm calling the cops!" Steven yelled, as he shoved the man towards the driveway, then hurried to Amber's side. She buried her head in his chest and clung on for dear life.

"Call the cops? I was just asking to use her phone, and she went berserk. I didn't do anything. She just started yelling."

"Just get out! Go use a pay phone!" Steven hollered.

"No, thanks. I'm not going to live next to some freak."

The man stormed off and screeched away from the curb. Amber saw a realtor's business card on the floor of the garage as Steven pushed the button for the door to go down. She reached for the card, realizing it was what the man had tried to show her. "I'm sorry. I overreacted. He showed up out of nowhere, and startled me."

Steven reached out to hold her, but she didn't want to be held. "It's okay, Amber. He had no business approaching you like that."

Steven tried to calm her down, but she was angry she had let it happen. Again. She had allowed herself to lose control. And it wasn't the first time.

"I'm so stupid!" she ranted as she started to pace. "I am such an idiot! I just made a fool out of myself and for what . . . because some guy wanted to use my phone?"

"Enough, Amber," Steven raised his voice slightly.

She continued mumbling to herself.

Finally, Steven pulled her close and pressed a finger to her lips. "That's . . . enough."

She looked at him with wide eyes and swallowed. He leaned down and replaced his finger with a gentle kiss.

"Now, let's try to forget about what just happened and concentrate on what's going to happen in a few days."

Amber wanted to argue, but Steven again quieted her with a well-placed kiss. One kiss led to another, and then another. He was doing his best to make her forget.

"If this is your way of scolding me, I could definitely get used to my punishment."

Steven grinned. "Just following doctor's orders."

Amber was thankful she hadn't had a full-blown meltdown. Each time she experienced one of these episodes, it took less time for her to recover. Dr. Stuart had warned her she could experience lapses of paranoia, but Amber refused to allow the episodes to take her captive.

"So, how did things go with the dressmaker?" Steven asked as Amber continue to go through her stuff.

"Oh, you should've seen Jaime. She loved every minute of it."

Steven laughed. "Well, too bad Jarrod doesn't share her opinion of dressing up. When I showed him what he had to wear, he just moaned."

"He doesn't have to do it if he doesn't want to."

"Nah, he'll be fine. He was just acting like every other man I've ever seen in a tuxedo shop."

Amber laughed. "So, can you think of anything we might be forgetting?"

"I don't think so. We've got the church, Craig to officiate, the license, and two consenting adults. That's all the important stuff."

Amber imagined how everything would look. Steven in his morning coat, the church lit only by candlelight, Scott by Steven's side and Stacy by hers. Other than Steven's mom, Connor, and the kids, the guest list was pretty minimal. Rosa, Wendy, Craig's wife Sara, Dr. Stuart, Hastings, Cooper, Jones, and Armstrong.

It would be small and intimate, just like she wanted.

Two more days.

SIXTY-THREE

The evening had finally come. Amber was in the bride's room with Stacy and Jaime waiting to hear the music that would signal the start of the ceremony. She glanced at the clock on the wall. It was time for Steven and Scott to take their places with Craig. Just then, there was a faint knock on the door. When Stacy opened it, Amber saw Jarrod standing there pulling and yanking on his tie.

"Uncle Steven told me to wait with you guys."

"Did he and Scott already go in?" Stacy asked.

"Yeah." Jarrod pulled on his tie some more.

Stacy bent down to straighten it. "Okay, you and Jaime remember what to do, right?"

"We walk slow and Jaime throws petals," Jarrod said, sounding less than enthused.

Stacy kissed his cheek. "Perfect."

Scooting Jaime and Jarrod out the door, Stacy turned to Amber. "I'm going to get the kids in place. I'll see you up front, okay?"

They exchanged smiles, then Stacy quietly closed the door. Amber looked at herself one more time in the mirror, then closed her eyes to pray.

Thank you, Lord. Thank you for Steven. Thank you for bringing us together, and thank you most of all for this day. I know I wouldn't be here if it wasn't for the protection and strength You've given me.

Amber had turned the corner spiritually. She no longer questioned God about what had happened to her one Saturday in the park. Instead, she recognized it was God who had saved her—saved her because He had an incredible plan for her life, a plan that included Steven.

Amber made her way to the back of the church and stood where she couldn't be seen. She stole a look at Jaime and Jarrod as they headed down the aisle. Jaime allowed each pedal to flutter to the ground before taking her next step. Amber giggled. At the pace they were going, she hoped the music didn't run out before the kids made it to the stage.

Amber listened to the music, remembering the day she and Steven had spent in front of the stereo listening and laughing as they chose each song. When the tempo changed, Amber realized it was her cue.

She stepped to the center of the sanctuary doorway and just stood there. Amber wanted to take it all in. She wanted to remember this moment for the rest of her life.

The huge stained-glass windows showered the room with multi-colored light while the Candelabras lining the aisle illuminated the church with a warm glow.

It's just like I remember it.

But when Amber looked at the front of the church, she saw gorgeous, white poinsettias filled the stage. The sea of flowers looked exquisite—like nothing she'd ever seen before. She was awestruck by their beauty.

Then she saw Steven.

When her eyes met his, her heart stopped. Amber had promised herself she wouldn't cry, but seeing Steven standing there—his eyes riveted on her—made it difficult not too.

Amber quickly brushed the tears from her eyes and took a deep breath before starting down the aisle. She listened to the soft swoosh of her dress as it trailed behind her, and clung to the cluster of calla lilies that made up her bouquet. Lilies had been her mother's favorite flower. Holding them now made it feel as if her mother was with her on her special day. *I love you, Mom. I hope you can see how happy I am.*

When Amber saw a tear roll down Steven's cheek, she almost lost it. Knowing she had to distract herself, or chance losing her composure, Amber looked from side-to-side at those who had stood when she entered. Steven's mom, Connor, Maria, and Wendy were on her right. Across the aisle, Dr. Stuart and Sara smiled at Amber, while Hastings, Cooper, Jones, and Armstrong stood stoically next to each other.

When she reached the foot of the stage, Steven stepped forward and extended his hand to her. She took it, and carefully ascended the steps.

"You look incredible," he whispered in her ear, as he led Amber to center stage.

"So do you," Amber said, under her breath. "But the flowers. I don't know where . . . or how . . ."

"Do you like them?"

She looked at Steven, realizing he didn't seem surprised. "Well, yes, but—"

"Poinsettias symbolize joyfulness and celebration. I thought it was only fitting."

Amber threw her arms around Steven's neck and held him tight. "They're beautiful."

Craig cleared his throat and smiled. "We haven't gotten to that part in the service yet. I would skip ahead, but some of this other stuff is pretty important," he said as he pointed to the small folder in his hand.

Amber and Steven laughed, as did everyone watching them.

"Sorry about that. I guess I got carried away," Amber said as she took a step back and handed her bouquet to Stacy. When she turned to face Steven, she reached for both his hands and held them tight. "I'm ready."

Craig went on to perform a traditional service, but before having Amber and Steven recite their vows he added some words of his own.

"This wedding is truly like no other I've ever officiated. Most people turn the most special and intimate day of their life into a celebration for their friends. But Amber and Steven only wanted those who were instrumental in helping them get to this point in their relationship. I am honored to be here to witness and solemnize this union."

He turned to Steven. "Steven, Amber stands before you and God, giving herself to you. Do you promise to love her, honor her, keep and protect her, always bringing your relationship before the Lord, being faithful only unto her as long as you both shall live?"

"I do." Steven's words were heavy with emotion.

"Amber," Craig shifted his attention. "Steven stands before you and God, promising to be your lover, your keeper, and your protector. Do you promise to love him, encourage him, honor him as the spiritual leader in your home, and be faithful unto him and God?"

"I do." Amber's lip quivered with emotion, as she whispered her answer.

"Then, as these witnesses stand before you, and you stand before your Lord and Savior, exchanging vows meant only for each other, with the power vested in me by the state of California, I pronounce you husband and wife."

"Steven, you may kiss your bride."

Steven cupped Amber's face in his hands and pressed his lips against hers. Amber reached around Steven's broad shoulders and embraced him as his wife.

Everyone applauded, the detectives whistling, adding a little light-heartedness to the moment. Steven kissed Amber again and again. And again.

"Steven, stop," she whispered and gave him a playful nudge. She felt mildly embarrassed, only because his affection was being witnessed by so many people.

"Just practicing," he mumbled in her ear, kissing her behind the lobe.

Amber was sure she was blushing for all to see.

"It is my pleasure to introduce for the first time anywhere, Mr. and Mrs. Steven Levitt," Craig said with a smile.

After another round of applause and whistles, Steven and Amber descended the stairs where their family and friends greeted them.

After offering their congratulations, Hastings and the guys said their goodbyes, wishing Amber and Steven the best of luck. Each man gave Amber a small kiss on the cheek and Steven a congratulatory handshake.

Amber watched as something passed between Cooper and Steven while Cooper shook his hand. "You're a lucky man, Steven. Screw-up and I'll drop you where you stand." Amber knew Cooper's good-natured bantering was meant as a joke but sensed a hint of truth in his statement. Cooper had admitted having feelings for Amber, but Steven didn't give him a hard time about it. He had just thanked him for all that he'd done to keep Amber safe. Even putting his own life on the line.

"How about some one-on-one after we get back?" Steven asked Cooper with a smile.

"Giving me a chance to beat you at something, that's very big of you," he said with a grin. "Call me." Cooper smiled.

"I will."

They shook hands again before the four officers made their way to the back of the church and disappeared through the door.

The photographer came down from the balcony, where he had positioned himself during the ceremony and began making suggestions for pictures. It was hard for Amber not to look through the viewfinder herself, setting up each shot, making sure it was perfect, but she relied on John—a competitor in the business—to live up to his reputation.

He clicked off several pictures with the family, then asked for a few minutes with just the bride and groom. Everyone moved to the foyer, talking joyously among themselves.

John positioned Amber and Steven, in close, intimate shots. The candlelight danced in Steven's eyes while a glow radiated from Amber's complexion. The church was completely silent, except for the clicking of the camera. The mood was so romantic, so intoxicating, Amber felt her flesh heat up with both excitement and anxiousness.

"I don't know about you, but I'm ready to go," Steven whispered as the photographer prompted him to kiss Amber's neck.

Amber only had to look in Steven's eyes to see what she was feeling in her heart.

They said their goodbyes to friends and family before getting into the limo waiting at the curb. Amber still had no idea where they were going on their honeymoon, Steven insisting it was a secret. He had even had Stacy do some shopping for Amber so he didn't have to give any hints regarding weather or climate. Amber had tried to get the information out of him, but to no avail.

But as she looked into Steven's eyes and felt the strength of his love surround her, Amber knew it didn't matter. It didn't matter where she was or what the future held. She had everything she would ever need in life. An amazing God who would see her through the difficulties she was sure to face, and an incredible husband who had promised never to leave her.

It was a promise Steven had made to Amber during the lowest time in her life—to offer her comfort and hope.

Who could have known then that God had meant it for a lifetime.

ABOUT THE AUTHOR

Tamara Tilley writes from her home at Hume Lake Christian Camps, located in the beautiful Sequoia National Forest. She and her husband, Walter, have been on full-time staff at Hume for over twenty years. Tamara is a retail manager and an active book reviewer. You can read her reviews on her blog at http://tamara-tilley.blogspot.com Along with reading, time spent with family, and crafting cards, she loves connecting with readers at www.tamaratilley.com.

Made in the USA
San Bernardino, CA
25 June 2019